Sweetly

Denise McKay

Manor House

Library and Archives Canada Cataloguing in Publication

Title: Sweetly : a novel / Denise McKay.
Names: McKay, Denise, author.
Description: Includes bibliographical references.
Identifiers: Canadiana 20240479734 |
ISBN 9781998938124 (hardcover) |
ISBN 9781998938117 (softcover)
Subjects: LCGFT: Autobiographical fiction. |
LCGFT: Novels.
Classification: LCC PS8625.K38843 S94 2024 |
DDC C813/.6—dc23

Cover Art: Young woman looking through boat window: Shutterstock

Cover design and interior layout: Michael Davie

Published in 2024 by Manor House Publishing Inc.
452 Cottingham Crescent, Ancaster, ON, L9G 3V6
905-648-4797 – All Rights Reserved.

Book Description:

Follow the misadventures of free-spirited young schoolteacher Betty Wheatley – or Sweetly – as she's nick-named by her handful of students at a remote school house in the Canadian wilderness. She soon encounters bears, risqué romance, revelry – and retribution from judgemental locals. An insightful engaging novel based on the real-life experiences of author Denise McKay, a former teacher at a one-room schoolhouse in the rugged British Columbia interior. Denise McKay was born in Vancouver and she now resides in Ancaster, Ontario. She studied creative writing at Ryerson University and Humber College. She is a gifted writer and a highly creative artist in oil painting, acrylic, sculpture and pottery with many awards to her credit.

Funded by the Government of Canada | Canada

For all the teachers who live for that moment when understanding lights up a student's face. It is one of life's greatest rewards, and your dedication makes this possible every day

Foreword:

There is a painting by **Denise McKay** hanging on a wall in our house. She is a successful artist of longstanding and a seriously creative soul.

When I heard Denise had written a novel, I was curious, but not surprised.

Once I started to read, the vivid world she was creating and the characters who lived there pulled me in. I couldn't put the book down.

Informed by a lived experience, Denise takes us on a journey back in time to the early nineteen-fifties in the interior of B.C. There, a nineteen-year-old girl accepts an impossible job of trying to teach three different grade levels all at once, in a one-room schoolhouse, with a wood stove, and no plumbing.

The close quarters of a small community, creates something of a crucible where this young woman seeks to find her way through patriarchy, gossip, twisted minds and naysayers, into the warmth of friendship and the gradual discovery of her own values.

Denise McKay is a gifted painter with oil or words. *Sweetly* is a truly enjoyable read.

- **Ian Thomas**, singer-songwriter, author: *Bequest* and *The Lost Chord*

Review:

Denise McKay has written an insightful engaging novel based on the author's real-life experiences as a former teacher at a one-room schoolhouse in the rugged British Columbia interior… A young, free-spirited woman walks off a ferry boat and into a new life dramatically different from anything she's ever known... it's a life-changing experience of bears, revelry, risqué romance, – and retribution from judgemental locals, for teacher Betty Wheatley – or Sweetly – as she's nick-named by her students at a remote schoolhouse in the Canadian wilderness..."
- **Michael B. Davie**, author: **The Late Man**

Chapter 1

There's small choice in a box of rotten apples.
—Apologies to Shakespeare

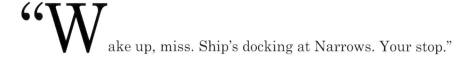ake up, miss. Ship's docking at Narrows. Your stop."

The captain reversed the paddlewheel, eased the Minto alongside the dock and cut the thumping engines. Backwash splashed the shore. The steward held a door open and Betty stepped over the high doorsill, straining to see beyond the single beam of light cast by the sternwheeler. She saw nothing, only blackness.

Where are the shacks? The lights? The people? Am I getting off the Minto to nothingness—or worse—into a forest of waiting bears? Every hair on her body stiffened with fear. She was about to throw herself on the mercy of the waiting steward when she saw the wavering beam of a flashlight farther down the dock. Two men gradually became visible as they walked into the sternwheeler's projected spotlight. Their footsteps resounded loudly in the inky stillness. A faceless voice called out from the boat to the two shadowy figures. "Hey, Bill, Jake, got a little schoolteacher on board for you."

"What, tonight? Lord Almighty..."

Betty held back. The steward prodded her down the steep metal stairs. "Move along, miss, no need to be afraid. That's Bill Trent. He'll help you out. Off you go." Betty stepped onto the dock.

The Minto's spotlight lit up the two men on the wharf. They were of a similar build: long and lanky, with weathered faces. Hunting caps on their heads, plaid shirts and loose woollen sweaters over baggy pants. Work boots. She looked to see if they carried guns for protection, but they did not.

"This what you're down here for then, Bill?" called out the same disembodied voice. A small package sailed through the air. Bill caught it, then turned to face Betty. He positioned himself for lecturing. Betty tensed, recognizing the move only too well.

"Young lady... piece of luck I'm here. You could've been stuck on this dock all alone, all bloody night long. No one meets the Minto when it's this late." He took a look at her city clothes — fancy dress and flimsy high heeled shoes — and then he tisked and shook his head disapprovingly.

Betty opened her mouth, but nothing came out. It was typical of her tongue to lose communication with her brain whenever they needed to work as a team. Except with Cameron, her beau, far away now —regret hit her with a sharp pang.

With a rude horn blast, the sternwheeler shoved off, returning the shore to blackness and a single flashlight.

The gruff voice continued. "The name's Bill Trent. School board trustee. This here's Jake Patten. God almighty, you schoolteachers are all alike. Full of the wrong kind of surprises. Who did you contact up here for room and board?"

"M–my father told me there's a hotel here in Narrows. I'm going to stay there tonight and f–find my way around in the morning," she managed. Ten hours on the throbbing, reverberating sternwheeler had not completely silenced her.

"The hotel? It's closed. A trapper and his wife are renting it for the winter."

Now Betty's voice really shut down. Dried up for good, she feared.

"Maybe they'd let you share a mattress with all of them cats they got. Must be dozens of 'em," said Jake Patten, the other shoreman, Bill Trent's companion. Jake grinned, looking to left and right as though a full house audience was applauding his wit.

Betty frowned and blinked back tears. How could he joke when her very existence was at stake?

"Why do schoolteachers always give me problems?" Bill Trent waved his flashlight heavenward, as though searching there for an answer. "I'll have to ask Granny if you can stay at her place tonight. I don't look forward to asking." A loud rumble emanated from his stomach.

"Well, good luck, Bill. Ee hee hee! She sure got mad at the last teachers she had. Them two who had the rip-snortin' parties," said Jake.

"No one else wants any teachers this year, either. What's your name? Miss Wheatley, isn't it? Let's go up to Gran's place, then," said Bill. The two men stepped into the dark night and began to ascend a steep road.

Betty scrambled to keep up with them in her best dress and favourite pumps, which were all muddy now. "H–how do you know my name?"

"You're from Trail." Bill ignored her question. "You related to old T.J. Wheatley? Wheatley's Billiards?"

The mention of her Grampa Wheatley—the solidness, the reality of him in the heavy darkness, calmed Betty somewhat. "T.J. Wheatley's Billiards and Tobacco Shop. That's my grandfather. He's a tobacconist." She emphasized the word because of its respectability. She hated being linked to the pool hall.

The ground levelled out. The flashlight beam highlighted a white picket fence. A few steps more brought them to a house. The three of them

6

walked up some stairs, Betty ending up on the lowest one, behind Bill and Jake.

"Here goes nothin'," said Jake, grinning down at her.

Bill knocked at the door. Black silence. Bill knocked again. From the depths of the house, a moving light appeared.

A woman opened the door. Short, plump, clutching a pale-blue chenille dressing robe around her, glaring suspiciously out at them. Holding a kerosene lamp. Watery blue eyes blazing at Bill. "What on earth are you doing banging on my door in the middle of the night?"

Bill's stomach rumbled like a cement mixer. "I–I'm sorry, Granny, I realize it's ten-thirty, but—"

"Ten-thirty? Bill, you know I go to bed early. I need my sleep."

"I've got a schoolteacher here. She just came in on the Minto. Granny, if you'll just have her for the night, I promise to find her a place in the morning."

"I've told you over and over, I don't want strangers staying here." Granny tried to peer around the men. "Where is she?"

Jake pulled Betty up to his step. "Here yuh are. Miz Wheatie. Just like the breakfast cereal, you know? 'Wheaties — the Breakfast of Champions'."

"Wheatley," said Bill and Betty in unison. Betty continued, "I'm Betty Wheatley—teacher for grades four, five and six..."

Granny pushed her lamp forward. "Why, you're too young to teach those big children. You're just a child yourself."

Betty, intent on the night's bed, struck a soulful expression. At the same time, she saw Bill looking down at her dubiously. It suddenly dawned on her that he is the school board representative. He's assessing me, she thought, assessing my potential as a teacher.

"How tall are you?" he asked.

"Five foot three," she lied, and reached up to hide her nose. Darn stupid baby nose, she thought. Well, at least having a too-high forehead is an asset—makes me look intelligent. So do my new glasses.

Bill remained skeptical and Granny looked as though she were swallowing castor oil. Betty self-consciously smoothed down her flaming red mane—the unfortunate result of a hair dying accident—and assumed as dignified an air as she could muster, considering her unfortunate circumstance. Granny gave a huge sigh, She pulled Betty inside and slammed the door on Bill's face. "Pick up your suitcases. Follow me."

As Betty awkwardly manoeuvred her bulky suitcases through a narrow space, following Granny and her kerosene lamp, she resolved to ingratiate herself somehow. "Your living room is very pretty." She rummaged for further tactical remarks, but her eyes locked onto the light switches. Why doesn't she turn them on?

"Humph, luckily you can't see it too well by this wretched lamp. When I came here from England I never thought I would spend so many years coping with these dirty things. Of course you know we're getting electricity this fall?" The question sounded like an accusation.

"Well. Uhh, yes. Of course," Betty lied again; it seemed the right thing to do.

"Rural Electrification programme." Granny spat out the words like caustic soda. "New power station out at Whatshan. Probably have lights by October. So they say. I doubt it. It should have been hooked up ages ago."

A chesterfield and two small armchairs festooned with crocheted doilies clustered around a potbelly stove. Next to the dining table a Chippendale cabinet, chock-full of assorted Spode and Wedgwood dishes, caught Betty's eye. Even her Gramma Wheatley, with all her money, her big house, didn't have this that much china.

They continued through a doorway into a dark kitchen. A Gurney-Oxford Range, polished to a high shine, dominated the shadows. Here, Granny held the lamp aloft so Betty could see into an adjoining room.

What a pretty bedroom, Betty thought. It's as decorative as a gift box.

"You can sleep here tonight, but that's all," warned Granny. She brought another kerosene lamp from the kitchen, lit it and shoved it at Betty. "Now goodnight. Close the bathroom door on my side. And flush the toilet. It's properly hooked up now. And," she emphasized, "don't you dare wake me up early by walking around. I need my sleep and I don't get up until nine."

Show gratitude, Betty decided. She flashed the widest smile she could make. Wide enough to counteract the dimness. "Goodnight, Mrs. Trent. Thank you very much for taking me in. I didn't relish the thought of sleeping on the dock."

"Well, it's probably where you should be." Mrs. Trent grumbled. She retraced her steps to her bedroom, leaving behind a wake of indignant darkness.

Some still-functioning part of Betty placed the lamp on the night table without dropping it. She removed only one layer of clothing and pulled on her pajamas over the rest — in case of sudden eviction. She climbed under the bedcovers. The room smelled clean. The blanket's faint odour of mothballs reminded her of home. *My dad was wrong when he talked about this place*, she thought,

8

this is no shack. She extinguished the lamp. She rolled around restlessly, re-living the events of the last few days, that fateful dinner just two nights ago with her family when she had to break the bad news of how she'd nearly flunked normal school and now couldn't find a teaching job anywhere—not in Vancouver near her handsome Cameron and, because she applied too late, not home in Trail either.

Gramma Beaton, with her cigarette, as usual, simultaneously yellowing her silvery hair and dropping hot ash onto her apron (adding fresh-ash polka dots to the random ones already there) watched, as Betty bustled about the kitchen helping her sister. Making dinner was Faye's jurisdiction. Faye, Betty's sister, was a carbon copy of Betty: the same too thin body, the same insignificant height, same long hair framing her heart-shaped face. Except Faye's hair was brown, not inferno-red like Betty's and her disposition was docile and sweet. Faye was the one to add the salt, smooth the gravy, time the vegetables. Trustworthy Faye—not Betty—performed tasty little miracles every night.

That night, Gramma Beaton looked bemused as she watched the normally indifferent Betty transform the plates of food into masterpieces. Her intelligent beady eyes crinkled with suspicion--she knew something was up. 'The food must be pure joy to the eye', Betty declared. Mashed potatoes diagonally balanced by minutely diced carrots and circled by green peas, curves of finely sliced beef, bedded in light swirls of gravy. Culinary Cubism bisected by slivers of ruby red beets. Gramma Beaton shook her head. Too much fuss; fuss meant trouble.

Nora, Betty's mom, already knew Betty's news. Tight-lipped, she impatiently jiggled her well-curved leg, waiting for her daughter's announcement, waiting for her husband's resultant, inevitable explosion. Betty flitted from the stove to the table, serving Faye's dinner that she had arranged so prettily on the plates. Betty's other contribution was a fresh-from-the-oven raisin cake, her father's favourite. The whole ambitious meal was designed to tranquilize Glen, to soften him up for bad news. The four women in the house knew they would witness his anger; it was the degree of rage they were conspiring to control.

"Pass me some more gravy, Betts. Damn fine meal you girls made."

As her dad chomped down his food, Betty twirled her mashed potatoes with her fork and thought about when she saw her dad earlier in the day. Walking home from the school board office where she received the bad news, she passed by the billiards and smoke shop her dad and Grandpa owned. Cigar smoke and guffaws drifted out from the backroom of the billiards hall. One familiar voice carried over the rumbling of male voices, carried over the click-clack of billiard balls. She could hear his swaggering bravado, followed by the tittering of female encouragement. Dad. Too-handsome dad. Playing up to some rule-breaking floozies who should be home waxing floors, not hanging about in a backroom billiard world, not dallying with her dad. Nora snapped Betty out of her reverie. "Betty has something to tell you, Glen." Speak up, commanded Nora's leg. Spill out the wretched news.

Mother's right. Make the plunge now, thought Betty. Now, while he's still mellow. But before she could blurt out her unpalatable tidings, the phone rang.

"Get that goddamn phone, Betts. Tell 'em I'm not home. A man should be able to eat in peace."

Betty ran to the hallway and grabbed the phone. In a deferential voice, she uttered a handful of terse yeses, a smattering of interrupted excuses and one sharp intake of air followed by a long exhalation. Although the phone call lasted only five minutes, to every hopeful woman in the kitchen — those three generations that Betty held most dear in all the feminine world — those five momentous minutes seemed to last forever. But finally, Betty hung up and called out: "I've got a job! A job!" She dashed back to the kitchen. "That was Trail's school inspector. He just got me a teaching job. I'll be teaching three middle grades at a place called Narrows. They need me right away!"

Nora's eyes rolled skyward in a prayer of thanks.

Glen didn't even look up from his plate. "Damn good thing, Betts, bloody well time you got some cash into your life and stopped being a noose around my neck. Christ, I'd been working three years by the time I was nineteen." Not a speck of impatience in his deep voice, and underneath the gruffness, maybe even a faint hint of pride. Crisis averted!

Gramma Beaton settled back and sipped a mouthful of tea. Faye smiled her relief. Nora unpursed her lips. "Narrows? Where on earth is Narrows, Glen?"

"To hell and gone. It's at the pinch point between the two Arrow Lakes. Just a bunch of shacks really." Glen jolted upright. "Hell! Narrows? That's near where Hop-along Freddie and Shorty and I met up with the grizzlies!"

Betty, lying in her bed, shuddered when she thought about the gruesome grizzly story her dad regaled them with over that dinner. She stared out the window, out into this new, Narrows' wilderness. Suddenly her eye fixated on the dim silhouette of a swaying, portly shadow—a bear? No, don't be ridiculous she told herself, it's just a dense shrub, she decided. Trying self-hypnosis, she willed herself to sleep to deaden her anxiety. Dog-tired, her eyelids soon fluttered shut. The shadow slipped away, on shuffling feet.

Chapter 2

The first duty in life is to be as artificial as possible.
What the second duty is no one has yet discovered.
—Oscar Wilde

Betty donned her mother-dictated garb—teacher-type suit, stockings and pumps—and waited for Granny to wake up. If this is the only place to stay, she thought, I must win over this miserable old woman. Either that or run away to Vancouver and sneak into Cameron's dorm. Stay there.

When she heard the kettle being filled, she took it as a signal to emerge. "It's another beautiful day out there, Mrs. Trent."

"No. It's not." Granny Trent moved her stiff lips as though she were chewing on gooseberries. She poked at the fire. "I make tea for breakfast. Toast. That suit you?"

"That would be very kind of you." Betty honeyed her voice.

Granny guillotined four slices of bread, shoved them between wire toast racks, slapped them on the surface of the stove and commanded Betty to guard them. The kettle sang nervously. Granny spooned tea leaves into the pot, filled it with boiling water and suffocated it with a no-nonsense tea cozy. "Sit down. I suppose you're used to fancy breakfasts."

"Oh, no, I usually have toast and tea, and this bread is delicious. Do you make it yourself?"

"Me? Huh! Never. Bill's wife makes it. I had a gentlewoman's upbringing in England. And until I met Bill's father during the Great War, I lived at home and a cook made the bread."

"Bill is a kind man," Betty's sales pitch continued, "a lovely man. Do you have any other children?"

Granny bristled. "Bill's not my child. He was Mr. Trent's by his first wife that died. I never, ever had any children." She looked repulsed by the idea. "Biggest mistake I ever made was to come here with Bill's father." Tears spilled over her soft cheeks.

Startled, Betty rummaged for comforting words. "You've got that beautiful English complexion that my Gramma Beaton is always talking about."

"Do you think so? Still?"

"Oh, yes. Both sides of my family are English, and we know a good complexion when we see one."

"Well. Thank you." Granny reached for a handkerchief from the recesses of her flowered house dress, wiped her eyes and scrutinized Betty. "Do you have a young man yet?"

"Yes, I do. He's a student in Vancouver."

"Last year, the teachers brought boy friends to my upstairs apartment time after time, until I could hardly face the community. Disgusting parties—drinking and smoking. Do you smoke?"

"Oh, no, definitely not. You've got an apartment upstairs?" That sounded even better than the gift box bedroom. "I'd love to see it."

~ ж ~

Dim light filtered through two small windows into the main room of the apartment—a partitioned attic space with walls of unpainted pine board. No gift box décor here, Betty noted. One unusable light socket dangled from the ceiling. A stove, a wooden table, four chairs and a single-tap sink—cold water only—with shelves above it, huddled in one corner. The rest of the room was empty, except for a worn-out chesterfield.

Behind the partition was another room. Here sagged two double beds, each covered with an old blanket to conceal the indelicate stains they had accumulated in their long-overdue lives. A tilted wardrobe. Two dressers with cloudy, useless mirrors. Cripes, thought Betty, everything looks like it's been rejected by the Salvation Army.

"Oh, this place is...uhh, so wonderful!" Lies of necessity, she had now decided, did not count. "I'd love to stay here."

"Sorry. I can't let you. The high school teacher, Miss Bradshaw, has got it. She sent me a cheque for the whole year. And Bill says she behaved herself well enough last year when she taught up the lake at King City. Too bad."

~ ж ~

Bill Trent waited for a long rolling belch to complete itself. "Two of my teachers out of action—both hurt and in hospital. Our Miss Bradshaw and her passenger—the teacher for down the lake, Miss Maleyna."

12

"Oh?" said Betty.

"Miss Bradshaw's van was hit by a truck near Slocan City as she was driving up here. She's got a smashed leg. Miss Maleyna's got whiplash."

"Oh?" said Betty. "Can I have Miss Bradshaw's apartment, then?"

Granny and Bill frowned. Shook their heads at this impertinent young woman with not even a pretense of concern about the accident victims. Betty, seeing the consternation on their faces, thought fast, then loaded enough anxiety on her face to make the Mona Lisa cry. "Of course, I'm sure they will recover quickly! What about your pretty little bedroom, then, Mrs. Trent?"

"Oh, my, no. No! That's my guest room. I've never rented it out."

Bill clenched his stomach. "Maybe she could stay upstairs until Miss Bradshaw arrives?"

Granny hedged. "But you've no pots and pans—that sort of thing, Miss Wheatley."

"Gosh, that'd be easy, I'd just phone my parents--- they're in Trail--- to bring up what I need." Inwardly, Betty cringed. Ask my dad to bring up supplies for a place I don't have? By long-distance phone? Wreck his new car, his precious Henry J, on these harrowing mountain roads? By God, I'm desperate!

Granny stared into Bill's agitated eyes, then nodded approval.

"Only phone is at the store," said Bill. The tightness was gone from his voice. "You can phone them from there. And about your school—Len, the janitor, has the key, but he's gone for the weekend."

"But I need to plan the lessons."

"Sorry, can't be helped. You're lucky to have a place to stay!" He shrugged, belched and rushed off.

~ Ж ~

When Betty opened the front door, she could instantly survey all of her new community. It consisted of a handful of houses under attack from encroaching aspen, birch and pine. Her dad was right that most of the houses were little more than shacks, but there were a few neat little clapboard buildings where the paint was not peeling too badly that made the town seem more habitable. A quietude, a drowsy sort of timelessness permeated the pine-scented air.

Granny pointed straight ahead. "There's Trent's Landing, Miss Wheatley. Over there. Across the lake. You can guess who that was named

13

after. You see that ferry? Bill and Jake run that." Betty saw an eight-car cable ferry crossing the narrow waters. Its diesel engine resounded throughout the stilled valley. Granny wiggled her helpful finger. "The store's down there, right by the dock."

Directly before her, across an unpaved road, a hand-painted wooden sign proclaimed a tiny structure to be Nina's Cafe.

"Bill's wife Nina runs the café. Only open for the two months of summer. Closes after Labour Day. Then this place gets really quiet. Mind you shut that gate!" Granny retreated inside her house.

Betty inched the gate into position behind her as though it were hand-blown glass. She could see only one house to her right. A large one. Two storeys fronted by a wood façade, which advertised words as faded as the wood was weatherworn: Narrows Hotel.

A blue Chevy pickup roared out of nowhere, bumped and jolted over the gravelled road, and skidded to a stop. A young man grinned out of the window. "Hey! Beautiful Red! Where did you come from?" The truck moved backwards, matching her walking pace.

Blue eyes under a shock of blond hair. Betty would have found him intriguing in any other time or place, but not here. Not now.

"Red?"

My God, how embarrassing! A pick-up. In my first five minutes of daylight exposure. If Granny Trent sees this, I won't even have a temporary place to stay. Betty scowled at the driver, spun her face away.

"Okay, Red, be stuck-up, have it your way." He sped off and the muffler of his truck roared its contempt.

She swept her campfire-red hair back as it blew in her face. Harlot red, she muttered. Another one of my mistakes. It should still be mousy brown like my sister's. Schoolmarm brown—in a severe bun, instead of show-off Rita Hayworth curls. If I'd dyed it right, there'd just be a hint of red. She smoothed her skirt, scrunched her curls, checked the seams of her silk stockings and continued on.

As she approached Nina's Café, the door swung open. Out waltzed a grinning girl about Betty's size and age. Betty stared at bleached blonde hair, black eyebrows, dark red lipstick, rolled-up blue jeans and a snug white blouse.

"Hey...you just snubbed Sparks Thornton—that truck driver. Best catch in the valley! Welcome to the sticks, Betty Wheatley. I'm Dorothy LaPointe...call

14

me Dot. I teach at Trent's Landing. Across the lake. Come on into Nina's for a cuppa Java and get acquainted."

At the Normal School, they had decreed: No sloppy speech, no slacks, no questionable behaviour. This girl breaks all the rules, thought Betty. Probably why she's here. And dyed blonde hair! Worse than harlot red by a long shot.

Inside the café, a curvaceous Nina Trent, Bill's wife, slid a cup of coffee along the counter. "Sit down, kiddo. You look like a nervous canary. Did Granny give you a bad time? Or Bill? Well, you just never mind. Granny's crotchety and Bill's a fusspot. Don't you laugh, missy," she said to Dot. "You found us hard to get used to."

Dot straddled a stool and dragged on a cigarette. "Last year I came over from Vernon lots of times. To see my fiancé, Lou Fielding. I'm only teaching in this dump because of him." She inhaled with a look of self-satisfaction. "Lou's an engineer at the hydro station. We're getting married at Christmas."

Betty felt rootless, cast adrift. Only one word cut into the numbness: fiancé. She savoured it; she had never before heard anyone call their boyfriend "fiancé". Trailites would have found it an affectation. But the sparkling ring on Dot's finger entitled her to the word.

"I'll betcha you never told School Inspector McIntyre you were going to marry during the school term," teased Nina.

"Of course not. I'm no fool. You have to stretch the truth like a rubber band, Betty, or they'll give you the boot. They expect you'll get pregnant right off the bat and quit."

"Well, most do, Dot," said Nina. She reached for a fly swatter. "I could tell you a thing or two about the schoolteachers and the other folks up here. Some mighty strange goings-on." Dot and Betty looked at her with interest. "But I'm not going to." Whap! Went the fly swatter. "People here have enough trouble trying to keep secrets—it's almost impossible." Splat! "Correction. It's completely impossible."

"I'll disappoint them all, then. I've got no secrets," said Dot.

"Neither do I," Betty lied, denying unbidden visions of herself coupling with Cameron. She focused on the flattened fly to keep her red face from betraying her.

"Your school and mine used to be one-room, all-grade schools, Betty," said Dot. "God. Imagine teaching twelve grades at once. Three is bad enough. I get the best deal. The little ones. Grades one, two and three. Is this your first year?"

"Yes."

"My second. The first is a nightmare, believe me. Last year, I taught the grades you've got. I hated it. Poor you. You get two of the Carson kids. Little savages. Cousin-marrying-cousin stuff, and now the whole family's a lulu. The kids throw fits in class." She tapped her painted fingernails. "You get Howard. He's a total wingding." Dot dismissed Betty's horrified look with a perfect smoke ring. A patronizing grin. "Don't let them get away with a single thing. Whack 'em with the strap.

"Except for Alec Detweiler. You've got him, too. Great big skinny bugger. Don't whack him with the strap. He might just grab it and strap you." Betty glanced again at the flattened fly. Winced.

Overwhelmed with this truckload of new worries, Betty downed a third cup of coffee before her caffeine-charged brain remembered her mission. "Oh, my gosh, I've got to phone my mother."

On her way down the hill, little puffs of fine dust lifted with each step she took. The ferry appeared to be halfway across the lake, and its pulsing engines sounded far away. Betty could hear someone chopping wood. The rhythmic axe blows echoed in the stillness. To the right of the road, at the end of it, was a one-pump gas station, the Narrows Garage. To the left, a dirt path between indifferent patches of dry grasses led to the Narrows General Store. The lake was only twenty paces farther away.

On the store's long porch, a blonde girl of about eight broomed away the layers of road dust that had settled on the greyed boards. As Betty entered the store they traded smiles.

Familiar smells from home assailed her: the compound chemistry of vanilla ice cream and Havana cigars. Addictive. Heartwarming. Just like at T.J. Wheatley's Billiards and Tobacco Shop.

A buy-here smile greeted Betty, revealing store-bought teeth: marvellously white and just a tad loose. "Welcome, Miss Wheatley, I'm Mrs. Johnson, and that's my daughter on the porch. She'll be in your class. I'll be right with you after I've helped Mrs. Sunders... Mrs. Sunders, this is one of our new teachers." Mrs. Johnson's teeth clicked approvingly.

The other customer continued peering at a list. Betty had never seen such a pale, sickly-skinned woman. Insect bites covered her face and thin arms.

"Mrs. Sunders' husband is a trapper. They usually camp in the woods.

This winter's going to be a real treat for you, dear, isn't it?"

No reply.

"Mr. and Mrs. Sunders have rented the hotel for the winter. Sammy, with God's help, must have got a good price for his marten pelts to be rewarding you so well." Mrs. Johnson spoke in a soothing, careful way, as though she were speaking to someone standing on the ledge of a cliff. "I do hope that all your cats have adapted well to the move, dear." While she talked, Mrs. Johnson packed can after can of cat food into Mrs. Sunders' basket.

Mrs. Sunders spoke as though she knew only one flat, hollow note. "Has anyone bought cat poison lately?"

"Cat poison? There's no such thing. I don't even carry rat poison," said a startled Mrs. Johnson.

"Good-bye," monotoned Mrs. Sunders. She restrained the screen door; it shut with a whisper.

"Poor soul, poor soul." Mrs. Johnson collected herself and honoured Betty with another gleaming loose-toothed smile. "Bill was just here filling us in, Miss Wheatley. There's the phone, over there. Not like your city phones, I guess. Just pick up the receiver and crank the handle to get the operator."

After a long wait, a raspy voice came over the crackling line. "Armour Shoe Store."

"Joyce, it's Betty. Is my mother there?" Betty shouted, summoning the necessary volume for a long-distance call.

"Betty? My gosh, long distance! Noraahh! Hurry, it's Betty!"

"Betts, are you all right?" The beloved voice made Betty want to cry. She filled her mother in with the briefest of information—not even mentioning the temporariness of her accommodation—and hung up. Long-distance phoning was nerve-wracking enough.

"You didn't have to ask your parents to drive all the way up here." Mrs. Johnson's affable dentures had retreated. "Whatever you need, we've got it, Miss Wheatley, our prices are as good as those great big stores in Trail. They don't give any bargains. They'd cheat the devil himself. And here, you don't even need to pay cash until your first pay cheque." She looked ruefully at a shelf of dust-covered kitchenware.

Betty wiped her sweaty palms on her skirt and almost phoned her mother once more. But she could not approach the intimidating hand-cranked phone again; she would rather suffer the wrath of her father. Besides, she had a worse problem. "Do you know of any places to stay, Mrs. Johnson?"

"No. I don't. No one wants schoolteachers." Mrs. Johnson's teeth snapped shut.

~ ж ~

From the porch of the store, Trent's Landing looked like a mirror copy of Narrows. Trees obscured a scattering of houses, and a few crooked farms crisscrossed the hillsides on either side of the town. Above them, densely green mountain walls rolled backwards, blending with higher, steeper ones: the Selkirks, topped with white spikes of perpetual winter. Betty shivered.

Her eyes fastened on the cloistered lake, traced it to the south, picturing where it became a river again, picturing the place where the river ran past Trail. Dear Trail.

A lump of homesickness filled her throat. The kitchen table at home had, unbidden, flashed before her—with her mother, grandmother and sister sitting around it, tossing forth ideas, opinions and secrets. On a map, they were only two lake squiggles and a river kink away, but they might as well be separated by an ocean.

The ferry had docked. A bullet-nosed Studebaker and a three-ton Ford truck rumbled off and sped up the hill, churning up clouds of dust. Betty received her share—up her nose, in her mouth. And her white blouse, now grimy, matched her mood.

~ ж ~

Nora waved a fluttery hand at her daughter, but Glen glowered as he drove his Henry J. off the ferry. "What a helluva drive that was—washboard roads damn near shook my new car apart, and bloody boulders at every turn. Get in, get in, for God's sake, Betts." Betty climbed into the back seat and Glen gunned up the hill in a whirlwind of dust.

"Dad, you won't be able to stay at the hotel. I couldn't."

"We'll see about that." Glen whistled as he strode up the hotel steps, his handsomely round and shiny head radiating confidence. When he came out, he announced that he had booked a double room.

"How did you manage that?"

"Soft soap and moola," said Glen with a wink. He had changed moods faster than he changed gears. Nora, too, looked relaxed and happy. It was a rarity for them to be in sync. "Now," Glen concluded, "let's go see this hole-in-the-wall you got yourself."

Everyone, including Granny Trent, clumped up the wooden stairs to the apartment. To Betty's relief, Granny Trent did not mention the transient nature of Betty's lodgings; she seemed to know it was imprudent. Nora and Glen, appalled by the primitive place, nonetheless pronounced it "roomy".

Nora unwrapped her parcels and gestured theatrically; she loved being on stage. "Oh, what a horribly frustrating time—yesterday I just worked my head and feet off! I was worried sick because I had no chance to get you anything, and I came home at supper time in total despair."

Betty listened with rapt attention. Drank in her mother's words as if they were nectar.

"But..." Nora paused for effect. "I had this marvellous brain-wave of phoning Fred Ross—you know him—the charming fellow your father insists on calling Hop-along Freddie, and he just opened up his whole hardware store especially for me!"

I can believe it, thought Betty. Mother's very attractive. Capable of making men jump through hoops—even a man with a bitten-off leg from a vicious bear attack. Any man, except Dad.

"And I got you these funny-looking Indian blankets and some pots, plus this kettle and teapot and little toaster and—" Nora stopped. "Where are your plug-ins?"

"There aren't any. There's no electricity in Narrows."

Nora's eyes widened. "Oh, my word, how really dreadful—" she began, then looked at Granny and reached for more tactful words. "I'm sure you'll be fine." She turned down the corners of her pretty mouth. "Now, Betts, you owe Fred Ross sixty dollars for all this stuff and you must pay him soon. I'd be terribly horrified if you let me down after Fred's thoughtfulness."

"Pay him a bit every month," said Glen. "As long as you keep sending Hop-along Freddie something, you don't have to pay it off fast."

"Oh, good, I can handle that." Betty was grateful. They had not, as she had feared, let her down.

That night, Betty thought about poor Hop-along Freddy and the gruesome tale her dad loved to tell about how he lost his leg in a bear attack.

"I knew to freeze, and Shorty did too, but old Freddie, he got the heebie-jeebies and ran like hell, the damn fool. Great big mother grizzly went after him...crunched on his leg, shook him like a rag doll."

Glen shook his head back and forth, reenacting the moment. "Couldn't shoot her. Freddie was in the way. Wasn't till I shot the cub that the mother dropped Freddie, then Shorty blasted her.

"Jesus. I can still hear Freddie's skin popping and his bones cracking when that grizzly sank her teeth in — see his leg bumping along, bloody bones sticking out as she dragged him through the bush..."

Betty had heard this story so often she could recite it. But as she lay in her bed, she shivered violently. Now the story had meaning. Her first job—in a place where animals feasted on humans.

"... and that damn bear meat tasted like jam. That bear must've eaten a ton of huckleberries. The sweetness sure couldn't have come from ol' Hop-a-long's leg meat…" Dad and his dark sense of humour, she thought.

Just then, Betty heard a rustling noise outside and could swear she saw a hulking shadow moving past her window again—a bear? She tried to force herself to go to sleep but tossed and turned restlessly until morning.

~ Ж ~

In the morning, Betty felt groggy and dirty. She wondered whether Granny would ever allow her to use the bathtub. How would she get clean for tomorrow, the first day of school?

And my parents—will they be leaving early, she wondered. The sun had barely peeped over the Selkirks. They might be; they had gone to bed early enough. She dressed quickly and crept down the stairs.

"God damn lemon of a Henry J. Why the hell didn't Kaiser put in a lid to the trunk like everybody else? Going through the back seats to load an ass-backward trunk is a pain in the neck." Glen rammed his suitcase into the trunk. "Your ma's not up yet. You go in to tell her to hoof it." This morning dad was more his usual self--a spring under compression.

It bothered Betty how harshly her dad always treated her mom. It was Nora who kept the family afloat with her job as a shoe store manager. Her dad mostly hung out at the billiards hall flirting with floozies. All while neglecting the only part of the business with an aura of propriety and prosperity—the cigar shop with its oak and glass cases filled with cedar-boxed cigars and tin-encased cigarettes. No wonder I'm hopeless, she thought—neither my dad nor grampa are ever at the cash desk. Anyone could clean the place out. Any of those billiard players. Any person off the street. All of us Wheatleys other than my mom: tarred with incompetence and feathered with mistrust. But her mom did have a way of rubbing in her superiority, making Betty feel like she never quite lived up to expectations. Perhaps her dad felt the same way…which was still no excuse for his terrible temper.

At that moment, Nora emerged, suitcase in hand, she moved slowly; looked tired.

"Did you sleep well?" Betty asked.

Nora did not reply. Her eyes investigated Betty's Dot-inspired outfit disapprovingly. "Where are your stockings? Your pumps?"

"They don't dress like—"

"Don't argue with your ma, Betts," said Glen. "She looks like she'd bite your head off. You okay, Queenie?" The venom in his voice made Betty's stomach churn. "Her majesty is used to sleeping in mansions—she tossed and turned all night. I'm surprised you didn't light the goddamn lamp and read." He jerked his head toward Nina's Café. "Let's go eat, bleary-eyes. You look like hell."

Nora, as always, ignored Glen. Treated him as if he did not exist, as if he were no more than a nuisance of a mosquito. "What a pigsty that hotel is," said Nora. "It reeks of cat pee and worse. And there's fleas there, too. I itch all over. What a horrid place! How in the world can anyone let a place get so disgusting? Your father's a fool to have paid them."

Now Betty knew what today's spat was about.

Betty lingered by the side of the car. "I wish you weren't leaving so soon."

Nora surveyed Betty's hangdog expression. "Really, Betts, we can't possibly stay any longer. Fred Ross invited us to his Labour Day celebration. If worse comes to worse, why don't you figure out how to get home for Thanksgiving?"

Glen's head swirled around like a traffic cop's. "How in the hell is she going to do that?" he shouted. "There's no bus connections and the Minto only goes south on Friday mornings. You should know she can't just pack up and leave on a Friday morning! And I'll be goddamned if I'm coming back up here again." He turned to Betty. "It's just a year. It won't kill you to rough it a bit. Put a smile on your face, kiddo."

Glen and Nora entered the Henry J without a backward glance.

Betty wanted to lunge at the back of the Henry J, pry its trunk lid open and jump inside. Hide in it all the way to Trail. But then she remembered: the

Henry J had no trunk lid. The car sped off. Damn Henry J! Just as callous as my parents!

She watched it debark from the ferry at Trent's Landing, watched it crawl up the gravel road, and disappear into the forests. With her parent's car out of sight, the obliging ferry drove her parents to the other side of the lake, where the silhouetted Selkirks stood shoulder-to-shoulder, blending into a craggy version of penitentiary walls. They soon disappeared from sight. And when she turned around, the Monashee Mountains loomed over her. Solid black-green pine.

I'm sentenced to a whole year in Hell and Gone. She kicked at a dusty grasshopper, missed it and banged her toes on a protrusion of rock.

She limped to a tree stump and sat. Her foot throbbed. Nobody cares. Nobody loves me.

Chapter 3

You've got to ac-cent-tchu-ate the positive.
—Johnny Mercer and Harold Arlen

J ake Patten stood outside one of the houses built on the down slope of the mountainside, one foot planted on a pile of freshly chopped wood. He waved up at her as if they were old friends.

"Hey, Miz Wheatie, are yuh lost? Didn't eat your Breakfast of Champions this morning I take it?" He grinned at his own annoying attempt at humour.

Betty refrained from reminding him that she had not been named after a cereal. His was the first sympathetic voice she had heard since her encounter with her parents, and it melted—just a bit—the frozen lump that was in her chest. She called down to him. "Is this the way to my school?"

Needing no further encouragement, Jake sprinted up the slope. In the daylight, he appeared much older and thinner than Bill Trent. His weather-beaten skin had the colour and texture of well-worn penny loafers. Despite the midday breezes, he exuded an odour of strong tobacco and sweat. "Your school? Yep, yessiree, it's just up that way 'round that hairpin turn."

"It'll be the first time I've seen it and I still don't have a key, and it's Labour Day and I need to get into my school pretty soon." More inner-slivers of ice dissolved as she poured out her anxiety to this stranger.

"Whoa! Take yer time, Miz Wheatie, there's lots of it—yuh got a whole year." He gestured toward his house. "I'd invite yuh in fer a spell—never let it be said Jake Patten didn't have no manners—but I'm s'posed to be lookin' after my granbaby. Hear 'im? Wanna borrow 'im fer a few hours? His hollerin' could keep yuh company up there scoutin' out yer school, keep yuh from bein' lonely. Want him? I'll run and git him." Grinning broadly, he feigned a move to go for his grandchild.

Betty grinned, too. The first time in days. "I'll take your baby up to my school if he can pick a lock, Mr. Patten."

"Mr. Patten? Mr. Patten? Who's he? It's just Jake." A louder wail travelled up the bank. "Hell's bells, I better git along to my grampa job and you better git up there to yer school. Yep, we built it just fer you." He hurried down the slope.

"Oh, Mr. Patten...Jake, one question. Have you seen any bears around my school?"

"Nary a one," Jake called up the hillside. "Other critters, though. Ee hee hee."

Betty's smile disappeared. What, she wondered, was so funny? What critters? Coyotes? Cougars? She continued on. Slowly. She knew there were bears; Narrows was the place where Hopalong Freddie had lost his leg to a hungry bear only a few years ago.

She turned onto the steep road that ascended to the school, and soon entered a hushed world of dense brush and tall trees. As effectively as a wall of stone, the impenetrable growth blocked her view of the lake and the little town. Other than the distant thrum of the ferry and the sounds of her own breathing, she walked in silence. Not one leaf rustled. A sense of aloneness, of disconnection suffused her, made her uneasy.

Farther along, on a cleared plateau, rested a house. Faded tarpaper and greyed strapping partly covered its sides. Like a shack in a ghost town: vacant, abandoned, neglected. A school bus was parked a few feet away. It had to be the home of Len, the absentee school bus driver/janitor, the keeper-of-the-key, she decided.

About two hundred paces farther, she saw a green schoolhouse. It was unremarkable — a clone of what she had seen elsewhere. She did not want to be in this place, this eerie stillness; yet the little green schoolhouse reached out to her. She drank in every detail of its insignificant façade.

An oversized bell hung above the scarred front door. She stifled a giddy urge to grab its stout rope and pull hard. Blast away the dead silence.

She spotted two shabby sheds a short distance from the school. Her nose told her they were the outhouses. Cripes, no flush toilets! She pinched open the door of one and peered inside. Up in the corners were spiders on tilted trampolines. Fat brown-speckled ones, ready to pounce. The critters, she wondered? Betty dared herself to swing the door wide open. Daylight beamed back at her through an array of poked out knotholes.

Good heavens, she thought, any student would be able to peek in. There's no way I'll ever use this place. If pupils saw me with my pants down, I'd die.

But the curl of disgust on Betty's lips departed—took off at great speed— replaced by fear, which rippled through her spine as she stared at one knothole—a knothole blocked by a white wetness that gleamed, gleamed like an eyeball, a rolling, bloodshot eyeball, that stared back at her! From the same source, she heard unmistakable sounds of shuffling and snuffling and panting, unmistakable lip-smacking sounds of a large tongue, rolling over the sides of a loose mouth. Her inner eye saw a heaving, huffing monstrous creature and her flesh could feel its rapacious caress, feel its ravenous spirit dissolving the outhouse; and every ounce of reason disappeared, all the self-control of the last fate-filled days deserted her.

"BEAR!" she screamed as she tore out of the outhouse and ran in frantic, useless zigzags. "Bear!" she kept hollering. Just as Hop-along Freddie must have done; no standing still for Betty.

An old Ford truck lumbered into view and creaked to a stop at the tar-papered house. A man and a woman with a baby stepped from the cab and stared at Betty, doing, what seemed to them, and for no apparent reason, a strange heebie-jeebie dance—all over the baseball field of the green school. The woman hid behind the man, clutching her baby tightly.

Betty fled to them. "A bear! Over there! Behind the outhouses!"

The man stood his ground; moved not so much as a facial muscle. His voice was as calm as if he were pacifying a skittery calf. "Don't see none. Couldn't be a bear, huckleberry season's over. Haven't ever seen one around the schools, anyways. It's a fella. Just a fella I reckon, Miss Wheatley. Probably wantin' to use the outhouse. I'm Len Wilson, janitor for your school. Drive the bus, too." He turned to the serious-faced young woman, who had returned to his side. "Vivian, this here's Miss Wheatley. Think you might make her a cuppa tea to calm her down a bit?"

"Tea?" Betty squeaked. "No thanks! I'm going to the dock. To the Minto. I'm going home!" No matter what Dad says. Gramma Beaton was right—there are worse things than Dad's words!

"Now, now, nothing to worry about. First-job jitters." Len Wilson clamped a friendly hand on Betty's shoulder and propelled her toward the school. "Bill tells me you're champing at the bit to see your classroom. Well, come on, then, I'll open up for you. Maybe afternoon tea then, eh, Vivian?"

"Tea? Later? Afternoon tea?" Vivian sounded as though he had asked her to prepare a ten-course meal. She was backing away from the truck and into her half-finished house as she spoke.

The big hand on Betty's shoulder was reassuring, coming, as it did, from such a sturdy, muscled arm. Her blood coursed less wildly. She scanned the outhouses and the woods, but stillness mocked her apprehension. Not one sign of the bear.

As Len unlocked the door, Betty stole a sidelong look at him. An extra-wide, generous mouth, a relaxed and gentle man. She instinctively trusted him, as one trusts a Clydesdale to pull its weight. She inched closer.

"You'll get your own key by and by, Miss Wheatley."

"Y–you can call me Betty."

He smiled down at her. "Don't look so worried, Betty. Coupla rough months, then you'll be in your stride. Most teachers we get are beginners like you. We don't get too many repeats. My wife taught up here for a few years, though. Before she married me, that is." There was great pride in his voice as he said the words, "my wife".

They stepped into the tiny cloakroom. Benches lined the walls on either side and above them coat hooks poked out like so many noses. Len opened the inner door. Betty inhaled the familiar musty smell: chalk dust, old wood and Dust Bane.

A large Quebec stove sat directly in front of the entrance. Betty eased around it to see the classroom.

The room was alive with shimmering light as the sun cast beams that lit up hyperactive dust particles. And shone on the scuffed little seats and desks attached to runners, aligned in neat rows.

Across the entire wall at the front was a blackboard. Above it, the mandatory photo of King George staring vacantly off to some grander place. Opposite the window wall, another long blackboard. Above it, a clock. It hung motionless, stopped at some other year's time: nine-twenty.

Instead of being at the front, the teacher's desk—her desk—was at the back of the room, right next to the stove. The solidity of it, the authority it represented, comforted her; she did not know why. She leaned against it; felt the first flickerings of teaching persona infuse her.

And then, something grander made Betty gasp. In the shadowed front corner of the room, almost obscured by the airborne dust particles, sat her dream: a piano! She wanted to run to it, to hug it, but she was afraid to leave Len's side.

"Now this old stove, she's a humdinger. Once the weather gets cold, you've got to tend her like a baby. Put one of the big boys in charge, but don't take your eyes off of her because she can quickly overheat. Once her sides turn red, you're in trouble. Keep your desk away from her. You don't want her to catch fire, or blister the varnish any worse than she already is. And don't move the desk to the front of the room or you'll freeze in the winter. That front wall gets mighty cold.

"When it starts to get chilly, I come in here before I start the bus up, and I make a low fire." He put his ear to the stovepipe and tapped it like a doctor checking out a chest cold. "I pick the kids up at three-thirty. Then I clean the schoolroom after supper, chop wood, throw a little lime in the outhouses. Today I'll prime the pump outside for you. Tell Bill Trent if there's anything you need. That's his job; he's the trustee. See you later at my place? This afternoon?" His eyes crinkled. "You'll like my wife Vivian. And don't worry about the fella in the woods. I tell you, he's as harmless as can be."

"It was a bear—"

"A fella."

Betty squelched the urge to run after him, to yell, "Don't leave me ALL

ALONE!"

Reluctant to remain in the dark classroom, afraid to go outside to bear country, she paced between the cloakroom and the stove.

My God, my God, I'm in purgatory! Punishment for my sexual sins! Her mind flashed to her handsome Cameron and how she submitted, rather too willingly, to his persuasive ways…and now here she was--no flush toilet, no running water, no Dad-controlled stove, no fellow teachers. All alone on a plateau, except for bears.

She circled the room restlessly, scanning the trees from each window. She cracked a window open, but heard no grunts, no growls. Only silence. It was siesta time, even for the birds. She began to breathe at a normal pace. Maybe the eyeball had been an illusion. A Hop-along Freddie panic attack.

Get hold of yourself, coward, you're stuck here. Get used to it. She locked the classroom door, slumped into the teacher's chair and gradually calmed down.

The teacher's desk had two drawers. The top one contained a letter from the previous teacher, detailing his work and pupil assessments. For Betty, it was too much, too soon. Her head hurt.

She opened the bottom drawer. Here, coiled like a snake, was the dreaded strap. She studied it, saw that it was bigger and thicker and meaner than she had imagined. She pictured herself raising it, bringing it down on a child's tender hand. She slammed the drawer shut. No matter what they do, I'm not using that.

She gave herself a pep talk. Look over there, coward. A cupboard loaded with supplies. Look at all these possessions. Mine! My schoolhouse, my refuge—a place where only kids can see my mistakes.

I could live here if I had to, make up a bed under the desk. Safe. Curled up like a cat. I could get a baseball bat to ward off bears and I'd buy a pee pot from Mrs. Johnson's store. She grew bolder; walked to the front of the room.

And I might even teach myself to play this piano in my free time.

Heintzman & Company Limited, the gold letters read. She lifted the lid. She had never had piano lessons, other than being taught at the Normal School to play God Save the King on a cardboard keyboard. The ivories were as yellow as tobacco-stained teeth, and the key she calculated to be middle C was missing its facing, which, she reasoned, would make playing easier. She pressed a few keys. None of the trebles worked.

A handful of readers and arithmetic texts occupied the front seat of each row. Where, she wondered, are the supplementary texts? And surely there must be books the children can borrow? A little library somewhere? I'll ask Bill Trent. He's the trustee.

She examined the cupboard contents, made lists, then, holding in front of her a piece of thick stove kindling—bear protection—she ran like a hunted deer down the hill for a lunch break at Nina's café. Not a bear in sight. She raced back and tentatively outlined a week's schedule on foolscap.

Only one more task remained. She wrote on the board, "Good morning, class. My name is Miss Wheatley." She slanted and rounded and curled every letter to please the legendary Mr. McLean, the Normal School's guru of penmanship, whose ghostly image hung over her shoulder. She stood back. Her writing slanted uphill. She rubbed it out twice before it was horizontal, then drew an elaborate, curlicued series of lines under the words and bordered the entire message with flowers.

Such efficiency! She was proud of herself: her goals set out, her work begun.

Now she could go for afternoon tea with Vivian, janitor Len's wife, and was eager to do so. She found she was not as frightened as before; she was almost brave. Familiarity breeds contempt, her Gramma Beaton often said. Maybe if she stayed here long enough, she could stride by bears without a care, stare them down like the inferior creatures they are. Maybe.

~ Ж ~

Vivian, baby still in her arms, opened the screen door. Now that bears were not filling her thoughts, Betty could focus on her hostess. Vivian was a slender, oval-faced, astonishingly beautiful woman. Movie star material, thought Betty. Maybe I could talk her into running off to Hollywood with me so I can fulfill my true potential as an actress... She could get acting jobs for us both. "Miss Wheatley, uh, Betty, please come in." Vivian motioned for Betty to sit at a lace-and-frill table setting, shifted the baby to her hip as though she needed three hands to do the job, and fumbled with a teapot.

She'll drop that baby on the stove for sure, Betty thought. Fry it to a crisp. "May I pour the hot water for you?" she asked.

"Here. Baby Harry doesn't make shy." Vivian plopped the baby into Betty's arms. Betty waited for the infant to wail, but he just criss-crossed his hands under his chin.

It took beautiful Vivian forever to make the tea. She wiped and rewiped the already spotless work area. Betty had plenty of time to look around. Every conceivable surface gleamed. Fresh floor wax scented the air. When Vivian finally brought the teapot to the table, perspiration beaded her forehead. She panted as though she had just run the four-minute mile. She sat on the edge of her chair, her eyes darting everywhere except at Betty. She drummed well-chewed fingernails. "Four years ago was my first year of teaching. Len was my janitor, too. I saw him every day at the school. We were married in Nelson, my hometown, two years ago. Do you have a boyfriend yet?"

"Yes. Cameron. He's studying to be a—"

"A year's a long time. You'll probably find a new fellow up here. I had a boyfriend before I came up here. He must have hated me for jilting him." She frowned and scratched at an invisible food stain on the starched cloth.

"Well, we've been going steady for a year and a half. I'd better not find anyone else." Betty travelled back to last Friday's good-bye to Cameron at Robson dock. She had known as she waved to him from the Minto's upper deck that she was going to miss him desperately, miss the nights of passion, the sureness of his presence. A lump was forming in her chest; her voice was thickening, ready to grow tears. She could say no more.

Vivian seemed not to have heard her; her roaming eyes had spotted a wayward cookie crumb on the floor. She ran for the broom. "You'll get lonely living up here, but not as much as I have. I just dread the thought of winter. I just get a little—" She dropped the broom and dustpan with a clatter. The defiant crumb rolled back to the floor. She seemed to have forgotten it existed. Stood there.

The change in the girl was startling. From a glamorous perfectionist whirlwind to a zombie, thought Betty. Perhaps she's—Gaahh! A warm wetness had infiltrated Betty's clothing, had seeped into her crotch. She felt invaded, defiled. She hoisted Baby Harry skyward and he responded by issuing another well-aimed stream through his drooping diapers, again soaking Betty's lap. Baby Harry dripped drool as he smiled down on her, marvelling at his body's ability to drain itself.

"I'm so sorry, Betty," Vivian cried, as she carried soggy Harry away, flopping him about as if he were an armful of mercury. "It's just that I can't stand to use plastic pants on him, they incubate germs, and..." her voice trailed down the hallway.

Betty fanned her wet skirt beside the stove, ate three cookies and waited. How long did Vivian need to change a diaper? Probably wiping and re-wiping Baby Harry's bottom raw. Just like the kitchen counter, thought Betty.

When Len arrived, Vivian returned to the room. Len swooped up powder-scented Baby Harry and wrapped his free arm around Vivian.

Len's arms made Betty think of Cameron's arms—arms that could be wrapped around *her*. And *her* son someday.

"Here's your key, Len. I must be going. I have to get to the store." She eased herself toward the door. She could not stay another minute. Vivian's strangeness had undone the last of Betty's composure and the couple's domestic completeness made her feel infinitely lonely. Besides, she reeked of baby pee.

~ ж ~

Betty carried a heavy grocery bag up the hill. She also carried a heavy heart. Vivian and Len's closeness had accentuated her aloneness, made her long for Cameron. His face kept looming before her. She stopped abruptly.

I can't do this. I can't go around constantly thinking of Cameron and feeling sorry for myself. I'm not Vivian; I have no Len. I have to learn to be self-sufficient. I'll go crazy if I don't smarten up; I've got a whole year ahead of me.

She tried to think more positively. Look at me. I'm buying my own food. I'm earning my own money. I've got my own school and even a piano, for God's sake.

She continued her climb and her new train of thought. I've got to bide my time. I've got to put my love gears in neutral. I've got to be strong enough and tough enough to scout out a new place to live. Or move into the school and get that pee pot. I'll never use that outhouse. Ever.

In the silent apartment at Granny's place, she kindled a sputtering fire, ate half a scorched hamburger and a nearly raw potato before she gave up. I should have done more of the cooking, she thought. Not left it all up to sister Faye. I can't even make an edible meal.

Hell. I'll buy ketchup, she decided. It compensates for anything. That's a positive approach. Then she remembered that her mother would not allow ketchup in the house. A sudden, triumphant, bull-moose rage arose in her chest. "I'm the boss here and I'll cover the damn food with anything I like," she shouted to the phantom mother, her own voice startling her in the silence. Still, the mutinous thought cheered her up. "I'll eat what I want, I'll wear what I want, and—I'll break Normal School rules if I want."

That's it, Betty, she congratulated herself, that's the way. Don't let life get you down. Get through this year somehow. Take it just one day at a time.

Chapter 4

Today is the tomorrow you worried about yesterday.
—Jack Miner

"And what grade are you in?" A hearty voice that Betty barely recognised as her own, spoke. The voice of THE TEACHER. Good. Sound like one even if you don't feel like one. Play it like a stage role. Use this life experience for when you become a famous actress someday.

"Grade four, Miss Wheatley," replied two angelic little girls in first-day finery: dresses of flower-sprigged cotton, stiff hair bows on hair braided so tightly it tugged at their eyelids. One was Ingrid Johnson, the daughter of the storekeeper.

A lumbering bus roared into sight. Len, the driver, cranked open the door, and wary students streamed out, stopped dead and stared at Betty. "Darn school board and their darn keys," muttered Len as he took the stairs two at a time to unlock the schoolhouse door. He geared the protesting motor and rattled back down the hill.

As soon as Betty disappeared into the school, the children began to talk. Quietly at first, but by degrees boisterous playground energy took over. Quarter to nine, by her wind-up Bulova. She wished that the clock worked. How did she know what the exact time was?

The playground was now in full swing. Betty peeked out the windows at the unruly children: pushing one another, shrieking, chasing, taunting. Oh, God. What if they don't stop? Can't quiet down? She put her hands over her ears.

At Bulova-nine, she rang the school bell. For a seemingly dull, insignificant chunk of metal, it had a powerful effect: the commotion ceased and fifteen pairs of chary eyes turned toward her. She rummaged for the voice of THE TEACHER again.

"Good morning, boys and girls, please line up." Get a grip, she told herself, it's curtain time. Act One.

She descended the stairs with as much majesty as King George reviewing the Grenadier Guards. "Grade sixes, here," she heard herself command in a regal voice. She stretched out both arms indicating a path. Several moved to this spot. Formed a line.

Thank you, God. They are obeying me!

She continued to organize them in rows and then marched them into the schoolhouse.

"My name, as you can see by the blackboard, is Miss Wheatley. I hope we will have a wonderful year together."

She moved up and down the aisles dispensing yellow pencils. As each in turn rose to go and sharpen the new pencils, others grew restless. They shuffled, giggled, kept checking her face, watching for signs of weakness. Her stomach had now formed a Gordian knot.

"I have some questions." Hah! I've got their attention! Thanks again, God.

"Does anyone know if the high school has a library we can use?"

Blank looks. The friend of the storekeeper's daughter raised her hand. Though she was only a grade four pupil, she spoke well, with assurance. "They don't have a library. They just have two rooms."

"Does anyone know if we have access to sports equipment?" Several hands shot up.

"The high school borrows us a softball and bat or we bring our own."

"Lends. Not borrows." What a sad place, she thought. Not one extra book, not even a softball. These poor kids.

She tore foolscap sheets into thirds, just as she had seen countless other teachers do. Waste not, want not.

"On your papers, I want you to print the following." She turned to the blackboard and chalked:

1. Name
2. Favourite school subject

A child snickered. Betty whirled around. A grade-four boy grinned at her, saying, "My favourite subject is recess."

"Mine is lunch break," added one of the grade-five boys, accompanied by a braying laugh. Tittering laughter swelled, body language became menacing.

She searched for the teacher voice, but this time it did not appear. "Th–that's enough." The regal tone had fled, leaving behind a thin reed, more like the squeal of a bagpipe.

They did not stop. They were pulling away. The tallest sixth-grader, Dot's 'great big skinny bugger'—at least six feet tall, decided Betty—sent his pencil spinning high into the air, caught it and looked to the class for approval. A ragged cheer. Desk beating.

She filled her lungs and tried again. "You better buckle down, or we won't get done." No effect. Flustered and alarmed at her inability to command their attention, and not knowing what to do, she simply turned to the blackboard and continued printing:

3. Address
4. Age
5. Place of birth
6. Birthday
7. Last school attended
8. Hobbies

She had no idea why, but they quieted and picked up their pencils. The steady writing seemed to settle them. Keep them busy. Was that the answer? She began to breathe again, walking up and down the aisles as they pencilled their information.

It dawned on her that her simple request had become an IQ test. Some finished quickly, some agonized over every point, other than their names. The grade sixes, three boys and one girl, were done first. They began to fidget—sliding about on their seats, turning around, warming up for mischief. She collected their papers and loomed over the six-foot pencil-flipper. She tried to study their answers with one eye and watch him with the other.

"Keith." She looked at the boy in the back seat. "I see that you went to school in Vancouver last year. Have you met any of your classmates during the summer?" Keith Evans: round shouldered, lethargic, with an asthmatic wheeze. He shook his head.

"I gather, from your address, you live at the construction site for the dam they're building. You're new here. Just like me." He stared down at his desk, shoulders hunched even more. She belatedly realized that she had inflicted upon him the worst of wounds: she had categorized him with herself. She let him slip back into oblivion.

"All the rest of you come from Trent's Landing?" The sixth-graders nodded.

As she scanned their slips of paper, she noted great age differences. Keith Evans was eleven, the average grade-six age. Alec Detweiler—daunting, pencil spinning, big skinny bugger—was fourteen. Fourteen, and only in grade six? Strange. He did not look slow. The only grade six girl, Margie Sloboda, was twelve. Bony and awkward.

Three of the fourth-graders were still struggling to answer the questions. It was now past nine-thirty.

She gathered up the fifth-grader's papers and examined them. "I see you all like playing softball. We'd better borrow that bat and ball from the high school really soon." They stared at her impassively. She gave out more paper, chalked a purchase list onto the blackboard and asked the class to copy it.

She went to see what was holding up the three remaining fourth-graders, and was aghast at the slow progress of the 'recess' boy—the one with the engaging grin. Large and unformed printing, assignment half-done. He was staring out the window until she approached, then he applied himself again. She looked at the paper of the little girl behind him. She wrote legibly, but had progressed no further. The last of the slow ones was also the tiniest. He barely showed above the desk he had chosen. She made a mental note to move him—he should be up at the front. All that he had on his paper was his name: Donny Rodman. What was the problem, here, she wondered?

"Finished or not, I must collect your papers. Start copying down your supply lists."

She analyzed the fourth-graders. A great difference in their abilities. The well-spoken one—Helena Stevens—was equal to the fastest sixth-grader. Tiny Donny Rodman was no better than a first-grader.

The rest of the class were soon done and testing their pencil-flipping prowess. Cripes, she wailed inwardly, I've got a class of budding anarchists.

It was now five minutes before bus time. "Everyone who is finished is dismissed," she declared. When they were out of sight, she helped the remaining three complete their lists. "Don't worry, you'll soon speed up." As she stood back and let them go, tiny Donny Rodman passed by her as if in a stupor. The girl managed the wan smile of the defeated. The 'recess' boy—Howard Carson—did not look defeated. His smile was broad and cocky. "G'bye, Miz Sweetly." The bus rumbled into sight. They were soon gone.

She collapsed into her chair and groaned. One hour. It had felt like ten. So much to assess, so much to do. She opened the folder of information left behind by last year's teacher. Studied his descriptions. Who would be her adversaries? She had better identify them: Alec Detweiler, big-bugger pencil flipper, held back for illness and unspecified reasons. With an opinionated father who did not believe in schooling, who would yank his son out as soon as he was of age, wrote last year's teacher. Two others, failed too many times: Raymond Whittaker and Howard Carson. The rest? A wide variety of abilities and backgrounds. They all seemed decent enough, yet all could be potential monsters.

Monsters. Oh, Lord, what am I doing here? I'll never get through this week, let alone a whole year. She was struggling with the next day's preparations, when school trustee Bill Trent arrived at the door.

"Here's your register and your key, Betty. I hope you've found things to your satisfaction."

"Oh, the students and I already get along well. Everything's positively wonderful, thank you, Mr. Trent," she lied. "Just a few teeny problems."

"Shoot 'm by me."

"First, the clock. I don't think my watch is that dependable."

"Well, as long as you're fairly close to the mark it won't hurt. Slow or fast, a watch can still mark off a six-hour day. Go by the bus times if you get too far out." Betty looked dumbfounded.

Bill explained, "I've had a requisition for a new clock for three years. This one's beyond repair. Len and I have both had a go at it."

"I need supplementary readers. I can see a great discrepancy in performance already. And some story books and some reference books and some—"

"Lord Almighty, you're asking for a whole library!" He tried unsuccessfully to suppress a deep belch. "There's no supplementary readers. Anywhere. Send a short list of library books you want to Inspector McIntyre. You might get them. Anything else?"

She hurried her words. Bill was drumming an impatient foot. "Yes. When does Inspector McIntyre visit the school?"

Bill sighed and his innards rumbled. "McIntyre's visits are surprises to us all. Keeps us on our toes. He just appears at any time. Never know how often, either. But," he offered, "not usually more than twice a year. That it?" She nodded. He left.

Betty slumped at her desk, her head in her hands. *How did I get to this god-forsaken place*—she thought miserably.

Her mind went back to a hazy classroom, the face and flippant words of the Trail High School guidance teacher. She frowned. *He's the one I listened to; he's the one I trusted. Yes, the one who told me that Vancouver Normal School was a snap, a breeze, as easy as pie. That anyone with half a brain got a teaching certification without doing a lick of work. Have fun, the guidance teacher had said. Misguidance teacher. What a liar! What a gigantic, diabolic lie! And I chose to believe him.*

Annoyance with both her duped self and the roseate guidance teacher made her shake her head. Resignedly, she picked up the arithmetic books. While studying the arithmetic review chapters, she suddenly heard footsteps. She walked to the door.

Approaching her stairway was a red-faced, overweight man, around the age of thirty, dressed in a rumpled grey business suit, wearing a fedora, carrying a bruised briefcase and wiping his damp face with a handkerchief.

When he saw Betty, he hastened toward her.

"How d'you do, Miss Wheatley. Edwin Chalmers. Ensconced for a portentous year further up the hillside at the high school." He swept the hat from his head and stretched out his hand to shake Betty's. She received his wet grasp, which was as slippery as a fish—a bloated, soft fish—but she managed to keep a civil face. Oblivious, he wheezily advanced.

"Would it inconvenience you if I entered your little schoolroom? It is customary for beleaguered educators to search for kindred sustenance."

She stepped back. "Come in." She could not understand why she felt so put off by this man. It was unlike her to feel so unfriendly to someone who seemed so harmless.

His warm bulk dwarfed the doorway, caused the student desktop to moan as he dropped his mass onto it. He continued to mop his face with the soaked handkerchief.

"The first day, the first breath, is the beginning of death. Cobwebs and indifference. Pearls to the swine. Do you think you'll get used to it?" She resented the instant familiarity in his voice.

"This is a damned lonely place. You won't mind if I intrude on your privacy occasionally?" He seemed not to need an answer. "Some of those fellows...pure savages, I should say." He shook his head. Sweat sprayed from it. "Bewilderment reigns. A nightmare prevails on the upper hillside. I need the other teacher, the invisible Miss Kate Bradshaw, to appear soon, because I'm fielding both classrooms and all the students. Every grade from seven to twelve. Teaching in such chaos is comparable to swimming in treacle." He shifted his weight. The desk groaned.

"How can one person teach two classrooms?"

"Ah, forbearance—at this time I must plough my furrow alone."

"Have you heard anything about Miss Bradshaw and her car accident?"

"Mr. William Trent told me a mere hour ago that he is expecting the unfortunate Miss Bradshaw tomorrow or Thursday."

"Oh no... She's going to take away my apartment. I don't know where I'll end up."

"So William Trent informs me. I trust he will soon find such a well-countenanced young woman as yourself something suitable. I'm residing in the last available room in the Trent's Landing boarding house and so is the Trent's Landing teacher, the aloof Miss Dot LaPointe. It's an adequate arrangement, with a commanding view of the lake and all passers-by, although I must say, I'd have preferred to have my wife and son here with me." There was the slightest crack in his wry manner. Wide enough for Betty to see he was masking deeper feelings.

"It must be difficult for you to be here without your family."

He entwined his thick fingers. Inverted them. Stared at them. "My wife says that such an outpost as this is quite unsuitable for our son." Irony tinged his half smile. "He's due to commence his education this fall, and she is determined to save him from the negligence of a country school. They will remain in Victoria."

Is he, she wondered, already resigned to failure? He's like a lifeguard who believes he's going to drown. "I think...I know...I'm a pedagogic misfit. I'm on trial this year."

Betty could not bear the burden of his lonely suffering on top of her own. She put her negative feelings aside. "I'm a misfit, too. I didn't perform well at Normal School," she confided.

"My misfortune also. If you don't mind, I'll disturb your threshold occasionally, for a bit of companionship?"

"Uhhh...okay, I guess."

He went to the door, then paused. "You don't play chess, do you?"

"No."

"A pity. But I'll teach you if you want, we could play right here, perhaps a couple of times a week."

Chess? With him? Her temporary sense of charity darted out the door ahead of him. "Oh, I couldn't possibly. I expect I'll be far too busy." I'll probably end up living here in my school anyway, she thought. No way I'm going to entertain strange men in my strange home.

"Perhaps. Who knows the shape of things to come? I'm going to my quarters for a rest." He returned the brand-new fedora to his head. It looked so eccentric here in Narrows. Betty repressed a smirk. "Until we meet again, Miss Wheatley."

She did not have enough interest to tell him her first name. "Good-bye, Mr. Chalmers."

What a day to choose for a social visit—the first day of the school year! "He can desert his ship if he wants, but I'm getting as prepared as possible," she muttered. She frowned at the piano. "Don't tempt me, I have to work."

She would have to have two-thirds of the students working independently while she taught the remainder. And she had learned one thing today: the more work there was for them, the better; leave them no time to plot her downfall.

As the sun cast slanting beams into the room, she looked around with grim satisfaction. The blackboards boasted work for each grade, in all the morning subjects. Spelling hogged the most space: questions needing full-sentence answers for the sixth-graders, fill-in-the-blanks sentences for the fifth-graders, match-the-jumbled-words-to-the-right-ones for the fourth-graders. Supplemental arithmetic problems and reading exercises squeezed into the remaining space.

At lunchtime, that work will be finished with, and I'll put up the afternoon stuff.

She had studied the review chapters in all three arithmetic texts and had chosen the science and social studies topics. She could carry on for one full day, but no further.

For now, she was done. As the sunrays slanted more, she raced down the hillside to Granny's house. To Granny's bathroom. No outhouses for Betty. She was even looking forward to her remaining scorched hamburgers. She carried home two thumbtacks.

~ Ж ~

Writing the letter to Cameron did it; the final straw, after her draining initiation into teacherhood. She could not summon the helpful internal pep talk of the previous day. Yearning for him weighed her down; the need for his comforting arms and words returned anew. And she was homesick. Tears rolled down her cheeks, she made no effort to stop them. "Softy," she whispered to her shadow on the unpainted pine boards. "Cowardly-lion softy."

On the bedroom wall, right beside her pillow, she thumbtacked a photo of Cameron. Kissed him and turned off the lamp. She could not get to sleep; the sight of him had made her think about their lovemaking, think about the first time they had kissed—the time when he had whispered to her to soften her lips, had taught her to make them send messages, to yield herself with them. And now, overtaking the classroom woes, her body ached with longing.

~ Ж ~

She double-checked the work on the boards, swallowed hard and rang the school bell. Today, this second morning, though they stared at her with impenetrable eyes, they seemed calmer. "Please stand at attention and bow your heads for the Morning Prayer." They droned the Our Father and sang God Save The King with the enthusiasm of sleepwalkers.

Although most of the class were clean and neat, a few reeked of barnyard smells; had dirt-laden fingernails and bird's nest hair. "Beginning tomorrow, we will have the daily health check. Remember: clean hands, face, fingernails and ears, neatly brushed hair and a clean handkerchief."

"Miz Sweetly, you forgot teeth. And I don't got no toothbrush." It was Howard Carson. The recess kid. One of the infamous Carsons that Dot had warned her about.

"I have no tooth brush. Not 'I don't got no tooth brush'."

"Our hired hand has got one; I could lend his."

"Borrow his...uhhh, no...oh, just clean your teeth with a clean rag and baking soda if you don't have a toothbrush, Howard."

There were no mutinous uprisings and at recess they filed out for their fifteen-minute break. She flashed the crammed blackboards a grateful look. All that preparation had paid off. There's not much to teaching after all, she thought, just hard work.

She watched them from the windows. The boys had brought bats and balls from home.

No girls were allowed in their game, she noticed. The girls played hopscotch. All but Daisy Whittaker, a tiny, blonde fifth-grader, who stood alone, hungering for the ball game.

The fifteen minutes flew by so fast that Betty cheated and allowed them another five before she rang the intrusive bell.

The sunshiny smell of their hair, the fresh sweat of their healthy bodies mixed into a distinct, almost pleasant odour as they filed in and slid into their seats. It was short-lived; the barnyard odour resurfaced.

A hand flew up. Howard Carson again. More of Dot's words echoed in her head: The Carsons. Little savages. They throw fits when they don't get their way. The brown-haired girl who sat behind Howard was a Carson, too: Jenny Carson, as shy and skittish as a deer mouse. It did not seem possible that this sunny boy would cause any serious problems, either. Maybe Dot had exaggerated.

Howard smiled at her as she acknowledged his waving hand. "Please Miz Sweetly, can I go out to the pump to get a drink?"

"I'm afraid not, Howard, you must know that a school rule is drinks at recess and lunch only. And my name is Miss Wheatley, not Sweetly." His sunny smile vanished.

Betty began her next lessons. She had worked through the spelling, concentrating on juggling the three grades, locating all the different levels of ability, before she realized that Howard was sending out troubling smoke signals: legs sprawled across one aisle, arm looped over the desk behind him, eyes staring moodily at the dead clock. She sucked in her breath. Please God, this morning has been okay. Please. Let it continue.

"Howard, you're not working."

"Ahhgrrrrrrr...!" From deep in Howard's throat came the guttural growl, the snarl, of a wild dog and it grew louder as he swept his books and papers from his desk, heaving with all his might, trying to overturn the entire row of desks to which his was joined. The row leapt out of place from his violence; the other children in it tumbled from their seats. What extraordinary strength! What an unholy sound! Finally, he dropped to the floor, kicking wildly, wrenching his vocal cords even louder. No words emerged, only an ear-splitting, feral sound.

Before Betty had time to think, she grabbed Howard by his shoulders and jerked him upward. Her hand positions on his shoulders were good. She held him fast. They lurched sideways, knocking textbooks and exercise books and pencils from the desks they passed as they stumbled all the way into the cloakroom. Betty still not reasoning; simply obeying some ancient, inner instinct of survival: separating the sick from the well, separating the insane from the angry, chaos from order. By the time they got to the cloakroom, his body was slack, his temper spent, and he was wailing in a broken, unnerving voice. She pushed him onto one of the benches.

"Now, sit here until you can regain your manners. You can't return to the class until you're in control of yourself." She shut the cloakroom door.

The shocked children gaped at her. "It's all right, class. Howard will be fine presently." He was already quiet. She walked to the front of the room, pushed up her constantly slipping eyeglasses and resumed teaching as though she carted off wild animals regularly.

The class tried to return to work, but all minds were on Howard, including her own. Her legs had become boneless; they could not believe what she had just done. She took stock of herself. Fortunately, her voice was not quavering and her stage-nature had surfaced once more.

After a long seven minutes and a hundred glances at her Bulova watch and a growing fear, a horrible vision, of Howard; now producing horns and breathing fire from his nostrils, she heard a tentative voice from the cloakroom. "Miz Sweetly?"

She deliberately walked slowly to the back of the room. "Yes, Howard?"

Silence. Then an almost whisper. "I'm in control of myself."

Oh, oh, oh, thank you, thank you, God! I promise to go to church!

She kept her voice cool. "Well, I'm glad, Howard. See that you don't carry on like that again in this class." She fished in her pocket for her handkerchief and wiped away his tearstains. Resisted an urge to crush the deflated, forlorn little fellow to her chest.

He returned to his row. She helped him pick up his books and papers. The three members of the first row pulled the seats back into line.

The tears on Jenny Carson's face told Betty that whatever Howard Carson might be, his sister Jenny would not be a discipline problem. Howard, to Betty's astonishment, made a miraculously quick recovery—had the audacity to grin at everyone.

Betty felt drained. She would have liked to go and hide under her desk. Crawl into her could-be bed.

~ ж ~

At noon, she and the students ate their lunch together. The children had milk in mayonnaise jars; sandwiches and cookies packed in lard or jam pails. They chatted freely, oblivious of her presence.

No rules at lunchtime and no problems either, she observed. Some lesson was to be learned from this situation, she felt, but she did not know what it might be.

Despite her violent confrontation with Howard, they did not look at her with fear or loathing. It was as though they knew she would have to undergo such a wild initiation with him.

For the last period of the day, she had scheduled a softball game, and she joined in. Betty swung the bat with all her might. Pinkk! The ball sailed high. Dropped into the pitcher's mitt.

"Wow, Miz Sweetly, you sure can hit 'em!" Howard called out.

But Grant, a freckled and serene sixth-grader, frowned. He was as tall as she. All the sixth-graders were her height or taller. She found this unnerving. "Are you going to be able to coach us for the annual game with Kokanee?"

"What annual game?"

"Every spring we have a softball game with Kokanee," explained Grant. "It's hard to beat 'em; they've got more kids than we do. Last year's teacher, he coached us and we nearly beat 'em for the first time. He was great." His easy-going face warmed to the memory of the previous year's near triumph.

"Uhhh...we can try hard," replied Betty. What on earth am I going to do? I've never coached anything. She forced a smile. "We'll practice and practice until we're top-notch." Grant looked as convinced of her abilities as trustee Bill Trent had.

A coughing bus muffler interrupted the game. Betty had lost track of time. "Hurry! Everyone back into the class to tidy up!"

They shoved their way into the classroom, jammed their new school supplies into their desks, grabbed their lard-cum-lunch pails and rushed for the bus. The big ones scrambled in first. Howard Carson, acting as though she'd never skirmished with him, was one of the last in. "G'bye, Miz Sweetly," he hollered. Fighting the desire to correct him on her name, she forced a smile and

41

waved. Several others, already in their seats, smiled back and waved, too.

As the gears complained and the bus rolled away, she shook her head.

I dragged Howard about like he was a wild beast; I penned him up like I was his jailer. What kind of awful person am I? And he's forgiven me! And the rest? They couldn't care less. I don't understand.

Dainty, tight-braided Ingrid and Helena—the only students who lived in Narrows, and therefore did not need to take the bus—followed her back into the classroom. "Please, Miss Wheatley, can we clean the blackboards and bang the chalk brushes?"

Betty gave her approval, returned to her desk and began her preparations for the next day.

Grunts. Then loud and fierce whispers. "Give them to me, you greedy—!"

"Let go. I want to—I got it first!"

Betty looked up just as the two fallen angels began pummelling one another with blackboard brushes. Chalk dust flew around the room like an invasion of gnats, settling on Betty's precious piano, clouding the face of King George and causing Betty to sneeze and cough and choke, all at once. "Stop!" She croaked, like an asthmatic frog.

The girls looked as if they had just clambered out of a flour bin. Betty, with weary arms, dusted them off as best she could, and shooed them home. Now her nerves were as shredded as the old chesterfield in Granny's apartment.

~ Ж ~

Static squealed and squawked from the Philco radio console. "I'm eternally grateful for this radio. It's attached to Bill's generator. On good nights I get stations in the United States. Sometimes even the UK."

Granny handed Betty a cup of cocoa. "You need outside news, Betty, or you'll get bushed. I subscribe to the Star Weekly and my English magazine, Woman's Own. Establish some sort of outside contact. You can't let the world pass you by. It gets too easy up here. Did you know that poor King George isn't in the best of health? He has..." She bobbed her head like an exclamation point. "...terrible troubles." She would not use that dreaded, awful word: cancer. "Mark my words, Princess Elizabeth will be Queen by her next visit."

They waited by the radio, sipping Fry's cocoa. Waited for any words from the rest of the world. An hour later, Betty bade her good night. Granny still sat by the radio, and still no sense came from it.

~ Ж ~

In the middle of the night, strange sounds woke her—a soft, scuttling hubbub coming from the other room: the sneaky sounds of invasive mice. She winced, sighed, then banged her arm on the wall softly, so as not to wake Granny. The noise stopped. But soon, it began again.

"Shoo!" she hissed. Silence. But not for long. She was afraid to get out of bed to investigate. What if one runs up my pajama leg...right up? She squeezed her thighs tight.

I'm not even safe in bed. They can climb; they can skitter over me while I sleep. Bite my ears. Chew my nose.

She pulled the covers over her head and listened. There was nothing cute about them. The filthy vermin sounded as though they were everywhere, investigating everything she owned, holding races.

Then she heard a louder noise. Grinding. Scraping. She had not a clue what it might be, unless they were now chewing on the leg of her bed. She lay rigidly, with blankets tucked tightly around her body and head. Eventually she slept.

In the morning, all was quiet.

Oh, no. Sometime in the night, she had thrown off all her blankets—no face and head protection. She patted her face, which seemed unharmed, and studied every inch of the floor before putting one foot out of the bed, then she swivelled her head left and right, up and down --checking for mice--as she tiptoed into the kitchen.

Mouse droppings by the sink. And something else—bits of shredded burlap. She poked at the burlap bag of potatoes that sat on the floor. It did not move. When she pulled the bag open with a fork, she experienced waves of indignation. *Little fiends! Eating my potatoes!*

More mouse excrement near the bread and cereal. She ate her Quaker Puffed Wheat with the scrutiny of a Mountie on a murder case, overturning each spoonful, searching for vermin evidence.

She made her lunch—a peanut butter sandwich of the life-threatening bread—and scribbled a note to give Granny. A simple will in case she died from accidentally eating mice droppings. She stared at it. *What am I doing?* She crumpled the note and threw it in the fire. The flames crackled-laughed.

Chapter 5

She has not a single redeeming defect.
–Apologies to Benjamin Disraeli

Betty read the obligatory What I Did On My Summer Vacation compositions. And felt sick. The finished results were as uninspired as the topic. Compositions, she knew, summed up all that a student had learned. And these compositions exposed stunted imaginations, puny vocabularies and laboured spelling. Only two students, Keith Evans and Helena Stevens, wrote at an acceptable level.

What can I do, should I do? She stared, blank-brained, at the scratchy writing, at the spiteful inkblots from the stiff metal pen nibs. She stared at them for an hour, but no solution magically appeared, no Normal School training came to her rescue. It was after five; she locked the school and descended the hill.

~ ж ~

Nina Trent, Bill's wife, collided with her as she opened Granny's back door. "I'm treating tonight, Betty. Supper at my house. Celebrating the closing up of my café until spring. Bill's working, so it's just us girls and my kids. See you about six, okay?" She rushed off.

How nice! No cooking!

Inside Granny's kitchen stood a newcomer. On crutches. One of her legs was encased in white bandage from thigh to calf.

"Betty Wheatley, no doubt. I hear you've managed to take over my territory while I was getting smashed up. Stealing my apartment!" It was Kate Bradshaw, the high school teacher. Come to serve eviction papers.

Betty's face turned red, then white. "There–there's not many places to stay around here."

"I'm well aware of that." The edginess in Kate's voice sliced as sharply as Granny's bread guillotine. "You owe me four days rent."

Betty took a quick survey of the unsettling interloper: piercing dark eyes, circled with black shadows of pain. A jaundice-coloured face. Kate's features were good; she was almost beautiful. But a simmering rage, wanting to boil over, marred them. She was athletically built: not an ounce of fat on her sinewy body. She wore no make up, and a pale sensual mouth drew attention even more to the dark eyes. Black curly hair hung down to her shoulders.

"I'm sure there's room for you both – it's a big space, so you could share the place," suggested spunky Granny.

"Share? No! That wasn't the arrangement. I had first dibs on this place. It's mine." Kate jabbed a crutch at Granny's browbeaten linoleum, then pointed it at Betty. "Unless... you make it worth my while. I'll accept a sixty-forty rent split. And as it's my apartment, I set the house rules."

Betty frowned. Began forming a protest. Searched for arguments, alternatives, bargaining chips. And found she had none. Her only alternative—a bed under a desk in an isolated schoolhouse—silenced her. The nest that was now her night-time refuge—the cozy, sunken nest in the middle of the saggy upstairs bed—silenced her.

She already loved that safe haven. Besides, it wasn't as if she had never lived with a tyrant; her father's explosive outbursts had conditioned her.

Still, I ought to at least try to negotiate. She concentrated.

Kate Bradshaw's impatient voice snapped across the room like a whip. "Take it or leave it. Co-operate or out you go."

"I—I agree," said Betty.

When Kate saw Betty's shoulders sag, she swagger-crutched off to the bathroom.

Granny scurried to Betty's side. "Ugh! What a nasty piece! That Bill. He couldn't have checked her out. She's going to be trouble. Don't you let her boss you around," Granny hiss-whispered. They jumped apart when Kate reopened the door.

~ Ж ~

Kate pulled herself up to the apartment, stair-by-stair. Betty followed and was amazed at the transformation of the space. Books sat on makeshift shelves, dishes and pots filled the kitchen, cardboard boxes crowded every corner.

"Wow. You certainly have a lot of possessions," Betty said, in as neutral a voice as possible. Non-incendiary.

"I've been on my own and in the CWACs for years."

That explains a lot, Betty thought. *A war vet. Probably a sergeant—a bossy drill sergeant.* "How did you get all this stuff here?"

"A travelling salesman brought my boxes in his car. Bill Trent set it up." Kate snapped her fingers. "I need a sweater and my purse. You carry them." Betty complied rather than face another outburst. "It'll be cool tonight," Kate decreed. Betty grabbed a sweater for herself. She suppressed an impulse to salute.

~ Ж ~

Savoury goodness emanated from Nina's kitchen as the door flew open. A junior Nina, her cheeks flushed and eyes sparkling, said, "I'm Phyllis.

I'm in your class, Miss Bradshaw."

Nina was tending pots and pans on a massive Moffat range. Above its cooking surface a warming oven's polished chrome door distorted Betty and Kate's reflections like a fun-house mirror. The child triumphed over the adult in Betty and she allowed herself one quick wiggle, fascinated with her bizarre reflection, while Nina's son hovered over his mother's shoulder. "We're having lamb chops. My favourite." A solid farm table dominated the roomy kitchen. Checkered cloth, Blue Willow plates, and a jug filled with daisies.

"Albert's in your class, too, Miss Bradshaw. I'm in grade nine and he's in grade seven," said Phyllis.

Kate winced when she sat. "I need a glass of water," she panted. Phyllis fetched water and Kate washed down two white pills, leaned back and moaned, kept sucking in deep breaths. They hovered over her. She finally spoke. "Don't...stare. I'll...be fine."

What's going on, Betty wondered. Kate has flipped from a hostile negotiator to a pathetic invalid!

"How did the accident happen, Kate?" asked Nina.

"Accident? Accident?" Now Kate's face became as distorted as Betty's image had in the Moffat range door. "Bloody truck deliberately jumped out of a side road and ploughed into us. My passenger, Elaina Maleyna, had her neck wrenched badly. The idiot of a driver smashed right into the front of us."

"The front? You mean the side?" asked Albert.

Kate's eyes narrowed. "What? The front, I said."

Albert persisted. "But... coming from a side—"

"Albert, mind your manners." Nina's voice was sharp.

"He rammed us. Full force. Stupid teenager. He'll pay for it; pay dearly. I'll see to that." Kate's face reshaped itself. And her voice changed. "I was bruised everywhere—it's fading now—and my knee is a complete mess. My van is totally destroyed. It will be ages before it's fixed."

The pragmatic Albert again: "If it was destroyed—"

"Albert!" warned Nina.

Kate ignored the boy. "The pain is terrible. I don't want to talk about it." She turned to Phyllis. "Who's been teaching you?"

"Mr. Chalmers. He's been teaching both classes." She grinned. "The first day he ran back and forth between classes like a fat Charlie Chaplin on an assembly line—he looked so funny we couldn't stop laughing. Now he just stuffs us all into the same classroom, two to a desk."

Kate looked irritated. "Ridiculous. Why didn't Bill get a substitute teacher?"

"You'll have to ask him," answered Nina.

"He could at least have asked that former teacher, what's-her-name, the janitor's wife," said Kate. "What foolishness. Trying to save a nickel."

Nina bristled at the criticism of her husband. To Betty, she looked ready to spear Kate with her knife and fork and heave her into the stove.

"Oh, no, Kate." Betty had to jump in. Give a logical explanation and save Nina. Nina was not only the wife of their school trustee, but she was also, obviously, a first-rate cook. And Betty hoped to someday be invited back. "Bill couldn't hire Vivian; she's married. Dot says you can't teach once you're married, and—" But the gathering ball of flame in Kate's eyes made Betty adopt prudence. She changed the subject. She asked the children about her school's annual softball game against Kokanee.

"Give up," groaned Phyllis, shaking her head. "Kokanee always wins."

Albert agreed. "Yeah, I had a home run last year and we still lost."

"Typical boy. Blame the teacher," said Kate.

Betty squirmed. "I heard there are community dances to look forward to," she said, trying again to move them to safer ground.

Phyllis chattered about the dances at the local community hall, the gifted local fiddlers and the potluck desserts. "Trent's Landing has dances, too, and sometimes even movies."

"It's not all work and no play," said Nina. Albert, his mouth full of lamb, nodded agreement.

"Well, it will be for me," sighed Kate. "I can't dance. Not like this."

"Even watching can be fun," Betty said.

"What do you know?" snapped Kate. "You're not in pain."

Thanks to the pall Kate spread, every conversation died before it began. Shortly after eight, the promising evening ended like a B-grade movie. No one wanted it to continue.

~ Ж ~

Upstairs, Kate gestured with one crutch. "Let's get down to business. Week one, you cook and buy groceries. I wash up and clean the place. Week two, we switch. Got it?" She shifted her weight and went on. "The cook, on her week, must have dinner prepared by five. It's healthy to have meals on time. Right?"

Betty, caught in Kate's web, merely nodded.

Kate continued. "The cook gets up at seven and lights the stove."

"I haven't been lighting the fire in the morning—a cold breakfast isn't too bad."

"The first frost will change your tune. Besides, you need hot water for washing yourself and dishes."

Betty had no stomach for arguing, especially with this very taut and coal-eyed, changeable creature. "Okay. But how do we do all this, when you're in such bad shape?"

"I'm used to a tough life." Kate lowered her head into the palms of her hands. Her hair fell forward and Betty could not see her face. She spoke so quietly that Betty could barely hear her. "I'll survive. I've survived worse. Much worse."

Betty noted the contrast between the caustic voice and the exhausted face, and despite the verbal blows she had received, she softened. "Perhaps, for the next few weeks, I can do the strenuous things. You do the easier ones."

Kate studied her for a second. Conceded. "I only need a few days. Then I'll even the score."

"That's fine with me, Kate."

"Then heat some water and I'll start on the food budget."

Betty made the fire, brewed tea. Put out Dad's cookies.

"How old are you?" asked Kate.

"Nineteen. I'll be twenty in June."

"My luck. Spend all day teaching teenagers and now I have to tolerate another adolescent at night."

And I, thought Betty, have to tolerate a mean old spinster. She must be at least thirty. "When did you join the army?"

"It was the CWACs—Canadian Women's Army Corps. Women aren't allowed in the real army. Bloody males. Same rank, paid a third more than us." She clenched her fists until their knuckles were white. "I sneaked in when I was sixteen, to get away from my stepmother. After the war, I finished high school and went to UBC on a veteran's grant."

"Are you on better terms with your stepmother now?"

"Are you always this nosy?" Kate hopped to the stove. Checked the temperature of the wash-up water. "My father and stepmother are strait-laced Baptists. It's impossible to live by their bloody, sanctimonious rules."

Betty waited for more. However, Kate crutched off to the bedroom and came back with her pyjamas under her arm. Betty transferred the basin of hot water to the table.

"Do you need help with undressing or washing?"

"Good Lord, no."

~ ж ~

Betty climbed into her bed.

"Kate?"

"Yes?"

"Don't be surprised if you hear mice running around. I hope you're not afraid of them. I forgot to go and buy some traps today."

"Good Christ. The last thing I'd be afraid of is mice."

Betty lay awake, waiting for the verbal bruises to stop stinging; Kate took less than a heartbeat to fall asleep. Betty counted the days until Christmas. To the day when she could flee from this brusque bully. "I hate being here," she mouthed to the darkness. She felt very sorry for herself. Especially when the mice returned to frolic and forage again.

~ ж ~

Betty had not yet opened her eyes when she heard Kate clumping her way downstairs to the bathroom. Thump! Drag...Thump! Drag... The military cadence broke the silence everywhere she went. Though she had only had two days of it, now, the beat was already tattooed on Betty's brain. Soon, Kate was back upstairs, lighting the fire. It was Saturday and Betty wanted to lie abed. But she got up. Kate looked at her with frustration. "I can't put the water on." Already the fire crackled. The stove had leapt into action; it, too, obeying Kate.

"That's okay. I'm supposed to do the hard stuff, remember?" Betty filled the kettle and wash pan. Placed them on the stove.

"Did you look at the mouse traps?"

"No, I forgot."

"We've caught three. One baby."

Betty swallowed hard. "A baby mouse?"

"For Pete's sake, Betty, they're nothing but dirty pests. Come, we've got to reset them."

Betty followed her to the open space behind the kitchen wall, where they had placed the three traps. She looked in horror at splayed out furry bodies, at bulging dead eyes.

"Go get a paper bag." Betty got one. "Open the traps and get them out." Betty's mouth fell open. "Now!" flared Kate. Betty did not move.

"Oh, Christ, what a bloody sissy. Hold my crutch." Kate bent over and

50

retrieved one-by-one each of the traps and emptied them into the paper bag Betty held.

"Put the bag into the stove and bring me some more cheese." Betty dumped the mice into the flames, engulfed with queasiness as she watched the flames twist and shrink and char them. Cremation, she thought. Like an execution pyre. Poor little criminals. She tore herself away, took the cheese to Kate.

"Set the traps. And wash your hands really well afterwards. You're not dealing with house pets." Betty followed Kate's orders, heavy with guilt as she prepared to trap more tiny creatures; flames and burning bodies now branded onto the back of her eyes.

Imagine. Me, Betty. Following orders to execute and cremate. Throwing children into closets. What dastardly deeds won't I stoop to?

~ ж ~

Storeowner Mrs. Johnson looked up from a large bible she was scanning—a deluxe edition bible, bearing the mystifying title of Pronouncing Parallel Holy Bible—and handed Betty a letter from Cameron. "Your beau?" her teeth clicked with waggish anticipation.

"Yes." Betty hurried from the store to a nearby, isolated rock and tore open the envelope.

Dear Bets,

Only a few days of separation and I'm already feeling miserable. What's the rest of this damn year of separation going to be like? Hell?

All day at work in the smelter I daydream about you. How much I miss you. That place, the grimy buildings makes life seem gloomy. I sure don't want to spend my working life there in that bleak environment, a pick and shovel existence. It makes me realize how essential it is to continue with engineering, so that, when I graduate, I can choose where to work; use my head, not my brawn. Can't wait to get back to UBC next week.

And then I wonder if I might lose you to some handsome local yokel in Narrows. God how I worry. I see you as the gold in my life, not unlike the gold bullion produced in the smelter, all shiny and precious, sitting unguarded for some thief to steal. I see my year without you like the lead ingots, grey and lifeless; tap them and one hears no sound, no music.

Please write soon. Your pal and lover,

Cam

Betty pressed the letter to her heart. *My Cameron. The only person I can count on in the whole wide world. And the only person who'd use metallurgical terminology to describe his love for me. My funny engineer*, she thought fondly.

~ ж ~

Saturday. At school, Betty spent a couple of hours planning lessons and making master copies for use on the ditto pads—the rural version of a hectograph machine. She laid each master sheet on a different jelly pad so that the ink transferred. After the prescribed waiting period, she removed it and proceeded to make copies one-by-one, laying a fresh sheet of paper on the jelly, smoothing it out, peeling it off. She finally decided she had enough prepared. Now she could visit the piano.

She barely touched the keys, so that her tentative sounds would not drift down into the valley. She did not want townspeople to hear her pathetic efforts. The afternoon flew by. Now she could play, with one finger, God Save the King and Pretty Bobby Shafto. She could even make the treble keys work if she pressed hard enough. A good beginning. Because she would have so much spare time up here, she reasoned, she could teach herself a lot in a year. At four o'clock, she went back to the apartment.

Kate had said she could borrow any of her Book-of-the-Month Club books, so Betty selected a novel, lay down on the aged chesterfield and cracked open the book's new cover. The room was warm, the house was quiet. She dissolved into the story.

~ ж ~

Later, she heard persistent knocking on Granny's back door. She went down to see who it was. A well-dressed man in a business suit and tie stood at the door. He looked out of place here in Narrows. Handsome in a florid, heavy-set way. Bryllcreem hair. Flirtatious eyes.

"Hello there, little lady. Where's Kate?"

"She's not here."

"Oh? Where can I can find her?"

"She's up at the high school."

"Well, I'll lend a little sunshine to her textbooks, I guess, hey?" He grinned, winked and left.

About an hour later, Kate returned. She had Mr. Bryllcreem with her.

"This is Roscoe Taylor, Betty. Roscoe is the kind person who brought down all my possessions for me in his car. I won't be having supper with you, Roscoe's taking me to Kokanee for dinner." Kate's tone had taken on sultry dimensions; the drill sergeant voice had gone AWOL.

"Well, that's very nice," said Betty. Good. Loneliness no longer seemed so bad; Kate's constant flow of orders and abuse ranked worse.

"Sit down for a minute, Roscoe. I'm just going to freshen up."

Roscoe sat on the frayed chesterfield and draped both arms over the back of it. A tuneless whistle kept escaping his lips. "So how do you like Narrows, Betty?"

"I'm getting used to it, thank you."

"I've been coming up here for about a year, now. It's part of my sales route."

"Oh. What do you sell?"

" Ah, well...rubber goods. I get down here about once every three months or so. I'm a true travelling man, little lady."

He watched the bedroom door and jumped up when Kate reappeared. She had put on a beige shirtwaist dress. Pinned a silk flower to it. It was the first time Betty had seen her wear pancake makeup and rouge; the effect was astonishing. The helpful crutches stretched the dress around her breasts, emphasizing them.

"Wow, girl. You sure are a sight for sore eyes," Roscoe said. Kate produced a quasi-girlish giggle. Betty marvelled at Kate's turnabout; Roscoe Taylor was a miracle worker.

They moved to the stairs. "Bye, little lady. As I always say, if you can't be good, play it safe. Roscoe to the rescue any time...for a dime." He gave Betty an exaggerated wink and followed Kate.

Betty had barely returned to her book when she heard Granny bustling up the stairs. "Now, who was that?" Granny's face was flushed and animated.

"His name is Roscoe Taylor. He's the fellow who brought Kate's boxes and luggage down from Nakusp, the day she arrived."

"Well I thought so, but I wasn't sure. Where did they go?"

"On a date for dinner."

The questioning was slightly annoying. It seemed as though there could be no privacy up here about anything.

"Do you want to go to church with me tomorrow?" asked Granny.

"Sure." Why not? She had no better offers.

"Good night. I'm going out for the evening."

Oh. Great. I don't even get my cocoa companion on a Saturday night. Betty ate her supper and read while she ate, read all evening and read in bed. It hurt her eyes to read by the kerosene lamp, but, unlike Kate, she still could not light the bright gas lamp. The book was Kate's newest: *Catcher in the Rye*,

53

and it had received rave reviews. At one-thirty Betty extinguished the lamp. She did not hear Kate return.

~ ж ~

The alarm clock rang. Eight-thirty. She jumped to silence it before it woke Kate. Kate groaned and sat up. "Where are you going?"

"To church with Granny."

Kate threw aside the covers. "I'm coming, too." The late night had taken its toll. Kate looked exhausted but made no mention of her date with Roscoe Taylor. They donned suits and hats, as befitted church attendance, even in the boonies.

The three of them walked down to the ferry and waited along with a body of Sunday-best pedestrians, tailed by a small line of polished cars and pickup trucks. A familiar figure, tall, dark and skinny, sauntered over to them. The dark eyes smiled out of the lined face. An odour of strong tobacco and sweat clung to him despite the direct breeze from the lake. It was Jake Patten.

"How's yer school, Miss Wheatie, think we built it right? How come you never came to get my little granbaby fer a pupil?"

Granny took on the role of hostess. "This is Jake Patten, Miss Bradshaw. He works on the ferry with Bill. Come here, Estelle, and meet my teachers. You going to church, Jake?"

"Hell, no. I'm goin' over to my brother's place. Church and me give each other indigestion." He turned to his wife, Estelle. "These here are the new teachers, Estelle. Better give 'em hell before they start. Scare 'em good." He grinned at Betty and Kate. Betty grinned back, Kate glared.

Estelle Patten, a plump, nicely dressed blonde, smiled at them. "Oh, don't you mind my Jake, young ladies, he's just a thorn in the town's side. No one knows how my girls and I ever put up with him." She gazed fondly at Jake. "If he wasn't such a good dancer, I'd have dumped him long ago."

Jake raised his arm and one knee as though to ward off a blow. "Holy smoke, how's a guy to cope with such a woman? Eee hee, hee." He wandered off to another group. Estelle Patten pushed forward her teenage daughter, Charlotte. As Betty stared at her, a vision of Grampa Wheatley's English flower garden flashed in her head: the garden in July, at its abundant best. Charlotte's body: a full-blown peony, Charlotte's face: an unfurled rosebud.

Estelle, almost as an afterthought, then presented her older daughter, Freda, a bedraggled copy of the overwhelmingly beauteous Charlotte. Freda carried a well-bundled baby boy of about three months. He wailed ceaselessly.

"Where's your husband, Curley, today, Freda?" Granny stood beside the young mother, who, with both hands, shook the baby to and fro, determined to distract and quiet it. Freda was too preoccupied to talk.

Estelle Patten looked reproachfully at her unsociable daughter, then took over for her. "Curley's working at the Kokanee mill, Mrs. Trent."

"Well that's nice. Is it going to be steady?"

"We don't know, we hope for the best. Curley and my Jake are just about finished building Freda's new home and then Freda and her family'll be moving out of our place." Estelle gave her other daughter Charlotte a fond look. "Charlotte will soon get her room back. Did I tell you she has applied to go to nursing school?"

"Why, isn't that wonderful. Good luck to you, Charlotte." Granny patted Charlotte's arm.

"Perhaps I'll get my nurse after all. That was my dream for Freda here, but, oh no, she wanted to get herself knocked up and married." No wonder Freda looks so sullen all the time, thought Betty. Estelle's making it a bit too obvious who her favourite daughter is.

The pedestrians walked onto the deck and found places at the rail. A soft wind blew. Sunbeams sparkled on the waves as the ferry chugged to Trent's Landing.

A short hike up the hillside brought them to a white building with a steeple. A black and white sign faced the road:

> THE NEW TESTAMENT TABERNACLE
> THE VENERABLE
> REV. JACOB CHRISTOPHER HANGINGER
> *GOD KNOWS WHY YOU SHOULD BE HERE!*

"Sit with us, why don't you?" asked Estelle. "The Pattens have first claim to the front pew—have since the church was first built. There's plenty of room since Jake never attends."

~ Ж ~

The portly minister wore dark vestments, sported Jesus-style hair, beard and moustache. But not silky, shiny hair like the pictures of Jesus in Gramma Beaton's bible. Reverend Jacob Christopher Hanginger's hairiness was as uncompromising as the ruff of a bear--and he was as big as a bear too. His large eyeballs were bloodshot as if he, not Kate, had been out late last night. Already the naked parts of the Venerable Reverend's face glistened from the heat of the densely packed room. In no time at all, he began spewing forth a long sermon, mouthing it with spit-laced fervour—exuding none of the usual ministerial detachment Betty was used to.

"...And–and why is it many young women today forsake that which is–

uhh modest, that which is moral?

"Is it not deplorable that young women—in the name of twentieth-century freedom—uhh–flaunt themselves? Wearing enticing attire, smelling of perfume–ahh, yes, perfume, painting their fingers, and–and displaying themselves like wares for the eyes of all men, pandering?" He rolled a long tongue over his teeth as though the words were deliciously chewable. Betty was sure she had seen him before. But where?

Along Estelle's pew there was an air of indifference to the preacher's impassioned words: Granny snoring, Kate reliving her Roscoe Taylor date, Estelle and sullen Freda hot-potatoing the miserable baby.

Restless beautiful Charlotte, sitting next to Betty, criss-crossed her legs again and again. Betty noticed a correlation between Charlotte's leg movements and the fervour in the minister's voice. His eyeballs bounced with each leg criss-cross, his lips smacked almost painfully. Betty perked up, listened, watched him closely.

"... And is it not surprising when girls are persuaded by false ambition, by uhh–misguided, ambitious parents to move away from here? Here, where they are safe? Head to immoral big cities, like Vancouver, yes, yes, yes, where they are prey to every salacious, slavering stranger?"

There was no doubt about it: he was aiming his sermon at Charlotte. And when Charlotte absentmindedly brushed her breast his voice rose an octave.

Betty, seated far to the side of the pew, could see around the protective podium that fronted the man. Could now see him fumble with his robes as though he was untangling his underwear, adjusting himself.

"...Do not be misled, I plead. Watch and–and pray, that ye enter not into temptation: oh, yes, yes the spirit indeed is willing, but the flesh is so, so, weak, my friends..." He looked relieved as he finally finished, and wiped his hot-fleshed, hairy face. Cleansed. In a voice filled with dignity, gazing at the oblivious Charlotte, he directed calmer words at her. "And we will now close with–ahhh: What a friend we have in Jesus..."

The drowsy congregation focused their attention again. Betty, continuing her observations of this strange little church, nodded her head. The singing works, she decided. Look at us now, how we respond! Swaying bodies, tuneless voices; participating, instead of just listening. What a finale!

With satisfied smiles, the congregation poured out into the sunshine. Many other males surveyed Charlotte's temptations, Betty noticed. She felt invisible by comparison.

Several friendly people introduced themselves to the teachers. A bull-doggish man approached Betty. No friendship on his face. "How do, ma'am, the name's Detweiler. You got a boy of mine in yer class."

"Oh, yes, that would be Alec." Alec was a headspan taller than his beefy father, Betty noted.

"Well, I don't aim to interfere, ma'am, but I jist want to tell you it's no use gettin' him all fussed up about no high falutin' ideas. My boys is goin' to take over my land fer me when I get too old, an' they needs book learnin' like a wild cat needs a stick up its arse."

Betty was only momentarily taken aback; Dot had warned her about Mr. Detweiler's narrow views and colourful language. And he was approaching her at an ideal moment: she was feeling calm and self-assured today. "How big is your farm, Mr. Detweiler?"

He looked at her suspiciously. "Big enough."

"Big enough for ten years from now when your sons take over? Can the farm produce enough to support you and the boys' future families?"

Her spiel had not budged him. "What I does is good enough fer my sons."

The grade six arithmetic guidebook was fresh in Betty's mind. "At my school, I'll be teaching Alec things like: how many feet in a yard, yards in an acre and quarts in a bushel, and how to multiply and divide with this information. With very little help, your son could calculate the yield of your land in bushels per acre. And when he becomes comfortable with reading, he could read about improved farming methods, Mr. Detweiler. Other farmers' sons are becoming educated, and Alec's got to be able to compete with them."

Anger spat out of Mr. Detweiler's eyes. "Don't you go and try and get me worryin' 'bout things that don't matter. And as fer Alec; he's nearly old enough fer me to get 'im outa school."

She could see her lecture had only put him on the defensive. She eased off. "Mr. Detweiler, I don't have any 'high faluting' ideas about pushing your son to be a poet or a plutocrat, and I promise you that whatever I do teach him, I'll relate it to how it will help him as a farmer. Will that be okay? He has to stay in school for two more years, anyhow."

Frustrated with her persistence, he shook his finger at her. "Now you hear me, miss; don't you fuss him."

"I promise. There'll be no fancy tales that will cause him to leave the farm. Besides, Mr. Detweiler, no one gets enough attention in a rural school, anyway." She was now determined to help Alec every way possible. She issued Mr. Detweiler a fake smile and strode off to Granny and Kate.

On the ferry ride home, they continued to chat. Other than Farmer Detweiler, Betty decided, après-church had been an enjoyable social event. No one cared to discuss the sermon. *I'll go every week. That dose of religion with its added sideshow was easy to take. As good as a movie.*

Chapter 6

Yes'm, old friends is always best,
 'less you can catch a new one
that's fit to make an old one out of.
—Sarah Orne Jewett

"**M**iz Sweetly, Miz Sweetly!" She'd grown accustomed to her pleasant misnomer. At least it was better than being associated with a breakfast cereal... She hurried to the door. Was someone hurt? "Miz Sweetly, we saw a skunk!"

"Wuh? Unnh ... where?"

"In the woods on the other side of the road."

"I-I don't want you playing over there. It's too far from the school. And stay away from skunks. You know what they can do. Play softball, why don't you?" By the time she had retrieved every student, recess was over. She repeated her warning with foreboding.

At lunchtime, after they had eaten and left the classroom, and while she was preparing board work for the afternoon, a distinctively strong odour wafted into the room. She threw down the chalk and strode outside. The children were scurrying back from the woods.

"The boys killed it, Miss Wheatley. They killed it with rocks." It was fearless Helena Stevens who tattled.

"That was a cruel thing to do. Come into class right now."

Excitement filed into the room alongside every child. "Oh, boyz, Miz Sweetly. Now you'll have to close the school!"

The stench in the room quickly became stomach churning. Betty flung open the side door, wrenched up a window and faced them with a wagging finger. "You knew when you pursued that poor creature you'd be sprayed, and I asked you not to. Now here, where I am, in front of the class, with a breeze in my face, it's not too bad. I can stand it. So you'll have to put up with it, too. We can't close the school every time something goes wrong. School is too important for your future. Isn't that right, Alec?" Alec Detweiler jumped.

"Uh ...I guess so, Miz Sweetly," he stammered. Betty had trapped him into the role of Teacher's Ally. For now.

In time, Betty's nasal senses dulled. She completed the day's lessons, then shut the school early. Thankfully, it was Friday. The smell would, she hoped, dissipate during the weekend.

A grumpy Granny, parting with her precious wood, had heated up bath water for Betty. The skunk scent had descended the hill and invaded the whole village, Granny announced. Now everyone would have to suffer. She grumbled under her breath about teachers who don't supervise enough. Betty washed, emptied the water, refilled the tub and scrubbed again. As she dried herself, shivering, she could not tell if the bath had done any good.

Kate thumped on the bathroom door. "Have you forgotten we have people coming? My friend Elaina Maleyna. You know, Elaina who was with me when that bloody truck ploughed into my car. She's bringing half of Kokanee with her, for God's sake—her school's principal and two villagers. They'll be here in no time and it's your turn to cook, remember? And we don't have anything for supper."

"I'm having a bath—"

"You don't have time for baths. Besides, you should know it takes more than soap and water to get rid of skunk smell. Get to the store!"

"I'll go, I'll go."

"And hurry!"

Betty rushed to the store and back, despite a dripping ponytail, despite having to listen to a drawn-out dialogue between Mrs. Johnson and Jake's wife Estelle on the merits of tomato juice as a skunk deodorizer. The odour had assaulted the store, too. Mrs. Johnson allowed that it might be gone by Monday. Their critical gaze followed Betty as she rushed out.

Betty had just plopped potatoes in a pot to boil and begun frying pork chops when she heard voices. Kate hobbled to the top of the stairs. "Elaina Maleyna! My God, what a bunch of bruises. You look terrible! Come on up, everyone."

A tiny, wizened woman, covered with abrasions and bruises, and talking at great speed, arrived upstairs first. Her head wobbled like a spinning top on its last revolutions. She wore a white medical collar but it did not support her careening head.

Behind her strode a lumberjack of a woman: firmly packaged plumpness. Short hair, plaid shirt, suspenders. Followed by two tall, good-looking fellows, about Betty's age: one curly-headed blond and one curly-headed brunette. They stared at Betty, and she fought the urge to stare back.

The bird-like, wobbly Elaina introduced them. "This is Georgika Standard. Owner of the Kokanee Restaurant. Serves fabulous Doukhobor food. And her gorgeous son Tommy." She patted the arm of the fellow with brown hair. "And this," she twittered at the blond one, "is my marvellous Leslie. Leslie Bedford-Jones, the principal of my school." She wrapped one loose-skinned arm around Leslie's muscled one, and from this coy clutch, she ballet-gestured toward Betty.

60

"And you, of course, must be the gentle Betty. It's nice to finally meet you. Oh, good heavens, we've interrupted your dinner. Darling Georgika made us a little picnic lunch and we ate it in the car on the way here. We'll just sit and wait for you, because—" she paused while her head twirled like a tilted merry-go-round, "tonight—we're all going to have a musical soirée at Georgika's house!" She clapped her hands and pranced over to the chesterfield. "Sit down, everyone. Kate, my dear, how is your poor leg?"

"Improving slowly, thanks. I have to get over to the doctor next week for more painkillers. I'm having trouble sleeping." This revelation surprised Betty; Kate slept as soundly as a hibernating bear. "How are you, Elaina?"

"I choose to forget these damnable headaches and all else from our accident for tonight, my dear. I need some fun for a change. Hurry, Betty, dear. We don't want to keep everyone waiting." Betty turned her attention to the stove.

Crunchy potatoes and over-cooked pork, but a hungry Betty cleaned her plate in no time. Kate and Elaina were reciting the details of their car accident. Betty tuned them out; she had heard Kate's jeremiad before and Elaina sounded like an echo. Kate finally reached for her fork. First the pork, which she chewed as though it were beef jerky, then the potatoes. "My God, Betty, how can you expect me to eat this pig slop!" She hopped to the stove and dumped her food into the fire. "Betty has had a stinking day, right, Betty?" Kate drag-thumped to the bedroom.

The light-hearted mood that had danced in with Elaina limped out. They all looked at the mortified Betty with dismay. "My–my class killed a skunk today."

"The boys and me have all worn skunk perfume at some point in our lives, isn't that right, boys?" prompted Georgika Standard.

Leslie Bedford-Jones nodded. "My pupils have not attacked skunks, but I must admit I do have my own assortment of embarrassing stories."

"And if he don't tell them, I will." Tommy Standard's braying horselaugh startled himself, and he fixed his red-faced gaze on the floor as if the neighing had come from there.

"It's Friday, and we're going to forget the trials of teaching and have fun, fun, fun." Elaina's breeziness blew away the tension in the air, and Betty could smile again as she rinsed the dirty dishes. Georgika Standard, despite Betty's protests, helped her with the efficiency and speed of restaurant hands. The gentle voice and sweet smile of the woman did not match her manly garb. Betty wondered why she chose to dress as if she were heading to a construction site; neither her son nor the teacher, Leslie, wore such workman-style clothing.

Soon Kate came out of the bedroom: powdered, rouged, and lipsticked. "I'm ready."

"Tally ho!" called Elaina, heading to the stairs.

Georgika had Betty sit in the front seat, squeezed between herself and her son Tommy. Kate sat in the back with the other teachers. Betty was disappointed; she would have preferred Kate's spot—next to curly-blond Leslie Bedford-Jones.

As they drove along the incredibly bumpy and rutted road, which no one except Betty seemed to notice, Tommy chatted with her; eyed her closely. He was, he said, between jobs right now, so he was helping his mother in the restaurant. Soon, he was sure, he would be back at work at the box factory. Then, with an effort to sound nonchalant, he asked, "Do you have a boyfriend?"

"Yes, I do. He's a student at UBC."

Tommy's shoulders drooped; he moved slightly away.

"My dear fellow-teacher Leslie is Inspector McIntyre's fair-haired boy," announced Elaina. "Leslie's only taught one year, and during that year, he took a partially completed school and turned it into a marvellous success story."

"Elaina, please," Leslie murmured.

"Oh, now, I'm not saying you're perfect. I can teach you a few things, I'm sure, can't I, Leslie?"

"You're making me quite uncomfortable, Elaina."

Betty rolled his words around in her head. 'Un-com-for-ta-bul', he'd just said. Speaking the way they taught us at Normal School. Consistently. Doesn't even slur a single syllable. I've got to start trying again. It's been so easy to slip back.

Eventually, after about a three quarters of an hour drive, Georgika pulled the car up in front of her house in Kokanee: a rambling Tudor style, with vine-smothered walls and a thistle-dominated garden.

"Your place looks very historic, Georgika," said Betty.

"Thanks. It was built about nineteen hundred by a remittance man."

"A remittance man?"

"One of those younger sons of English aristocrats. The firstborn son inherits the land and the title, and then what the heck do you do with the others? Send 'em off to the colonies with a regular remittance."

They entered a side door, into a large kitchen. A grand stove dominated the room. The stove was bigger than any Betty had seen before, with The Wilson Engineering Company imprinted on its central firebox. Hugging the firebox on either side were ovens that looked like bank safety vaults. Hansel and Gretel, Betty thought, could fit in either one of those ovens. And the moveable iron plate over the firebox was massive, too. That firebox, she concluded, could eat logs whole.

The fire crackled out just the right amount of warmth, a kettle hummed a welcome, and a coconut cake waiting on the counter exuded an eat-me scent.

Betty helped Georgika serve coffee and cake. As she carried the coffee cups into the living room, she looked around. Oversized and ornate antique furniture crowded the large living room, and dusty books, tarnished trophies, scrawny plants covered every flat surface. The room had an air of decaying grandeur.

"You have a magnificent home, Georgika." Betty had never been in a mansion, decayed or otherwise.

"We've had some real good times in this place. My home has always been a gathering spot for the teachers. I want you to join us whenever you can." Georgika smoothed back her short-cropped hair, causing her ample bosom to strain against the buttons of her shirt. She wrapped her plump arms around Betty and squeezed her. "I know what loneliness can be like," she whispered.

Elaina Maleyna plunked her sprightly body down at an upright Steinway and metamorphosed. "Friends, Romans, lend me your voices!" she tremeloed in a staged, cracked and husky voice. Now she was a cocktail lounge performer, and her fingers trilled background music. Perfect accompaniment to coffee and cake. Then with a keyboard flourish she sang out:

Five foot two, eyes of blue
Oh, what those five feet can do...

Elaina was captivating. Bewitching. She rocked side to side, bouncing her feet on the pedals, while her shaky head beat out a counterpoint to the music and her shaky voice belted out a semblance of the tune.

Soon, Tommy was drumming cautiously on the top of the piano, a tentative Gene Krupa;

Georgika grabbed a self-conscious Leslie and improvised a jitterbug do-si-do; and Kate, surprisingly, leaned her head back and belted out the lyrics—a lean version of Kate Smith.

In a corner, Betty sang quietly, danced alone. Swinging her arms a bit, swaying her body a tad. Until she began to relax; to feel free and, finally, carefree. Now she was part of a movie musical; now she was on stage—now she was snowballing into Dinah Shore and Ginger Rogers rolled into one!

They all relished song after song, each engrossed in their own release, their own intoxication; Elaina's music their common bond.

Finally, banging her hands down on the piano keys, Elaina groaned, "That's it! I'm pooped. I can't play a darn thing more!"

"Elaina, you're the most wonderful entertainer ever!" exclaimed a fervent, flushed Betty.

Everyone laughed, clapped, cheered and grinned at one another.

Georgika reluctantly looked at her watch. "I don't want to end a great night, but I've got to get you good folks home and get to my restaurant early in the morning. And, Tommy, there's several cords of slab wood you've got to chop."

"Oh, don't remind me."

"Okay, everybody, to the car, then?"

Elaina patted her neck brace and now spoke in a little girl voice. "May I be excused? I can't take that ride again. I'm exhausted. Leslie?" She cocked her bobbling head coquettishly. "Could you walk me home? I'm sure Tommy and Georgika can deliver our guests safely home without you." Leslie did his best to cover up a look of disappointment.

~ ж ~

"That was the best party I ever went to," Betty said, on the drive home. "And that Elaina is the most entertaining old lady I ever met. She's amazing. Do I ever like her!"

"I had a good time too, but my knee is misbehaving terribly; it was throbbing all night." Kate's voice was fretful; all her short-lived party mood had vanished.

Betty tried to give Kate the attention she seemed to be asking for. "You better get to see that doctor soon, Kate," But images of the party won out. "I just love that Elaina! But gosh, her poor head sure shakes. She really got damaged in your car accident, ah... crash, didn't she, Kate?"

"I doubt if that's from the accident. That condition is not uncommon in older folk," said Georgika.

"Are you implying she's faking it?" Now Kate's voice hardened into her familiar quenched steel sound.

"Well…. I realize she got hurt, but she sure doesn't behave like someone suffering from long-lasting neck damage." Georgika sounded reasonable.

"She was seriously injured. Her head wasn't shaking like that when we drove up from Vancouver!"

"I'm sorry. I didn't mean to upset you," said Georgika, a hint of huffiness now in her voice.

"You didn't upset me. You just don't know what you're talking about."

"Well, Miss Charming, I may not have all the answers, but neither do you," snapped Georgika. A thick silence reigned the rest of the drive.

As Betty and Kate got out of the car, Georgika called out. "Betty, would you be kind enough to phone me Wednesday? Maybe we can get together again soon."

Betty waited until Kate swung off to the house. Then she called back. "Sure. Thanks, Georgika." What a wonderfully kind woman, she thought. And what's more, she's the first person up here not to kowtow to Kate.

~ ж ~

The following week—after the school day was over—the Kokanee school bus driver let Betty off in front of Georgika's restaurant. Georgika came rushing outside, enveloped Betty in a bear hug, and hefted her suitcase. It was Friday. Betty was to spend the weekend.

"Now, I have to work until seven. I hadn't planned it that way. I hope you don't mind?"

"Mind? I'm delighted to be here." Betty looked about as they crossed Main Street. She liked the confident, assuredness of the Kokanee business district, busily fighting back against the encroaching wilderness. Narrows gave the impression that the wilderness had won.

Opposite Georgika's substantial restaurant, next to the Kokanee Farmer's Co-Op, Betty could see a combination blacksmith shop/gas station, and next to it, a small hotel with an adjoining beer parlour. Facing the beer parlour, self righteously, was the Fire Valley Gospel Church; its two windows as accusative eyes. Sounds of a nearby sawmill cut the air with whines and filled it with a forest pungency. The town, she noted, with its advantage of being on a plain, had streets arranged in a civilized grid, complete with street signs. Nice.

Georgika stowed Betty's suitcase in the restaurant's kitchen and told her the back booth was reserved especially for her.

"Hi. Wanna cuppa Java?" The waitress, Olga, waved a greeting with a red, soap-damaged hand.

Between customers, Georgika sat with Betty, beaming admiration. Her son, Tommy, she said, was back at work again at the box factory. Leslie was still at his school.

About five-thirty, the place started to fill. Betty ignored Georgika's objections and helped the waitress Olga wait on tables. It was fun serving Pirozhki heaped with sour cream. Fun exchanging banter with the men from the hydro project and the sawmill. It was even fun towelling steamy dishes pulled by Olga from finger-scalding water. At seven, the worst of the crowd had gone and a stolid village woman arrived to take Georgika's place. They drove to Georgika's house.

"Will we be having another music night with Elaina?"

"Nope. A little of Elaina goes a long way. She was over here night after night taking over my house. Bossing Leslie one minute and practically sitting in his lap the next. Silly old cow. I don't know how Leslie can stand her." Betty was disappointed and Georgika sensed it. "We'll have a good time, you'll see."

In the kitchen, a flushed-face Tommy was closing an oven door, releasing the aroma of roasting beef. "I done my share, Ma, now you have to make the Yorkshire Pudding."

"You probably wonder, Betty, how a Doukhobor girl could make Yorkshire pudding. Tommy's dad can take the credit for that. I had to learn the English ways. No borscht for him."

Leslie poked his head around the door frame. "How is the Narrows delegation? Where is Kate?"

"I didn't invite her," Georgika said. The edge of testiness in her voice forestalled any reproach.

Leslie had set an elegant, small table in the living room, next to the fireplace. He had lit just enough lamps to show off the beauty of the room, and cast flattering shadows on its shabbiness.

"I have a special wine for us. Californian. It is Christian Brothers' Cabernet Sauvignon. Allow me to pour you a glass."

Wine? The harsh grappa produced by the Italians who lived in Trail was all Betty knew. But she would have drunk poison rather than spoil the ambience of the occasion.

Leslie wore an ascot tucked into the open collar of his shirt, and a lock of hair dangled on his forehead. He leaned against the stone fireplace holding an unlit pipe, stabbing the air with its stem to accent the points he was making. "I believe the Californian wines are a match for any we can buy from Europe... ."

How wonderful he is, thought Betty. It was hard for her to take her eyes off him. Urbane. Like a blond Peter Lawford dressed for a British movie.

~ Ж ~

"What a meal! I've never eaten anything so delicious," Betty said. "And the mushrooms! Where did you buy them?"

"They grow wild. Pine Mushrooms. Ma and me picked them," said Tommy.

"Chanterelles," Leslie Bedford-Jones corrected. "Much in demand. They have a pleasantly unusual odour."

"Oh, Leslie, what a wonderful place for you to live," said Betty. Tommy laughed.

"We don't eat like this except on high days and holidays, and sometimes not even then," smiled Georgika. "I'm too busy most of the time."

"Yeah. If you weren't coming, we'd probably just have supper down at the restaurant," added Tommy. "Now we pay the price. We gotta do the dishes."

"And that we can all do together," said Betty. An even more relaxed mood set in while they worked in the kitchen as a team.

~ ж ~

Later, as they exchanged childhood reminiscences, their voices tumbled over one another. Betty told them of her life in Trail. Leslie expounded on the advantages and disadvantages of his life as an only child. Tommy told tales of village escapades. Georgika sat and listened and her puppy-eyes followed Betty's every move. Finally, Georgika announced it was time for bed and Tommy settled the embers in the fireplace.

"That was fun, Georgika," said Betty.

"I told you we'd have a good time. My little waitress Olga rents the guest room, Betty, and Leslie and Tommy have the other bedrooms. I hope you won't mind sharing my bed with me? It's a big roomy one."

There was a slight jerk in the pit of Betty's stomach. Share a bed? With a woman she barely knew? She brushed it away. I am spoiled, she thought. It's just that I've never shared a bed.

Georgika's ornate bedroom was as opposite to her mannish appearance as a room could get: peaches and cream, and flounces and curlicues. Georgika disappeared into a cavernous adjoining space.

Betty pulled her flannel pajamas from her suitcase, clutched them to her chest, and waited. When Georgika returned, she was wearing a lace and satin nightie. Her large bosom rolled under the revealing satin. Betty was startled: mannish by day, all-female by night? Georgika could not have looked more indecent if she had been nude. Betty averted her eyes.

"Dressing room's all yours, Betty."

When Betty returned and climbed into her side of the bed, Georgika pulled Betty toward her and gave her a loose-lipped, wet kiss. "Peaceful night, little one." She extinguished the last gas lamp. In the dark, Betty wiped her mouth. She lay as rigid as a corpse until she heard the sound of Georgika's steady breathing.

When she awoke, Georgika was gone. Bright light outlined the opaque window blinds. In the semi-darkness, she had to squint to see the time. Quarter to nine! She hurried downstairs. Georgika, girded in a coverall apron, was braiding mounds of bread dough. Cooling pies, breads and cakes loaded the counters.

Georgika's face broke into a warm smile when she saw Betty. "What would you like for breakfast: Pirozhki? Pancakes? A slab of ham and some eggs?"

Georgika catered to Betty as though she were the Empress Catherine come to visit, before she finally poured herself a cup of coffee and sat. Leslie had gone to his school to take charge of field day practices.

"Am I holding you back from work, Georgika?"

"No, Betty, I make the bread and pastry for the restaurant. And I'm done."

As they sipped their coffee, Betty did most of the talking, telling Georgika of the traumatic night of her arrival, of her confrontations with Kate.

Georgika listened with wide, warm eyes. When Betty told her about the piano and her latest one-fingered success, Georgika motioned Betty to the Steinway in the living room.

"I've got just the book for you." She rummaged in the piano bench. Pulled out a yellowed book: E. Warner-Smythe's Teach Yourself Piano. "I tried to teach myself once. You can have it. I don't intend to try again."

"Oh, Georgika. What a perfect gift!"

Georgika's eyes welled up with tears as she savoured the pleasure on Betty's face. "Don't pay any attention to me. I'm a great big crybaby. Can't help it." She fumbled for a handkerchief from her pant pocket. "I've got to go to the restaurant for an hour. Will you be okay on your own?"

"Sure. I can try out your piano book, unless you'd like me to come and help."

Georgika shook her head. "It's not proper for a teacher. Besides, you're my special guest. I'll be back at noon."

Betty followed her to the back door and passed her the baked goods, which Georgika piled into her car. Then, with no warning, Betty found herself corralled against Georgika's bosom, receiving yet another cloying kiss. "I'll see you soon," said Georgika as she closed the door.

Betty wiped and rewiped her mouth, like Vivian cleaning her counter. Such an emotional person! So demonstrative. Annoyingly so. Maybe it's a Russian characteristic, a cultural thing, to slop kisses about.

She tidied the kitchen and went to the piano with Georgika's teach-yourself book. Concentrated on trying the beginner's fingering exercises. She liked them, finally playing with two hands, up scale, note by note, carefully moving her thumbs and forefingers as directed, and then reverse fingering down scale. She played with feeling; she felt her efforts sounded quite melodic.

She became aware that someone was watching her.

She turned. It was Leslie Bedford-Jones. She smiled with pleasure. "How did your sports morning go?" She felt self-conscious, almost blushing, now that she was alone with him.

He sat on the edge of a chair near the piano. Drummed his right knee up and down. "I probably would have had a great morning; I enjoy coaching and I excel at it, but not when I have an unasked-for assistant."

"Oh?"

"Elaina... . Elaina Complaina. One would think, with that neck brace, she would be resting on the weekend." He said the words softly, speaking more to himself, than to her. "Everything I do, she watches and advises. Everything I say, she finds time to correct." He finally looked at Betty, his face taut. "And I cannot stop her, she phrases her advice oh-so sweetly, and everything she says sounds so right. Yet I did just beautifully on my own last year. Rob McIntyre said so. Rob McIntyre... our school inspector, Betty. He said I had great potential. That I, too, was inspector material."

He looked down at his hands for several long seconds. "I pride myself on doing things to perfection. And I do, as a matter of fact. But she doesn't see it. Too wrapped up in herself." He shook his head dismissively, stood up and smiled down at Betty. He looked as though he was going to pat her on the head.

He's pleased I've listened so attentively, thought Betty. She had been nodding and smiling and frowning and listening with all her might. Almost like man's best friend, she thought. *Silent and wagging for approval. I hope he doesn't think of me as some empty-headed Red Setter.*

"Shall we have some coffee?" he asked.

Betty followed him to the kitchen where, with all the precision of an apothecary, he measured the coffee and water, perked a fresh pot and poured it into stemmed china cups.

Savoir-faire in spades. On a first-name basis with the inspector and handsome as all get out. And a great future. What a catch! The best catch in the valley. Not like that rude truck driver friend of Dot's, the fellow who called me "Red". Leslie: truly the best catch in the valley.

"Do you miss your family?" she asked, pulling her thoughts away from dangerous directions. She felt a stab of guilt, thinking of Cameron, studying so hard at UBC. Alone with his books.

"Quite frankly, I'm too busy. And my mother, bless her bossy ways, is highly ambitious for me. She wants progress reports, not visits."

"I get a little homesick, already. Some of the locals are very good to me, but still, I..." Betty smiled apologetically; she didn't know why.

He smiled back. "I wrap myself up in my work. It is always easy for me to adjust. Anywhere."

"Lucky you. I was even homesick at Normal School. That's probably why I ended up teaching in Narrows. I didn't apply myself." Betty avoided mentioning her usual blame-person, Cameron.

"Mother was determined that I should go to UBC. But after Father had his

69

heart attack, that was not feasible. You can imagine her pride when I excelled at Normal. I could've taught at the coast, but when Rob McIntyre—you know? The school inspector—was at our house and offered me the position as principal in a brand new school, you can picture my delight. And Mother's, too."

"You must be a very well-balanced person, Leslie. And your mother must have done a good job. My grandmother says good plants only grow in well-fertilized soil."

"I suppose I am well-balanced, Betty. Thank you for the compliments."

~ ж ~

The oppressiveness of the evening air finally lifted, then rain flayed the windows and thunder rattled them. Leslie and Betty stood side-by-side, looking out at sheet lightning as it lit up the valley.

Leslie moved closer to Betty, almost touching her. She could see, from the corner of her eye, his chest, lifting and falling as he breathed. A strong surge of excitement filled her body. He stared at her in an intent way. She fought the desire to let her eyes hold the gaze; Cameron-guilt made her turn away.

Leslie lit a fire. It was crackling when Georgika returned from the kitchen with three glasses of sherry. She grinned. "Are you ready to play us a piano concert, yet, Betty?"

"Give me a couple of more sessions and who knows? As long as the concert is just finger exercises."

Georgika had a Sonora gramophone. She wound it up and put on some Glenn Miller tunes. The conversation was relaxed, then, as the fire and sherry slowed them, desultory.

Betty watched Leslie through veiled eyes. She admired the way the flames highlighted his profile, the way his long legs spread so gracefully. Time could suspend itself forever, she thought. The moment was perfect. The view of Leslie was captivating, sensual.

It was Georgika who moved first. "Ahh," she sighed, stretching. "All good things must come to an end. Tommy and Olga sure missed a nice evening. Too bad they had to work." She picked up the sherry tray and took it to the kitchen. Leslie and Betty rose. Again, he stood near her. She pushed Cameron from her mind; held her breath. He looked down into her eyes for an electric second—then bade her goodnight in a strained voice and dashed up the stairs.

Betty girded herself to face the bedtime routine: the risqué nightie, the moist kiss, the loving look before Georgika turned off the gas lamp.

As she lay in the dark room, disturbing, alternating visions of Cameron and Leslie played with her mind.

Georgika made a festive breakfast of pancakes with preserved huckleberries from the nearby mountains.

The waitress Olga chattered away as she helped Georgika.

Leslie glanced at her each time she chalked up yet another double negative. Olga caught his impatient look. "What's the matter with you, Mister Leslie-ain't-ain't-in-the-dictionary? Didn't you get enough sleep?" She turned to the others. "I heard him up half the night, goin' in and outa his room." Leslie flushed bright red. Stared at his plate.

"Oh, Olga, you exaggerate," said Georgika. "If you heard all that, you'd be tired, too."

Leslie excused himself in a tumble of words. "I must say à bientôt, Betty. I suppose I am obsessed with my job. And I promised my fellow teacher Elaina to meet her and map plans for a school choir. I'm steeling myself to put up with her; after all, she took honours in musicology." He rushed from the room.

Georgika shook her head. "He's sure not his usual self. It's that Elaina Maleyna. That woman has got a hold on his life. I wish he had the gumption to tell her off." She glanced at her watch. "We'll have to hurry a bit, Betty. I have to deliver you safe and sound before I open my restaurant at eleven."

When they arrived at Granny's, Betty submitted as Georgika slathered on another wet kiss. It was, she decided, a small price to pay for such a perfect weekend. "I really enjoyed your company, Betty. Will you come down again next weekend? I'll cook you up a real gourmet feast."

"I wish I could, but I can't. I'm getting really behind in my preparations for school. Perhaps after Thanksgiving?"

"Oh, no, are you already invited out for Thanksgiving?"

"I'm going home."

"I'll miss you. After Thanksgiving, I'll leave you a phone message at the store and maybe you can come then."

Good. Something to look forward to after Thanksgiving. Leslie jumped into her mind—a vision as large as a movie screen: his lissome body, his lips, his blondness, his spine-tingling blue eyes. The electricity that had bounced between them still crackled through her.

She tried to shrug off the spell, the magic of the encounter. *It's Cameron I love.* But she had trouble conjuring up his face. She hurried to her bed, to the tiny photo of him thumb tacked to the wall.

Chapter 7

It's worse than wicked, my dear, it's vulgar.
—Punch

"I had quite a to-do with that bossy Kate Bradshaw on Friday. She's learned she can't get the best of me," said Granny.

"What happened?"

Betty had to wait for a reply. Granny could not speak—would not speak—until she had obeyed the rubrics of the tea ritual: a rolling boil of water, a scalded pot, a generosity of tea leaves, a tea cozy thick enough to ward off arctic blizzards.

Only after handing Betty the cream and sugar, after carrying the life-giving pot back into the living room, only when they finally had their tea in hand, could Granny continue.

"Miss Hoity-toity came in from her school Friday, early. And she told me, in an unpleasant way, that she was tired of cold baths. And she wanted me to make sure there was hot water for her every day. Not asking, mind you, no by-your-leave, more like a straight demand. Well, I told her if once a week was good enough for me, it was good enough for her, and if she didn't like it, she could get out."

She smoothed her skirt, and let out a pent-up breath. "Now I've told her, Betty, just as I've told you, it takes quite a while to heat up that tank for a bath, and it takes a lot of wood and elbow grease doing all that chopping. Our Albert's been a good little chap, cutting all my daily wood, and his mother's; I can't ask him for any more than that, and I don't intend to."

She poured more tea, steaming as much as the scalding brew. "She probably thinks I should go out and cut the wood myself."

"Where is she?"

"In Nakusp. Over night. She had some appointment there, she said, and that slick-looking salesman Roscoe Taylor came and got her yesterday and took her up there. Hah! I must say I can't imagine who you can have an appointment with on a Saturday night. However, she's old enough to take care of herself."

"Granny, don't let her get to you. I'm starting to realize that her bark is worse than her bite."

"Don't count on it. Her bark is dreadful."

"I've got to go to the store. Can I get you anything?"

"I'd like to walk down with you. I'll pick out my own things." Betty was flattered by Granny's offer of company.

As she went upstairs to put away her suitcase, she wondered how it was that of all the people she had met up here so far, it was this old lady whom she was closest to, understood the best, and trusted the most. Despite Georgika's pampering.

~ ж ~

"The Wicked Witch of the West is in Nakusp? Shacked up with the rubber salesman from Oz, I'll bet. In that case, you've got Dorothy for lunch for sure. I've done loads of classroom prep," Dot LaPointe said as she helped Granny and Betty carry their purchases back up the hill. "There's going to be a dance on the weekend after Thanksgiving. Are you going, Granny? Never know when you might meet some nice bachelor."

"And what would I do with some broken-down old fellow? I'm too old for that nonsense."

"What dance?" asked Betty.

Dot nudged Granny. "You can't go, Betty. What would your boyfriend say?"

Granny humphed. "What he doesn't know can't hurt him. There's little enough to do up here without missing what does come up."

Betty grinned. "Thanks, Mrs. Trent. I like your logic. I love to dance."

~ ж ~

Dot plopped herself down on the chesterfield. "Well, well, well. Kokanee again? God, Betty, it can't be that Leslie who's the attraction."

"Why not?"

"I wouldn't be surprised if he was a queer. He's such a prissy know-it-all!"

74

"A queer? Oh, Dot! Definitely not! I've met a homosexual. At the Normal School. He fluttered about and giggled—more effeminate than any girl I know. Leslie's not like that. He has gorgeous muscles, the deepest, most thrilling voice... ." *God,* thought Betty. *Listen to me. Talk about getting carried away!* "So how are your wedding plans, Dot?"

~ ж ~

After their Prem and pickle relish lunch, Dot took Betty to see the house she and her fiancé were planning to rent. Baby-wails floated up the hillside from Jake's house as they passed by. His married daughter Freda was outside, shaking her crying baby like a bartender preparing a martini. Jake hovered uselessly. Once he saw Betty and Dot, he darted up the hillside.

"Lookit the schoolmarms, wandrin' about with nothin' to do. Hear yer gettin' hitched, Miz La Pointe. Rentin' a house. Rentin', by geez! Why doncha put yer spare time to use? Build yer own place, like my son-in-law Curley."

"Spare time? Jake, we teachers don't have any. We're too busy whacking all the brats," retorted Dot. "Besides, we've no tools."

"I'll lend yuh my tools. And get Miz Wheatie here to help yuh. She's got nothin' to do but eat her Breakfast of Champions and play the goldern piano ten hours a day." He winked at Betty.

"Is that so, Jake," replied Dot. "Well, lend Betty your tools. She can start on Len's house for practice."

"Good thinkin'. All that janitorin' and bus drivin' is more'n enough fer Len." Jake chuckled at Dot's joke, then reluctantly returned to the noisy baby and its sullen mother.

"Freda reminds me of the Duchess in Alice and Wonderland, the way she shakes that kid. She sure has it rough. Her husband Curley didn't even marry her until she was seven months gone," said Dot.

"How awful. I sure hope Cameron doesn't do that to me."

"It won't happen to Lou and me. There are some safe ways to let off steam. 'His and hers finger exercises', if you get what I mean."

Betty was astounded. Was Dot launching into No-no land? Into the taboo subject, into that most intimate, forbidden secret world?

Dot's eyes danced. "A couple can have fun without risking pregnancy. Oh, Betty, the look on your face! You're a real prude!"

75

"I'm far less of a prude than you give me credit for."

"I bet you keep that Cameron in hospital restraints. Come on, admit it."

"Dot, you have no idea, you—next to me, you're the prude. I've gone a way lot further than you...all the way." She had just started down a greased hill, she realized, admitting things she had never expected to tell anyone.

"Really? Holy Smoke!"

Now that Betty had begun slipping, she could not stop. Could not stop telling her most shameful secret to a near stranger. "With Cameron. All last year. While I was at Normal School."

"A year? God, Betty, how come you didn't get pregnant?"

"You have to...I mean, he has to, uhh, withdraw." Betty's voice was thick with tension. "You can't...oh, gosh, you have to uhh...stop, sort of, just when—"

"I get it! I'm not stupid. Coitus interruptus. God, and you're not even engaged! Talk about Russian Roulette! And to think I had you pegged as a Goodie Two-Shoes. Instead, you're hot to trot. Wow!"

"Oh, Dot, you pegged me right in the first place. I'm not 'hot to trot'. I'm ashamed of what I've done. Sex. It's great while you're having it, but it's torture to the conscience. And if my mother knew, oh boy. She says no man will accept used goods. You have to keep your virginity as a wedding present. Let's not discuss it any more, okay?"

"I think you're calling the shots like a man. To heck with old-fashioned notions!" Dot's new admiration galled Betty beyond words.

Dot quieted when her house-to-be came into view: unpainted, small, commonplace. But Betty and Dot looked at it with reverence. "Imagine. It'll be my wedding home."

"Your own home, you lucky thing."

"You'll have one too, Betty, some day. With your Cameron."

~ Ж ~

They called on Len-the-janitor's wife, Vivian, who asked them in for tea. Vivian focused her restless eyes long enough to give Betty a look of reproach. "I thought I would have seen more of you." Her voice was thin, listless. Almost not there.

"Uhh...I'm always so busy. I can't get ahead of the game, yet," said Betty.

Dot picked up baby Harry. "Boy, I sure want a baby as soon as I can."

"I sort of want to start another one. I guess," said Vivian. She squinted at a fly speck on the wall. "Baby Harry is four months old."

"Why the heck so soon?"

"I just have an overwhelming need for something more. Harry doesn't keep my mind busy enough. Maybe two babies would. Having babies is the most important thing in a woman's life. I guess."

"Yeah, but you have to give your baby machine a rest," said Dot.

Vivian fastened dilated pupils on Dot. Raised her voice from a whisper. "I know, I know, but I have to have something to look forward to. I can't stand—" Vivian began her repetitive counter-wiping again, rearranging the shine.

"I want babies, too," said Betty, "but there has got to be more to life than just them." Vivian dropped her washrag. Stood staring at the sink. And Betty regretted her words.

Len arrived. Dot joked with him as he cuddled his baby and kept a protective arm around Vivian. As they were leaving, Vivian attempted to smile but failed.

"Something's wrong. Very wrong." said Dot, as they descended the hill.

"She was that way the last time I saw her, too."

"Well I can't figure her out. She's got everything a woman would want. A husband, a baby and even a home. And she's not like poor Freda; she even has them in the right order!"

Dot giggled and continued:

>First comes love
>and then comes marriage
>and then comes Betty
>with a baby carriage!

"I sure hope so, Dot. I like that order."

Dot left on the ferry. Betty hurried up to her school to get some work done before daylight retreated behind the Monashee mountains.

Later that evening Betty reflected on her conversation with Dot—and how shocked she'd seemed about Betty's pre-marital hanky-panky. And she thought about her Cameron. *My Cameron, damn him*, she thought.

Besides the guidance counsellor, Cameron was partly to blame for her bad marks in normal school. Mostly Cameron, with his take-off-your-clothes eyes, she mused. He distracted me from my school-work. And I trusted him most of all. Trusted him with the most important thing I had. And, what's worse, wanted to trust him.

At tryst after tryst, moonlit nights on the boulder strewn mountainside among runty birches, Cameron, breathing sweet breath, mouthing sweet words, tutoring sweet urgings in Betty's willing body. Cameron, eloquently pouring forth his limited knowledge of current sex practices, like some Jesuit-in-training trying to use logic to convert an atheist.

"Easily sixty to eighty percent of girls your age are doing it, Betty. They just won't admit it. But it's a fact. Everyone knows it."

Betty thought about how different things were now from the last time she saw Cameron, before she got the fateful call about the teaching job in Narrows.

She remembered holding the receiver of the payphone with trembling hands. "Cameron? I–I'm down–downtown. I need you desperately. I'm too late. My life's ruined." Ruined. A cooler, split-off part of herself savoured the drama of the word.

"Oh, no. Late? Are you sure?"

She blinked back tears. "Yes. We need to talk. Meet me at the Crown Point. Right away." Thank God for Cameron, always running to me when I need him. Except it's his fault I'm in this mess in the first place she thought—so he'd better run.

~ Ж ~

Betty lugged two bags of Safeway groceries over to the Crown Point Café and instantly spotted Cameron. Spotted Cameron in a booth, flipping through the listings on the jukebox. Cameron: Sun-tinged brush-cut. Tall, tanned and muscled. Sybaritic, darkly brown eyes and sensuous mouth.

Betty dropped into the booth opposite him, plopped the paper bags onto the wooden tabletop, sending the salt- and pepper-shakers bashing into Cameron's coke float.

Cameron whacked the coke foam off his pride and joy—a bright red UBC Engineering sweater. Whacked at the foam as if it were splashes of molten lead. The precious sweater flaunted those damn numbers, those red-flag-at-a-bull numbers—1954. Three more years of separation, they jeered. Three more years of school claiming his attention, keeping him away from her. She hated the taunting sweater, had hated it the first time he wore it, that night when she had dared to hint at marriage and babies.

"I never promised to marry you," he had said. It was more than the words; it was the guarded way he distanced himself with them that had stung. When he had seen the liveliness draining from her face, he had backtracked. "Just kidding," he had said; a jest, mere semantics, he claimed.

And she had picked up the fragile pieces of trust that lay strewn about, stared at their lost gleam and willed herself to transfer her qualms to the new sweater; she had buried them in its woollen folds.

"How late are you?" The normally sunny and calm Cameron was flipping the jukebox listings as fast as if his life depended on help from the titles.

"Oh…far too late. I should have applied to Trail schools at Easter. But I wanted to teach school in Vancouver. Near you. Nowhere else. The inspector gave me a lecture instead of a job."

Cameron exhaled. His tension evaporated like a July rain cloud and sunshine returned.

He leaned across the table, gently wiping a daub of dried ice cream from Betty's chin. He grinned. "Whew…Jeez, I thought I'd have to quit school and we'd have to have a shotgun wedding. You had me scared shitless—"

"Oh, Cameron! What? You think… are you saying…?" Betty pulled away from her school inspector predicament.

Her eyes blazed, then dulled. Typical Cameron, only focused on his own career.

Nevertheless she desperately wanted him to be hers, to be safely bonded to her by church documents, wanted to become respectable, aproned Mrs. Cameron McDonald.

Betty remembered her limp Coke float turning coffee-coloured. Curds of vanilla ice cream coated the walls of the glass… like clouds of disappointment on her soul.

~ Ж ~

So much for trusting lovers and misguidance teachers, she thought as she brushed her teeth and readied herself for bed in her meagre surroundings.

As she lay in bed, she could swear she heard a rustling outside her window again, but by now she had resigned herself to being surrounded by voracious wildlife and fell asleep easily.

Chapter 8

Time solves every problem and in the process
adds a couple of new ones.
—Richard Needham

"**M**iz Sweetly! Miz Sweetly! The boys are throwing pine cones at each other!"

"Well, that's not so bad."

"They got pitch on my sweater, and I'm gonna get it from my ma," complained sixth-grader Margie Sloboda. Before Betty could reply, they heard snuffling noises, the quiet sounds of a boy taught not to cry. It was fifth-grader Raymond Whittaker, his pale face even paler. His hands covered his eye. He had trouble walking up the stairs.

"Oh, no, Raymond, let me see!" No cut, just puffed flesh around his eye. She wet her spare handkerchief and pressed it onto the swelling.

"Sit in the classroom, Raymond." She stomped to the front door, clanged the bell; summoning the children in early.

"We have just about had a major catastrophe. Someone could have cost Raymond his eye. I don't want anyone to throw pine cones here again."

Howard Carson squirmed in his seat.

"Do you have anything to say, Howard?"

"Well, we always throw those things, and they don't hardly hurt."

"I would have thought so, too, until ten minutes ago. But just look at Raymond's swollen eye. No more pine cones."

In a few days, there was again the same shrill girls' cry of tattling: "Miz Sweetly! Miz Sweetly!" She was growing to hate this strident use of her altered name. She put down her red marking pencil and strode to the front doorway.

The same three girls. Bits of grass and streaks of dirt decorated their cotton dresses, adorned their hair. "The boys are throwing dirt at us!" She rushed to the back door, in time to see a large clump of yellowed grass with soil attached, go sailing from behind the school toward a group of excited

81

boys, who screeched and scattered, trying to avoid contact.

"Stop that this instant!" It was nearly the end of lunch hour. "Line up at the front door!" The students marched in sheepishly.

"You're all filthy! What will your mothers say?" She looked at them with dismay. Even the usually prim Ingrid and Helena had telltale dirty hands.

"I'll just say I fell down the hill. Don't worry, Miz Sweetly, I won't tell on you." Why Howard with his lesser intelligence had become the class spokesman, she would never understand.

Ingrid was indignant. "It's not Miz Sweetly's fault, Howard." Then, Ingrid, surprised at herself, pressed her hand against her mouth and moved herself as far back in her seat as she could. Like a chain reaction, her remark released the tongues of others.

"Yeah, Howard, you nut. Miz Sweetly didn't throw any." Confused input from fifth-grader Timothy Brentwood, who rarely spoke.

"I know who started it." Tattling from Helena.

"You were doing it too!" Jeering from several of the boys. Anarchy breaking out.

"Quiet, class. That's enough. By the looks of you, with your dirty clothes and hands, all of you have been misbehaving. Now just sit in your seats with your hands behind your backs until I'm ready to start teaching again."

They complied with Betty's order, other than sharing sly looks.

When she sensed heightening restlessness, she began the lessons early. She remembered only too well how uncomfortable it was to sit in those hard little seats for so long, with arms pushing backs forward in an unnatural way.

~ ж ~

"Grass clumps? Pine cones? Outside? You think that's bad?" Kate said. "Try coping with high school. In Edwin Chalmer's class, they throw their erasers so well, they can pocket shoot them off the corners of the room and wing him. By the time they rotate to my class, they're hopped-up fruitcakes. You don't have a clue what tough is. Quit whining."

~ ж ~

A growing friendship between Mr. Detweiler's son Alec, and Bruce Irwin, a mature grade fiver, were a new threat to Betty's slim hold on discipline.

Whenever Betty used any words that even remotely had a scatological connotation, the boys would catch one another's eyes and laugh. Double p's in spelling, innocuous words such as prick, bush, come, cream, juice, hard, screw, sent the boys into convulsions of repressed laughter. Betty had no idea how to handle this. Other than hard looks directed at them when they got noisy, she did nothing. But this new problem nagged at her.

Howard Carson threw another tantrum, and this time the cloakroom banishment had little impact. If he threw any more, she would not know what to do. Lock him in the outhouse? There was always the strap, but it seemed as severe as lashing him with a cat-o'-nine-tails.

~ ж ~

"Hello, Betty, did you send that library list up to Inspector McIntyre?"

"I'm working on it, Mr. Trent." Damn. I suggested it, and I haven't done a thing.

"Good. I expect to see McIntyre soon."

Betty shivered. "Soon?"

"He's not coming here. Relax. I'm going up there."

"Uhh...Mr. Trent. My tooth..." Betty-the-actress cradled her jaw. Made a face. "I must go to Trail this Friday, Mr. Trent. I need to see a dentist. I have the most terribly painful toothache. I thought I could ask Len's wife Vivian to take over for me for the two school days until I can get back on the Minto—she's an ex-teacher; Len says it's possible. I'll pay Vivian from my salary, of course."

Bill gave her a worried look. Belched. "Well, I guess...yeah, okay."

"Oh, great! Thank you." She hurried away, delighted, but nervous.

Kate was in the process of preparing supper.

"I'm going home this weekend to Trail, to the dentist!" Betty announced. "Mr. Trent says it's okay."

"Dentist? What dentist is open on Thanksgiving weekend?" said Kate. "You think you pulled the wool over Bill Trent's eyes, do you? Hunh. He wasn't born yesterday."

Chapter 9

It is the unexpected that always happens.
—19th Century proverb

All 830 tons of the Minto sat low in the water like an oversized houseboat, an impressive sight as it steamed toward the wharf, blasting out Indian war whoops, disgorging thunder clouds. The Minto: Betty's personal saviour arriving to carry her off. She reached for her suitcases.

The no-nonsense first deck, darkly scarred from countless hurried commercial heavings, held cargo and cars. The genteel second sported a Ladies' Saloon, Dining Saloon, Men's Smoker and many staterooms. The upper deck housed more passenger staterooms and the crew quarters. Perched on top like a peaked cap was the pilot's cabin, where the captain and first officer held sway. Three prominent flags flapped in the breeze: the house flag of the Canadian Pacific Railway, the Union Jack and the Red Ensign. Two energetic and noisy 17-horsepower engines waited impatiently for Betty and her fellow passengers to board so they could continue their single-minded thrusting of the shafts that spun the paddle wheel.

Soon Betty was leaning on the polished brass and wood rail, savouring the beauty of the fading fall colours, marvelling at fractured reflections on the rippling waters. She sauntered to the stern and watched the huge paddle wheel churning the water into foam. Later, she delighted in the damask-covered tables of the dining room, ordered from the engraved menu with the aplomb of a remittance man and coveted the abundance of heavy silver, emblazoned with emblematic motifs of the CPR house flag.

Hooky. She was playing hooky. And it felt great.

At Robson, she boarded the Greyhound bus for Trail and reflected on her good fortune. The end of September had brought her first paycheque: one hundred and seventy dollars. She still owed Grampa Wheatley fifty dollars from her Normal School days, but she hoped he would let her pay him back slowly.

~ ж ~

At home, Betty fanned out ninety dollars in her sister's face. "Faye,

85

look at my extra money! I'm rich!"

"Gee, Betts, you really are. Come on, then. Let's go!"

From the crest of the hill near their home, the girls, if they had paused, could have studied the whole of Trail. Seen that the town was a rock bowl carved from the Selkirk Mountains. A bowl split in half by the swift Columbia River and dominated by a sprawling smelter—the great Cominco—which reigned over the downtown from an elevated alluvial perch. They could have marvelled at the townspeople's use of bold colour to counteract the persistent greying caused by the ever-present smoke; the stucco-coated downtown stores and homes perched on the mountainsides were every hue of the rainbow.

But the girls flew down their mountain street, heading for the joys of clothes shopping. Before they had even reached Marlatt's Clothing, however, a voice waylaid them. "Betty? I thought you were up the Arrow Lakes. How did you like the stuff your ma bought at my store for you? She's a real good bargainer; you got a lot of stuff for your sixty-odd bucks. Those Indian blankets were a good buy. So was the toaster. Yep, sixty-odd bucks...." It was Fred Ross, the owner of Goodman's Housewares, the purveyor of all Betty's home assets. Grizzly-food, wooden-legged Hop-along Freddie Ross.

Trapped! "Everything's absolutely great, Mr. Ross. I was just heading right to your store, going to come in and pay you." Betty pulled out sixty from her precious horde of cash and reluctantly handed it over to Hop-along Freddie.

"Sixty? This soon? Now that's the way to do business, Betty. Your dad could take lessons from you. Sixty will do the trick; I'll forgive the rest—all in the interests of future business." He beamed a gold-toothed smile at them. "Oh, say hello to that lovely mother of yours." Fred Ross pocketed the money. Limped back into his store.

"You panicked, Betts. You didn't have to pay him the whole shot, Dad wouldn't have," said Faye. "He wasn't asking for it; he's always friendly like that." Faye's remarks made Betty feel like a country bumpkin, unaware of city-ways.

Now they were in front of Wheatley's Billiards and Tobacco Shop, and Grampa Wheatley was calling out to them. Grampa Wheatley, who had paid so much money out for Betty's education, waved to them, "Oh ho! My two handsome beauties! Come in, come in."

Betty's payday joy evaporated as they entered the aromatic shop, evaporated as Betty looked at the loving face and realized what she had to do. Do what was right, no matter how painful, no matter what Faye thought. "I can't pay you back all the money you lent me, Grampa, but here's thirty." She pulled out the last of her money and felt like a pauper. Now, no shopping spree. Not until Christmas. Unless she settled for hunter's garb or house-print dresses from Mrs. Johnson's store.

"Oh, no no. Put it away. I'm pleased with you, Betty. That's repayment enough. You don't owe me one red cent." He moved his fat cigar to the side of his mouth and scooped them each a large cone of ice cream. The thirty dollars took on new significance; Betty felt rich again. Debt free!

They visited every store in town. Blouses at two dollars apiece. Shoes. A skirt. A winter coat on the lay-away plan. Then: "Come on, Faye! Let's celebrate! Hamburgers and a movie!"

~ ж ~

Sunday morning at the kitchen table: the sanctuary, the refuge, the place—with any luck—to replenish frayed nerves and weakened egos. Amongst the women Betty loved. Brunch had devastated the stylish kitchen, but no one moved to clean; they were too engrossed in listening or expounding. Betty's dad haunted the cellar, squaring off against his treacherous sawdust burner, spooking it into submission for winter.

Betty wooed them, gained centre stage by making light of her classroom peccadilloes, and they laughed. But when she grew serious, when she described the peculiarities of Kate, the frankness of Dot, the clannishness of the townsfolk, Gramma Beaton – ashes spilling from her cigarette onto her lap and smoke curling up and yellowing her hair as always — moralized, as she was wont to do. "You dwell on the petty, daily pinches of life, my girl. You must learn to look to the skies and lift your mind to higher planes."

It was a dictum that Gramma Beaton practised herself. She lived in a house of conflict, with a son-in-law who hated her, who treated her daughter spitefully much of the time. Gramma Beaton took her thoughts elsewhere. Did not, as she said, "dwell on daily pinches". Betty studied her; wished she had the same attitude.

Nora took over the lecture circuit. "Oh Ma, you're so right. It sounds like an odd place, Betty. But surely you can take tremendous pride in your teaching?" Betty listened attentively. Every piece of advice Nora had ever given, Betty had absorbed and tried to use, and had been rewarded accordingly. Nora's love and approval went hand-in-hand with unquestioning obedience. "You're giving these thirsty children knowledge; you are enriching their lives. Don't you realize that teaching is the most noble of all the professions? The most rewarding?"

Betty nodded. "Some days, Mother, I do see a flash of enlightenment on their faces. And maybe even a little pleasure in the fact they've accomplished something. But, boy, it's sure rare. Most of the time they're restless, putting in time like prison inmates."

"Oh, that makes me so very sad. I felt that way as a child in school. I had hoped times had changed and a kinder, more understanding generation of teachers would be out there." Mother looked downcast, theatrically deflated.

Betty tried hard for the right words. "They told us at the Normal School that if you always kept your lessons interesting you wouldn't lose their attention. But it's impossible to always be interesting, just as it's impossible for someone's mind to never wander. I think it's only the ones who learn easily where that might even remotely apply. I think intelligence and attention span are related. The already gifted learn more and the short-changed absorb very little and get restless. I think that a teacher mostly just waits for the next rebellion. That's me. That's what I do, any way."

Mother looked unconvinced. "Oh come on, I can't believe my ears. You sound so cynical; it's not like you. And it's self-defeating. Perhaps you just don't try hard enough." The reproach in her voice stung. An uneasiness suffused Betty. A rare time in her life: she pulled back from her mother; saw gaps in her logic.

Faye was bored with the conversation. "We sure had fun yesterday. We shopped all over the place. Betts bought me a blouse and she got the greatest pair of green shoes!"

"Clothes? When you've got debts?" Dad, emerging from the cellar, was black with soot. When he walked into the brightly lit kitchen, he looked down at his dirtiness

88

with disgust. "I heard all that nonsense. Betty, you're a bloody spendthrift. Clothes. For Faye, too? Jesus."

"I haven't any debts, now, Dad. I paid Mr. Ross and Grampa says I don't have to pay him back another red cent for my schooling. Ever."

"My dad let you off the hook? For a bunch of clothes? He never, ever was so generous to me—and you? You fritter away his money on stuff you'll throw out in a year. Christ almighty, you and your mother are a pair!"

As usual, Betty's father had transformed the sanctuary into a war zone. As soon as his ranting abated, Betty and Faye hastened up to their bedrooms. Away from any further verbal bombardment.

~ ж ~

She was to take the night boat back; she would have a berth. On Monday evening, the Henry J carried her and her parents to the Robson dock.

"I'll try to get back again soon. Somehow," Betty said.

"Don't jeopardize your job, Betts. No more phony toothaches," said Mother.

"No."

"And stop splashing your cash around like a drunken sailor," added Dad. "It doesn't grow on trees!"

On board, she nestled into her cubbyhole cabin, with its starched bed linens and 15-watt ceiling light. She bent open a new pocket book. A cerebral snack to take her mind off her family.

As she lay there, relaxed, enjoying the ship's motion, the comforting throb of its engines, she saw something scuttle along the baseboard: large, fat-bodied, beetle-like. Then she saw another, and another. Cockroaches. Cockroaches for sure. Now she felt itchy and vulnerable. She spent the night with the light on, and between periods of snatched sleep, checked her bed for six-legged predators.

But bugs were a minor skirmish for Betty. She had survived Mother and Dad, mice and skunks, phantom bears, and Kate. Besides, she had new clothes. She was up and dressed in them, ready to disembark and go to the school when they docked at Narrows. It was early dawn. She scratched at fleeting itches all the way up the hill.

~ ж ~

"It's the highschoolers," said pupils Helena and Ingrid. "On Halloween, they usually cart away the two outhouses from the green school. Our outhouses."

"What? Where do they take them?"

"They usually topple them and roll them down the bank. Sometimes they get really mean and take them 'way off into the woods."

A whole set of new problems. Betty could imagine days, or weeks, when her students would have no outhouses. They would have to scoot up the hill to the high school, would malinger enroute, and find worse things than skunks to distract them. She knew she would lose the flimsy bit of control she was just managing to establish if they were so far out of sight.

From Trail, she had brought a cookbook containing a recipe for candy apples. She had even had the foresight to go to Campion's Drugstore to buy tongue depressors to use as sticks for the apples. Two days before Halloween, she went to Mrs. Johnson's store and bought the basic supplies and an assortment of candies. The candy apples were going to have jellybean mouths, sugar-dot eyes, and black-licorice hair.

Betty was alarmed at the cost of everything, but excited by her creative venture. She had always wanted an excuse and the money to try this out. Besides, she hoped, a bit of bribery might make life easier for her. Might make them behave, like her more, and maybe even pull down that wary, isolating barrier that was always between her and them.

The process took longer than she had anticipated. One evening to make the glaze and coat fifteen apples, another to stick on the candies. She worked on them until after midnight; Kate, after proclaiming that Betty had gone nuts, had long since retired.

On the morning of Halloween, Betty surveyed the results. The decorations had slipped, had twisted the faces into bizarre nightmares. But there was no time to fix them. She packed them in boxes as if they were pieces of Granny's precious china, carried

90

them up the hill and hid them under newspapers until the end of the day. When she presented them to the students, her face was flushed with expectancy. She wondered if they would laugh at the cartoon faces, or exclaim over the menacing ones.

They accepted the apples, studied them, and carried them outside to wait for the bus. No reaction, none at all.

Disappointed, pushing the ever-slipping eyeglasses back up her nose, Betty hung back, peering around the door frame, careful to stay out of sight.

Helena and Ingrid, bless them, held their candy apples in front of them as if they were gems. Several of the others began tearing off the jellybeans and sugar dots and stuffing them in their mouths.

Bruce Irwin, after a backward glance to see if Betty was looking, pushed Howard Carson's apple, which Howard was contentedly licking, knocking it to the ground. It rolled in the dirt. Howard gave an angry roar, picked it up and threw it with all his might at Bruce, catching him on the side of the head. Alec ran to defend his buddy, Bruce, and accidentally caught his candy apple in Margie Sloboda's hair. Margie hammered him in the back with hers.

Ingrid Johnson and Helena Stevens froze on the spot, gaped at the uproar, then scurried off behind the outhouses to the pathway that led down the hill.

Jenny Carson and Daisy Whittaker shoved their prized apples under their fuzzy wool cardigans. The treats would undoubtedly reappear, later, looking like they needed a shave.

Candied apples flying through the air, being ground into the dirt, rubbed on faces, stuck into hair. Children yelling, shrieking, swearing, moaning, crying.

"I'm gonna punch in your face!"

"Yah? You and what army?"

"Just wait, you chicken-shit!"

And when the bus arrived, they did not stop; they shoved, slapped, hollered at one another even when they were seated.

Betty collapsed onto the top stair, lowered her aching head into her hands. Back to ground zero. Wasted money! Wasted time! Damn the little savages!

But the next day, the outhouses still stood in their usual places.

Chapter 10

Merry is the feast making till
we come to the reckoning.
English Proverb

They went to the dance together, Betty keeping step with Kate's crippled gait. In their apartment, Kate discarded the crutches; in public, she dragged about on them as if she were paralyzed from the waist. Betty went along with the ruse.

Outside the Community Hall, the liquor-swiggers clustered.

"There's the schoolmarms. How do, young ladies." Jake swooped his cap off and bowed before them like a rakish Sir Walter Raleigh. As usual, he smelled of sweat and tobacco, but tonight, his breath was worse. Boozy enough to kill flies.

"Goin' to save a dance for me, Miz Bradshaw?"

"I don't dance."

"Well, hell's bells, Miz Bradshaw, how are yuh goin' to have any fun? Me and Miz Wheatie could go and get my wheelbarrow and ride yuh 'round the floor a bit, eh, Miz Wheatie?"

"Keep going the way you are and you'll be riding home in your own wheelbarrow," retorted Kate.

Jake slapped his forehead. "Hoo-boy, Miz Bradshaw, yer quick on the trigger. No, young ladies, old Jake may tip his arm back once in a while, but he don't ever take too much of the sauce. How about you, Miz Wheatie, yuh game to do-si-do?"

One refusal was all Betty could bear to see him receive. "Sure, Jake, I'm not too good at do-si-dos, but I'm game."

"Okay! Catch yuh later when Jimmy comes. Oh reservoir, mamzelles." He again bowed elaborately and rejoined the tipplers.

As they entered the room, the band—two fiddlers and a fellow with drums—was playing a sedate waltz. Several couples glided by, dancing with graceful swoops and polish. The less-gifted happily shuffled about, feet splayed, bodies rocking from side to side. Children darted amongst the dancers. Babies, strewn about on reversed benches butted against the walls, slept or screamed. But neither the wailing babies nor the wild children could divert the attention of the dancers for long.

The band struck up a two-step. One-two, one-two, the feet complied. Kate took refuge with other seated folk.

Bill Trent whirled Betty around the dance floor with smooth, fast footwork. Next, a gawky highschooler stick-walked her. He beamed, proud of his audacity.

A tall farmer entered the hall. Tanned face, dark wavy hair, blue eyes that shone right across the room. When he selected a young woman to dance with, and swung by Betty, her eyes glommed onto him. God, he's just... so...handsome! She thought, before she chastised herself.

"Jimmy!" the crowd near the door shouted out. "Jimmy! Make room for Jim, It's Jimmy McCullough, the caller."

A short, wiry man entered the room. A whiff of rye whiskey wafted along with him, like randy perfume. With a showman's swaggering walk, he headed to the fiddlers and stood on a small platform. "Who's ready?" Cheers greeted him. "All right! Find a partner and form a square!" Alec, Betty's big-bugger troublemaking pupil, approached her and asked her to be his partner. She wondered what she had done right to merit his attention.

Ho, greet your partners, short and tall
Listen to me make a call
Allemande left to your partners all
Do-si do and have a ball!

Awkwardly at first, but with quickening agility, Betty and Alec wended their way through the dance, concentrating on the caller's directions, copying the better dancers. Next, as promised, she danced a Virginia Reel with boozy Jake, who, despite contorting his body with more abandon than anyone, took honours as the most graceful dancer in the hall.

A waltz. Jake's son-in-law, Curley McCloskey, asked Betty to dance. His wife, Freda, stood at the side of the room with her baby. The red-faced bundle screamed every time Freda put him down.

Others, including his grandmother Estelle Patten, tried to hold him but he would have only his mother. So Freda stood at the side of the room, once more being the Alice-in-Wonderland duchess, shaking the baby up and down until his eyes rolled, as she watched Curley dance with other women.

Freda's sister—the voluptuous, angel-faced Charlotte, the girl who drove the preacher wild—was dancing with a highschooler named Steve Waterbrook, an assertive and cocky newcomer to the valley. He moved city-style slow: not a shred of space between him and Charlotte's perfect body. Overbearing smugness plastered his face; adoration etched Charlotte's. She alternated between enjoying his embrace, and keeping an eye out for her parents. Jake had gone outside again, but Estelle saw them, and watched with tightened lips.

"I don't like that Steve Waterbrook," the woman next to Betty said. "He's too forward. I'm glad he hasn't taken a shine to my daughter. Poor Estelle."

Betty resumed her inspection of the handsome young farmer. He, warming up to the polka spirit, began to call out falsetto-pitched "ah-hahs", thumping his heavy work boots to the beat of the drums as he clod-hopped about. How unsophisticated! What a disappointment!

The other young men took up the beat of his heavy boots. Thump! Thump! went dozens of thick soles, making the sturdy floor bounce as if it were constructed of green saplings. The music took on urgency; the dancers whirled faster. The older folk retired to the sidelines. Betty longed for someone to ask her to join in, but all the men had their preferred partners.

The women were placing food on a table. Kate and Betty had attempted to make some cookies for the event, and Kate motioned Betty to take the anemic results from her knee, where she had been guarding them, and place them on the table.

The musicians went outside, backslapping all the way, for a swig or two of something raw and uplifting. One or two bolder women joined them. The rest of the revellers crowded around the food table for its sandwiches, cheese, pickles, coffee and ambitious cakes.

After their reinforcements, the musicians wooed the dancers back. From the sidelines, Betty watched Jake and Estelle enjoy a two-step. They circled the floor as expertly as ballroom instructors.

Kate noticed Betty looking at her watch. "Are you ready to go?" A few others were leaving.

"Yes, I guess so." They found their coats. Went out into the cool night air.

"Feels like snow," a bodiless voice announced. It was cold and damp. Both girls felt downcast, missing not being partnered.

"What did you think of that really handsome guy, the one with the black wavy hair?" asked Betty.

"What handsome guy?"

Betty described him.

"Oh, him. He lives near King City. He's a dull clod."

"Well, perhaps he might be dull, but what a face."

Kate shrugged. "Each to his own. Not my type. I prefer Bill Trent to him."

"Bill Trent? Gee, Kate, he's ancient."

"Humph," said Kate. "That's youth speaking. How little you know."

As they neared Jake and Estelle's home, they spotted a cluster of teenagers on the roadside. Giggling, staring down at Jake's house. They moved off when they saw Betty and Kate approaching. Curious, Betty and Kate looked down the hillside to see what had caused the laughter. A large picture window framed a view of Jake's living room. There, on the chesterfield, were Jake's daughter Charlotte and Steve Waterbrook, last seen dancing far too close; now seen in a horizontal embrace. Their clothing was askew. And Steve's hindquarters were bobbing up and down like two apples floating on a wind-swept lake.

"Good God," said Kate. "Foreplay on the dance floor, fornication in the living room."

"Oh, Kate, I hope her poor mother doesn't see this. Or Jake."

"Well, we all play with fire at times." There was a surprising amount of tolerance in Kate's voice. They walked slowly back, wrapped in their own thoughts, wrestling with their own past indiscretions. They missed seeing a dark, portly figure slipping from tree to tree, hiding in shadows, creeping toward Jake's house.

~ ж ~

By mid-November, winter had changed their lives. When Betty and Kate awoke each morning, they saw ever-thickening frost dendrites on the windowpanes. When they breathed out, anywhere except right by the stove, their breath turned to fog. They were sleeping in everything warm they owned: flannelette nighties and sweaters, woollen undershirts and socks. Once they were under the covers, they pulled their winter coats on top of all the blankets. Mornings, they instantly donned the coats. It took twenty minutes to warm the kitchen up enough to take off anything. Then they dressed under their nighties, using them as tents to hold in body warmth. Ice formed on water left in the sink overnight.

Betty dreaded her weekly chilled-to-the-bone bath. Kate, a true Spartan, continued bathing every day and Granny, with bulldog determination, refused to warm up any extra water for her. Kate would rush back upstairs, crutches under one arm, lips blue, shaking from head to foot, wet hair streaming down her face.

Betty concocted a crude bath of her own. She would stand on top of the wood box, lean over the stovetop and wash herself from a large tub of preheated water. Face first, progressing down the body; feet last. Twice as messy, twice as long, twice as awkward, and dangerous, but at least she did not turn blue.

~ ж ~

When the first snow arrived, the annoying chant resurfaced.

"Miz Sweetly! Miz Sweetly!" All the little girls, bright with excitement, slipping on the snowy stairs, eager to tell on the boys. "They're throwing snowballs!"

Betty looked at the girls with revulsion. Had she been as persecutory in her youth? She hoped not. She sighed. Left off writing on the blackboard. The girls could see her reluctance.

Helena spoke. "They're icy snowballs." Betty picked up her pace. Helena, encouraged, spoke again. "And maybe they've got rocks in them."

Betty clanged the school bell. The boys, like overgrown puppies, ran toward the front door. Laughing, rosy-cheeked, skidding in the fresh white covering. They were getting used to Betty's early summoning and lined up without apprehension. Pretending to slip, trying to make one another laugh. They came inside, clothes steaming, full of the elation a first good snowfall brings. What was the best way to handle the situation? School kids always made snowballs.

She waited until they were seated and then waited a few seconds more for dramatic effect. Trying for perfect timing.

"Winter is a wonderful time." She emphasized each word. "We can build igloos and snow forts and magnificent snowmen, even giants, because there are so many of us. But, we CAN NOT THROW THINGS AT ONE ANOTHER. HEAR ME?" They flinched at her harsh loudness.

"No rocks, no pine cones, no dirt clods, no ice balls—nothing. Not hard or middling hard or even soft things. And not just in the winter; in the other seasons as well. Do you have that straight?" She glowered at them, her mean eyes moving up and down the rows.

"Now, here's paper and on it you write, in your best McLean's penmanship, these sentences." She turned to the blackboard and wrote:

I will not throw things at my fellow students.
I will not take the chance of hurting someone.

"Write it thirty times." They groaned. "Stop it! I could have said a hundred."

She wished she had a solution other than this timeworn punishment, this mindless repetition that would make them hate writing. They were not scholars; they had been sired by workmen and farmers. Classroom demands exercised their brains but rarely their bodies. And now even their brains were stilled.

~ ж ~

One day, after staying at the school longer than usual, urgency insisted she forego the ploughed road. She took the perpendicular route, directly down the hillside to Granny's

98

bathroom. The steep, snow-covered pathway on the hillside appeared to be passable. But she soon learned why woodsmen wear snowshoes: Each footstep broke the snow crust and plunged her into bottomless softness, not unlike stepping into clouds. Slow-motion progress. Cold whiteness climbed up her skirt to her thighs and filled her rubber galoshes. Each step was slow motion frustration. Halfway down, the solitary cloud-walker suddenly stopped. Stood still as steam rose around her. Several seconds of ignoble ecstasy ... . Now her galoshes sloshed and her clothing began to stiffen as the warm liquid cooled into ice. She reached Granny's, unobserved, safe from sharing an encore to the skunk story. Safe from being this week's topic, this week's joke.

For the rest of her stay in Narrows, she decided, she would use the outhouse after the children left, whether it was coated in ice or smelled vile. Despite her knothole-phobia.

~ ж ~

"Want to go to Nakusp on Saturday?" Kate was light-hearted, even enthusiastic.

"Sure!"

Roscoe Taylor, Bryllcreem hair glinting in the afternoon sun, met them as they stepped out of the mail truck. "Two good lookin' babes for me. How can I be so lucky? What's on our agenda, little ladies?"

"Register at the Leland Hotel, then shopping. Betty and I are going to stock up on groceries at the Overwaitea."

"Whoa, baby! Count me out of that! I'll treat for supper at the Leland. Maybe a few beers before and after? Or a movie? Swim at the hot springs? I'm game for anything."

Kate's eyes shone. "We'll settle for a beer and dinner and then decide what else."

"Okay, ladies, I'll meet you at four-thirty outside the Ladies and Escorts door."

Betty and Kate strolled down Broadway, sizing up the six stores. Betty stopped at a display window. "Oh, wow, just look at those, Kate." Pristinely white leather snow boots beckoned to her. Black or brown was all she'd ever seen before. Movie stars would wear such boots.

Kate scrutinized them. "You like those? They're huge. And impractical. Awfully showy."

"I love them! They're a dream come true!"

The suited salesman cradled them. "Latest style, designed to be a female version of aviator's boots. Top-quality leather. Lined in genuine sheepskin. They'd look good with your black coat, miss."

Up close, they did look huge. But, she reasoned, they certainly had to be the heighth of fashion. " Oh Kate, I've never seen any as nice in my whole life! And guess what? They'll fit over both high- and flat-heeled shoes."

Kate shrugged. "It's your money. Do what you want. Just hurry up."

"How much?"

"Twenty-two fifty."

"Twenty-two fifty!"

"Built to last forever. And you'll never have cold feet again, I promise you."

They continued down Broadway, Betty staring down at her splendid new boots. They were heavy and wide, and made her gait awkward; but she did not care. She spent no more on clothing, preferring to watch Kate, who picked up some satin lingerie. They carried back heavy sacks of groceries, and Kate's rare, free-wheeling laughter echoed all over Nakusp as a grinning Betty, boots spread apart, slid and stumbled in the snow like a sailor on rough seas.

~ Ж ~

"Say, Betty, did you hear the one about the preacher who raised sheep?" Roscoe told non-stop, off-colour jokes as he quaffed glass after glass of beer.

"Drink up, folks," said the bartender. "It's five. We'll open again at seven."

After dinner, on the mark of seven, Roscoe herded the girls back to the beer parlour. More beer and more   beery   jokes;

laughter and giddiness until the bartender announced closure at eleven.

"Oh, Roscoe, where did the time go?" Kate said. "It's time to go to bed, Betty."

"Sure. I've got my boots, tha'sh a good enough day for me."

~ ж ~

"Roshcoe. Whadda card," said Betty, as she swayed toward their room.

"Betty. Sober up," commanded Kate. "You cover up for me and keep your trap shut. I'm going to stay with Roscoe tonight. I'll see you in the morning."

Betty's beer-induced euphoria vanished. She felt betrayed. All I am, she thought, is Kate's cover-up, her phony chaperone. The hand of friendship, so recently, so gratifyingly extended, picked up a suitcase and left.

Loggers, miners, and other footloose men were now swilling beer in their rooms, downing whiskey chasers; Saturday night was their night to howl. The ill-fitting door to Betty's room rattled every time the drunken men thumped by. They roamed about, bowled beer bottles down the hall, laughed, hollered, cursed. Betty was afraid to go to sleep, but the alcohol won and she drifted off.

Suddenly, she bolted upright. Some drunk! Trying to open her door! Making an eerie, sniffling throaty sound that turned her spine to ice. He jiggled the doorknob. Betty searched for a weapon. My boots! She sprang from bed; stood as far from the door as she could and as it opened, she raised a heavy boot in each hand, ready to heave them.

The intruder tottered into the room, a pitiable figure uttering deep sobs. It was Kate. She leaned against the door and collapsed. Between heaves, she gasped for air.

Betty's heavy boots thundered to the floor. "Kate! What's wrong?" Kate could not speak, could not stop the waves of hurt. Down on her knees, Betty patted and stroked Kate's arm. Finally, Kate, her emotions spent, took a deep sigh. Betty found her a handkerchief. "Can you talk?"

"He's married. Roscoe. He's married. He has kids," she moaned.

"What does he intend to do? Get divorced?"

"Nothing. Nothing. I don't really enter the picture." She blew her nose, gained a measure of composure, and spoke with derision. "He says he loves me. He still wants to see me. Maybe about once a month. Here. In Nakusp. I'd be his once-a-month mistress. His shack-up." More tears.

"The dirty creep! What on earth are you going to do?"

"Cut him out...like surgery." Kate pounded her chest. "Cut him out of here. I won't play destructive games. I've dealt with enough male beasts." The tears stopped. Her eyes did not glare as they usually did; they had become black velvet holes, capable only of absorbing light.

They lay awake on their beds. Kate did not move, did not cry. Her hands rested on her chest like those of a prepared corpse. She wishes she were dead, thought Betty.

Fortunately, the mail truck was leaving early. They returned home to Narrows with only the most minimal of verbal exchange.

~ ж ~

Betty coped with a period of parade-square-orders from Kate for several days after this incident. Betty had been learning from previous experiences, that every time Kate opened up to Betty, Kate would later resent it, and chew-out Betty in one way or another. Betty kept out of her way as much as possible. Eventually, Kate lapsed into a somber silence, and the case of Roscoe Taylor snapped shut.

~ ж ~

A few weeks after the Nakusp fiasco, they sat together, working on their first joint project: a song sheet of Christmas carols for Jake's son-in-law, Curley McCloskey, who was organizing a Christmas concert.

"I don't look forward to working with him, do you Kate?"

"I don't want to work with anyone."

102

"My mother says all men are Casanovas, and Curley didn't marry poor Freda until she was seven months pregnant. And Freda's sister Charlotte is going to get in the same mess. Ever since you and I and those kids saw her and that Steve uhh...copulating in Jake's living room, there's been gossip galore. Even I'm privy to their activities."

Kate nodded. "They're indiscrete, the ninnies. I caught Charlotte and Steve in the act at school, in the girl's washroom. God, I wish we had outhouses. Then I'd be none the wiser."

"You saw them doing it again?"

"Heard them. I just stood outside the washroom door. I called out, 'Charlotte and Steve, please return to your classrooms as soon as you are presentable.' I didn't know what else to say. For me to say anything else would be like the pot calling the kettle black."

"I guess so, Kate. Perhaps you should tell Charlotte's parents?"

"Would you want anyone to tell your parents if it were you?"

"Good Lord, no!"

"Me neither. I just hope to God she doesn't get pregnant."

"It's awful that such a special human act can be considered sordid. All because they aren't married."

"Betty—you miss the point, as usual. It's they who make it sordid, doing it in public."

~ Ж ~

A week after their discussion of Charlotte and Steve, Betty and Kate went again to another community dance. They stomped the snow from their boots and entered the boisterous hall, momentarily blinded by bright gas lanterns. Whirling merry-makers, panting exuberance, were egged on by two sweat-soaked fiddlers and an accordionist. Kate, as usual, hobbled to a seat in a corner.

Again, Betty hoped she would be asked to dance by the handsome, black-haired farmer from King City. She had given him no thought between dances, but now that she was in his presence, she kept staring at him, examining every part of him. In detail. Now she liked the way he had rolled up his plaid shirt sleeves, displaying the white sleeves of his long underwear, liked the way he

103

wiped his hands on the back of his pants before he took the hands of his current dancing partner; now his stomping to the music and his yelling of cowboy "heehaws" sounded like the heighth of virile manhood. She wanted to be held by him. But he did not seem to see that she existed.

I'm bushed. Thoroughly backwoods, she told herself. Calf-sick over a cowboy.

She danced with several partners, including Curley McCloskey. Curley, the Casanova, she kept thinking. Ruiner of poor Freda's chance to become a nurse. She feared the sexuality radiating from the man. It had been so long since she had been held in an embrace, been kissed. The closer she got to Christmas, the more she was allowing herself to think of Cameron. And the nighttime thoughts of delicious animal exchange were gnawing at her reserve. But Curley did not pull her to him. He simply danced.

The same way highschooler Steve Waterbrook now danced with Charlotte. Indifferently. He danced with many girls. But Charlotte's eyes rarely strayed from him.

Betty and Kate remained until the end. The townswomen allowed Betty to help with the clean up, a sign that she was being accepted.

Kate had temporarily put aside her broken heart, and they walked home in a happy mood. Kate was now very adept with her crutches. Their overshoes—Kate's practical rubber pullovers and Betty's impractical aviator boots—made satisfyingly crunchy sounds in the damp snow.

"Curley isn't as bad as I thought he might be. Never tried anything wrong when we danced," said Betty.

"Why should he? Don't flatter yourself; you couldn't get him away from Freda; you're no Gina Lollobrigida."

Betty ignored the insult. "And your student Steve Waterbrook is behaving himself with Charlotte." They were passing Jake and Estelle's house. No lovemaking taking place on the living room chesterfield this time.

"Well, even though Charlotte's a raving beauty, I suspect Steve's fallen out of love with her. High school romances don't always pan out," said Kate, as she concentrated on the snow. "Sexual encounters alone don't cement a relationship. I should know."

When they arrived at Granny's, they turned onto the side path that led to Granny's back door. Moonlight illuminated a dark figure, bumping shoulder first from the hotel. It was Granny's next-door neighbour Sammy Sunders, the trapper, exiting from his and Mrs. Sunders' winter abode: the cat flea-infested Narrows Hotel. Two heaped pails weighed down his arms as he laboured to a spot near Granny's property. Plopff! Shisss! Went the contents of his pails as he dumped them.

Kate screwed up her nose. "What a stink!"

Another dark figure emerged from the hotel, wearing a tattered kimono and cradling a kitten. A black tabby perched on the narrow, kimonoed shoulder, a Persian rubbed against the bare, skinny legs. The light from inside the hotel silhouetted the figure; it was Mrs. Sunders.

"Shut off your flashlight, Betty," whispered Kate. The two girls stood stock-still in the safe shadow of Granny's house.

"God damn...filth...I'll put a stop to you and your crap!" Sammy Sunder's voice carried over to them on a putrid breeze.

"Oh, Sammy, Sammy...no...no, please don't—"

"...turned our place into a shithouse. Damn worn-out bag of bones, I—" His voice was cut off as he shoved Mrs. Sunders inside and slammed the door behind them.

"Don't breathe while we go by that slime pile. Imagine him carrying it out by the bucketful!" Kate whispered. "She must let the cats poop wherever, whenever... and leaves the clean-up to Sammy. Yech! Disgusting."

As they rounded the side of the house, without warning, the cold, quiet night air split open with unexpected, heart-stopping blasts— Crrrack! Crrrack!

Both girls froze. "Gun shots! His hunting gun! He's killed her!" shrieked Betty.

"No. A man wouldn't shoot his wife over cat shit. Would he?"

Kate's voice was unsteady.

"My dad would," wailed Betty. "What should we do? Get Bill Trent?" They looked at Bill and Nina's house; their lamps were already extinguished.

"No. Absolutely not." Kate had regained her normal voice. Almost.

"Mrs. Sunders could bleed to death by morning. Oh, Kate, we have to do something!" They crept back toward the side of the house to look at the hotel again, their hearts pounding. All of the hotel's lamps were out.

"We are not going over there and we are not waking Bill." The back door of the hotel bashed open again. Betty and Kate rushed pell-mell into Granny's house, like two terrified rabbits escaping the claws of a cougar.

"Do you think he saw us?"

"I hope to God not."

They slunk up the stairs in the dark and burrowed into bed. Both imagined Sammy Sunders prowling about; gun in hand, intent on silencing witnesses.

Betty awoke in the morning to see blue-lipped Kate, shivering from her cold-water morning bath, getting dressed in her good grey suit.

"Where are you going?"

"To Nakusp. On the milk truck. And if you're going to Kokanee, you better hurry up."

"What about the murder?" Betty whispered.

"What about it? She's dead by now, if she wasn't dead instantly."

"Oh, Kate, we're guilty, too, by reason of silence. And what if he saw us?"

"We're still alive, aren't we? If we say nothing, he'll never know we saw it all. And besides, I've got my own court case coming up after Christmas, and I think it would look bad for me if I was involved in a murder trial at the same time."

Betty put her coat over her nightgown and peeked out the window. All was deathly quiet. Elongated early morning shadows patterned the hotel's backyard like steps up to newly framed gallows. Betty looked in vain for the bloody footsteps of a fleeing victim. Saw only a man's footsteps breaking the pristine snow. Footsteps leading away from the hotel. "There's no sign of life at the hotel. Oh, God, Kate, we shouldn't have panicked, and now we should—"

"Smarten up, Betty. We are not getting involved. And don't tell Bill. Keep your yap shut." Kate grabbed her crutches and hurried off.

Betty watched Kate boarding the milk truck for Nakusp, watched daylight climb above the mountains. The light snow ended and a pale sun tinted fluffed clouds. The skies couldn't care less about murder, not now. Mrs. Sunders, the cat lover, was dead.

Betty looked over at the spot where Sammy had dumped the cat mess. Dung. A cold cairn, Betty decided, in memory of passive, forlorn, unrevenged Mrs. Sunders. Snuffed out by a raging man with a gun. A man who was now, no doubt, dog sledding away from the scene of his crime.

She straightened her shoulders. "Pull yourself together, you lily-livered coward," she whispered. Kate had said not to bother Bill Trent, but she hadn't said anything about Mrs. Johnson, the storekeeper.

Oh yes. Me and Mrs. Johnson! On a mission. We'll phone the Mounties and help them get their man! Get the Infamous Narrows' Wife Shooter! To hell with Kate's upcoming court case, to hell with Kate's warning. And then I'm getting the mail truck to Kokanee. Getting out of this dangerous place, too.

She waited impatiently until Mrs. Johnson got off the phone, then approached her. "Mrs. Johnson—"

The bell over the door tinkled. Someone was entering the store. Betty wheeled around, ready to project her exasperation onto the clueless shopper who dared slow the pursuit of justice.

Instead, Betty's jaw dropped open and would not close. Her eyes bulged and her eyelids forgot how to function.

Holding Mrs. Johnson's screen door so very carefully, letting it shut without a sound, approaching the counter with apologetic footsteps, emitting a steady moan of sighing tears—in came flea-bitten... Mrs. Sunders!

"Oh, Mrs. Johnson, my husband Sammy's gone crazy. Last night he killed my darling Peppy, my old father cat. Shot him! Then he just pushed him in a gunny sack and took him away!" She pulled out a handkerchief and sobbed into it. Mrs. Johnson rounded the counter and placed her arms around Mrs. Sunders. Gingerly.

"There, there, Mrs. Sunders. Don't cry so. You said yourself the old cat was in terrible misery. It was an act of God's mercy. And if, as you told me, he's given the germs to the other cats, you've got enough cleaning up to do, without having to deal with one whose old insides are misbehaving, too."

Betty, still pumped up with get-your-man fervour, could not close her mouth or control her bug-eyed stare. The bell over the door tinkled again. In came the driver of the mail truck.

"Mail time ladies! Going to Kokanee with me this bright a.m., Miss Wheatley?"

Mrs. Johnson waved good-bye to Betty over Mrs. Sunders' shoulder. Cat stench permeated the store. Mrs. Sunders' shoulders were still heaving; her tears still fell.

Chapter 11

Of all sexual aberrations,
 perhaps the most peculiar is chastity.
—Rémy de Gourmont

Only soft winds ever blew in the valley. The snow, when it came down, coasted from side to side as falling feathers do, but it was never buffeted severely as it was on the plains where the strong winds live. Down, down, softly it came, and it piled up ever higher. The cars, trucks and buses wore steel chains on their wheels to help them dig into the quick-changing face of the snow. First the slush and ice and then the rising soft depths, followed by yet more ice.

Steadily the cold thickened the shores, reaching out to choke off the narrows. The ferry, with its steel hull, and twice-hourly voyages could keep open its passageway through the ice mass, but the Minto could not. Regular through service came to a halt. Betty experienced a sense of overwhelming isolation, a frequent desire to hibernate in her coat-covered bed, like some weather-weary grizzly.

She often joined Kate next to the high piles of snow at the front of Granny's house and waited for the school bus. Kate, ever mindful of her upcoming court case, and still loving any sympathy she could get, persisted with the crutches in public, though when they were alone upstairs, she now moved with as much ease as Betty. Granny knew of the deception.

"I could forgive those crutches bumping about up there. But these days she stamps around like some storm trooper goose-stepping in his jackboots. Ah, me, I think God is punishing me."

Betty and Granny and Sunday afternoon tea. Kate at her school preparing lessons. Betty procrastinating, knowing she should be at hers. Despite layers of sweaters, despite woollen skirts, Granny and Betty hugged the living room stove. Granny wore men's brown plaid carpet slippers. She tried to persuade Betty to get a pair. "They have them at the store, Betty. You don't even have to send away for them, and they're so warm!" Granny and Georgika can wear all the men's clothing they want, thought Betty. That's what comes of living in

109

the backwoods. I'll bet no Vancouver woman would wear men's slippers. Me neither. I'd rather freeze to death. Granny rocked in the afghan-lined rocker, teacup and saucer in hand, the well-behaved tea only occasionally slopping over to swim in the saucer.

~ Ж ~

Betty had just returned from yet another visit with Georgika. She went there almost every second weekend, arriving Saturday on the mail truck and staying for just one night; otherwise, she got too far behind in her classroom preparations. The visits were predictable but immensely satisfying: good food, kind words and laughter. Georgika catered to Betty's every need. Long hugs and sloppy kisses were the only negative factors. She saw little of Leslie Bedford-Jones, though, which always disappointed her. A little spice, a soupçon of flirtation would add colour to her nun-like existence. Leslie, however, remained dedicated, addicted to teaching. The few times he was around, they were never alone. Sometimes she would catch him looking at her, but he did not let himself indulge in eye contact. Georgika's son Tommy, ever since the first mention of Cameron, did not seem to have much interest in Betty. Georgika never invited Kate, and Kate never talked to Betty about the slight.

Kate had perked up ever since they had put together the Christmas Concert song sheet. Every evening, during chores, they sang carols. Kate, a melodic coloratura, had had singing lessons. She led, Betty echoed. Granny told them to sing even louder; they were a joy to hear.

~ Ж ~

"How've you been, Dot?"

They had met while watching the adult portion of the concert rehearsal, and now Betty and Dot walked together towards Granny's house.

"Punk. I think I'm getting the flu. Every one of my grade-one kids has it. I've felt like puking for two days, now. I can't even stand the smell of a cigarette, let alone smoke one."

Betty moved away from Dot. She could not afford to be sick; she was too busy. Most days she had the students practising for the concert during their lunch times, and therefore, she had more evening work to do. She could rarely do any marking at recess, either;

on frostbite days they had to stay inside and she would read to them from her first Book-of-the-Month Club purchase. They didn't like Winnie the Pooh, though. Sometimes, they played 'Walking the Dog', 'Hide the Letter' and 'Pop Goes the Weasel', but the older boys complained. "We don't wannna play no pansy games, Miz Sweetly." They preferred to be outdoors whenever the weather allowed.

"So far no one in my class has the flu," said Betty.

"Are you still having trouble with them throwing things?" asked Dot.

"Well.... yes. They're still throwing snowballs at each other. My punishment didn't work. I'm hopeless as a teacher. I shouldn't even be here."

"Betty, you've got to get the little buggers under your thumb."

"I wish I had never listened to my parents. They made me be a teacher. I wanted to go to Hollywood; be an actress."

"An *actress*? Who *wouldn't* like to be an actress? Cripes, why not a queen...or an heiress? Touch the ground, Betty. Reality. Like it or not, you're a teacher."

"If Cameron and I were—"

"Forget Cameron. He's way off in Lotus Land. You're here in the sticks. Who knows what he's up to in a university filled with flirty co-eds? Right now, you've got to get a hold on today."

"That's easy for you to say, you've got your fiancé Lou." They watched the ferry dock and unload its few passengers. A blue Chevy pickup slowed as it neared them. The driver looked familiar to Betty. He waved at Dot, she waved back and shouted, "Hi Sparks, you good lookin' devil, you." The fellow grinned at Dot, avoided looking at Betty, and sped off.

"Yeah, I've got Lou now, but I had to wait, too. And I work hard at being a darned good teacher. I joke a lot, but in reality, I give it my all. Tackle it, Betty. Face it squarely. And don't look so gloomy!"

"If you and I could get together more often, that would help, but I rarely see you."

"I don't have any spare time, between Lou and the school. But....when I'm married and living on this side of the lake, I'll give great big dinner parties and invite hundreds of perfect bachelors for you, and you'll be so grateful to your wonderful friend Dot...." Dot left Betty at Granny's gate and skidded down the hill to the ferry. The sound of her laughter trailed off, soaked up by the roadside snow, which was humped and clumped like old mattress stuffing: stale coloured, lumpy textured, waiting for a fresh sheet covering.

I really like her, thought Betty. I could do with her in big doses, but she doesn't need my friendship. Too bad. Thank God I've got Georgika.

~ ж ~

Betty returned home to volatile Kate, marking papers by gaslight. She stopped when Betty arrived. "You hopeless twit. You didn't buy any matches. I had to go and get them, or we'd freeze in the morning."

"Oh." Betty resisted an urge to kick Kate's bad knee. Kate, she thought, must be the meanest sub-landlady in the world.

"I had a note from my teacher-friend, Elaina Maleyna. Her shaky neck is improving," Kate continued in her drill-sergeant voice, "and she's coming here Saturday so we can talk about our court case. It's less than two weeks before we leave for Christmas holidays and the court case is just after that. And...." she suddenly switched to an atypical voice—softer, more like a sweet-talking army recruiter—"my fixed-up van is being delivered to me Saturday! We don't have to ride on the milk truck and the bumpy Greyhound bus when we go home for Christmas; we can leave right after school on the Friday and I'll drive you straight to Trail. I also promised that God-awful, pathetic teacher I'd drive him to Vancouver—don't look so half-witted! I'm talking about Edwin Chalmers. I'll only charge you each a share of the gas. Now isn't that good news?" Her face radiated satisfaction.

"Really? That's swell! Thanks."

"Well, it's on my route and I need your cash, so no thanks are needed."

They prepared for bed in a happy mood, singing carols. They had a shared goal: getting out of Narrows for Christmas.

Kate was brushing her teeth at the single tap sink. She moved aside so Betty could do the same. "Oh," said Kate, "I forgot to tell you something. About Jake's daughter Charlotte. Remember the horizontal tango in Jake's living room? And my school washroom episode? Well, I heard Charlotte telling one of the girls in the classroom she's pregnant. Either she thinks I'm deaf, or she wants me to know. And now Charlotte and her mother have left for the coast. I bet you Estelle will have Charlotte get rid of it."

Betty dropped her toothbrush and stared at Kate. She began to shiver, but not from the cold. She didn't know why; did not want to think about such a drastic concept. "You mean abortion? Poor, poor Charlotte! Really? Are you sure?"

"Think about it, for God's sake, you dough-head. Her mother has all her hopes pinned on Charlotte. She doesn't want her to end up like her sister Freda, saddled with a baby. Charlotte's only seventeen. Someone's supposed to become the nurse in that family, remember?"

"Oh, yes. Of course. But an abortion, Kate?"

Kate shrugged her shoulders. "Yeah. I know what I'm talking about. Vinegar douches and slippery elm and coat-hanger abortions are way more common than head colds. Dangerous as Hell. I bet there are more abortions than live births. Fortunately, there are some doctors in Vancouver—God bless 'em—willing to defy the law—keep you from ruining your insides or dying. If you've got the money."

As usual, they layered themselves well and banked the fire up with extra wood to get through another bone-chilling night.

Kate spoke in the darkness. "Betty?" The friendly tone was gone.

Betty tensed. "Yes?"

"You don't take good enough care of my books. You mess up the book jackets, so I'm putting them away. Don't touch them again."

Now Betty seethed. *One of these days I'll kill her. I'll stuff my rent money down her throat.*

Chapter 12

The smyler with the knyf under the cloke.
—Geoffrey Chaucer

B etty clumped reluctantly over to janitor Len's house, after deciding it was time to make a duty call on his wife Vivian. She walked in valleys between the drifts to protect her white aviator boots. She smiled down at them. Such beauty! Such elegance! So citified! However, their low-cut fronts let the snow in, and their Sasquatch-size caused her to trip despite her wide-legged gait.

She knocked twice before Vivian answered. "Oh. Betty. Uh, er, come in."

Betty's snow boots made a puddle on the floor. "What a mess I'm making! Sorry, Vivian."

Vivian stared at the slushy water, unmoving. There was a dirty cloth on the floor. Betty stretched for it and sopped up the mess, wondering why Vivian did not run a hundred-yard dash for the floor wax.

But the room had changed since Betty's last visit. The floor was scuffed and spotty. The once-immaculate counters and corners were cluttered.

Vivian wandered to the stove, pushed the kettle onto the firebox and spoke as though she were unbearably weary. "Tea?...Teatime? Len will want tea, too..."

Betty hid her uneasiness. "Where's your beautiful baby?"

"Harry's asleep. At last." Vivian rallied a half-smile and reached for her good china cups, reached for them with hands that shook. She started to rummage for a tea cloth, then gave up, gesturing indifferently.

"See? Len still hasn't finished off the woodwork. Len never finishes anything.... He takes too long with all his jobs. I tell him, but he does nothing. See?" She ended with a humourless giggle,

115

wrapped her arms like a straitjacket around her chest and forced vivaciousness into her voice. "Tell me about your Christmas concert. I hear from Len it'll be simply fabulous."

Betty took over the tea making. "My class is reciting short poems I wrote. One of their mothers is playing the piano for background effect. And we—"

"Wonderful." The lilt in Vivian's voice mocked her slammed-shut face. "I didn't know we had a poet in our midst."

"Hardly. Kate's the only one capable of teaching singing. So I—"

"Len tells me you design intricate art projects and clever little assignments. I had to subscribe to children's magazines. You don't even need the kind of books I had when I taught."

Betty felt uncomfortable with the accusatory praise. "How about you, Vivian, what have you been up to lately?"

"Nothing. Len gets the groceries. I can't go anywhere with the baby in all this snow. We're going home for Christmas, and–and I can hardly wait to get out of here." Her teacup rattled as she settled it on its saucer. "Having a demanding baby and a messy house and winter time is so...." Betty waited. After minutes that crawled, Vivian lifted her eyes to Betty. Clung to her with them.

"I'm not ready...just not ready for another baby. I'm not....not a good mother." Each word exploded, like a popgun inside Vivian's throat. "There's nothing to do up here.... No one to talk to.... If I stay much longer, I'll jump out of my skin.... And run...."

Alarmed, Betty searched for helpful suggestions, anything to divert Vivian, to pull her back from the darkness she seemed ready to embrace. "What about going to the dances, or shopping at Nakusp, or you could help at our Christmas Concert?" Vivian remained silent. "I don't see you at church, or at the monthly movies, either. Can't you find a baby-sitter?"

"I can't leave Harry with strangers."

Betty persisted, in a calm and coaxing voice. "Well, the other women bring their babies to the dances with them."

"I can't. The place is full of smells and smoke and germs." Vivian drummed her chewed fingers against the tabletop. She looked as though she was going to make another confession to Betty, when they heard the sound of the school bus pulling up. Vivian jumped, refilled the kettle, and opened the door.

"Hi, dear." She gave Len a peck on the cheek, then darted an anxious look at Betty. Play my game, the look on her face pleaded. "Isn't this just the most lovely surprise, dear? Betty and I are having a wonderful chat. She's asked me if I wanted to help with the concert."

Len studied Vivian warily while she spoke. Kept them on her as he answered Betty. "Hi, Betty, good to see you here. Help with the concert? Are you going to, Viv?"

Now Vivian started breathing hard, in little gulps. "No. No. No! I told you! I'm too busy."

Deflated, Len stared down at his snow-clad rubber boots, pooling on the wet floor cloth. Then his natural optimism surfaced once more. He glanced guardedly at Betty. "Gee Betty, what were you thinking she could do? Maybe—"

"Stop, Len! I've got Christmas cleaning to do before we go to my mother's. I can't."

Len stiffened. Again, he fixated his eyes on his boots. His last bit of optimism had, Betty realized, just melted totally away along with the snow. "Sure, honey, I understand. I just thought—"

"Stop doing my thinking for me. I'm all right." Vivian stared vacantly ahead. The kettle began to shriek.

Betty couldn't stand the tension in the house; the forlorn look on Len's face. She stood up." I've got to be going."

Now Vivian's pleading eyes flew open wide; her eyebrows pulled high enough to take off in flight. "Oh, Betty, stay for a fresh cup. You've barely arrived." She looked ready to cry.

"I always have so much to do, and if I forget anything, Kate gives me heck. I'm supposed to go to the store." Betty was backing towards the door, edging Len from the exit.

"But you haven't even seen baby Harry, yet. You'll have to come back soon, Betty. Don't wait so long; I have to talk. Please!"

Again Vivian's eyes bore into Betty's.

Betty's smile was forced. "I'll do my best."

~ ж ~

The sky was darkening when she left. She shook her head as she looked at her watch. Night came so early, now. A heavy snow was falling again, blurring the landscape.

Coming down from the high school was bulky Edwin Chalmers, huffing and puffing, tightrope walking in the slippery snow tracks left by the bus. When he saw Betty, he skidded to a stop, and adjusted his crooked fedora. Snow cascaded from it and piled on his rounded shoulders.

"Upon my word! It's my neglected fellow-teacher Miss Wheatley." With an extravagant flourish, touching first his forehead, then his lips and then his chest, he bowed, skidded and righted himself. "I'm sorry not to have popped in to see you. I have been quite derelict in my duty."

"I'm sure you've been as busy as I have, Mr. Chalmers. I've never been up to your school, either."

"Ah! 'East is East and West is West and never the twain shall meet', my dear, to steal from Kipling. Tell me what you are up to. Surely you don't keep your pretty head in your classroom night and day. Where are all the lucky swains?" They walked side-by-side down the icy hill.

"What swains, Mr. Chalmers? Do you think I should find myself an unmarried farmer?"

"Fine madness, I'm sure, unless you have fallen in love with the place."

Betty shoved her hands deeper into her pockets; kept her eyes on the slippery snow ruts. "That would be the biggest overstatement of the year. I'm surviving. I never see you at the dances, or the church, or the movies. What do you do in your spare time?"

"I read. And I write." Now, his voice was guarded.

"Letters?" Betty momentarily roused herself from her weather-watch; wondered if she should prod Edwin into a more active

118

social life, prevent him from becoming like Vivian.

"Well, yes, those too. I am writing a paper on William Blake, the English poet—an ambition left over from my student days."

"My goodness! That's wonderful. I wish I could say something as great about the use of my time." She looked at him with new respect. No helplessness, here. No Vivian-type problems.

Edwin Chalmers allowed himself a brief self-congratulatory smile. "I hear we will be travelling companions with the delightfully benevolent Miss Kate Bradshaw."

"Yes." Betty ignored his sarcasm.

"That will no doubt be a pleasant trip."

"Yes." She wondered if he wanted to bring Kate up as a subject. If so, she was not going to co-operate. "Do you ever hear from Inspector McIntyre?"

"I had a letter recently. There will be a meeting of the local teachers in Edgewood, possibly in late April, and at that time we will receive the benefit of his consummate wisdom."

"Is that when he will judge our teaching?"

"Judge? Would you worry about the judgment of one man?"

"Of course. He holds our future in his hands." Betty became annoyed with herself. She was beginning to sound like Mr. Chalmers.

" 'Judge not, that ye be not judged', Miss Wheatley."

"I'd like to hear you say that to Inspector McIntyre."

"Are you laying down a gauntlet?"

"No, I'm certainly not." She could not help smiling.

"Good. The vicissitudes of teaching untutored minds are burden enough. Your good friend Miss Bradshaw has no doubt apprised you of the behavioural liberties of my young rascals."

"She is not necessarily my good friend." Betty wished she had bitten her tongue. "Kate and I get along just fine."

"Well, good for you, Miss Wheatley, I am sure you are a cautious diplomat." He glanced toward the lake. "Yonder arrives my trusty conveyance." He was looking at the approaching ferry. "Good day, Miss Wheatley." He tipped his snow-topped city hat to her. "Until we begin our journey to civilization."

~ ж ~

A persistent tapping at the back door woke Betty and Kate. It was Saturday. Kate sprang out of bed. "My God! It can't be bloody Elaina already! What time is it anyway," she said, trying to focus on her watch. "Hell. It's not even eight o'clock!" She yanked on her coat. It was still dark. Kate, sans crutches, descended the stairs, storm trooper style again. "Hang on, I'm coming!"

A wavery voice responded: part crow, part canary. "Wake up, you sleepy heads! Pick up your socks! The sun's nearly up—the day's half over!"

"Half over, my eye. When did you leave Kokanee, Elaina? Last night? You sure couldn't have had any sleep."

"We left at six." Stamp! Stamp! Elaina was trying to stomp off her snow accumulations. "Brush me off, Kate!" Unwilling, effort-making grunts from Kate. Patient sighs from Elaina.

"This darling young milkman had only five stops on his way here, so the trip wasn't bad. You'll have to give me some breakfast. I'm starving! What a strange morning get-up for you to wear, Kate: coat and scarf; you'd swear it was snowing in here."

Elaina peered around the doorway into Betty and Kate's bedroom, where a barely-dressed Betty was discarding her warm tent of a nightie. "Caught you, Betty! What a pair of lazy bones. Most Saturdays by now, Leslie and I have half a day's work done."

"Yeah, yeah, you're truly wonderful, Elaina…." Kate and her cynicism headed to the bedroom.

Betty moved alongside Elaina to the stove. Elaina, she noticed, had shed her protective neck collar. Elaina stage whispered. "Just kidding. See if I get a rise out of Kate!" She winked, and her shaking head appeared almost to pirouette. "I'd make the coffee for you, but I make dreadful coffee, everyone says." She raised her voice.

"Kate! Why didn't you and Betty come to our Christmas concert?"

Kate called out from the bedroom. "We have more things to do than to run down to Kokanee every other day. I'll bet you're not coming to ours."

"Well, of course we are," said Elaina. "All of us. Really, you should have made an effort. My choir was magnificent and Leslie's class performed a clever little play I found years ago, when I was teaching in Saskatchewan."

Kate reappeared in the doorway. "Concerts aren't my cup of tea. I'd rather concentrate on the essentials. How about a math performance and a stage setting for a spelling bee? It would do more good."

"How like you, Kate." Elaina waved her hand in a hyperbolic, dismissive manner, and turned to Betty, who was making coffee in an open pan. "You should have come without her, Betty. My word, you girls really do live primitively. No coffee pot?"

Betty smiled. "No coffee pot. I'm sorry we missed your concert."

Elaina Maleyna kept up her sprightly chatter throughout breakfast. Betty enjoyed every word.

"Betty, you can visit with Elaina for awhile. I have to scoot down to the store for the mail. After that, make yourself scarce for a couple of hours. Elaina and I have to talk about our court case."

"That's fine. I should get up to my school, anyhow."

"Get on your way, Kate." Again Elaina waved off Kate. A perfect stage gesture, thought Betty. So graceful. Like an aged ballerina. "Take your time. Betty and I shall just have a lovely little tête-a tête."

How lucky! One-to-one conversation with Elaina.

"It's fortunate Kate is giving us time alone. It's essential that I have a chat with you." Elaina's cheery banter had metamorphosed into hushed tones as somber as a mortician's. With a pained look on her face, she paused for a long while, as though gathering up some sort of inner strength. "Betty. You are a very dear girl, which makes it doubly hard for me to say to you what I feel I must." Another long pause. A long sigh. "However, because I am so fond of you, I will say it. I must. Someone must."

As Betty tipped more coffee into their cups, she rummaged through a headful of guilty thoughts. Is she going to bring up my lack of discipline? Can she read my mind about Leslie?

"Betty, there are some—some…. complex types of people in this world. People with… different tastes. Your… ahh… friend, Georgika. Oh, dear, how shall I put this?" She closed her eyes, ran her hands over her temples as if to remove incalculable stress and then plunged onward. "Georgika is a pursuer of young women. A pursuer." She bobbed her loose head at Betty, waiting for a flicker of understanding. "Crushes, Betty. Georgika gets crushes on young women. The talk in town this year is of you, Betty. You are Georgika's latest love interest." She scanned Betty's blank face, searching for comprehension. Saw none. "The word is, you share her bed, and she has been seen fondling you."

Fondling? Betty felt queasy. Her skin prickled.

"Of course, I know you're an innocent, Betty dear. But unfortunately, the damage is already done. Everybody is talking about… about your affair."

An affair? Elaina's tidings began to coalesce, to infiltrate Betty's mind and saturate it, to ransack it for stored memories. A mental projector flashed image after image onto an internal screen: Georgika's soulful glances. Bosomy hugs. Wet kisses. The images swarmed about, overwhelming Betty's capacity for rational thought. Sexual? Are Georgika's advances sexual? A buzzing noise began resonating inside her ears and spread, it seemed, throughout her entire skull. "I–I really don't think Georgika is like—like that."

"I'd like to be as charitable as you, but people talk. She's been 'cultivating' innocents for some time, they say. Other teachers. Other years. Only the lonely outsiders, never the locals. She's more than a bit twisted, you see. She's calculatingly prudent. Mind you I've nothing against her." Elaina, with a bitter expression on her face, bent forward, as though she was going to reveal worse revelations, but instead, she clamped her hand over her mouth. "Perhaps I shouldn't have told you."

"No….no, I guess, oh, you're right, someone should tell me. Thank you. But I—I don't know what to do, what to think. I can't think. This stuff you're telling me is just too confusing."

Elaina tapped Betty's arm. "The last thing I want to do is interfere, but I can't help feeling it's in your best interests to… just stop seeing her."

Betty moved to the stove as if she were a zombie. "C–coffee?"

"No. I can't handle your pan-coffee. It's too harsh, and I'm all a-jangle. I'm so sorry, I—"

Kate announced her return by stomping the snow off her boots in the lower hallway. She rounded the doorway in her two pairs of man-socked feet with a satisfied look. "I've got the papers from the lawyer. Do you mind getting out of here, Betty?"

"No." Betty's reply was faint. She prepared to leave. Kate watched her impatiently, eager to have her gone. Time to plot court case tactics.

At the door, Betty turned to say good-bye, but they had their heads together, examining documents. Betty no longer existed for them.

~ ж ~

A light snow. A silent world amongst the stilled pines on the mountainside as Betty trudged upwards towards her school. But in her head, a cacophony of damning whispers: fondle… share bed…everyone talking… and unwanted images: flimsy night clothes, melon breasts, wet lips…

~ ж ~

She unlocked the school and made a fire. Cut red and green crepe paper into strips, fashioned the strips into neck bows for her students, for the concert. She could not concentrate on marking the spelling tests. Her head ached.

She knew Elaina wouldn't be gone yet, and didn't want to face her again; what more information might the compassionate Elaina be privy to, feel obligated to reveal? So she sat in the class and stewed, again and again rehashing every visit, turning every nuance of Georgika's effusive behaviour over and over. She sat. And sat. And this idleness agitated her even further. At one o'clock she deemed it safe to go to the store. Perhaps there would be some mail to divert her, to silence the repetitive voices and unasked for images within her.

Hands plunged into her sagging coat pockets, she plodded through the light layer of new snow. Even the cherished boots looked unhappy: the white dye had thinned from the constant wetness, revealing the greyish-yellow colour of the natural leather. Her feet were cold, and her teeth chattered. Yet her neck—under a knitted scarf—was sweating.

Jake's beautiful young daughter, Charlotte, approached her on the hillside. Charlotte turned the corners of her mouth up into a listless, polite smile when she saw Betty. Betty responded in kind: mechanical, and wondered if Charlotte had an abortion, as Kate had conjectured. Probably, she decided. Life is always playing tricks on us all. Funny, her face looks as pure as ever. Still a rosebud. Still angelic. The only give-away is her sadness. Pariahs. We're both outcasts. If we were Eskimos, they'd make us walk out onto ice floes and never come back.

"I'm sorry I haven't contacted you about the concert, Miss Wheatley. I'm available to help you any time now. My teacher, Mr. Chalmers, has given me permission to take some time off school for the practices." Charlotte spoke without animation.

"I really could do with your help, Charlotte." Betty didn't need help, but she did not want this sad girl to face any further rejection. While she was trying to think of some uplifting Gramma Beaton motto, Charlotte plodded past her. Betty barely suppressed a spontaneous sob of anguish that transformed into a strange hiccup. Was I going to cry for her or for me, she wondered.

There was no mail for her. She bought Arrowroot biscuits and went back to the apartment. Neither Kate nor Elaina was there. She tried to read for a while, then gave up.

~ Ж ~

"Betty! Come and see my van!" Kate called. Betty put down a half-peeled potato and went to the top of the stairs. "My van is here. Do you want to see it?"

In her present mood, Betty did not give a hoot about Kate's van, but she feigned interest and joined her.

Kate clutched her mittened hands together, as if in a prayer of thanksgiving. "I don't know how they did it, but it looks brand-new again. It's an Austin Hillman; it's a great little van. What do you think?"

Betty knew nothing about cars; it looked very ordinary to her. She mustered up a typical male-talk response. "It's a beaut."

"I'll ask Bill where I should park it. He'll want to see it."

Betty went back inside. When the potatoes were boiling, she opened a can of green beans. Put them in a pot. Kate returned just as Betty placed thick slices of smoked ham in the frying pan. "I've got to do some practice driving before we leave Friday. I'll at least take the van to school every day. Good God, Betty, you look awful! White as a sheet. Are you sick?"

A mental image of Elaina, her head shaking and swivelling, mouthing those damning words: "She has been seen fondling you", returned to Betty. "Kate, did Elaina say anything to you about Georgika?"

"No. What's wrong with Georgika?"

Betty stood over the stove, trying to keep blurred eyes on the various pots and pans. She poked a fork at a potato and missed. "I don't know. That's the problem."

"Don't talk in riddles, Betty."

"I'm not!"

"Don't you get sore at me. Do you want to talk about what's bothering you or not?"

Betty dropped the fork. "Elaina says Georgika is a pursuer of young women, and that she is pursuing me, that she's in love with me and that the whole town of Kokanee is talking about us."

"Good God. Trust Elaina to walk where angels fear to tread."

"Do you think she knows what she's talking about, Kate?"

"How should I know? I hardly know Georgika. She's snubbed me, as you well know. What else did she say?"

"She said my reputation is compromised." Betty used a potholder to wipe tears away.

"What are you going to do?"

"Do? I don't know...I can't believe it of Georgika. No one in Narrows has ever said a thing against her. Not Nina, not Granny, no one."

"Hunh. They wouldn't share secrets with us outsiders. I'll bet it's true. And I bet you don't even know that Georgika isn't a regular Doukhobor; she's one of the Sons of Freedom sect. One of the group who paraded nude in Nelson!" Betty gaped. Nude parading? More kerosene on an already blazing fire. Kate persisted. "Are you going to confront her? Get it out in the open? You should."

The thought horrified Betty. She didn't reply.

Kate continued. An increasing bitterness spilling out as she spoke. "I can see why Elaina thinks Georgika is sexually interested in you. Georgika goes out of her way to look like a man. She even swaggers like one." She pursed her lips into a cynical sneer. "Humph.... what a person can get away with in a city is not the least bit acceptable in farm country. Biblical morals are paramount. Any talk of sinning is latched onto. Hahh! All this gossip would be lost in a big population. But huge news in this.... claustrophobic, skinny valley. All the people here are news-starved. I bet they're all talking in Narrows as well as Kokanee." She scrutinized Betty and shook her head. "You truly are an unbelievable mix of innocence and ignorance!"

Betty's rapid breathing made her take gulps of air.

"God, I wouldn't want to be in your shoes, Betty; Inspector McIntyre will hear about it."

Even the Inspector? Now, Betty reeled dizzily above the hot stove. "What's wrong with you, Betty?" Betty could not speak. Her mind had emptied. "Say something, Betty, don't just stand there. What's wrong? You look weird. Don't tell me you're going to pass out?"

A pounding noise—like horse's hoofs—accompanied Kate's words into Betty's ears. She could barely hear.

"What a hellish mess you've got yourself into." Kate stared steadily at Betty.

In the back of Betty's mind, in an area still able to make judgment, she realized there was not an iota of sympathy in Kate. And Kate, like a heavy weight champion, was now delivering blow after blow. Betty quailed when Kate's eyes narrowed; searched for a final knockout. "You have to solve this fast, you know. Or you'll be dismissed. Turfed."

The hoof beats escalated, became a clattering, ear-splitting stampede. Betty struggled to find her way through the tumult. "I– I'm finished. I'm truly ruined," she whispered. A fearful picture of her father's disapproving face flashed before her and delivered another blow. "I should have known I would screw things up."

Kate pushed her aside. "Sit down. Next thing we know, you'll pass out on the stove and fry yourself like that slab of ham. I'll serve the food." Kate ate the meal with enthusiasm; Betty could not eat at all.

"You better get a grip on yourself, Betty, or you'll have a nervous breakdown." There was a smirk on Kate's face. As if she was recalling some unrevealed, similar situation from her own past.

Betty did, for a moment, catch the barely hidden triumph on Kate's face. A cold breeze of clarity possessed her for a brief second. Who's carrying the biggest chainsaw up here, Betty wondered. Sweet Georgika? Messenger Elaina? Or is it Kate?

~ ж ~

Dot's fresh-faced babies: angelic and well rehearsed. The audience loved them.

> Away in a manger
> No crib for a bed...

they sang. Nativity scene costumes made from sheets and towels, sheep and donkey face masks made from papier-mâché. Clever, thought Betty.

Then Betty stood in the makeshift wings watching her class flounder, watching as her ambitious skit crumbled. There had been too much to memorize; too little time. One-by-one, like dominoes falling, the students lost their rhyming lines and improvised until they were in complete disarray. As they left the stage, several of them tore off their perky neck bows and looked at her with reproach.

Join the club, class. Point at me, you and the whole town. I'm a failure. A failure and a pariah.

Georgika and the Kokanee contingent were there. When Betty and her agony approached them, they tried to bolster her. "The audience didn't know it was supposed to rhyme, Betty. Looked just fine to us."

While the others socialized around the refreshment table, Georgika pressed a small gift-wrapped package into Betty's hands. "I'm sorry we can't celebrate Christmas together. Give my regards to your parents and have a good time." She kissed Betty on the lips and hugged her. Over Georgika's shoulder, Betty could see people watching. Alert storekeeper Mrs. Johnson, spying them, grimaced, her mouth stretched taut over her too-perfect, albeit floppy, teeth. The sharp scrutiny unnerved Betty, reinforced a newfound sense of shame.

"Phone when you get back, okay?" Betty had an intense desire to shove the gentle Georgika away. At the same time, she felt contempt for her own lack of faith in her friend.

Later, in the bedroom, while Kate puttered in the kitchen, Betty opened the gift-wrapped package. It contained a delicate, feminine nightie, a twin to Georgika's own. Betty sat with it on her knees, unmoving, as it slid to the floor.

Chapter 13

Sex alleviates tension.
Love causes it.
—Woody Allen

A black precipice on the left, sheared rock face on the right. The single-lane road, not much wider than a pathway, hugged the contours of the mountain face. Only where topography allowed it had the plough cleared two-lane swaths: the only passing lanes for oncoming traffic.

It was snowing again, heavily. "Damn," said Kate, turning to Betty, who sat next to her. "I don't think the Hillman's heater is working. It should be warmer in here by now. Are you cold?"

"Well, yes, I am. But at least we're on our way home." Betty was trying not to shiver.

"Shakespeare, if he were accompanying us, might pronounce it to be 'as cold as the hand of death', Miss Bradshaw," added Edwin Chalmers from the back seat, up near the car's roof where he lay on his stomach, astride all their luggage. He seemed cheerily oblivious to the discomfort of his situation.

"It's a good thing he isn't accompanying us, or there'd be no room for you. There's nothing I can do about the damn rotten heating system in this bloody van until we get to Nakusp." A tense Kate leaned forward, gripping the steering wheel tightly, peering with squinted eyes through the tiny windshield clearing Betty was managing to scrape free of ice.

Darkness came fast. Now Kate squinted even more, thrusting forward her neck to peer through the iced and fogged windshield, through the pelting snow. As the van rounded a sharp bend, not that far from Trent's Landing, a car appeared out of nowhere, heading straight for them. On the one-lane road. Kate stomped on the brakes and skidded to a stop, inches in front of the car.

Kate jumped from the van and slammed the door. "Jesus Christ!" She shrieked as she slipped and slid and skid over

129

the road to confront the other driver. "Don't you know how to drive? Where are your bloody lights?" She harangued him until he signalled surrender and began backing up. Kate returned to her van. They crept forward, almost pushing the other car back, until it reached one of the passing swaths. Then Kate gassed the van and fantailed past, muttering non-stop. Betty, for the first time, appreciated the merits of Kate's vitriolic nature.

Hoarfrost formed on all the windows. Betty kept scraping, keeping a tiny view hole open for Kate. She glanced at Kate's speedometer: Kate was travelling at 10 miles an hour.

Only one gas station was open at Nakusp. "Can't get you no help fer yer heater till Monday," said the attendant. "Bet there's nothin' wrong with your van anyways—these goll-dern English cars ain't made fer no Canadian winter."

Nothing could keep out the biting cold. Pain stabbed Betty's feet and fingers and she shook uncontrollably. Her arms ached from the constant windshield scraping efforts. Edwin remained a paragon of stoicism; he neither complained nor shivered. It's his bulk, Betty decided. The layers of fat help. Betty fantasized about having rolls of comforting, protective fat.

Cold. So, so, cold…. Betty was only dimly aware that there were a few small towns along the route. She barely saw them; the blood in her neck and brain, she concluded woozily, had probably become ice-slush, making it too hard to even turn to look out the window. Besides, she had to keep concentrating all her remaining energy on clearing that tiny peephole for Kate. The only other movement in the van was Kate's arms stiffly maneuvering the steering wheel. Not a peep from Kate. Not a peep from Edwin. He could, Betty realized, be, by now, frozen solid back there, all alone. Even if he were still alive, she reasoned, she couldn't offer a single word of encouragement; her cheeks held her lips in a frozen grip.

They chugged on and on and on—hours became eternity. Three frozen figures in a Hillman chugging ceaselessly, chugging forever along the long, lonely mountain ledges road. Cold, cold, colder…coldest… .

"Castlegar," said a hoarse voice. What? Who? Betty tried to focus. What an arm I've got! It has a mind of its own, she marvelled, as it kept scraping the windshield. "Castlegar. We're   finally   at

Castlegar," Kate grunted. "The ferry's here. Christ. I feel like I'm half dead."

"The f..f..ferry! A..a..nd….c..civilisation, with that most ch..cherished marvel of Edison's: e..electric l..light…" said Edwin, his teeth now chattering loudly.

Once the Hillman halted on the twenty-four car ferry, Kate stepped outside. She swung her arms around, and jumped up and down to regain blood flow. Betty and Edwin refused to budge.

"Sh..she'd survive us in a c..concentration camp, Mr. Chalmers."

"Sh..she'd have made it to the North Pole with P..Peary, Miss Wheatley. In a swim suit."

They drove off the ferry to a ploughed, two-lane highway and Kate speeded up. She sped through the towns of Robson and Castlegar, past their reassuring lights and continued onward into thick darkness. With her increased speed, an iota of heat issued forth from the Hillman's heater. The windshield began to thaw just barely enough to see through, of its own accord. And Betty could finally drop her arm to her lap, where it commenced a steady complaint by shooting pins and needles in all directions. Still it was a great relief. Betty sat back against her seat at last.

Without warning, blinding headlights—the first they had seen since Trent's Landing—glared at them. Kate spun the steering wheel; the Hillman responded and—rammed itself into a packed snow bank. Betty and Edwin, at the mercy of momentum, sailed forward like rag dolls.

~ Ж ~

"My God! Are you folks okay?" The driver of the other car beamed a flashlight in at them then pulled open the door on Kate's side of the van. The usually caustic Kate didn't even look at the rescuer. Said not a word. Betty reached up from somewhere near the floor, from under an unbelievably heavy weight, and shook Kate's arm, but there was no response. Betty's gelid jaw dropped. Oh, my God! Kate's finally frozen to the wheel!

"I've received no injury but my fedora has suffered great insult," shouted Edwin from above Betty, as he extricated himself from a squashed position against the wind shield, and squeezed out of

131

the other side door. He tried to straighten his flattened hat. "Sorry to have squashed you, Miss Wheatley, are... are you still alive?"

"I...don't...know." Betty disentangled herself from the luggage which was pinning her down. With a great effort, she tried to analyze where all her body parts had ended up. Then breathed many pent-up sighs of relief. Every part of her throbbed, but nothing seemed broken or broken off. Maybe you don't break when you are nearly frozen, she rationalized. "I... can't tell for sure, I...I think I'm all here, but Kate, though...Oh God, Mr. Chalmers....she may be a goner ...." Betty's voice was as quavery as Elaina's.

The rescuer focussed his flashlight on rigid Kate, stared at her intently, seemed satisfied, and turned to study the high snow bank that was doing an efficient job of swallowing the Hillman's nose.

Betty and Mr. Chalmers scrutinised Kate, still frozen in her driver's position, clenching the steering wheel. And each breathed a huge sigh of relief. Although there was, they saw, a small, barely bleeding cut above the bridge of her nose, her chest was moving... she was breathing...little wisps of breath issued forth from her nostrils.

The Good Samaritan called back from the snow bank. "You definitely need a tow truck. You'll never get out of there, otherwise."

"Ohhh....this is the last straw.... Wait for a bloody tow truck...." Kate whimpered and dropped her head onto the steering wheel.

She can still speak! Thank all the Gods! Betty clasped her mittened hands. *But...possible brain damage?*

 From deep within Kate a weak voice ventured out. "I'm okay. For God's sake quit staring at me, Betty," she said. Betty breathed a big sigh of relief. *Good. Crankiness is a good sign!*

Edwin leaned in towards Betty and scrutinized Kate. "Upon my word, I do believe you are alright! Amazing woman! Now is not the time to despair, Miss Bradshaw." He spoke very gently. "Be thankful that you have not been hurt. Over yonder are farm house lights. No doubt they'll have a telephone, and we shall get assistance."

The roadside Samaritan test-patted the Hillman's hood. "Be glad you're all alive! Good thing that snow bank's fairly soft. Look, I'll drive you all over there, and we'll see what can be done. If need be, we can find a hospital and get you fully checked out," offered the roadside Samaritan.

No hospital care needed, thankfully, and once the van was free of the snow bank, they continued their interminable journey. Mr. Chalmers drove. Betty reclined upon the luggage. Kate spoke not a single word for the entire journey. Finally, the first faint lights of Trail. Finally, the signature clouds that rolled upward from the towering smelter smoke stacks.

Betty was overwhelmed with emotion. She barely resisted breaking into rolling sobs of gratitude. Good old Cominco smoke stacks, she shiver-whispered. Beacons of welcome to the homesick and the lost, symbols of home and family!

Mr. Chalmers, not much better than Kate, braked all the way down the treacherous smelter hill, while an emotion-choked Betty marvelled at the wonderland of Trail, glittering Silver City, bejewelled with fresh snowflakes.

Into the Kootenay Hotel tottered Kate and Edwin. A taxi delivered Betty to her home. She dragged her two suitcases up the front stairs, and dropped them in the living room. She looked at her watch: they had taken twelve hours to travel one hundred and fifty miles.

~ Ж ~

Oh Lord, it's the phone. Gramma Beaton hates phones. She'll never answer it. It could be Cameron. Betty leapt from her bed and flew down the stairs.

"Betts! Where the hell have you been?" Cameron's voice was loud and tense.

"Oh... Cameron, have I ever missed you." Now the tears burst forth. More like hiccupping sobs.

"I've been worried sick about you! Are you okay?"

"Kate is the worst driver in the whole world. What a horrible trip! Ughhh!" She sneezed and suppressed an urge to wail and keen with self-pity.

Tenderness gradually replaced Cameron's tension. With a tad of indignation. "I've phoned your house I don't know how many times. I've never been so worried! I could picture you frozen in a ditch, under a ton of snow."

"I actually was." Betty shivered as though an Arctic wind was blowing through her. Her whole body ached. Especially her windshield-scraping arm. She glanced down. There were bruises on her arms and legs. She felt her forehead. Bruises there, too, she suspected. "When are you coming over, Cameron," she pleaded.

There was gratifying fervour in Cameron's voice. "As fast as I can."

She filled the bathtub with hot water and slid into it. Bliss, even though the hot water tank had failed to provide enough heated water to cover her thighs. The water line divided her body: goose flesh above, boiled lobster below.

Gradually, she shook off thoughts of the abrasions on her shins inflicted by Kate's eccentric driving; then began to shake off memories of the bruises to her self-respect inflicted by Elaina's unbridled tongue. She lay there, soaking up heat.

And finally, finally, Betty allowed herself to luxuriate in her feelings for Cameron. Feelings she had suppressed for nearly four months. Euphoric, she spent a few seconds thinking, with gratitude, about the intensity of their relationship, on the harmony of their minds, but dwelt mostly on the bodily pleasures they had shared. She recalled the first time he had touched her. And she had not stopped him, had welcomed his explorations. Her body pulsated and despite the steaming water, she shivered with remembrance and anticipation. Mrs. Cameron or not, she knew that she longed to be with him.

Betty heard the noise of a car door closing: The Henry J. Mother and Dad arriving for lunch. She left the cooling water without regret; she could not bear even the slightest hint of cold. She checked her forehead: no, no bruises. Just pain. Just tender bruises on her back, chest, legs and arms. She put on slacks and several sweaters and came downstairs. Dad was coming out of the bathroom, shaking his head.

He's mad, thought Betty. I used up all the hot water and I haven't cleaned the tub. I... She waited for the usual stream of censure. But his voice was mild. "You're red as a beet! It's not healthy to bathe in such hot water."

Mother pulled food from the fridge. "Let's hear what on earth you've been up to." Betty helped Nora arrange sliced ham, cheddar cheese, pickled beets, bowls of cold canned tomatoes, all the while recounting details of the arduous trip. She had to hurry through it, following her mother around the kitchen as she recounted the main details. She knew they were in a hurry. No one asked to see her bruises, even though she offered.

"Jesus Christ! You could have been killed! Don't go back with that girl after Christmas. Stay out of her car. She's jinxed," said Glen, as he aligned his precision-angled cutlery on his emptied plate. A signal for Betty to jump up and clear the table.

Betty nodded. "She is jinxed. I'll take the bus to Nakusp and the mail truck down the lakeside road to Narrows."

Mother rose reluctantly. Her sympathetic eyes clung to Betty. Made her feel like crying again. Mother patted her on the arm. Looked at her watch. "Tomorrow is Sunday. We'll have time to really talk then."

Betty's fast thinking really surprised her: "May I invite Cameron for supper tonight?"

"Of course, but you'll have to cook it; I absolutely have to work late."

"I'll be 'working' late at the Legion, bending my elbow." Glen gave Betty his charming grin, then changed his face abruptly as he looked at Nora. "Don't forget. We're going to Hop-along's shindig tonight."

"I haven't forgotten. No chance of that. There's meat in the fridge, Betty. Steaks. I thought you might be wanting to invite him over."

Gramma Beaton cracked open her bedroom door. "Betty? Good! I see you are in one piece. You should have phoned. Your poor mother was in a tizzy."

Fastidious Glen curled his lip in disgust at Gramma Beaton's untidy white hair, at her once-impressive dress and apron pockmarked with food spills and cigarette burns.

Poor, half-blind Gramma Beaton. Unwanted because she's another drain on Dad's wallet, concluded Betty. Her Narrow's sojourn was giving her a touch of insight into her family, she realized.

"Put on the kettle, Betty," said Gramma Beaton. "Good-bye,

Nora." She ignored the hostile Glen. Nora and Glen hurried off.

It took Gramma Beaton forever to light a cigarette. Her quavering lower lip and shaky hands made the meeting of flame and tobacco a near impossibility. She launched immediately into her version of small talk. "The Chinamen are swarming all over Korea, you know, Betty." She leaned forward and wagged her gnarled finger. "Didn't I tell you that the Dragons of Asia, the yellow hordes, would conquer the world? Blow it up! Atomic radiation. Then the Plague. It's all in the Book of Revelations."

Betty waved her bruised arms about trying to get a bit of attention. Gramma Beaton seemed not to see them. Betty gave up her quest for sympathy.

Gramma Beaton could distract anyone from their near-death plight, thought Betty. Even Satan would take time out to listen to her. Betty needed attention and if she couldn't get it by telling Gramma about her plight, then she would get it by other means. She pulled up a chair next to Gramma Beaton and launched into her own world views; feeling so much wiser, after her three and a half months as a salary earner. It helped. The pain subsided. "I've got a subscription to Time magazine, Gramma Beaton; it's more up-to-date than the Bible. We won't have a World War III, Gramma Beaton. The Korean War is nearly over. A United Nations team and the Communists are at the negotiating table. "

"They won't succeed. Just delaying the inevitable. It's written. In a book nearly two thousand years old and written by God. Your Time magazine's no match for that. Ah, well, the fat is in the fire, Betty. Make the tea, that's a good girl."

Betty sighed and gave up. Gramma Beaton was too old and opinionated for enlightenment. Too old and downtrodden to give someone else pity. "Do you want something to eat?"

"Yes, a bit of bread and butter with treacle would be nice."

"Not many vitamins in that, Gramma Beaton," said Betty as she placed white bread into the toaster and brought out the butter and syrup.

"Good. Vitamins are dangerous. Whenever they let me cook I boil the vegetables thoroughly to kill the wretched things."

A knock on the front door. Betty rushed to it, her heart skittering.

Cameron stood waiting, with his coat collar pulled up against the cold. Tall, slender Cameron, a light brushing of snow on his brown hair, on the long eye lashes that framed those bedroom eyes, those sensual eyes; busily drinking her in. After the three, nearly four months they had been apart, he was even better looking than she remembered. Those hungry eyes and that sensual mouth pulled her into orbit. "Who's home?"

"Just my grandmother." Betty ran her eyes possessively over his clean-slate face, felt them fasten onto his lips.

He pulled Betty outside, pulled her inside his coat, wrapped his arms tightly around her, and kissed her repeatedly. "God, how I missed you."

Paradise. Inside Cameron's coat. I will stay here forever, she vowed, savouring the maleness, the confidence and strength that emanated from him. But her out-of-whack body temperature regulator soon caused her to shiver uncontrollably.

"This is crazy. Let's get you into the house, or you'll get sick." He ushered Betty inside.

Gramma Beaton stood waiting for them. She squinted her cloudy eyes. "Well, young man, it's a long time since I've seen you. You were in this house every evening, last summer." She followed them into the living room.

"I've been away at school, Mrs. Beaton."

"Are you taking anything useful, or are you going to end up a learned parasite?" Now Gramma Beaton trailed them into the kitchen. She could not be shaken loose.

He grinned at Gramma Beaton; he liked her. "I'm studying engineering. You can't get much more useful than that."

"What about history, young man, the rich history of socialism?"

Cameron straddled a chair opposite Gramma Beaton; she had attained her goal: to lasso him with her leftist views. Yet he had a full view of Betty from his seat and he did not take his eyes off her.

Betty was impatient. Get away, Gramma. He's mine!

"Aren't the words rich and socialism contradictions, Mrs. Beaton?" he asked, as he looked into Betty's eyes.

"You're playing with my words, young man. You know the rich feed on the poor."

Cameron flashed Gramma Beaton a wide smile. "Yes, big fish eat little fish but I don't intend to be a minnow. Like it or not, life is exploitation. If I were a rich man's son, with no hunger for money, I might be studying socialism; but I'm not."

Betty turned on the kitchen sink taps full blast, rattled the soaking dishes and clashed the cutlery, but Cameron continued. "But I do take some courses you'd approve of. I've brought two of my English Lit books for you. Short stories and poetry. You can get a little second-hand university." He signalled to Betty over Gramma Beaton's head. Betty stopped making war-hoop warnings with the dishes; waited to see if Gramma Beaton would take the bait.

Gramma Beaton butted out her cigarette in the sloshed tea that lived in her saucer, ignoring an assortment of ashtrays. It was an ugly practice she stubbornly maintained, a defiance. It irritated Glen. "Good! New books! I'll need to take your books to my bed where it's warm. You must forgive an old lady. I don't mean to be unsociable." She went into her room and shut the door.

Cameron and Betty moved to the living room. They stood in a shadowed corner embracing with intensity, making up for the long months of dammed-up sexuality.

Just as she had daydreamed, Cameron covered her lips, her eyes, her neck, her bruises with warm sympathy-murmuring kisses. Reached under her sweater. Cupped her breasts. Eased off her slacks, her underwear. Pressed his body against hers. There, in the corner, between the dining room buffet and the umbrella stand, at long last, truly together. Swept away by the heighth of all sensations.

Time stood still. Of course. Until approaching footsteps galvanized them. She grabbed her clothes and fled to the bathroom. He barely had time to do up his zipper before the front door opened. With nowhere to hide, Cameron stood in the centre of the room as

Betty's sister Faye opened the door. A witless grin spread across his face, now an interesting shade of crimson.

Faye smiled at him. "Long-time-no-see, handsome. Where's Betts?"

Betty soon breezed around the corner, trying to act as though nothing extraordinary had taken place. "Where have you been, Faye?" Betty patted her dishevelled hair; hoped that highschooler Faye would not have the slightest idea of what had gone on.

"At a pajama party. We never slept all night! Guess who asked me out?"

"Hmm let me guess...was it Hop-along Freddie or the bear who ate his leg?" joked Cameron.

"Ewww, Cameron!" laughed Faye.

Cameron had an easy, teasing way with Faye, and she liked him. They sat around the kitchen table while Betty made more tea. Gramma Beaton and her books joined them. Her eyes were filmy, but her nose could smell fresh tea a mile away.

"Mimi's taking Gramma Beaton to a show tonight. You two are going to be alone here, all evening. You'd better behave yourselves," Faye teased.

~ Ж ~

Dinner passed without explosions, suggestions or rebukes—Betty's parents both adopted an elaborate civility whenever Cameron joined the table, which, Betty recognized, meant they approved of him.

As soon as the last straggling watchdog had gone, Betty turned down the lights. "Come up to my bedroom and visit my web, Mister Fly."

"I'd love to, Miss Spider."

~ Ж ~

She poured Gramma Beaton and Nora another cup of tea and continued. "...and, oh, I don't know...now, when I go to the store or the dances, or even when the high school bus passes by, I wonder if they're staring at me. Because of the gossip."

"Didn't you say this Georgika is Russian?" asked Gramma

139

Beaton. "Is she orthodox Doukhobor or Sons of Freedom?"

Betty didn't want to tell them what Kate had said. Did not want to admit that Georgika might be one of the radical Sons of Freedom Doukhobors, might have paraded nude down the Main Street of Nelson. "Georgika's my only one hundred percent dependable friend up there. She's a very open-minded person. What she does is she—"

"Has she ever talked about burning the schools or organizing marching protests? If so, she's a Sons of Freedom Doukhobor," insisted Gramma Beaton. Betty wondered if Gramma Beaton was reading her mind.

"Oh, Ma, really. Mimi next door is a Doukhobor, for heaven's sake, and she's just like us."

"She's Orthodox, Nora. Anyhow, I don't trust anyone who isn't of English parentage. Even Mimi. She's generous, but she's a Russian who won't even admit to a shred of socialism. Something false, there."

Betty sat back, refusing to get tangled in her grandmother's Anglophilia, her illogic.

"It's got absolutely nothing to do with nationality. Mimi doesn't hug and kiss women," said Nora. "Actually, no one hugs and kisses friends except French people." She nodded an emphatic agreement with herself. Then piled up a layer of advice for Betty. "And... for future reference, Betty, you shouldn't even kiss babies too much. Germs. Plus you end up spoiling them rotten." She pointed her manicured forefinger at Betty and shook it in time with her next words, to emphasize her seriousness. "Stay away from that peculiar Georgika—no ifs, ands or buts."

Betty had, she realized, been holding her breath. Now, surreptitiously, she allowed it to flow outward. The slow release of breath exuded by a moth's larva after it changes into a pupa. No winged stage for Betty. Not yet, anyway. She frowned at the salt and pepper shakers until her thoughts coalesced. All my life, she realized, I've taken my mother's word as gospel. And she's not God; frequently she's given bad advice. Now she aligned the S and P shakers with hypercritical care. Why can't I make up my own mind? Why do I need her blessing for every single thing I do? At last, she and the shakers leaned back and took a deep breath. She was ready to communicate the rationale of

140

her beliefs. "It's… just not that easy, Mother. Georgika has made me part of her family, her life. More than anyone, she makes it bearable up there. I can't just drop her. I can't. I need her."

Nora grabbed the aforementioned shakers and put them behind her on the counter. No back-up props allowed. "That's ridiculous!"—" Nora scowled at the irresolution that instantly resurfaced on Betty's face. "Betty." Nora's voice was steely. "You've got to fight this tendency to be timid. I know you've inherited it from me, and it's a most terrible curse."

"Oh, Mother, you're not timid, you're—"

"You can't let others manipulate you, or use you. Stand up to them. Or you'll grow up as submissive as I am, dominated by a petty man."

Betty attempted to interrupt. She could not see how the problem had anything to do with timidity or manipulation. But Nora, in a voice anything but timid, continued. "So far, nothing alarming has happened. But what if, on your next visit, with you in her bed, she makes an… improper move?" Nora had not posed her question for a reply. The discussion was over. "Let's clean up the breakfast, Betts."

Improper moves? A cacophony of disturbing visions climbed all over Betty's active imagination. Dismayed, she resolutely pushed them back. But although she was filled with turmoil, Betty could not divine any flaws in her mother's reasoning. So she gave up. As always.

~ ж ~

Betty partied, shopped, visited friends. Joy-filled days and impassioned nights which all passed far too quickly. As the holidays drew to a close, the headaches and dizzy spells she had incurred in Narrows—after the alarming revelations dispensed by Elaina— resurfaced. She knew why. She did not want to go back to Narrows: to the privations, to the responsibilities of teaching, to Kate and her crotchety nature, to Georgika and her ambiguity, to being the focus of village gossip.

Two nights before she was due to return, she sat with Cameron in the Crown Point Restaurant, watching him drink a Coke, eat French fries.

"What did you say your roommate's name was?" asked

Cameron.

"Kate Bradshaw."

"I think that's the name. Dad just told me that last year, the RCMP up there had to put a teacher in a straitjacket. Dad says she'd gone berserk in the general store at Edgewood, throwing canned goods through the window."

Betty shook her head, brushing off the alarming vision. Kate? In a straight jacket? "It couldn't be her. She's not that bad. She's never thrown anything."

"Dark hair, dark eyes, dark skin? Almost as though she had Gypsy blood in her?"

Betty concurred reluctantly. "I guess that's what she looks like."

Cameron persisted. "About thirty?"

"Yes."

"I think you'd better get yourself another roommate."

"Cameron, I've told you what the place is like. There's nowhere else to stay. Even if there were, it would set the whole community on its ear if I moved out."

"So what? What would you care? You don't want to be with someone who can easily go berserk. You don't know what she might do next. It sounds like she hates your guts."

Panic welled in Betty. Again, the dizziness. Pounding hoof beats overpowered Cameron's voice.

"Betty. Betty." He reached across the tabletop and held her hands, massaging them. "Betts, you're scaring me. Say something. Hell, I should have kept my mouth shut."

Abruptly, the hoof beats subsided. She had a solution, and it was so easy. "Cameron, I won't go back. I'll come to Vancouver and get a job at Sears Roebuck, I heard my mother say they need clerks."

Cameron selected his words as carefully as if he were sorting eggs. "I'd give anything to have you in Vancouver with me, for my sake. But Betty, be reasonable, do you want to be labelled as a quitter before you're even twenty? If you quit now, you'll never be able to teach again. You'll never get your permanent certificate; you'll have nothing to fall back on. Maybe you'll end up always being a quitter when things get tough. Besides, even if you got a job at Sears, you'd never earn enough to support yourself in Vancouver as a clerk. And I haven't even got enough to take care of my own needs; my parents have to pitch in. I can't help." Cameron's face was filled with anguish.

Back came the roar in her ears, and tears rolled down her cheeks. Cameron looked guilt stricken.

He rumpled his hair; he pulled at his shirt collar as if it were choking him. He looked around the room. "For Pete's sake, don't cry, Betty, people will think I'm pinching you or something."

The tears stopped dead in their tracks. Betty wiped her face on her sleeve. "You say don't cry, don't be a quitter, go face people who say nasty things and a roommate who may be insane? Back to those wild kids and icy outhouses... Oh, you don't really love me, Cameron, you just love my...my stupid body."

Cameron reddened, stood abruptly and motioned for her to get up, too. "Let's get the hell out of here."

~ Ж ~

Behind the Crown Point Hotel and Restaurant, past the esplanade, flows the fast and treacherous Columbia River. At night, its swift currents and eddies take on a menacing appearance: here and there, the quick flowing water, black as tar, will suddenly swerve and curve into whirlpools before shooting away downstream. In other spots, the water appears to sit, at least on the surface, in dead calm. The river is so deep and so fast, townspeople say it is bottomless. Betty and Cameron leaned against the rock wall that bound the almost non-existent shoreline. Cameron stared at her helplessly, while she unsuccessfully tried not to cry.

"I wish we could get married." There. She had said it.

He grabbed both of her hands tightly. "We will. But not for a long time. I've got to get my degree. Do you want me to spend the rest of my life as a labourer up there in the smelter? Getting lead in my blood? It would kill me. Mentally and physically." They turned from one another and stared at the black water. Each involved with their own black thoughts.

"I hate teaching."

"Betty, you said only yesterday you found it fulfilling."

"Tonight, I hate it."

"Geez, Betts!" Cameron looked so agonized in the moonlight that Betty began to laugh and cry at the same time. Cameron reached and held her fast. "I'd like to just look after you, Betts. I love you. But I must get that magic piece of paper, or I'm nothing."

"I'll go back," she said in a flat voice. "It will be six more months."

"Save some money and come to Vancouver at Easter. You get ten days off."

"When is Easter?"

"Second week of April. Will that help?"

She nodded her head. He wiped the tears from her face, though they continued to fall. Then he wiped away tears of his own.

Chapter 14

The main difference between men and women is
that men are lunatics and women are idiots.
—Rebecca West

T he first bus took her as far as Nelson, the second to Nakusp.
She stayed overnight at the Leland Hotel. In the morning, she
found Tommy, Georgika's son, waiting for her, pacing the
lobby, looking tired and worried.

It did not occur to her to wonder how Tommy knew she would be at
the Leland. After all, she was back in the Valley, amidst an isolated
people whose main preoccupation was the doings of their neighbours.
Strangers in any of the towns made people stop in their tracks. The
Arrow Lakes News reported even the most mundane of happenings.
Even a trip from Narrows to Nakusp was reportable, listed under the
earnest heading of News From Narrows. The Narrows Christmas
concert had been reported in detail. Every trip she took to Trail
garnered space, had enshrined her in print for posterity, for future
valley historians to discover. She was a local celebrity with nothing
to celebrate.

"Ma is here, in the hospital, Betty. Real sick. She wants you to visit
her. I can drive you to Narrows later."

The Nakusp hospital did not have the same stench of ether as the
Trail hospital did, although disinfectant did a good job of taking its
place. Somehow the hospital-green walls seemed brighter and
cleaner. *Probably,* she thought, *because the Trail hospital, sitting
directly below the smelter, got a daily shower of smokestack grime,
got engulfed in sulphurous fumes.*

Georgika — tightly tucked in white sheets with only her head
showing — opened her eyes as Tommy and Betty entered, and
pushed herself into a sitting position.

"Don't, Ma," said Tommy. "They told you to lie still."

Georgika ignored him. Her pallid face came alive. "Betty!" She held
out her arms. The sheet slipped away, revealing her large

145

breasts, flimsily held by a thin-strapped nightie. Betty tried not to look at the soft flesh. Tried not to think about buxom, Georgika marching through Nelson in the nude. Georgika seized Betty's hand, yanked her forward for a kiss, then dropped to the pillow, her face contorted with pain.

Betty's initial distaste changed to concern. "Are you all right? Shall we get the nurse?"

"No! I'm okay." A gasp. A whisper. "I can control pain."

"What happened?"

"My rotten female bucket of bolts. Docs think I need an operation. Gonna take me down to Trail to the big hospital there. Specialists..."

Tommy left to pace up and down the hallway. Georgika watched him leave. "Poor Tommy. I sure scared the heck out of him. Maybe it'll help him grow up a bit, but. I'll be okay, Betty. Lots of women get hysterectomies, get little lumps removed."

Did you know my store helper Olga's gone? She's waitressing in Castlegar." Georgika's emotional eyes welled up. "I hate going by her room. Makes me feel so lonely. But at least I've got a spare bedroom. When you come down, you won't have to listen to my snoring."

Betty tried not to show her relief about the bedroom arrangement; it eased her problem somewhat. She wondered if Georgika knew of Elaina's accusations. Yet the mention of the bedroom seemed innocent enough. "You don't snore. Did they give you medicine for the pain?"

"Yeah. It works a while. Forget the pain. Tell me about Christmas."

"How's Leslie?" Betty did not know why she asked about handsome Leslie Bedford-Jones; she had barely said good-bye to Cameron.

"Leslie's back from his holidays. Came back for New Year's Eve. It was right after that I got into trouble. In more ways than one. Not just my innards. I had a real set-to with that nervy old Elaina. Telling me I have an unnatural hold on Leslie. Telling me who I can and can't associate with. She's crazy! I told her to stay away from my house. And my restaurant." Georgika's voice was weak, but matter-of-fact.

Betty winced. The two of them, Georgika and Elaina: the most fun people in the entire valley. What a shame to chafe each other! And both of them lonely. If only Elaina didn't go around analyzing and dishing out advice, if only Georgika would try harder, they could be tolerant of each other; no one can have too many friends, reasoned Betty. But Georgika, Betty decided, was too sick, too emotional to deal with a lecture from a nineteen-year old. She offered, instead, a litany of superficial subjects until Tommy poked his head around the corner. "We gotta go, Ma."

Again the sloppy, wet kiss Betty hated.

"I'll be back home soon, Betty, I know how you count on me."

"Trail's got some top-notch doctors. They'll take good care of you," said Betty. A nurse tucked Georgika back under her covers. Betty and Tommy left.

"She'll be lonely in Trail, Tommy."

"I know. But I have to stay up here and run the restaurant. Do my jobs." He did sound more adult.

~ Ж ~

"Come in, come in! My goodness, you're loaded down with Christmas spoils! There's so much to tell you. First, Nina's invited you and me over for dinner."

"What about Kate? Isn't she back yet?"

"That's one of the things I have to tell you! Come on, we can have some tea!" Being the news giver instead of the receiver energized Granny. She bubbled like milk froth. "Kate's not coming back for six weeks. She may need further surgery on her knee, and her court case isn't over yet. And, I happen to know that salesman Roscoe Taylor is down there in Vancouver with her. Don't ask me who told me, I can't tell."

Apparently, Granny doesn't know that Mr. Bryllcreem has a wife and two kids. "Hmmm. I wonder what that signifies, Sherlock Holmes?"

"We'll see, we'll see. That's not all the news, not by a long shot."

"Boy, I leave this place and it really gets lively! What else?"

"Your fellow teacher Dot has quit teaching."

"Oh?" Good for Dot, thought Betty. She's not waiting for the inspector to fire her just because she got married.

"Bill had to get someone really quick. There's a retired teacher coming up from Nelson to take her place. She's a widow. I told Bill he could give her my guest bedroom. She can share the upstairs kitchen with you and Kate and I'll give you girls a total reduction of ten dollars a month to make up for it. I'm looking forward to having her here. Inspector McIntyre says she's very nice; she's my age, and she was born in Birmingham—in the Midlands, just like me!"

An edge cut into Betty's smile. Lucky woman. Right age. Right nationality. And she gets the best bedroom. The gift-box bedroom. "What's her name?"

"Mrs. Allan. She'll be here Friday. That's not all." Granny dumped a treat load of sugar into her tea. Stirred it so vigorously the cup began to wobble. "Georgika's in the hospital. There's something wrong with her heart. She's always looked too ruddy, to me."

"You're full of news. I just saw Georgika in Nakusp. It's her female parts, not her heart. Any more changes?"

"I should think that's enough for only a fortnight."

"What about the electricity?"

"Now, now. I told you we had enough changes. They say we'll get it at the end of this month. I doubt it; I've given up on the whole business." With her little finger raised, she sipped tea and gazed at her unused wall switches.

~ Ж ~

It's not so bad, she mused, rooming alone. Not having Kate around was a plus, not a minus. A too-quiet apartment was way better than one filled with unpredictability.

Monday and Tuesday she left the school, went to the store for supplies, made supper for one and began reading her very own Book-of-the-Month Club selection. Both nights she read while she ate, then continued reading all evening long. She would soon exhaust her meager collection. She wished Kate's abundant supply of untouched books were not all bound up like virgins in chastity belts, preventing her from making that first, deflowering move, that cracking open of pristine cover. Still…. Life was not anywhere as bad as she had feared it would be. So far.

Wednesday after school, when she was part way through planning her lessons, a visitor rapped at the classroom door, then entered. It was snow-covered Dot.

Betty brushed the snow from Dot's parka, fussed over her, immensely pleased to see her. Dot somehow felt like a very dear, life-long friend. "How's newly-married life, Mrs. Fielding."

"Don't call me that. I don't like being a Missus anything. Call me stupid, I'd prefer that."

Betty laughed. "Why do you want to be called stupid?"

Dot slumped into a nearby student seat. "Remember when I told you I had the flu? About a month ago?"

Betty vaguely recalled.

"Well, I didn't. It was morning sickness." She stared moodily at her feet, encased in dainty fur-trimmed boots.

Then Dot's words sank in. "Dot! You're going to have a baby! That's great!"

Dot stamped her prettily clad feet. "God, Betty, sometimes you're so thick; I've only been married three weeks! I wouldn't give a hoot, except for living up here. Everybody watches everybody else like hawks. These old biddies are going to be doing the backward count."

"Backward?"

"The nine month's count, dummy. And it's your fault. Telling me about you and Cameron. I figured if you could play with fire, then so could I. And Lou, too. He was all in favour. We did what you said, and now look at me: I throw up every morning and I'm tired all the time. I should have talked to Kate and her boyfriend Roscoe Taylor, not you."

"Why Kate and Roscoe?"

"Rubber goods, condoms, French safes. You know---he sells Trojans. I'll bet Kate won't get into the same mess. Dorothy slid her feet through a muddy pool of slush on the floor. Betty resisted an urge to get down on her knees and wipe away the edge of mud that now rested on Dot's foot finery. Probably a Christmas present from her non-student, affluent husband, Betty thought.

Dot's comments sunk in as Betty reluctantly pulled her attention away from boot-envy. "Roscoe? Roscoe sells—those things? Up here?" He now took on an even more sinister characterization in Betty's eyes. Condoms. In cartons, wrapped in brown paper to hide their tell-tale labels. Hidden under the counter near the cash register, asked for in self-conscious whispers. Roscoe. Living, breathing, dealing in sex. No wonder he cheats on his wife. Poor Kate. How doubly embarrassing.

"Why not? Probably everyone in the world under the age of fifty uses them every time they do it, except you and me."

"I'm sorry, Dot, I—"

"Oh, it's not your fault, Betty. I'm an adult. It's just that Lou is always asking for you-know-what, and it makes me feel nauseated when he's doing it." She shuddered. "Boy, it sure didn't take long for the novelty to wear off."

Betty didn't understand Dot's new attitude. Pregnancy—early or not—ought to be wonderful. She had assumed that once a girl married, her worries evaporated. Unless she married a crabby man like her dad.

"Oh, well, what's done, is done, and at least I've got my own nice little house. I love it. It's beautiful. And I've baked a pie—my first one—it took me nearly all day, and I want you to come have supper with us."

~ ж ~

Betty marked a series of workbooks and scribblers for an hour, then left for Dot's new home. Between the leafless trees, she could see the ice-covered lake where Jake Patten and his son-in-law Curley McCloskey rhythmically sawed long straight cuts into the ice. She stopped to watch. A workmen's ballet, a graceful dance of moving arms, bent backs and tiny steps to the music of slicing saws: a hushed cello voice, as if the men were cutting   aspen   with   a

150

bread knife. For a grand finale, they tonged out triple-icebox-sized blocks, stacked them—separated with layers of sawdust—onto a waiting sled, and hauled them away.

Dot pulled her in before she even knocked. "Tuh-dah! Welcome to my castle. Great, eh?"

"Gee, Dot, you sure have some nice stuff."

"It'll look even better, soon. Here, look!" Betty tried to remove her coat and boots and keep one eye on Dot's issue of Better Homes and Gardens. "It's the latest thing." Dot pointed to the raw pine walls. "We're going to paint them just like in this magazine. They'll match my new Fiesta Ware dinner set." On a maroon tablecloth of rough woven fabric, Dot had paraded the 'Fiesta Ware': chartreuse, maroon, dark green and gold-coloured dishes.

"Ooh!" Betty's eyes lit up. "What sophistication! Like a movie set."

Even Dot's tough-pastried pie seemed special in this wedding-gift world. This Better Homes and Gardens future.

~ Ж ~

Betty walked home from Dot's house in a cheerful mood. The Northern Lights lit the sky with a dance of veils and the benign face of the moon smiled down on her. An autumn memory resurfaced and she reacted to it with excitement. The ideal night. Yes! The night to be Sonja Henie! Barbara Ann Scott!

At the apartment, she donned warm clothes, unpacked her skates, grabbed her three flashlights and skip-skidded down to the edge of the frozen lake. Between drifts of snow, the icy surface of the waters reflected the moonlight. The clear swaths looked as smooth as the ice at the Trail Arena, after the iceman had planished it with a canvas bag of hot water.

She sat on a log, yanked off her shoes and boots and pulled on the skates. They were cold. She would have to skate fast to warm her toes, which had instantly surrendered all their heat. She tied one flashlight on top of her head, under her woollen headscarf; had one for each hand. They were more for effect than for light; the moon was uncommonly bright. She decided to head downstream, with the gentle breeze at her back. Not planished. Not this ice: crevices, crusts, alligator-back knolls. But if Sonja Henie could get such pleasure from pond skating, so could she. She waved the flashlights in circles, tried simple jumps, swirls and bunny-hops. But each time she gathered up speed, the rough surface sent her sprawling. She skated past the dim lights of the community. Now, out of sight and alone, she painted the ice with flashlight, she bellowed out like Ethel Merman:

> I got rhythm,
> I got music,

She picked herself up after another fall.

> Old Man Trouble,
> I don't mind him—
> you won't find him
> 'round my door...

She broke off, too winded to continue, too cold. Sonja Henie and her skimpy sequinned skating dress, Ethel Merman and her orchestra were gone, leaving behind only a bulky swaddle, whose enthusiasm had skedaddled off into the darkness.

She turned back. A cold bone-ache suffused her feet. Now her fingertips—the little cowards—were beginning to complain; now she was facing the wind, now it took far more effort to get back to where she had started her Ice Follies. A grim anxiety took hold of her as she scraped her blades along. At last she arrived back at the log. It was difficult to remove the skates, difficult to put on her even colder shoes and boots—her whole body was stiff with cold. Not as bad as when she'd journeyed to Trail in Kate's Hillman van, but bad enough.

Every step up the hill was laborious; she was made of lead. Leaded, like a workman in the Trail smelter.

Reaching the top of the hillside, near the ferry dock, she smelled sweat and tobacco; heard a familiar voice. "Ee hee hee! I jest knewed it was you, Miss Wheatie, cain't think whut other durn fool might take to the lake with a buncha flashlights. Yuh need one a them Saint Bernerd dogs from the Switz Alps and his keg a rum around his neck. Might put some heat back in yuh!" It was Jake, leaning on a snow shovel.

As soon as Betty caught her breath, she spoke. "What are you doing out so late, Jake? I thought I was truly alone."

"Shovellin' some a that snow the durn guvmint plough puts in all the wrong places, tryin' tuh make life hard fer the ferry goers. An' enjoyin' yer concert."

Betty was searching for a retort when a cacophony of voices blared down the hillside. A frenzied race toward the ferry: a bulky, black-robed man in the lead; a plump, blonde, white-night gowned woman in vicious pursuit. She was lugging a baby under one arm and dragging with the other something that clanked over the iced road.

Betty stared in disbelief at Jake's wife Estelle, who was screaming at the top of her lungs. Estelle's gone berserk, thought Betty. She's chasing the Venerable Reverend Hanginger with an axe!

"I caught him staring in my precious Charlotte's bedroom window! You pervert! Pervert! Lecher! Peeping Tom!"

Under Estelle's arm was Freda's baby, who also screamed at full volume. In front, losing ground, the New Testament Tabernacle minister was panting, pleading, begging on the run: "...my flock, just checking ...blessed faith...the path of Jesus...have mercy in Lord's name woman, have..."

Estelle was unconscious of her night-gown-and-slipper's condition: "Poor Charlotte, getting ready for bed! I'll chop his bloody neck off— Pervert! Pervert! Pervert!"

"...never harm a hair on her head...God's child...my duty to protect her from damnation...have pity...in the name of our Lord on High!"

The baby's diatribe matched Estelle's. In volume, if not in kind. And now the approaching ferry, with its hooting, joined in with equal indignation.

"Jake, help!" pleaded the terrified black-gown, "Estelle has gone mad, I was—"

"Betty. Take the babe!" Estelle plopped the baby into Betty's arms, where he continued his screeching. Estelle brandished Jake's axe high over her head and, with a Viking's war cry, went for the minister, who cowered behind Jake, moaning uncontrollably. Jake seized the axe, threw it to the side and wrapped his arms around Estelle.

"He–he calls himself a man of the cloth—God's Instrument! I thought it was a bear outside and went out to shoo it away. Standing there, he was, Jake, nose against our girl's window, rubbing the front of his robe. Like a dog with fleas!"

"Estelle, hon, it ain't no use to kill the preacher. Hanginger ain't worth doin' time in the Oakhalla pen fer, now is he? And what would I do fer a dancin' partner, eh?" Calm words, warm arms. Jake pulled off his plaid jacket and covered Estelle with it. Jake: sporting a Doctorate in Common Sense, a Ph.D. in Christian Behaviour, thought Betty.

The Venerable Reverend Hanginger had dashed onto the waiting ferry. To the far side of it, to the darkest spot he could find. Still moaning. Only his agitated lips showed under his windblown black-bear hair, his frightened-stiff beard.

"I'm comin' over tuh see you tomorra, preacher," Jake called as the ferry took off.

"Never come back to Nah–Narrows again, you per–pervert! Pervert!" Estelle sobbed over Jake's shoulder; shivered. The baby hooted semi-words in staccato bursts.

"Amazin' woman! Put any man tuh shame! You sure fixed his tail Estelle, didn't she, Miss Wheatie? Come on, woman, up the hill and home with you. Come on, Miss Wheatie, yer shiverin' like a wet pup."

Betty carried the heavy baby up the steep hill, behind the linked couple, and listened closely to the baby's loud and insistent prattle.

"Berbert. Berbert..."

His first words. How ever would Estelle explain this to Freda?

~ ж ~

In her apartment, aware once again of her frozen self, she put her stinging feet in a pail of lukewarm water and flinched. The blood hurt as it reached her outer skin, thawing the frost-bitten cells.

Eventually her frozen face broke into a grin. It was a night better than any movie, a stellar performance: melodrama, ice magic, intrigue. And friendship. Yes. Life in Narrows could be great! Sort of.

Chapter 15

There is nothing stable in the world; uproar's your only music.
John Keats

E dwin Chalmers placed the note, written on textured, ivory-yellow paper, in Betty's waiting hand. "As you can see, Miss Wheatley, the vile pronouncement is addressed to me. Strange indeed are the pathways cowards walk. A plague upon all of them, I say."

The letters were poorly formed, as if produced with the left hand of a right-handed person. As she read it, Betty blushed, then turned pale.

> *January 5, 1952.*
> *Nakusp, BC*
> *Att: Mr. Chalmers:*
>
> *It is my duty as a God-fearing Christian to inform you of an unnatural relationship between a Mrs. Standard, restaurant proprietor at Kokanee, and Miss Wheatley, one of your teachers at Narrows.*
>
> *Parishioners at Fire Valley Gospel Church in Kokanee tell me they have watched your Miss Wheatley being taken in by the deviant Mrs. Standard. Our Lord has expressly said: 'Women shall not wear that which pertaineth unto a man'. Mrs. Standard persists in wearing men's clothing, cutting her hair like a man, behaving sexually as if she were a man. Scandalizing her community over and over!!*
>
> *It is common knowledge in Kokanee that Mrs. Standard and Miss Wheatley lie together; an abomination says the Bible, that surely will force the Lord to punish them with brimstone and fire.*
>
> *I call on you to do your duty! Do that which is required of God-fearing people everywhere. Put a stop to sin. Stop the foolish Miss Wheatley from associating with the She-devil of Kokanee! Restore the good names of the communities in our valley!*
>
> *- Yours in True Belief, A concerned Christian.*

Betty was shocked. "Oh, Mr. Chalmers, I didn't do those... She's not a–a —"

"I believe you, Miss Wheatley. Just because I bury myself in the mustiness of old poets, doesn't signify that I am oblivious to life."

"W–why? How–how could someone write something so cruel?"

Edwin Chalmers' usually benign face was grim. "Anonymity gives cowards courage, Miss Wheatley. Using biblical language likely emboldens them more."

"It's–it's like a nightmare; I don't know what to do." Betty's voice was thin, high, trembling. "Everyone gives me advice, but it all conflicts. Kate says I should confront Georgika. My grandmother thinks Georgika is a mad Sons of Freedom Doukhobor. My mother says to drop her like a hot potato. And my boyfriend? I don't dare ask his advice. He might think it was true and drop me."

"I wouldn't presume to advise you, Miss Wheatley. For you to do as I do would hardly be suitable. I would disinvolve myself from the community. Turn to my inner resources. Inner communication is far more trustworthy and less deceptive. Read more. Write more. Hardly the prescription for a young lady."

She nodded. "I'm already feeling too lonely up here, Mr. Chalmers, I need my few friends. And Georgika is special—a very kind and good friend." Self-pity stung the back of her eyes.

Edwin Chalmers reached out one of his chubby hands and patted Betty's hunched shoulder awkwardly, as if he had never touched a human before. "Forgive me for saying so, Miss Wheatley—I know your family attempts only to succour, but second-hand opinions are as worthless as the air they displace. We are all too quick with glib solutions. Only you, Miss Wheatley, are privy to the reality of this situation. Let your own conclusions prevail."

He chewed on his lips, appraising the situation. "I could be of use, however. Perhaps I could search out this vile letter writer."

Edwin Chalmers would be useless, she concluded. He keeps to himself even more than Kate and I. But he's right that I have to solve this problem myself. Who, she wondered, is filled with such vindictive biblification? Is the Venerable Reverend Hanginger associated with the Fire Valley Gospel Church? Hanginger knows the bible. Lives and breathes immorality—but he has no motive. He barely knows me. Who else? Betty rubbed her temples. Tried to push back the pulsating beat of hooves rounding cranium curves. "Thanks for the offer, Mr. Chalmers, but you and I are outsiders." Her voice was husky with misery.

"Outsiders. True. Nonetheless, there are advantages to being 'a stranger in a strange land'—to quote from your persecutor's source. I shall give the matter my undivided attention, Miss Wheatley." Edwin Chalmers compressed his cream-coloured eyebrows. "And whilst I pursue this matter, do not allow anonymous words an ounce of your attention."

His views and pronouncements seemed like papal blessings. The pounding subsided. But that night, and for many nights to come, after Betty extinguished the last light, the headrace began anew.

Chapter 16

The oldest body may harbor the youngest soul.
Joy Forever

"Well, what sort of things do you want to know?" Newly married Dot's teaching replacement—portly, white-haired and wrinkled—disappointed Betty. Though she had been told that Mrs. Edna Allan was retired, she hadn't thought to put an age to the word. Now she would be living with three old people: Kate, Granny and Mrs. Edna Allan. Damn, I'm living in an Old Folks Home: Shady Acres By-the-Lake.

"I need to know what I have got myself into," said Mrs. Allan in a jolly way. "I hear you've been friends with Dot, the teacher who resigned. Are the kiddies a lively lot? Do you know what reading levels they've arrived at? That sort of thing."

"Dot never talked much about them, but she just lives a short distance from here—"

Mrs. Allan shook her head. "I'm too tired to go anywhere today. I'll find out soon enough, tomorrow." She sighed contentedly. "I'm just so pleased that our Mrs. Trent has made me feel so welcome. It's cozy, here, by the fire."

Betty looked at the two women. They were both wearing their stockings rolled down to their ankles, both scratching their freed sides, where, throughout the day, corset stays had imprisoned their surplus flesh. Mrs. Allan, instant pal and peer, easing herself into the house with none of the trepidation Betty had experienced.

"I just love my pretty bedroom, Betsy."

"Betty. It's Betty."

"What? Oh, I'm sorry. My niece's name is Elizabeth, and we call her Betsy. As I was saying, I love my new bedroom; it's so toasty warm. I had really worried about leaving my own little apartment in Nelson, but I already feel better."

Betty masked her resentment. She would gladly change places with Mrs. Allan, swapping the refrigerator compartment she shared with picklepuss Kate.

"My nephew drove me up here. He was dead set against me teaching again. 'Auntie Edna,' he said to me, 'You retired two years ago. Why do you want to go up there?' I said to him, 'Rusty, young Robbie McIntyre has grown up to be the school inspector now, and he needs me. Besides, I could do with a little adventure. I don't want to curl up in a corner and try to learn to knit.' "

Granny nodded. "Just like me. I don't want to knit either." She beamed approval at Mrs. Allan. Such harmony. Betty felt like an outsider; nose pressed flat against a windowpane, staring in at the residents in Shady Acres By-the-Lake.

After teatime, Granny offered a suggestion. "Perhaps you can show Mrs. Allan around upstairs. She'll be sharing the kitchen with you; I think you remember, Betty? Show her the routine. Watch those stairs, Mrs. Allan, they're steep. Help her, Betty."

"Oh, sure," said Geriatric-Nurse Betty with false cheerfulness. "Come with me, Mrs. Allan."

Upstairs, Betty's misgivings multiplied. Mrs. Allan praised the sparsely furnished, roughly finished rooms with ebullience. "Gracious, Betsy, it's so roomy! So bright! Just look at the sun pouring in so late in the day!" She must be senile, thought Betty.

Granny had followed them upstairs. She looked pleased. She liked Mrs. Allen's comments. "I'll leave you two on your own to plan your dinner."

This was the last straw. Now she would have to cook for this person, too? Mash her vegetables? Cut her meat? "I have to go to the store for food. There's nothing here."

Mrs. Allan moved to the open shelves where Betty and Kate stocked their food, and peered at the contents through the lower part of her bifocals. "Oh my. I'm sure you don't want to go running out. You just came in. Surely there must be something we can eat out of all this." She fingered through a clutter of paper bags, cans and boxes. Reached for a bag of macaroni. Held up a can of fish. "Tuna Surprise! Do you like Tuna Surprise?"

"I've never had it." 'Tuna Surprise' sounded like the perfect euphemism or a practical joke.

"Absolutely delicious and cheap. You've got all the fixings, even the cheese and the Worcestershire sauce. Plus a can of peas. It'll be done in a shake of a lamb's tail, Betsy, and I'll bet you'll like it. You open the cans. I'll light the fire. We can be a team and we'll have food in no time." Betty reluctantly did as she was told. In less than half an hour they sat together eating.

"Only one dirty saucepan, Betsy, and the meal is well-balanced nutritionally."

A welcome change from Betty's usual fare since she'd been living alone: fried Spam and eggs. Betty had two helpings. "It's tasty," she admitted.

"I've got a trick or two up my sleeve, you'll see. You can't be as plump as me and widowed as long as I've been, without picking up a few easy recipes. Ever had Porcupine Casserole?"

"No. What's that?" Perhaps, beyond this gastronomic sobriquet was another tasty, easy-to-fix meal.

"Campbell's tomato soup, onions, rice and hamburger. Wonderfully delicious. I'll make it tomorrow." Mrs. Allan was now wearing the nurse's uniform and winning Betty over, to boot. She hated cooking.

Mrs. Allan scrutinized the food shelves again. "What do you eat for breakfast, Betsy?"

"Just toast and tea."

"That's all? I have, all my life, had porridge and cream."

Betty looked at Mrs. Allan with enthusiasm. This was senior's food she loved! "Porridge and cream? Let's get some tomorrow."

As they did the dishes, Mrs. Allan chatted about her sister's married children, explaining that she had been unable to have any of her own. She asked Betty about her life and her students in a kind and easy manner. The age gap closed. Shady Acres vanished. Betty did not even mind being called Betsy.

~ ж ~

On Monday after school, Mrs. Allan returned from her Trent's Landing class fuming. "Betsy, I just can't believe how behind their level these children are. The second-graders can barely read, and the third graders are more like second-graders. What a shambles! I don't know where to start. I'm really upset."

As soon as she had downed her mouthful of leftover Porcupine Casserole—a fabulous concoction—Betty replied. "I have the same problem, Mrs. Allan. There's just not enough time to teach three subjects at once to three grades and do a first-rate job. Not to mention all the preparation and marking. And I can't teach three histories, three geographies and three sciences. I muddle along." Betty helped herself to a third serving.

"Teach only one subject in each of those category to all of them. Pick and choose from the curriculum, and leave next year's teacher a list of what you've covered. She can pick up from there. But I'm not going to teach any of those frill courses to my poor little tykes. They can always pick up history and all the rest later, when they are older, if they know how to read. But if they can't read, their lives are hopeless, and if they can't successfully do simple arithmetic, they are at the mercy of all the crooks of this world.

"Even their printing is almost unintelligible. They will be drilled and drilled by me, just on the basics, until they start to reach their grade level. Then, and only then, will I teach them about Dutch girls with tulips and how clouds form and why fish aren't mammals.

"It won't be boring, Betsy, if that's what you're thinking. I've got a hundred ways to make the basics fun. I'll tell you about them if you want." Betty, mouth full again, nodded. "I suspect Inspector Robbie McIntyre won't approve at all. I don't give a dash what he thinks. I taught him when he was no more than a boy in knee pants. I'm not afraid of him. He can fire me if he wants."

She stopped her impassioned monologue and looked at Betty, astonished. Her face burst out in a surprised smile. "I think I'm going to enjoy myself up here more than I thought, Betsy. I love a challenge."

Betty pushed her plate away at last. "I'll gladly take you up on your offer of a 'hundred ways to make basics fun', thanks."

~ Ж ~

What would Mrs. Allan say? "What a shambles! Poor little tykes!" Academic progress: marginal. Except for Helena, Ingrid and Keith. They listen well, they understand and learn. Steady progress. But if I had time for individual instruction, I could challenge them, push them to excel, get them to think for themselves.

Margie Sloboda, Daisy Whittaker, Grant Keiffer, Bruce Irwin, show adequate progress.

The rest? Little Donny Rodman, pale-faced and red-eyed, acts like he's brain-dead. Is he sick? Does he have learning problems? Or maybe he just finds me boring? Probably the latter.

Though Howard Carson has had no tantrums lately, he and his sweet sister Jenny are always waiting, yearning for compliments for every meager success.

Newly cued by Mrs. Allan, she spread praise around like fresh jam on stale bread. It helped, but did not overcome the basic problems: slow reading, poor comprehension, weak arithmetic skills, atrocious spelling. But she had to keep the class moving or she would never finish the year's curriculum. And the slower children could not handle the pace.

Many a night she lay awake, feeling inadequate: too little time, too many grades, too many levels of intelligence. And their progress, she knew, was hampered and thwarted by her own inexperience and inadequacies.

Mrs. Allan was a godsend and Betty began to adopt more of her advice, embellish it with her own innovations.

~ Ж ~

Thunk-bam! A hard chunk of snow hit one of the side windows. She jumped. Icy snowballs again.

Damn kids, I'll make you toe the line yet! The new me, mirror-image of Mrs. Allan, rising to challenges, too.

After school, she went to the store to pick up her Eaton's catalogue order: three softball mitts, two bats, three balls and a can of red paint.

"Class! Line up on the softball field. You—Alec, Keith and Bruce! Get a helper each and build a snowman on each of the bases. And give each snowman a catcher's mitt when you're done.

"Margie, Helena and Ingrid, you make one at the home plate and the rest of

161

you each make one large snowball, as big as you can. Use this red paint to put targets on them. Softball season is here!"

Not a puzzled look among them. Full practice in less than an hour—pitching to the snowmen's bats, throwing to the frozen catcher's mitts, aiming for the red bull's eye targets.

Under Mrs. Allan's tutelage, she adapted other games. Channeled their energy, rolled with their interests, took charge. In short, just like Mrs. Allan, she was enjoying herself.

~ Ж ~

Constrained laughter. Smirks. Giggles.

"Come, come, now, Alec. It's hard enough for the class to concentrate as it is. There is nothing funny about a spelling test." More giggles.

The game of the double-meaning words had returned anew. Bruce and Alec, Associate Professors in Scatology, were lecturing to all.

"Appear: A-PEE-PEE-" Alec began, and then snorted.

"Try Mississippi, Alec," called out Bruce in a stage whisper. More giggles and snickers.

"Bruce and Alec. I want you to stay after class today."

"We can't. We'll miss the bus," said Bruce with a sly smile.

"I realize that, but I have a very important subject about which I must speak to you." She had rehearsed these words in bed, the previous, sleepless night.

After the rest of the class had left, she made the two boys wait as she flipped through papers, letting tension build. Then she moved to a desk directly in front of them and sat on it, her feet on the seat. An intimidating position.

"I have a serious problem. I need your help. Several of your classmates are not doing well. If I don't concentrate on them and bring them up to grade level, they will fail.

"You are big and strong and the little ones look up to you. If you provide them with a good example, they will copy you." She leaned forward and whispered, drawing them in further. "I leave this problem in your hands, boys. I am counting on you to be...the class heroes."

They looked relieved and flattered. Especially Alec. She was lucky: the bus, which was usually prompt, arrived late. It would have been a long, cold walk.

"Did you get the strap?" She heard little Donny call out. Though he never spoke in class, his mouth worked overtime outdoors. "Mind you own beeswax," called out Alec.

After this episode, she was careful to thank the two boys whenever they did anything positive. They ceased the adolescent leering. Fresh jam on fresh bread.

~ ж ~

As Betty and Mrs. Allan were about to leave the apartment for their schools, Granny called up the stairs like a town crier. "The king is dead! He died in the middle of the night."

They scrambled down the stairs. "I've just got the news on my short-wave radio! It's working so well; the BBC is coming in loud and clear. You'll have to make sure your flags are at half-mast. That pretty young girl is going to be our queen. Don't hold me back, I can't talk, I've got to get back for more news!"

~ ж ~

Betty donned a solemn face. "Class. I have an announcement to make. Our king, George VI, died last night in his sleep. He was quite old: fifty-six. We now have a queen. Elizabeth II. Please stand and give her three cheers."

"Long live the queen!" They called out self-consciously. When they began the morning rituals, she reminded them of the change. "We will now sing God Save our Queen." Helena hissed at the ones who still sang 'king': "It's 'queen', stupid," and swung her head to catch whoever would be the next one to err. One by one they lost their trains of thought. Even Betty. The previously well-mumbled anthem became a shambles.

Just a matter of time, she thought, and they'll get it right. She was learning when to react, and when not to.

Shortly after three, trustee Bill Trent appeared at the classroom door. "Because of the death of our king, there will be a day of mourning on Friday and the schools will be closed."

All eyes lit up with pleasure. Betty's too. And once the children left the classroom, they shouted: "Wow, we get a holiday. The king is dead! The king is dead!" Betty ignored them. Their callous reaction to the sovereign's death must not take up her precious time. So much to do! As the bus pulled away, she concentrated on marking their work.

She felt chilly. She piled more wood into the stove, widened the stovepipe damper. Sporadic crackling noises broke the stillness of the empty classroom, as the combusting wood swelled, split and burst. The only other sound was that of Betty's persistent marking pencil.

As usual, Betty wore her snow boots and extra sweaters. On these cold and dark days, when the snow was settled and deep, most of the students, both boys and girls, wore two pairs of heavy grey woolen socks and high black gumboots with felt soles inside them. Just like Betty, they did not take the boots off in the classroom; they all needed them for warmth. Air space between the inner and outer schoolroom walls provided the sole insulation from the outside cold, and frigid air seeped steadily in, crept along the floor and nipped at their toes. The Quebec heater roasted those students sitting near the back of the room and ignored those near the front, leaving them to freeze.

The experienced team of Alec, Grant and Bruce, the bigger boys, fed the heater at a suitable rate. They did the best they could with the green pieces of wood janitor Len provided. Surprisingly, despite the unevenness of the heat, the students rarely missed school because of illness. They did not even catch colds.

Betty began marking arithmetic workbooks for all three grades. So many errors! Like Flanders Field: crosses row on row.

She mulled over Mrs. Allan's radical idea of dropping the 'frills' and concentrating on the basics. Upgrading the students' skills would be a huge challenge because of the years of glossing over by previous teachers; six years, in some cases. Impossible, she thought, for me, a beginner.

She heard unusual sounds: Len's school bus roaring up the hill, screeching to a halt and Len running toward the school. A chemical smell assailed her nostrils. She looked up. The sides of the stove were cherry-red; the varnish on the side of her desk was bubbling like boiling porridge.

Len burst into the classroom, dashed to the stove, and shut off the stovepipe damper and the door draft. He rushed outside again, with Betty scurrying after him. He stopped a short distance from the school and stared up at the roof.

The chimney had transformed into a jet engine. Flames roared skyward. "Oh, golly, Len, I'm so sorry, I wasn't watching the sides of the stove!" He did not answer. Instead, he charged back inside and yanked Betty's desk away from the inferno. She followed him, feeling inept, ashamed. "I'm sorry, I just didn't—"

"It's me, Betty, I haven't been keeping up with things. I should have cleaned the soot out of the darn chimney last week. It's the soot and creosote that're on fire." They hurried outside again and looked up at the chimney. The jet flames were less threatening, now; the flying sparks dying as they landed on the snow-coated roof.

"Holy smoke," Len muttered. "The whole place could have burned down."

Betty, still awaiting a torrent of blame, began her apology anew. "I was so busy, I just didn't—"

Len ignored her words. "I can't seem to get myself up to snuff." He shifted on his big-booted feet and did not speak again until the flames subsided. They re-entered the classroom. The stove had returned to normal and the side of the desk had ceased erupting. They left the outer door ajar to diffuse the odor of burnt varnish.

Finally, Len turned to her with a sheepish, defensive look. "Did you know my Vivian didn't come back with me after Christmas?"

Not being castigated was a new experience for Betty. She produced a chatty voice, assuming it would be appropriate to Len's sudden change of topics. "No, I didn't, Len, is she staying on longer with her mother?"

"Sort of, yeah." He leaned against the blackboard. He looked forlorn. "She says she doesn't want to come back here." Impatient with the way his hands were betraying his controlled voice, he shoved them into his pockets.

"Why not, Len, is it the length of the winter days?"

"She won't say. She just kept crying when I was trying to find out. I don't know what the heck to do."

"Have you talked to her mother?"

"I've phoned and asked to speak with Vivian, but her mother says she doesn't want to talk to me."

"Didn't her mother explain any further?"

"That old biddy doesn't want her to come back here. She was upset that Vivian married me in the first place."

"Oh, Len, I'm so sorry. I can't think of who you should talk to for help. I don't know what to say."

Betty remembered Vivian's words of loneliness. They had been cries for help that she had ignored. Maybe if she had been friendlier, Vivian would still be around. She felt guilty. "I wish I could help. What are you going to do?"

"I'm going to drive down there this weekend and see her." Len stood up to go.

"Good luck. I guess that's all I can say, Len. I sure hope she's ready to come home."

"I just hope she's ready to talk. I'll clean the chimney up real good tonight, just to be sure it's okay. It won't happen again." He walked dejectedly to the door.

"And I'll be careful not to put in too much wood." What a relief not to have to take the blame!

Betty watched him from the doorway as he eyed the chimney before he climbed back into the bus. She waved as he left.

Poor Len. Gramma Beaton had once said, "Love is hardest on the one who loves the most. That person never has the upper hand in affairs of the heart." Maybe Len doesn't have the upper hand. Gramma Beaton also says, "appearances can be deceiving". Maybe Len has done something wrong. She wondered if she would ever find out which saying applied in this case.

It's strange how a person reacts, she thought. I'm blasé about the king's death not unlike my students, fearless about the fire; but I'm all tied up in knots about Vivian and Len.

She headed for the piano. She was making progress; she could play several simple melodies from Georgika's book. She played with no self-criticism, reveling in her meager accomplishment, not allowing herself to wonder how the villagers regarded her stumbling efforts.

When the skies became so dark that she could barely see the yellowed keys, she straightened the blistered desk, locked up the school, sucked in a deep breath of outdoor air to clear the burnt varnish from her lungs. Skidded down the road. Huge piles of snow lay everywhere. Stray flakes were nuisances, pushing past her eyelashes and landing in her eyes.

Suddenly, she became conscious that the town had changed. The light from the three houses on the lakeside of the road shone brightly. Every room in Nina and Bill Trent's home was aglow.

Granny was waiting for her at the back door. "The electric light has just come on! Hurry up and get your boots off. We have to see if all the switches work!"

"Did you see my school's chimney fire?"

Granny was too excited to answer. Betty trailed around the various rooms as Granny, in ecstasy, switched on all her lights. She charged upstairs, pulled the chains of the swaying, suspended bare bulbs that hung in the middle of each room.

"My goodness, I never knew how much I missed real lights. This is so...so... momentous!"

"Hah," said Betty, "I've never forgotten how much I've missed them."

Suddenly Granny stopped short. "Put them off! Quickly!" she demanded.

"Why?"

"Because they'll be so costly! We mustn't waste the light. Just one on at a time! I haven't the slightest idea how much they will be charging me for this. It's probably very expensive."

Betty helped her undo the mad excitement of the first few moments. Soon, all the lights but the one in Granny's kitchen were off.

Granny fanned herself with her apron. "I don't know what got into me, for goodness sakes."

"It's a big moment, Mrs. Trent; it's a time to celebrate."

Granny shook her head. "I don't usually indulge in foolishness."

Mrs. Allan burst through the back door, her arms full of groceries. "'And let there be light, the good Lord said.' I say, hallelujah! No more of those fragile gauze mantles to break! Good-bye, gas lamps!"

"I'll say double hallelujahs," added Betty.

Granny still looked apprehensive. "I don't know about that, it could be very expensive."

"It won't be, Maudie, dear. You'll see. Living right near the source—the hydro station—will make it quite reasonable. Cheaper than your gas or oil lamps."

It was the first time Betty had heard anyone use Granny's first name.

"I suspect you're right, Edna. You do make a lot of sense." All Granny's doubt evaporated. Edna Allan had great credibility in Granny's mind, too.

"I'm cooking dinner for all three of us, tonight. Come upstairs to help celebrate, Maude." The inexhaustible Mrs. Allan and Betty gathered the bags from the floor. They traipsed up the stairs.

"Did you see my school's chimney fire?"

"Oh, yes, Betsy, dear, I've seen many in my day. Now, I've got nothing fancy, just creamed salmon, but I've got the makings of Peach Melba for dessert."

"Sounds wonderful. What's in it?"

"Canned peaches wearing a crown of raspberry jam, topped with ice cream. The recipe's from Chatelaine, if I remember rightly. I know it's extravagant, but this is a special day, for heaven's sakes. I just couldn't resist a gourmet touch. There I was, trying to decide in that dark store what to buy for supper, when, Bingo! The lights came on."

Granny's eyes gleamed. "It is special, there's no denying it. I've got something special, too." She disappeared down the stairs. Returned with a bottle of rhubarb wine. "Nina makes it. It's delicious. I only have it on special occasions."

"Well, now you're talking, Maude. We'll have a first-rate party here."

Betty reached for three glasses.

"No, Betty, be a good girl and go and get my best glasses, the ones with stems, from my china cabinet. And my Spode plates. No halfway measures tonight."

Along with the creamed salmon and canned peas, and the makeshift Peach Melba, the three of them drank the entire bottle of sweet and tangy wine. They were soon in a laughing, jovial mood. They interrupted one another, loudly spilling out their pleasure.

They did not hear a car pull up. Or the bumping noises on the stairs.

"Well, well, party time. What the heck is going on?" Only Kate's dark eyes and disapproving brows were visible as she peered over a swath of scarf. Still using the crutches, leaning on them like an old crone.

Fuzzy-headed Betty and Granny looked like children caught in a naughty act. A quicker responding but slightly unsteady Edna Allan jumped up.

"My goodness, you must be Kate. Here, let me help you, you poor thing." Mrs. Allan unwound Kate's scarf, took her coat, and hung them up. Kate relished the attention and continued to stand in the doorway looking helpless. Granny and Betty watched the scenario with great interest, occasionally exchanging significant glances. Mrs. Allan hovered with concern. "Let me help you to the couch. I'll move this junk. Stretch out, dear. I'll put this pillow behind you." After hobbling across the room, Kate collapsed on the couch, groaning with either pain or pleasure from Mrs. Allan's administrations.

"Oh God, what a long and cold trip. I hope to never do it in the winter again." Kate lay back and closed her eyes.

Betty found her voice. "We didn't expect you back for several more weeks. This is Mrs. Allan, by the way. She's taking Dot's place."

"Hi, Mrs. Allan. I wasn't expecting to come back so soon, either. I was going to have more surgery, but the doctors finally decided it could make my knee even worse."

"What about your court case? Is it over? Did you win?" asked Betty.

Kate shot Betty a hard look. "What is this, the Narrows Inquisition?"

"Oh, Betsy, put the kettle on. We should make her a cup of tea. Have you had your supper yet, you poor thing?"

"No. I only had a bite in Nakusp, but I'm not hungry, thanks. Tea sounds great." She leaned back and shut her eyes again. She's trying to look like Greta Garbo, thought Betty. Camille. The role looked irresistible. Betty coughed. Twice. But no one looked at her. Mrs. Allan bustled, adding wood to the stove and jiggling the existing embers into a livelier fire.

"When did you get the electricity?"

Granny answered. "Just tonight, Kate. Just before dinner. That's why we were having a party."

"I can smell the booze in here. I thought you didn't believe in wild parties, Granny."

Granny's face flushed even redder than the wine had made it. She looked agitatedly at Betty for help.

"This is not quite a wild party, Kate. You shouldn't joke in a serious voice; it's too easy to take you the wrong way."

"Sorry. God, I feel awful."

"How did you get here? Did you drive your van?"

"No. I'm not taking that icebox up here again until spring. I got a ride."

"Oh." They stood, looking at her, until the kettle began to boil. Mrs. Allan made the tea.

"Would you like some toast, dear?"

"No. Nothing, I said. Don't stand there, all of you, just staring at me. I'm not a sideshow freak. I suppose you all want to know about the court case. Well, they've postponed it until Easter. I could just kill those dumb lawyers." She stared gloomily ahead.

"Let's do up these dishes, Betty," said Granny. Betty and Granny retreated to the sink to get as far away from Kate and her black mood as possible. Mrs.

Allan served Kate as though she were a fragile flower and Kate milked her role as invalid.

Once the dishes were done, Granny gathered up her goblets and plates. "Oh, Edna, Betty, that was the loveliest dinner. I did so enjoy myself."

"Just don't make these parties a habit, you bunch," said Kate from her invalid's position.

Granny hustled to the doorway as quickly as her good manners would allow. "Good night, all."

"I'm coming down too, Maude, unless you need some help, Kate."

"No thanks, Mrs. Allan."

"Good night, girls. See you for breakfast." The two older women departed.

Kate sat upright. Glared at Betty. "What does she mean, see us for breakfast?"

"Just what she says. She's renting Granny's downstairs bedroom and sharing this kitchen with us. It's not a bad deal. We get a reduction in rent and she's very kind, as you can see."

"Who foisted her on us? That damn Bill? They sure have a nerve. Why the hell didn't you object? Honest to God, Betty, you're a real pushover."

"It's okay, Kate, you'll see."

"It looks as though I don't have any choice, do I? I sure as hell don't need any more problems to cope with."

"What other problems?"

"I get talked out of surgery, can't get the court case finished up, spend three weeks fighting with my parents, and you say what problems?" She put her head between her hands. "I didn't feel like coming back up here, I can tell you. I wouldn't have, if I'd had any other option."

"I felt the same way, Kate, and everyone told me 'Don't be a quitter', so here I am. Now I'm finding it's well...not so bad. You'll see. Mrs. Allen's a real asset to us, not a nuisance. She may be old, but she pulls her weight."

"She'd sure better."

"A good night's sleep will help you, Kate. You look tired."

"Right now there isn't a thing in the world that could help me."

"My whole school nearly caught fire today. There was a huge chimney fire." Maybe Kate would be impressed; no one else had been.

"With you at the helm, it's a wonder it wasn't burnt to the ground."

Betty, who was banking the fire for the night, suppressed an urge to whack Kate with the hot poker.

Later, in bed, she was still seething. Kate hates me. She wrote the She-devil note! She hates Georgika, too.

She thought again about Cameron's story of Kate going berserk, throwing cans through a store window, being carried away in a straitjacket. I don't believe it. If anything, she's going to push me into going berserk and ending up in a straitjacket. Black Kate, turning me into a human time bomb. Tick, tick, tick.

Chapter 17

Why be disagreeable,
when with a little effort
you can be impossible?
Douglas Woodruff

The girls stood in a huddle, smirking, holding in giggles with mittened hands and staring at the boy's outhouse. The outcasts, asthmatic Keith and a sad-faced pair, young Howard and Donny, stood staring, too. Thin trails of smoke curled out of the outhouse knotholes.

Cigarettes again. Betty's mind was still racing to find the best means to deal with this test, when the outhouse door banged open and Raymond Whitaker reeled out, his face as white as the stick of chalk Betty gripped. Bruce followed, looking the same.

The chalk snapped as inspiration hit her. No direct attack. No. I will outflank the enemy forces.

She made her move later in the afternoon, during the Health lesson. "...and one of the dangers of smoking, a filthy disgusting habit, is the ruination of your lungs. It takes away your wind. That's why no athlete smokes. Not one. Anywhere. Especially baseball players." It did not bother her that she was speaking without the burden of knowledge. "How many of your fathers smoke?" Up went most hands. "Could your father run around three bases if he had to? Fast? Without panting?" Each one shook his head. "No? You see, it's the cigarettes. Robbing them of their very breath!" Drama, she was realizing, played very well. She would try it more often.

"I believe you will agree we cannot have smokers on our softball team. None. Smokers will guarantee that we lose. Do you intend to smoke, Raymond?"

Pale Raymond flinched. "Not me, Miz Sweetly. Never ever."

~ ж ~

Betty watched Kate and crutches being assisted from a stately black Packard. By a solicitous man with a slight stoop to his shoulders. He wore strange clothes for Narrows: a formal and severe black suit, a white shirt, a black overcoat. He conversed with Kate for some time.

When Kate came upstairs, melting snow flakes, sparkling despite the yellowish, single-bulb overhead light, decorated her hair. Her cheeks glowed.

Most attractive women, thought Betty, have moments when they're almost ugly. Take Kate. Some days her beautiful face is just like a hawk's. But not today. Today she's got a face as serene as…. the call of a dove. Still, no peacock radiance like when she was first dating that condom salesman Roscoe Taylor… . Good heavens! Was she becoming analyzer of people-person—like her mother Nora? She was impressed with herself.

Betty's intent look annoyed Kate. "What are you staring at?"

"You. Who's that fellow that drove you home?"

"Mind your own business."

"Suit yourself." Two can play this game, thought Betty, copying Nora.

"His name is Kurt Guttemann."

"Guttemann? Huh! Isn't he engaged to the daughter of the cheese factory owner?"

"Not anymore. And at least he's not married. He showed up at the school today and asked me out for dinner at Nakusp."

"Nakusp? You've got to stop seeing Roscoe Taylor, then."

Kate looked shocked. "Who told you I was still seeing Roscoe?"

"I have my sources. Seeing Roscoe is an awful mistake, Kate. What if this Kurt sees you with him?"

"I'm sure he hasn't. He looks at me as though I'm some sort of angel. I want to play this thing with him very carefully. He's a good catch. He co-owns a funeral parlor and sells headstones."

"Do you find him attractive?" He looked much older than Kate. And his clothing! Betty frowned. Anyone dressed in black from head to foot had to be a Gloomy Gus.

"He has money. Who cares about the rest? I'm holding really good cards. I'll dump Roscoe."

"Good, Kate. Once burnt, twice as careful, or something..."

"What do you know about getting burnt? You seem to have your boyfriend under control."

"Six hundred miles away?"

"He writes you every week."

Betty shrugged her shoulders. "Yo-yo letters. One time full of love, the next telling about his dates with some girl named Kathy. Inconsequential diversions from study, he says. To which, he says, he is indifferent. It's quite understandable. He says he only goes to please his friends, because they're worried about him taking his studies too seriously and becoming a recluse." As Betty listened to her own words, she felt a sense of uneasiness, but resolutely pushed it aside. She had to. Optimism was survival. "What are we talking about him for, anyway? I thought we were talking about this new fellow, Kurt Guttemann."

"We're done talking about him. You're a slow enough cook as it is. You get those potatoes on, or we'll be eating at bedtime again."

Pushed back to square one. Betty filed her Nora-style analyzing away to try out on a lesser being. The potato.

~ ж ~

"If Inspector McIntyre's organizing this conference in Edgewood, then that's when he'll inspect us, too. He'll kill two birds with one stone." Kate spoke as one seasoned to the ways of school inspectors.

New problems. Betty winced. "I hope those words 'killing two birds' don't bring bad luck." Her stomach made a loop as she envisioned the all-powerful and sneering Mr. McIntyre, watching her make mistakes, seeing her class misbehave.

"Gosh, girls, I used to teach him when he was just a babe. He's a real pussycat. Don't worry," Mrs. Allan said.

"We know you taught him when he was a babe—you've told us a

dozen times. Anyway, it's easy for you to say: you're retired, with a fat pension and teacher's pay to boot," Kate replied.

"It's easy for you, too; you've got tenure, now, don't you? It's Betsy who has to worry." There was a shade of tartness in Mrs. Allan's voice.

"And worry, I will. That's the problem. I'll probably get stage fright and spell everything wrong." Betty chewed on the arm of her glasses, then drummed them on the table.

"It's time you pep-talked yourself into a bit more self-confidence, Betsy, dear," said Mrs. Allan. "You've come a long way in a short while."

"It's Jake's daughter Charlotte who's come a long way," said Kate. "She's been accepted into the nursing program at Royal Vic Hospital. What a change. She and that ex-beau of hers, Steve Waterbrook don't even glance at one another anymore."

"He flirts with the younger girls at the dances," said Betty. "I hope they don't follow Charlotte's footsteps."

Kate snorted. "One advantage of small towns: word gets around fast. You can bet your clunky aviator boots that they'll be careful."

I hope so, thought Betty. Unwanted pregnancy: the killer of romance. So far, I've been safe. So far. Russian Roulette, Dot had called it. How true.

~ ж ~

At one of the dances, Jake's son-in-law, Curley McCloskey, came up to Betty as she stood by the food table, sampling a Nanaimo bar. "I guess you heard I'm organizing the Spring Concert?" He was there alone. His wife, Freda, was pregnant again and not feeling well. "I wondered if you would be my partner for a jitterbug act for the show."

Betty, after a nun-like existence these past few months, flushed as though he had invited her to go to bed, but Curley stared her right in the eye. "I'm not trying to start up some kind of flirtation, Betty, I'm married. But I surely want to make a good show, and you're a good dancer."

Betty relaxed. There was no mistaking the earnestness in his face. "Okay, Curley, I'll be your partner. When do we start?"

"Late April, after Easter."

When Betty left the hall, she walked lightly. April! We're already talking about April. And I thought I'd never get through the winter.

~ ж ~

"Yoo-hoo, Betsy?" Mrs. Allan handed her a note. "This is from your friend Georgika, Betsy. Her son came to the door. He says she's back from her surgery and wants you to come for a visit."

Betty sensed Granny scrutinizing her. Had she read any of the hate notes? Three of the ivory-yellow notes had been sent to Edwin Chalmers, now, and the last one hinted of extra copies being distributed. With Granny as judge and the rest of the town as jury, who would plead Betty's defense?

~ ж ~

Saturday morning. It was Betty's turn to make the breakfast. She had made oatmeal for herself and Mrs. Allan as usual; for Kate she had made toast. She and Mrs. Allan were now contentedly sipping tea.

Kate had eaten her toast without speaking. Then, as dishwasher-of-the-week, she sulkily moved to the sink.

Betty, sensitized by her father's rages, recognized the black clouds forming over Kate. First, the heavy air, then the storm. Suddenly, like Zeus in a rage, Kate turned toward them from the sink and hurled a thunderbolt. Betty ducked under the table.

"God damn you two!" The porridge pot winged across the room, narrowly missing Mrs. Allan, and crashed against the far wall, spewing its glutinous contents. "I'm bloody well sick and tired of washing out your sticky porridge pots!" Then Kate grabbed the oatmeal from its shelf and threw it into the stove, where the eager flames licked up the new fuel. "That's the end of this shit!" she screamed, "Don't you dare buy that crap again!" The smell of burning oatmeal permeated the room.

Omigod, mouthed Betty, still under the table, next it's cans through the window! And the RCMP is miles away! Not a straitjacket anywhere!

Mrs. Allan, unencumbered with Betty's knowledge, had not lost one iota of composure. "My goodness, we've got out of the bed on the wrong side today, haven't we?" she said.

"Don't patronize me." Kate's voice descended a decibel. Betty crept back into her chair. "I'm sick of you two siding against me."

"What do you mean? Betsy and I do no such thing!"

"Yes, you do. I see you giving one another knowing looks."

No cans, no broken windows... . Betty dared to muster her tongue. "Kate, what's wrong? It can't just be the porridge, what's really wrong?"

Kate flailed her arms around like a frenzied choirmaster. "Jesus, you little nosey-parker! There's nothing wrong! Nothing!" She glared at Betty, who prepared to duck again, if need be. Then Kate spoke in a defeated voice: "I s'pose you think you know everything. My life is jinxed. I've been charming to that damn Kurt Guttemann almost every day for six weeks, now. I've even gone to The Fire Valley Gospel Church with him. Then this morning, I saw him drive by with his old girlfriend—off on the ferry to god-knows-where!"

Betty stopped worrying about where to get a straitjacket. Love problems. She was familiar with those.

"Does it really matter, Kate?" asked Mrs. Allan. "Sometimes, when he comes to call, I feel as if he's a chore for you. I know it's none of my business, but I haven't seen any special spark in your reactions to him."

"Grow up, Mrs. Allan. There aren't always sparks in mutually beneficial relationships."

"I'd never marry without them. My husband and I were always romantically in love."

"Well, bully for you. Some of us aren't so lucky."

"You're too young to settle for a 'mutually beneficial arrangement'."

"I'm sick of looking for the other kind. I'll take whatever I can get,

178

now, and I want Kurt."

"He's a nice enough fellow, Mrs. Allan." Betty tried to find some conversational compromise.

Mrs. Allan knew when to back down. "I'm sure you're right, Betsy. However you feel, Kate, I think he cares very much for you. It's written all over his face. Maybe you're jumping the gun about this other girl. Wait until he returns. Maybe things'll be better than you think."

"Maybe so," said Kate wearily. Then she glared at them again. "But I still mean no more of that bloody, slimy porridge!"

~ ж ~

The visit to Kokanee was just for the day. Betty found a tired-looking Georgika: weak and slow moving. Leslie and Tommy cooked a special dinner for them all. They toasted Georgika with glasses of sherry.

When Betty was finally alone with her, she spoke with concern. "Are you all right now, Georgika?"

"Sure. I did have a hysterectomy; they found a little lump or two they didn't like. I'm all cleaned out now. Don't even have to worry about periods anymore. Praise God, I'll be as right as rain in a couple of weeks." She smiled her soft, mushy smile and gazed fondly at Betty. "I'm a tough bird, Betty. They can't get rid of me easily, you'll see."

Shortly after, Tommy ushered Betty out and drove her home, apologizing for rushing her. "My ma isn't in good shape yet, Betty. Maybe next time you can stay longer. She sure was anxious to see you."

Leslie, always too busy, was not with them in the car. During the evening, Betty had sensed him staring at her repeatedly, as before, but she could not develop eye contact with him because he was in constant motion the whole time. Even conversation had been impossible; he had run about, waiting on them all, never sitting for long. She decided to test Tommy. "I don't think Leslie likes me."

"What makes you think that?"

"He really avoids me."

"Shucks, Betty, he's a busy guy. So am I. I hope you don't think I

179

try and avoid you. It's just that I'm working harder than I used to."

She smiled. "No, Tommy, I think you've always been really nice to me."

"Les is cracker jack at everything he does. He can't take time out for fun. It's not personal."

"You're probably right." But she could not get Leslie out of her head, and it happened every visit.

———

Chapter 18

The Church after all is not a club of saints;
it is a hospital for sinners.
—George Craig Stewart

Outside there was a quickening; an uplifting of atmospheric spirit so strong that Betty became acutely aware of it. First, the lake ice disappeared, then the mountainside snow began turning to water, trickling over the rock faces. Daily, the outdoors came alive with new sounds: the cracking, shrinking static of melting ice, the gurgling music of new-born streams that filled every rut and descending curve.

By the middle of March, shoots of green sidled up against the remaining ice, coaxing winter to retreat. The final, most delicious signal of spring and its accompanying freedoms was the first triumphant hoot of the returning Minto.

The change in the weather excited the children as much as it did Betty. They ran around giddily, coats undone, faces red and sweaty, feet skidding from the remaining ice into mud. The classroom floors were constantly wet and dirty. She worried about what janitor Len might have to say. However, when he appeared, and she apologized, he smiled. "Happens every year, Betty. Nothing to worry about. Part of the job."

His wife Vivian had still not come back from Nelson. But he would not give up on her, and went down there nearly every weekend, trying to coax her back. In his spare time he steadily transformed his house. Shiplap now covered the tar-papered walls and the house was looking forward to a spring coat of paint. Although the house looked happy, he looked haggard.

~ Ж ~

It was not just the weather that had changed. The atmosphere in the New Testament Tabernacle Church had changed, too. Estelle and her family now sat in the back pew. Estelle's eyes burned nonstop at the New Testament Tabernacle minister like some competitive religious force, like Christ in the temple overturning the tables of moneychangers. Betty could not understand why the minister was still around. Although Jake's family owned the front pew, it seemed he had neither the gumption nor the influence to have the Venerable Hanginger ousted.

Betty turned this strange irresolution over and over. Why hasn't the congregation let him go? Everyone in the valley must know about his peeping-tom exposé. And, she speculated, many of them must know about the accusations levelled at me, and yet no one does anything about those, either. How long would I survive in a city, if letters accusing me of immorality were being scattered about? Not long. Someone would insist on my discharge. Unfit to teach young minds, they'd say. A dangerous influence, a bad example for the young. But here? Not a murmur. Is no one in charge? Is that the reason? Or is it the alternative they face if they let the minister and me go. Where would they find replacements on short notice? Would replacements be any better? Worse? Or is the community unusually tolerant? It certainly isn't because they're too lazy to take action. Hardly: Bill. Len. Jake. Nina. Mrs. Johnson. The opposite of lazy. She could not recall seeing a single lazy person in all her travels around the tiny community. Maybe they're waiting. Waiting for our replacements to arrive, and then they can grab us both by the scruff of our necks and toss us out. She cringed.

It was awhile before she could slough off this new fear, could notice other changes in the church: the sermons had changed. It was hard to make any sense from them. They were short, jumbled and dwelt on the sins of women, beginning with those of Eve. He must be the anonymous writer; he's obsessed with the evilness of women.

Betty still sat in the front pew with Granny and, from her near-the-wall position, she still could observe the minister's pulpit-hidden gestures. His hands had strayed under his robes that first Sunday she had attended, and now they strayed again—more so than ever. Too bad he doesn't have a wife, thought Betty. A wife to salve his itch, give his robes a rest.

My God. Now he's looking at me while he's doing it! He's definitely heard about Georgika and me! He's positive I'm a pervert like him. She shuddered at the grossness of the situation and settled her face into a mask, pretending to be oblivious. Then a thought dawned on her…the regular rustling outside her window and at the outhouse…could it be?

~ Ж ~

"What's that sour look on your face for, Betsy?"

"I'm trying to write a play for the spring concert and I don't feel like it. My Christmas effort was a disaster."

"I'm using an old chestnut that I've taught for so many years, it's etched on my brain. Some of the children will be trees, some will be spring flowers, et cetera. And, of course, one'll be the blue bird of happiness," said Mrs. Allan.

"I promised myself I'd work extra hard at everything. I am. I've never worked so hard in my life. And now this concert to do. I wish it was Easter break."

"Life passes by so quickly, Betsy, don't wish it away. In the wink-of-an-eye, you'll be as old as me, and still wishing for the future. Try Spring through the Alphabet. Keep it simple."

Betty began to write in a tepid frame of mind:

> A is for Apples trees, abloom in alpine white,
>
> B is for Blueberries, the black bears' delight.
>
> C is for Cats that cry all through the night,
> Yowling and mating and getting into a fight.

Cats made her think of the unearthly noises emanating from the hotel yard, as Mrs. Sunders' cats expressed their springtime urges. Mating made her think of her upcoming trip to Vancouver to see Cameron, being in his arms again...

She shook off the lethargy. Joan of Arc wouldn't whine about writing a playlet.

It was after six when misanthropic Kate slammed her way upstairs and flopped on the chesterfield. Betty and Mrs. Allan glanced at one another: two friends facing a common foe.

Kate had had a showdown with her new beau, Kurt Guttemann, about the cheese maker's daughter. "You think your friendship with her is over?" Kate had shouted. "You think? Don't come back to me until you're one hundred percent positive it's over." She had told Betty about her outburst. Since then, she had been more ill tempered than ever.

"We were just discussing what we are going to have our classes do for the spring concert. What are you planning, Kate?" Mrs. Allan ventured.

"Having a cussing contest, or a fist fight. Whichever they vote for as their favourite." Kate slapped her forehead. "I don't know, for God sakes. I told old Edwin Chalmers to organize it. He tried to get them to enact excerpts from A Midsummer Night's Dream, but they refused, and now he's pouting. I don't care what they do. They can stand there on stage and be jackasses; they're good at that." A grey cloud hung around her, identical to the misty shrouds circling the Selkirk mountaintops.

"Oh, well. At least the grasses are green and all the trees are in full bud. I love the approach of spring, don't you, Betsy?"

Before Betty could reply, Kate barged in: "Oh, get your feet on the ground.

To hell with spring. I hate it; it's the season of lies."

~ ж ~

After supper, Betty walked to the store, zigzagging around patches of oozy mud. As a black Packard came up behind her, she leapt to the roadside. Mud splashed her boots and her coat. Who, she wondered could be such a thoughtless speeder? It was Kurt. Kate's new beau. Kurt Guttemann and the cheese maker's daughter, speeding down the road as if no other person existed or mattered. Betty knew another period of stormy weather with Kate lay ahead.

~ ж ~

Storekeeper Mrs. Johnson's ornate bible, an embossed, massive tome, was near Betty's elbow as Betty placed her order. The bible was open, facing Betty. A coincidence? A message? wondered Betty. She studied the black and white wood cut of Moses. Was he pointing his finger at her, pushing the inscribed stone tablets toward her? *Moses descending from Sinai*, read the inscription below the illustration. Is Mrs. Sunders using Moses to remind me of the Ten Commandments? Are she-devil lesbians mentioned in the Ten Commandments?

Betty struggled to recall the ten holy injunctions; she recalled two of them: Thou shalt not kill. Thou shalt not steal. But then her mind filled with Thou-shalt-not question marks. Fornication, she reasoned, must be mentioned in one of them. And sleeping with someone of the same sex. The tablets must have that detailed someplace. Otherwise, why did the thought of the possibility upset her and everyone else so much?

Pregnant Dot entered the store to buy writing paper. She chose a pad of textured, ivory-yellow paper and matching envelopes. The same type used by the hate-note writer! Dot? Writer of hate-notes? Never, thought Betty. Definitely not Dot. Betty sighed. She had to stop being so paranoid!

"How come you don't visit me, Betty? I thought when I was on this side of the lake, we were going to be buddy-buddy."

"Oh, Dot, I've been creating a ton of ditto sheets! Special homework, supplementary worksheets—I've got six class projects on the go, and—"

"Is that so! Some friend you are. What about me? I'm alone all day. You have no idea how awful it is to be pregnant and sick. A bunch of housework to do all the time, and never seeing a single solitary soul except my animal husband." She plunged her hands into her raincoat pockets, hastily removing them when she realized that the action outlined her growing stomach. "I hate looking like Mrs. Santa Claus. And I hate this place. I wish I wasn't pregnant. I want to go home. I phoned my mother one day and told her I want to leave Lou, and she said if I came home to her, she'd lock the door in my face. Said I needed a good spanking. My own mother!"

They were walking home together through the drizzling rain. "Poor, poor, Dot," said Betty, and pushed aside her personal paranoia in order to cheer up her roly-poly friend: "Guess what, Dot? I'm going to visit Cameron at Easter. In Vancouver. I told my mother I'm staying at a girlfriend's house, and just visiting Cameron, but it's the other way around."

"Hunh. I thought he was seeing some girl named Kathy and you were giving up on him."

"Oh, that was just platonic. Just his chums setting him up. His letters are wonderful. Really romantic."

"Are you sure it's platonic?"

"Positive. Oh, Dot, it will be so wonderful! Five days. Four nights. We're going to stay in a hotel. Just like a married couple."

"You can't, if you're not married. They won't rent it to you. Not a respectable hotel."

"They will, they will. I've got it all figured out. We'll get some rings. At Woolworth's. I've seen them, and they're just as beautiful as the real things. When I come back here, I'm going to wear them around my neck, in secret, on a little gold chain. And every night, in the dark, I'll put them on my finger again. Just like a secret marriage!"

Dot's face was inscrutable. "Good luck. You'll need it."

A half hour later, Dot came up to the apartment. She checked to make sure neither Kate nor Mrs. Allan was around, and pulled out a bulky envelope.

"A going away present, Betty. Roscoe Taylor specials. Just so you don't come back carrying one of these." She pointed at her growing stomach, broke into peals of laughter and hurried off.

Betty opened the envelope. Little packets spilled onto the table. TROJANS. Lubricated ones. Feeling twinges of both excitement and embarrassment, Betty stuffed them inside her laid-to-rest aviator boots, buried in the farthest corner of the bedroom. Next to her going-to-Vancouver suitcases.

~ ж ~

Teacher Edwin Chalmers put the latest anonymous letter into Betty's hand.

"Oh God, will this never stop? I'm sorry whoever sends them insists on involving you, Mr. Chalmers."

"I'm in no need for sympathy, Miss Wheatley. Save it for the creature who writes such poppycock."

Betty plummeted into renewed panic. Everywhere she went—the store, the dances, church—she watched people. If they spoke softly, if they didn't look her in the eye, she worried, she wondered.

~ ж ~

"Mrs. Allan, each one gets worse. This note calls me a fornicator of the worst kind: she-devil sleeping with she-devil. Oh, poor Georgika! Poor me! My life is ruined!" The noise like the galloping of horses in her ears blasted at full volume.

Run with the horses, Betty, said an inner voice.

Run where? Home? To Cameron? I tried that at Christmas. Got nowhere.

Mrs. Allan read the note. "Betsy, crooked hearts are everywhere. Ignore this preposterous piffle! Go and visit Georgika all you want."

Without Mrs. Allan's reassuring presence, Betty would have run. Anywhere. Far inside her own head, if need be.

Chapter 19

What we anticipate seldom occurs;
what we least expected generally happens.
—Benjamin Disraeli

"Six times six is thirty-six...six times seven is forty-two...
Donny, stop fidgeting. What's got into you?"

Alec placed yet another log in the Quebec heater. "No more for the rest of the day, thank you, Alec. The place is too warm as it is. Six times eight is forty-eight...six times nine is fifty four..." The fourth-grade voices droned along comfortably. The fifth-graders were immersed in their workbooks. The sixth-graders copied bushel-and-peck problems from the blackboard. Ever mindful of Alec's father, the dour Mr. Detweiler and his admonishments, she had adapted the math problems, aiming them at farming concerns. She walked to the supply cupboard at the back of the room in time to the fourth-graders' singsong: "six times ten is—"

Whurumph! Brrang! Brrang! The Quebec heater hiccupped, burped, leapt crazily from the floor onto, in turn, each of its legs. "...sixty," whispered a spellbound Betty as she watched the stovepipe separate into segments, watched each segment collapse and spew a rain of soot, watched the heater door pop open, as if pushed from within by some invisible, hellish hand fencing with shooting flames. Brrang! Another explosion: this time, sparks racing toward her, zeroing in on her. "Duck, Miz Sweetly!" called out one of the older boys—Alec, perhaps, "Bullets! Bullets in the stove!"

Gut instinct took over, bringing with it adrenaline-fed courage; she became galvanized. The captain leaves last, she told herself. She shouted through the din: "Everyone! Go! Out the side door!" While she stood her ground.

More explosions. Sparks and glowing chunks shooting everywhere: onto her clothes, into her hair. She swatted them; stomped on them like a deranged folk dancer trampling hot coals from hell. Smoke...then silence.

She cautiously approached the berserk stove, wary lest it attack her again. Not a trace of fire. Not a single ember left. Just a blank-faced, empty cylinder.

"You can come back in, now," she called out. She stood before them at the front of the room, trembling, one side of her covered in white ash. Bullets. Bullets in the stove, he had said.

"Am–am I so bad a teacher that you want to set me on fire?" Silence. Her chest heaved, her heart pounded. She did not wait for an answer; she passed them by, walked past them, out the side door. Stared at the sky. Tears streamed down her face; they made pink tracks in the white ash.

She did not hear their whispers or their feet scurrying. Did not hear them sweeping. Scraping. Admonishing. It was Ingrid who finally tugged at her skirt. "Miss Sweetly. Please come back in." Betty wiped her eyes as surreptitiously as she could. They were all there, all fifteen of them, standing inside the doorway, soot-stained and anxious.

"It's okay, now, Miz Sweetly. We swept up the worst of it. Wiped it, too. There's hardly even a burn mark on the floor." It was Alec.

They returned to their seats, still watching her, wide-eyed. She stood under the portrait of deceased King George; she had no idea how long. Not a word passed her lips. When the bus rumbled up the hillside, they slipped away one-by-one. Although she did not move from the far end of the room, she could still see them, framed by the classroom entrance.

See them crowd around little Donny. See Alec shaking him. The little fellow more stunned than ever as they collectively cursed him. "Dim wit! Shit-for-brains! Burn our teacher! Why did you do it? Dumb bell!"

Shock gave place to astonishment. There had been no ring-leading saboteur at all. Just Donny—the last one I would have suspected.

Fresh tears stained her cheeks, but tears no longer stemming from betrayal, fire and fear. They had called her *Our Teacher*. Acceptance, at last!

It was Len who showed her: bullets embedded into cracks in the firewood. Undetected by Alec, the stove loader.

Great big bugger Alec, she thought. My ally. My defender.

~ Ж ~

Two days later, while Betty was teaching Language Arts, the explosive fire now far from her mind, she heard voices outside the schoolhouse. And a distinctive belch. Bill Trent was speaking in a formal, deferential manner. She froze. Omigod! Bill's brought Mr. McIntyre, the school inspector! She swung around the room in horror, seeing it through the inspector's eyes: textbooks in disarray, scrawlings across the blackboards, loose papers on her desk, mud streaks on the fire-damaged floor. And herself, with her pathetic boots, mud stains zigzagging up their sides. Unpressed blouse. Porcupine Casserole-stained skirt.

188

"Good morning. May we come in?" She nodded dumbly. Bill entered, followed by a man in a Mountie uniform. This was not Mr. McIntyre! Relief flooded through her and she began to breathe normally again.

"Miss Wheatley, this is Constable Kayke. He's down from the Nakusp detachment for a little visit."

"How do you do?" Then, remembering her teacherly etiquette, she added, "Class, stand and welcome Constable Kayke."

The class greeted him with the correct, classroom chant. She could have kissed them—they had done it right.

Constable Kayke, a huge beefy man, as massive and fierce as an Angus bull, pawed the ground and snorted. "It has come to my attention that someone in this class has been playing with bullets, eh?"

Fear and anger raced through Betty. Len the janitor! That darn Len! She had felt sure he would keep the incident a secret. He hadn't reported the chimney fire to any one, as far as she knew.

"Who's the culprit? Who's been playing Sons of Freedom here, eh?"

Not so much as a face muscle twitched. Constable Kayke turned to Betty. "Got any ideas, Miss Wheatley?" Betty shook her head. Little Donny in reform school? Locked up with the Sons of Freedom? No! She wouldn't tattle on a baby.

"Boys. Girls." Constable Kayke methodically eyed each student as though they were in a police line-up. "You were lucky no one was killed. Or burned. Miss Wheatley could have been scarred for life!" Donny slunk down in his seat. "And you're lucky the bullets were only .22s. Shotgun shells or .303s could have killed half of you. Legs and arms flying out the windows! I'd be hunting down the offender like it was Judgment Day. I'd take you away in chains like a wild dog. I'd keep you in prison until you rotted! You better have a talk amongst yourselves. I don't want to come back here for any stupidity again, eh?" He ran a steely eye over each of them and landed it with double-strength on Betty.

"Good. Now take these papers home. Tonight, up at the high school, I'm giving a lecture on first aid. I want at least one of your parents to attend. You be there, too, Miss Wheatley, eh?" His voice became even more ponderous. "My lecture could make the difference between life and death, any day in your life." He lowered his eyebrows and zinged them one more stern look. "After what's happened in your school, this lesson is most timely."

"I–I'm sure the children will pass on the message, and I will be happy to attend, thank you. Class, stand and say good-bye to Constable Kayke."

This time, the singsong voices were weak and rattled. Just like Betty's.

~ ж ~

Once the students were gone, she reviewed the unsettling visit objectively. A policeman. Next a school inspector. Ho boy. From one hurdle to the next. I'm against the wire, she concluded. A disgrace. And time is running out. If I don't perform way above the call-of-duty, I've got no future at all.

And...and I actually like being a teacher! Our teacher, they'd said. "Our teacher," she whispered to the doorframe; it nodded agreement. "Our teacher," she sang to the blackboards; they shimmered with delight. "Our teacher!" she shouted, and dead King George radiated down his royal approval.

She stared at the ceiling with religious fervour. I vow to any presence who cares, that I'll be ready for the inspector, and I will become the best teacher in the entire Dominion of Canada! I'll make more time for the fine details, even if I have to stay here all night. I'll pull them up to grade level and beyond! Amen. She was Joan of Arc again, speaking to the angels.

She stepped down from a golden cloud and looked around. What a slovenly room! What a terrible impression! I must start now. Today.

~ ж ~

Constable Kayke had a large audience at the high school. "Ladies, Gents, I'm here on behalf of the Red Cross. It's a long drive to Doc Porter's office, and a longer drive up to the hospital. So it's up to you to save your own lives. And I'm here to help you." He bent his stiff mouth into a smile. "You may wonder, why old Constable Kayke? Well, some of us have to be Jacks-of-all-trades, especially up here in the backwoods, eh?" He laughed in a self-congratulatory way.

"I need someone to be the accident victim."

Betty-the-would-be-actress, who normally would have jumped at any request to play a part, studied her dying aviator boots instead. Not me, she said to herself. Let you slam me with more reprimands? In public? No sir, Constable Kayke.

Constable Kayke's searching stare halted at a gaunt, sallow complexioned woman who was standing next to the minister of the New Testament Tabernacle. It was Mrs. Sunders, the trapper's wife, owner of a hundred cats. Constable Kayke's probably wondering if she needs first aid for her flea-bitten skin, Betty thought. But Mrs. Sunders took his attention for a command and walked to the front of the room as though hypnotized by the Constable's

190

authoritative gaze. Mrs. Sunders and her perfumes: Eau de cat pee, Parfum de mothball. Kayke flinched.

Mrs. Sunders straightened her rounded shoulders and became a woman with a purpose. She telegraphed a look of pride to the Venerable Reverend Hanginger of the New Testament Tabernacle. Betty was positive she could see an aura of light surrounding the blissful woman.

Constable Kayke began to discuss sprains, cuts and broken bones, wrapping the accommodating Mrs. Sunders in a variety of splints, bandages and tourniquets. Frequently, he turned from her to draw in fresh air.

Artificial respiration he described rather delicately. As a prudent constable, he could not, although she smiled encouragingly, bring himself to straddle the back of the prone and obliging Mrs. Sunders, or to place his hands on her rib cage.

He discussed heart attack symptoms and the handling of epileptic fits. He demonstrated supportive handholds for carrying patients out of the bush, described the search for and removal of wood ticks and lice, the treatment for bee stings and snake bites. First, second and third degree burns. The listeners, awed by the litany of catastrophe, tried valiantly to keep up with the flood of information.

"Now for the eyes. If someone has got something stuck in their eye, they shouldn't rub it. They could tear the eyeball, resulting in blindness. If Mrs. Sunders has something in her lower lid, this is what she does." Constable Kayke whispered in Mrs. Sunders' ear.

Mrs. Sunders, loving front stage, beaming her pride to the minister, obliged by pulling forward her lower lid and pantomimed wiping it with a handkerchief.

"If she gets something under her upper lid, she lifts it, wiggles her lower lid, and allows the lashes of the lower lid to remove the object." Mrs. Sunders obliged.

"However, if Mrs. Sunders still cannot remove the object, there is another procedure." Constable Kayke produced a wooden matchstick. "I will roll Mrs. Sunders's eyelid up and around the stick until I can spot the object. Once seen, I can remove it with the handkerchief and then let down the lid." As he spoke, Constable Kayke performed the technique, rolling Mrs. Sunders's eyelid up on the matchstick. Her grin became transfixed. After an imaginary swipe with the handkerchief, he unrolled the eyelid and stepped forward, as if to receive the applause one might get as a magician after an amazing trick. The audience, however, gasped in horror. Some inner part of Mrs. Sunders' eyelid had slithered down from its lair and shrouded her eyeball with its red, wet, thick membrane.

"Blink your eye, Mrs. Sunders, blink!" Constable Kayke looked shocked. The brave Mrs. Sunders did so without success. Each time she reopened her eye, the offending, unsightly inner skin remained down on her eyeball. "Keep your eye shut, Mrs. Sunders, for a bit."

Still to no avail. Now Mrs. Sunders, too, looked frightened. Tears glazed the offended eyeball, sliding out from under the trembling lid. Every witness was frozen; in a state of shock—except for the New Testament Tabernacle minister, the village pervert, who elbowed his way to the front of the room.

Constable Kayke's composure, like the core of an aged cottonwood tree, was disintegrating. "I think I uhhh ahhgh —"

It was the New Testament Tabernacle minister who uttered calming beatific words, who threw Mrs. Sunders' coat over her shoulders, who ushered her out the door to Constable Kayke's patrol car. Gravel flew as the threesome sped away.

"Crikey, that Kayke's an arse. He couldn't pour piss outa a boot, if the instructions was printed on the heel." It was a voice from the rear of the crowd that had pushed toward the door in the trio's wake. "I don't intend to pay no mind to what he says about nothin'."

The dazed audience filed out of the schoolroom. Betty and her two fellow teachers followed the walkers down the hill. The procession of flashlights lit the slush underfoot.

"Hope she don't go blind. Sure as ther's shit in a dead dog, they's hauled her down to Doc Porter's." The same voice. Betty turned to see who had spoken. It was Alec's father. Mr. Detweiler.

Constable Kayke never did return to finish the course.

Chapter 20

Go directly—see what she's doing,
and tell her she mustn't.
—Punch

The Vancouver sun shone brilliantly as Cameron cupped her face in his hands. "I'd forgotten how stunning you are."

Stunning! Betty bathed in the word, tasted it. Stunning. She twirled her long hair and expanded her chest. "Wait until you see my new clothes."

He grinned. "I prefer to see what's under them."

Hand-in-hand they stowed her suitcases in the bus stop lockers, hand-in-hand they walked to the Honey Dew Café, where they ignored their lunch, engaging instead in a pas de deux: feather-touch of hands, curve-invitation of shoulders, soft-whisper of lips—body language in total sync.

"...and then I even visited the Trail school inspector. He was really nice, this time. He's giving me a teaching position near town. Next year I can live at home."

"And you'll be closer to Vancouver. To me." Cameron's voice, his eyes caressed her. So few words, so much said. Betty reached out her hand; Cameron enveloped it in his. Here, now, with in-the-flesh Cameron, Betty felt sublimely confident, infinitely safe.

"And I've made wonderful plans—four whole days of them! Including a hotel room. For four days and nights." She lowered her eyelashes, he arched his eyebrows: pas de deux.

Perfection. Bliss. Almost, thought Betty, too good to be true.

~ Ж ~

As they approached the corner of Granville and Georgia, Betty took a deep breath and plunged into the pivotal point, the key element, the crux of her plan: "Before we go to the Avalon Hotel, I thought we should go to Woolworth's, and we could purchase an imitation wedding and engagement ring, and when we go to the hotel, they'll think we're married, and we can register as a couple."

Cameron stopped dead, as if he had bumped into an invisible wall.

"Woolworth's? That's a crazy idea, Betts. Be reasonable. Any fool could tell the rings are fakes."

Betty's smile slipped away; the tidy strings around her fantasy began unravelling. "But if we don't look married, then how can we register together?"

Cameron retied Betty's strings, tied them into knots of his own design. "Easy. You register; I'll sneak in later. Besides, it'll cost less and you don't have much dough. It's the only logical way, Betts."

Betty's winter-long dream now lay in shreds under Cameron's brown oxfords. What did logic have to do with her plans?

The hotel was seedier than what she expected. "I'm scared. What if the desk clerk catches you sneaking in and calls the police?"

"I doubt it. This place is so run down I don't think the clerk would do guard duty, too. Probably even let whores use the place."

Whores. Betty hated the ugly word and its implications. She flashed him a look of concern. "Will the clerk think I'm a prostitute?"

He shrugged. "Piss on him. Why would you care what he thinks?"

"I do care." Her eyes welled. "Do I look like a prostitute? Do you think I look like a prostitute? Do you think that me coming down here like this makes me a prostitute?"

Nineteen year-old Cameron looked bewildered. "Geez, Betty, I think you look absolutely wonderful; I can't even begin to imagine how lucky I am to get you. It's just that I don't give a shit what some clerk thinks."

"Please, Cameron, don't get angry and swear."

His voice rose. "I'm not swearing; I'm not angry." He shook his head. "How do I get myself into these fixes? All I want to do is get up there and be alone with you."

"Okay. As long as you aren't losing your respect for me. I couldn't stand it if you thought I was a dyed-hair brazen hussy."

His eyes opened with astonishment. He set down the suitcases, put his hands around her shoulders and drew her close, then gently removed her eyeglasses and looked into her eyes. "I love you. Every inch of you. Red hair and all."

"Oh, Cameron." He had said the magical words. Encouraging echoes of pas de deux.

"Besides, it's almost brown again, the way I like it. Let's get going, or we'll spend all our precious time out here on the sidewalk."

~ Ж ~

A baggy-eyed desk clerk looked up at Betty from his books. "Whaddya want?"

"A room for four nights."

"One person?"

"Yes." She wondered if her face was a give-away.

"Nine bucks a night."

"Nine?" It seemed a lot.

"Take it or leave it. You gotta pay up front each day. Gimme the nine now. Stairs over there. No elevator."

She clunked the suitcases up three flights, getting breathless as she reached the top. *Maybe I shouldn't have packed everything I own.* She found the room. Tried to unlock the door. Couldn't. She tried again, with no luck.

Finally she heard footsteps on the creaky wooden stairs. It was Cameron. By now, she was crying.

Wordlessly, he took the key and the door instantly opened. They entered; he closed the door with his foot, ending up slamming it. He dropped the suitcases and folded her in his arms. "I thought of something after you left."

"What?" Tears turning to relief as he wrapped her close to him.

"Prostitutes don't carry two suitcases."

~ Ж ~

Betty opened her eyes and smiled at Cameron's arm draped over her shoulder. *What a miracle to wake up and still have him with her, his body entwined around hers.* She nestled closer. Cameron stirred. She turned to face him. "Hello." She ran her finger over his ear, his cheek, his lips.

He groaned. "Damn thing's hard again. It'll be the death of me." He kissed her. Moved his hands over her body. "Christ, you feel so smooth. I'll never get enough of you."

Betty smiled. *From famine to feast. No sex since Christmas, and now my lover keeps the bedsprings singing all night long.*

Betty ran herself a bath, the deepest she had ever had. No Granny here, to remind her how much wood it takes to heat water. No Dad to complain, either. She even stopped up the overflow drain on the tub to fill it as high as its curved edge would allow. She stepped into it and sighed. What heaven, she thought. She closed her eyes, then opened them as she felt waves forming in the tranquil water.

"I couldn't resist," Cameron murmured as he settled on top of her. At first they created tiny ripples. Then the ripples became waves. The waves became surf. And the surf slopped over the tub edge.

A loud, insistent knocking on the door of the hotel room pulled Betty back from climactic reverie. She pushed off Cameron-the-wave-generator, climbed out, slipped on spillover water and pulled a towel around herself. The pounding was now accompanied by a loud complaining voice. Was it the police? Did they know she was here with an unregistered guest? Her heart was beating like a tom-tom. She opened the door and peered around it, hiding her barely covered body.

The baggy-eyed desk clerk was now much more lively looking. "What the hell are you doing in the bathtub?" he shouted.

"Uhhh practising," she stammered. "Practising the breast stroke. I–I'm a life guard." No skepticism on the baggy-eyed desk clerk's face. So she grew bolder. "I'm practising for the Olympics. I'm going to Helsinki." Some buried instinct from childhood, left over from all those years of self-preservation in a house of conflict, was advising her. When in doubt, lie big.

"Water is dripping down into the room beneath yours! Down into the light globe! Down the walls!" yelled the desk clerk. "You play seal in some other swimming pool or you're outa here, miss."

Betty drew herself up to her full five-foot-two. "Well, if I must, I'll quit. But don't blame me if I lose in Helsinki."

She shut the door, dropped the towel, and skidded back to the tub. And Cameron.

They ended up having breakfast at Woolworth's. She had looked longingly at the fake diamond section of the jewellery counter as she passed it, but Cameron seemed not to notice. They wolfed down bacon and eggs, ordered extra toast, beaming satisfaction at each other non-stop.

~ Ж ~

I'm a city girl at heart, thought Betty. Happiest when I'm where Man has triumphed over Nature. Jostling crowds, their perfume and sweat. Noisy traffic. Arcing trolley buses. Multi-storied buildings butting up against one another. The smell of fresh tar pothole patches on Granville, of vinegar-soaked fish and chips at English Bay, of caged bear stench at Stanley Park Zoo—so many reassuring signs of Man in control.

The civilized interlude was speeding by.

On the third morning, when she opened her eyes, she found Cameron lying awake, gazing at her. "I'd like to stay here with you forever. Hunh—only once last night then I slept like a baby—I guess a guy could eventually get used to sleeping with a pretty girl."

Today, instead of touring, they went shopping. At least Betty did. Cameron followed like a well-trained Spaniel. She bought some clothes, had her hair done, went to Purdy's Chocolates to buy Easter eggs.

This was the big night, their special, last night. Dinner at the Vancouver Hotel, then off to the Commodore Club.

The Commodore, epitome of her dreams: huge and ornate, with polished, springy floors, and an urbane dance band that deftly translated the current waltzes, fox-trots, rumbas into 'big band' sound for a tuxedoed and beaded crowd that could be extras on any Hollywood night-club set.

What a contrast to the Narrows dances! No sneaking outside to drink booze behind the hall. No do-si-dos and cleated boots. No heehaws. No clothing washed until every colour blended. Then the kind, outgoing faces of the Narrows dancers flashed in her head and she experienced waves of disloyalty.

~ Ж ~

"Cam. We have to pretend that tomorrow is Easter Sunday, because Easter Sunday I won't be here," she said, once they had returned to their room. "And we're going to have an Easter egg hunt first thing in the morning. You hide some for me to find. I'll hide some for you."

"What? You're crazy. Me run around looking for bunny droppings?" Even the adoring Cameron had his limits. She knew this; but she persisted.

"You have to. I've bought the eggs. First class chocolate."

"No. Be reasonable. I'd feel like a Tinkerbell—a goddamn fool prancing around in my birthday suit."

Her smile disappeared; her shoulders drooped.

"Betty," Cameron said in a pleading, coaxing voice, "I can't."

"Yes, you can. Just be like a child again."

"I can't."

She hung her head.

He sighed. "Oh, okay, give me the stupid eggs, I'll hide them, but I'm not going around hunting for them in the morning. The whole idea is ridiculous." He climbed off the bed and while she covered her eyes, he wandered around the room, hiding the eggs. She was elated. It was a sign: he cared enough to override his inhibitions. When he returned, he jumped on top of her. "That's going to cost you at least a kiss."

She imitated Mae West. "Try and get it, Big Boy." The egg business had put them both in the mood to play.

Betty awoke at dawn. She could not sleep any longer. In a few hours it would be over, and they would part again. It would be far, far harder than ever before, now that they had had four days of such closeness. She lay there, memorizing Cameron's features, listening to his breathing, savouring the intimacy.

After a while, she blew gently in his face. He opened his eyes and smiled. "Happy Easter," he said.

She sat up. "Can you imagine, I had forgotten about the eggs!"

He grinned. "Now that is a fairy tale."

"Yes, I did," she said as she circled the room, looking for the hiding places. She wore nothing, and his eyes roamed over her body as she searched. He just sat in bed, grinning ear-to-ear.

A strange seven o'clock breakfast: chocolate eggs and sex.

~ ж ~

"Your bus doesn't leave until evening. Do you mind if we spend the day together at the university? I'm worried about taking so much time off; my finals start next week."

She nodded emphatically. "Sure. I've got some important things I should do, too—make up a list of library books for my kids and study about softball."

~ ж ~

From the campus bus stop, Betty and Cameron strolled down Main Mall, a wide boulevard of groomed grass, trimmed hedges, a fountain and a reflecting pool. So civilized, Nature fully tamed, so absolutely perfect,

198

thought Betty. On either side of the boulevard stood grey Haddington stone buildings: stately, conservative, befitting their academic importance. Pacific dogwoods in full bloom. Chestnut, oak, Sitka spruce, Douglas fir stood tall and proud, like sentinels guarding the buildings, protecting academic freedom. Betty nodded approval. All of this. Put here by Man. No overpowering wilderness here. She inhaled the faint whiff of seashore, of ancient rain forest. Just enough. Perfection.

Cameron steered her toward one of the buildings, set back from the Mall, with a large green commons in front of it. Students lounged about, talking, reading, soaking in sunshine as they gazed at the bright blue sky. An arched, massive doorway beckoned. Above it, emblazoned in stone: The University of British Columbia Library. As impressive as a castle, a home for King Arthur and every one of his knights, thought Betty. But when they entered the building, it was the thousands of books that overwhelmed her. There must be enough, she decided, to educate every person in the world.

At noon they ate at the university cafeteria, a new experience that she enjoyed. More people passed by in a minute than she saw in a month at Narrows. She stared at them wistfully. How nice it would have been to be a student here. But it had never been an option in her life.

"Cam. How come there are so few girl students?" she asked as they returned to the library.

"Most girls come for one year. Two at the most. They come to get their 'MRS' degree."

Maybe I look like a student, here, too. Me and my pile of books. She sat at the far end of the same library table as Cameron. In front of her were strewn books on softball. She was studying coaching techniques, when a girl approached Cameron.

"Hi, Cameron. Hard at it, no doubt?"

"Oh, ahh, hi, Kathy... Yes. I am." As he rose, he knocked a pile of books onto the floor. "Kathy, I'd like you to meet...ahh...a friend of mine from home. Betts. Betty Wheatley."

"Hello. Studying...softball!" The girl flashed Betty a look of condescension. Turned back to Cameron. "Cam, I wonder if you have time before exams to help me with my spherical trig?"

"Uhh, well, I'm sorry, Kathy, but I'm kinda short of time right now. Could you find someone else, maybe?"

"Oh, sure, I just thought I'd ask you first, Cam. See you later. 'Bye." She sashayed off to a nearby table, where, with her books propped as an excuse, she could watch Cameron's interaction with Betty. Betty shot her enemy a look of resentment. She's as transparent as water, Betty thought, she doesn't need help with her math.

A shivery feeling infused Betty as she sat there, watching the pretty, well-dressed girl. She looked the epitome of the campus belle. So this was the Kathy, the so-called temporary date his chums had found for him. The Kathy he had taken to parties and danced with. Closely, no doubt. Just like high school students Steve Waterbrook and Charlotte Patten.

She studied Cameron's face as he concentrated on his work. Not once did he look at the girl. But the sight of this Kathy so near to Cameron unnerved Betty, gnawed at her. As it conjured up Steve and Charlotte's window-framed coupling, it threw her into turmoil.

~ Ж ~

They walked through an endless drizzle to the bus station. "Cam. I have to ask you something." He was holding her hand. Betty pulled it away. "That girl, Kathy. You didn't even tell her I'm your girlfriend."

"I told her you're my friend, that's the same. She could see you're a girl." But when he saw the expression on Betty's face, he hurriedly added, "Betts, she couldn't hold a candle to you. It was just as I told you: two dates, then the Engineer's Ball. I never took her out again. It's you I care for. I love you."

Betty persisted. "She's so pretty. So perfectly ladylike. Classy."

Cameron shrugged, reached for Betty's hands again. "She's a swell girl. A friend. I admit that, but it's you I love, not her. What more can I say?"

A loudspeaker blared. "... 23 in Bay 6 now boarding for Hope, Penticton, Grand Forks, Trail,"

"Cameron." She plunged into her previous night's thoughts. "Lots of students get married before they graduate. Maybe we could get married this summer." She held her breath while she awaited his response.

A worried frown replaced the look of affection. "That's out of the question. I can't support a wife. I can't even support myself; my parents have to kick in money after Christmas every year."

"I can support us."

He stared down at the concrete platform, at the splayed cigarette butts, at the blackened chewing gum. "Betts, I have to work like crazy to get top marks, you know that. The best jobs go to those with the best marks. And the responsibility of a wife—I just couldn't handle it. Besides, if we were living together, we'd probably end up having a baby, and that would be the end of my schooling. I've got to get that degree. I don't want to slave away in the Trail smelter all my life, and that's what I'd have to do."

"I love you. Please be patient with me. I've got two more years of this pressure-cooker life." As always, despite the persistence in Betty's voice, despite the fact that she had brought this subject up one way or another over and over again with increasing desperation, Cameron replied with the same calmness, the same gentle but persistently unassailable explanations.

Betty blinked back tears. "Could we get married in secret then, this summer, and not tell anyone, so that I'd have something to hang onto?"

He semi-smiled, then shook his head sorrowfully. "Betty, that's not possible. Be reasonable. That wouldn't work, either. There's no logic in what you're asking."

The tears came. She could not stop them. "Two years is a long time to be apart."

He shook his head. "I can't help the way things are. The world doesn't turn for just you and me."

"Maybe you'll find someone else. Maybe the next girl your buddies find will be more attractive to you."

The light in his eyes dulled. "Maybe you'll fall for some lumberjack or that teacher, Leslie. It cuts both ways. Please, Betts, don't end our wonderful time like this!"

Pas de deux: completely vanquished. Overwhelmed by the exhaust-pipe fumes of bus terminal reality.

~ Ж ~

Betty could not shake the feeling of despair during the entire ten-hour bus ride to Trail. Despite the glorious four days, despite the reassurances Cam had tried to give her, she did not feel their relationship was secure. The letter-references during the early spring had been hard enough to rationalize, but confronting the living, breathing Kathy was another matter. Now, disquieting Kathy images vied with one another inside her aching head.

Kathy, with her perfect oval face, her unmistakable aura of a well-bred, moneyed background, her strategic advantage: she was six hundred miles closer to Cameron. And she radiated virginal purity that gave Betty an uncomfortable sense of being a tarnished object. Used goods.

Betty rehashed the conversations she had had with Cameron. If only he had come up with some sort of commitment to her, other than just an avowal of love. Why doesn't he understand that the Woolworth rings would have been something palpable for me to hang onto?

The idea of waiting for two uncertain years was unbearable, especially in rural school limbo. She began to resent his pragmatism, his ambition. Surely they did not have to wait two years? Others married while still at school.

Or maybe he doesn't mean to marry me at all; maybe he doesn't really even love me. I'm just an Easter convenience who pays her own way and his, too.

Finally, tiring of conflicting, tangled, emotions, she began to sort through her options: if he doesn't come up with a tangible commitment, I'll plan a new life. To hell with Cameron! To hell with becoming the best teacher in the world! I won't teach school any longer than one more year. If he isn't meant to be mine, I'm going to become an actress and mix with the dregs of Hollywood society. Your fault, Cameron. Leaving me for a rich society girl. A virgin. I'll punish you; I'll be Betty-the-Quitter with a capital Q!

She calmed down.

~ Ж ~

Back in Trail, her mother's oratory filled the kitchen. "Betts, I'm so surprised at you. You should hear yourself. How could you have such a defeatist attitude: your roommate is terrible, your students are naughty, your Cameron is untrustworthy. And now it's crazy dreams of becoming an actress again. Running off to Hollywood."

"It's time you took hold of yourself. You'll be twenty in June, for goodness' sake. And besides, you've only got two months of teaching left."

Betty's facial muscles tensed. She clenched her fists and fixed on her mother's mouth as it opened and closed. Like a merciless talking machine.

"Don't be so timid, Betts. It's a terrible curse. Speak up for yourself! Tell off that roommate Kate! Tell off that odd Georgika! And this business with Cameron? Oh, Lord! You and your absolutely crazy imagination, at it again — you're wrong about him, I'm sure. You should send him a letter of apology, you should..."

Betty snapped like a too-taut elastic band. "Sh–shut up, Mother! Stop giving me so much damned advice. You don't listen right. You don't have a clue how I feel!"

Nora's mouth behaved like that of a gasping fish, before it clamped itself into a grim line. Her choked-off words were almost inaudible. "By God — you're as blind to reason as your father. All I've ever tried to do was help. Go ahead, live your own life and I'll live mine." She stalked off to her bedroom.

Lord, Lord, I've gone mad; I yelled at my mother; I told her to... shut up! She'll never forgive me. All because of Cameron! He's turned me into some kind of crazy crab-apple like Kate—him and his new girlfriend Kathy—and now he's made me lose the love of my mother! She felt, for the first time in her life, completely, totally alone. All her bridges cut off from the woman she loved, had clung to—before this Cameron fiasco—with total, uncritical obeisance.

Her father, as if on cue, surfaced from the basement and stood in the doorway until his eyes adjusted to the spring sunshine that flooded through the windows. She realized that he had heard her mutinous words; heard her cut her beloved mother beyond redemption.

The corners of his mouth curved upwards. "Now you've done it, Betts. You better hang out in the cellar with me from now on. Where'd you get the guts to tell her Highness off? Listening to me?"

Betty was confounded to hear him including her in his camp. Appalled. Does rejection by one mean acceptance by the other?

Glen stood there, owl-eyed, with a sorry sweep of soot on his forehead.

Betty saw him in a new light: He hides down there, hides from everyone, in a dark cellar with only a sawdust burner for company. Comes upstairs to counter-attack by bluster and bully, runs down there again, or runs off to the Legion. Guerrilla warfare, hit-

and-run. Like Mao Tse Tung.

"Make some tea," he commanded his perceived ally.

Betty bristled, but only momentarily. She made his tea. Then, like dipping a toe into an untested mountain pond before diving in, she tentatively consolidated the new alliance. "I'd like to thank you, Dad."

"For what?"

"For driving up last fall and bringing me my supplies. I had no idea at the time what a horrible drive it was for you."

"Someone had to do it."

"And it must have been hard on your Henry J," said Betty.

"Yeah. The finish got its share of dings."

She swallowed hard. "I could pay for the damage."

"No need. It's not that bad..." His tone changed to one he normally reserved for friends. "You've nearly done the school term, Betts. You hung in there. Survived winter in Dogpatch."

"Thanks."

"Did real good, just like I'd expect of a...a son." He returned to the basement.

Adult-to-adult conversation. This is the first compliment—sort of— he's ever given me, she realized. It feels good. So he's equating me to a son? The son he never had?

Poor Dad. A legacy of four women and a sawdust burner. Poor Mother. A bully for a husband and an ungrateful daughter. It's a good thing she still has one obedient daughter: Faye. It's a good thing I'm taking my miserable self back to Narrows. I belong with Kate. We're two of a kind. Bêtes noires.

~ Ж ~

It was dark when she got off the Minto. She lugged her suitcases up the hill.

"Hello there, Betsy, dear. Did you have a good time? I've got news

204

that you won't want to hear. Inspector McIntyre is heading our way." Mrs. Allan and Granny greeted her in the kitchen. The warmth in the eyes of the well-padded, comforting figures made Betty feel less alone.

She tried to muster a smile, but the weight of Cameron's infidelity, the shock of the battle with her beloved mother would not allow for such a luxury. Not a successful Easter. Not at all.

"Are you all right, Betty? Didn't get sick from tearing 'round the country, did you?" Concern in Granny's face.

"I'm okay. I just need some sleep. It's nice to see you both. But I certainly don't relish facing Inspector McIntyre." It had taken her three days to get back to Narrows, three days of coed Kathy-thoughts.

They tried to erase the forlorn look on her face. Granny bustled to make fresh tea. Mrs. Allan began a litany of reassuring chitchat.

"Kate's back. She never did go to Vancouver; she only went as far as Nelson. She's bought some great new clothes. I had a few days in Nelson myself. Had a lovely time with my nephew's family. We've missed you around here. Don't you worry about Inspector Robbie McIntyre, he's nothing special, I can assure you. You'll see for yourself Saturday when he speaks to us at the meeting in Edgewood."

Betty had forgotten about the teachers' luncheon.

Good. An excuse to dress up will help. I can wear the knitted dress I bought in Vancouver. Maybe fellow-teacher Leslie will be impressed—no Kathy-types trying to distract him.

A bouquet of tulips sat festively on the dining room table along with four Aynsley cups and saucers and a plate of fresh biscuits. They had obviously been looking forward to her return. She was grateful.

Brisk footsteps. Kate appeared, sporting an air of self-satisfaction. It took Betty only a split second to notice that something was missing: the crutches.

"Hi, Betty, good to have you back. Did these two tell you my news?" She looked expectantly at Granny and at Mrs. Allan.

"Heavens, Kate, it's not in our place to say anything," said Mrs. Allan.

"Certainly not," echoed Granny.

"Well, my case with the boy who smashed into my van is over. His parents settled out of court. And I've finally got the whole business out of my life." Betty had never seen her so happy.

"Are you seeing that new fellow Kurt Guttemann at all these days?" Betty asked.

"He wants me to. I'm still of two minds. It doesn't hurt to keep them dangling." Kate looked pleased with her cocky response. "How was your trip to Vancouver? Did you have a good visit with Cameron?"

Betty disciplined the tears. "I nearly decided to give up being a teacher. I was going to become an actress, but I changed my mind. I don't care if I become an old maid teacher, anyway."

Just in case spinster Kate spit out a sarcastic reply, Granny brought up a more immediate, important subject: "Who wants the first cup— the weak one—of tea?"

They asked Betty no further questions.

~ Ж ~

Strains of The Volga Boat Song broke the silence of the valley. It was not too unpleasant to listen to; the pianist did not falter or repeat the same stanzas. But the refrain was being played in its most simplistic form—a beginner's book rendition.

The townspeople were tolerant. They went about their business, annoyed only when they found that they could not erase the song from their own minds and hummed:

> Duh, duh, duh, duh-duh-duhh,
> Yo ho heave ho.

It was then, when they caught themselves, they wished that Miss Wheatley would progress to a new song.

She had tidied the classroom, had marked the books, and had prepared a dozen extra ditto pad sheets.

She was indulging herself, playing the music that most mirrored her gloomy mood. It took a knock on the door to stop the repetitive tune.

"I've got Ma out there in the car, Betty, we're just back from the hospital in Vancouver." It was Tommy. "She's wondering if you have a few minutes for a visit."

Betty was shocked at the sight of Georgika's yellowed skin and drawn face.

"Sit in the car for a bit with me, Betty. I don't have the energy to come into your schoolroom." Georgika's smile was forced.

Betty slid into the driver's seat. Tommy sat on the school steps, drawing aimless circles in the sand.

"I'm just back. Had to have a bit more surgery."

"Ohhh, I'm so sorry to hear that."

"Nothing to worry about, I'll probably be as right as rain, soon, you'll see." Georgika patted Betty's shoulder. "I'm so darned tired, but I just had to stop by on my way home to see how you are and to ask you to come for a visit. Don't just come for a day, though—come for the whole weekend. It's been ages since we had a real good visit." There was a pleading quality to her voice.

"I'll come as soon as I can."

She did not move to kiss Betty, did not have the strength. "You will come, Betty, won't you?"

"You've got my promise." The whole weekend. Against everyone's advice. Pity, reluctance, loneliness, fear, all fought each other; mixed unpleasantly with her pessimistic thoughts about Cameron.

After they drove away, she returned to the piano. The community braced itself as the same melody once more drifted down the mountainside.

Chapter 21

Progress is strewn
with the bleached skeletons
of discarded theories.
—Arthur Koestler

Props. She needed props. A Havana cigar to wave around. A plug of chewing tobacco and a brass spittoon from Grampa Wheatley's billiards room would have helped.

She tossed the annoying, constantly slipping eyeglasses aside and assumed a male stance; toughened her voice and became Casey Stengel. "The softball game is only a month away, class, and I smell a mood of defeat. Get rid of it! We're going to practice lots and lots of defensive and offensive plays. Bunts. The crow hop. Backing up each position in case of error."

"Thank you God for the softball manual," she muttered.

The class shifted an iota away from total pessimism.

~ Ж ~

Since her return from Vancouver, Betty had, for survival, increasingly wrapped herself up in her job; allowing herself no time at all to think of Cameron. Self-discipline at fever pitch.

Because she was acutely aware that Inspector McIntyre could arrive at the door any day, any time, she had her planning book up-to-date. Every exercise book and workbook was marked as precisely as Gramma Wheatley's cross-stitch samplers. She was as ready for him as was possible—with one exception. She had a major stumbling block, one she had been postponing all year. Every grade's guidebook had the same frustrating topic: Initiate and conduct explorative projects regarding local geography, history and commerce. She could not postpone tackling it any longer.

The only resource she had was a B.C. road map. On the blackboard, she painted a map of the Arrow Lakes. She took special pains with it to impress Inspector McIntyre. But, to help her with the rest, there was nothing in Narrows: no text books, no printed matter. The only sources of local history and commerce, she concluded, had to be residing in the heads of the children's relatives.

"Class! I have a wonderful, unusual project for you. A project that will be a surprise for the whole community. I want you to be the recorders of this valley's history!" Blank expressions. "Were any of your grandparents pioneers?"

Helena nodded. "My grampa was. He built the S.S. Nakusp. But it burnt down and sank two years later."

"Yes, yes, yes!" Both of Betty's arms waved about. She became Arturo Toscanini conducting his musicians. "Yes! A perfect project, Helena, you've got your story. That's what I want!"

Raymond, usually so quiet, spoke up. "My gramps says lots of things burnt down in the old days. Houses and boats and barns. His house burnt twice. His orchard, too. He was so mad, he nearly moved back to England. And he said some city slicker lied to him about comin' here in the first place. Showed him a picture of a tree loaded with apples. My gramps says the guy was a faker: the apples were tied on with string."

"Oh, Raymond, there's your project. Wonderful! You have to get your grampa to help you write it."

"My dad and his brothers were breeding cows, and—" began Alec. A snicker sprung up amongst the nonfarm children. Alec glared at them. "Bred cattle that won awards!" That silenced them.

"Yes! Commerce! The lifeblood of the community!" The classroom music was alive and flowing.

Ingrid's dad had worked on the ferry. She had access to photos of all the ferries. Grant's dad had once worked on the Minto. He chose that topic. Eric's cousin worked at the box factory. That was his choice.

Fruit farming, logging, gold mining, sawmills and shingle mills; stories poured out—even an intriguing one from Margie about her grandmother working in a luxury hotel north of Nakusp.

The power of praise! marvelled Betty. She exhorted, emoted, rhapsodized and swung her invisible baton with gusto, and as she did so, their enthusiasm grew to a crescendo.

"You have two weeks in which to complete your topic. You'll glue your write-ups and drawings onto big sheets of manila paper and we'll hang them at the spring concert for the whole world to see!"

~ Ж ~

On Thursday morning, she arrived at the school to find the door already open. When she stepped inside, she saw a squarish, ruddy-faced man seated at her desk, studying her daily planning book. He shot out his hand as she approached.

"Inspector McIntyre. Good map you've prepared, Miss Wheatley." The school inspector wore his cloak of authority with as much aplomb as Granny wore her men's slippers. "Glad to see you're tackling the local geography. That's a rarity. Too many of my teachers tend to neglect it."

"The children are asking their families for information. It's hard to cover the geography and history lessons with no reference books." She winced. Too negative a response. Too whiny.

His eyes flew around the room. It was as if they were two days ahead of his body. He rocked back and forth on his heels, taking in all the vocabulary cards she had drawn, coloured and placed above the blackboards. The children's artwork and compositions she had pinned around the room. The two blackboards crammed with work—and near-perfect McLean's penmanship—for each grade.

"Geography and history reference books? We rely, Miss Wheatley, on your previous education for such knowledge. All that these children are to be taught was, supposedly, taught to, and grasped by you in your fourteen years of schooling."

Is he serious? she wondered. How could I, a Trail girl, have knowledge of the Arrow Lakes District? Nobody could study every nook and cranny of this province—it's big enough to swallow up the British Isles and have room to spare! But she did not dare contradict him.

"Constable Kayke says you've had some discipline problems in your classroom."

"Yes, sir."

"And did you punish the culprit?"

"I don't know who put the bullets in the stove."

"I see-ee." His words were loaded with portent. "I'll give the children a history lesson—local history—first thing this morning, Miss Wheatley. Rearrange your schedule so I can hear your reading lessons right afterwards, will you, please? It gives me a feeling for the students' progress."

"Certainly, Mr. McIntyre, I'd be happy to." Her throat constricted.

The class behaved like frightened sheep en route to the slaughterhouse. They tiptoed into their seats. Betty loved the gratifying bonus: they thought the inspector was there to judge them. They had no idea that it was she who was on the witness stand.

Inspector McIntyre spoke while seated at Betty's desk—a deliberate move that forced the children to twist around in their seats, their taut bodies now stretched to the limit. "Where, Miss Wheatley, do you keep your strap?" he asked in a saccharine voice.

"Bottom drawer, Mr. McIntyre." The classroom was deathly quiet, the children petrified.

"Do you use it often?"

"No, sir." She could not tell him the truth. 'Never' seemed so feckless.

He pulled out the ugly thing from her bottom drawer and slapped it onto her desk. Whaapp! The eyes of everyone, including Betty's, fixated on it.

My poor kids. Mr. McIntyre and the strap: control by fear. If he tells them to jump, they'll willingly bash their heads on the ceiling.

Now Mr. McIntyre moved with a measured strut to the front of the room. "Our vast country, Canada, was discovered by great explorers. One of the bravest was the first to set foot in this valley. Who can tell me his name? No one? You, boy. Do you know?"

Alec dropped his pencil. "Me, sir? Ahh...a Mister Selkirk?"

"Lord Selkirk? No, boy. Good guess, though. Good guess."

Betty looked at Alec with new respect. Picking on the local mountain range was creative guessing. Her own mind, now paralyzed, would not budge beyond Christopher Columbus.

"David Thompson. 1810. Was there anyone before him living up here?" His darting eyes caught Betty's regularly as though to say: "Watch me, watch how much I know; how well I do this!"

Only Howard had the courage to raise his hand. "Indians, sir." Betty could have hugged him.

"Yes. Good boy. A mix of the Salish, Colville and Kootenai tribes. Called themselves the Sun-ai-ach-kist. Do you know that they lived here long before Christ was born? 1300 BC!"

The class stayed unnaturally attentive; afraid to breathe. Betty, too. She wondered how long he could hold them in this state of attention. Was this his only secret for discipline? Strap on view? Once a month? Daily?

By the time she began the reading lesson, she could envision him strapping her, too, if she faltered. But gradually, she got into a steady stride.

Somewhere between the grade four and five oral reading, she saw him leave. She suffered a mixture of relief and disappointment. She looked at her watch. He had been there for just under an hour.

So that was it. One hour to size up my skills, my intelligence, my year's work and all my previous training. One hour to judge me as a success or a failure. One hour. No criticisms, no praise, no suggestions. Betty was as drained as a marathon runner crossing the finish line.

But maybe he plans to come back again. Or maybe on Saturday, at the conference in Edgewood in a more congenial setting, he might speak personally to me. Just in case, I'll keep up all the extra preparations until I'm positive he's out of the area.

~ Ж ~

In the Arrow Lakes Hotel at Edgewood, the Narrows' teachers, along with compatriots from Needles, Fauquier and King City trouped into the dining room. Kokanee teachers Leslie and Elaina were sitting at the head table. Elaina, normally a marvel of animated body parts—rolling eyes, seesaw eyebrows, sweeping arms and swivelling head—was not competing for the inspector's attention. Or Leslie's. Betty had never seen her so still. Even her face was devoid of life. Poor old Elaina, thought Betty—the inspector must have been hard on her, too.

Leslie served as spokesman, saying grace and, after a lunch of glutinous chicken à la king, introducing Inspector McIntyre:

"Yes indeed, Mr. McIntyre needs no introduction, but I wonder how many of you know of his outstanding background in pedagogy?" Leslie rhymed off the inspector's academic credentials, his succession of promotions. He did so without notes. "... and Mr. McIntyre was on the senior advisory committee to the Minister of Education that recommended the current curriculum for B.C. schools. Mr. McIntyre's opinion, it is more than fair to say, is sought regularly by his peers throughout the province. Please join me in a warm welcome for our superior, our mentor and our inspiration."

Kate screwed up her face during the applause. "That Leslie sure can shovel shit."

Inspector McIntyre launched into an evangelical speech on the 'tomfoolery of the so-called progressive education' that wa now, he claimed, 'seeping insidiously into the system'.

"...that learning can be fun is pure tommy-rot! If learning is fun, it isn't learning. Learning is hard work, concentration, discipline and constant drill, drill, drill... Mark my words, these new educationalists who heed the babblings of so called 'progressives'; who advocate the abolition of all examinations, class standing, and oh yes, corporal punishment, will deceive the student and ruin him for the years ahead...

"Discipline. Some of you, it has come to my attention, are having discipline problems. There is no excuse for failure to maintain discipline in the classroom. I do not see how you can have a student body learn anything, unless you maintain it in a state of discipline. Corporal punishment. You have a strap. Use it!"

Inspector McIntyre was not all passion and punishment, though. Once he had unloaded his pet peeves, he leaned toward his audience, his arms outstretched, embracing the whole room. "I have visited, now, ten of your classes in progress. I can say in all honesty that I am pleased with all those I have seen. I wouldn't hesitate to have you all back with me again, next year." He radiated a pontiff's smile as he accepted their enthusiastic and relieved clapping. The only one in the room who did not clap, Betty observed, was Elaina, who sat as still as a tree stump. Even her head barely wobbled. Inspector McIntyre raised his hand to quiet the crowd and said, "Now I'll entertain questions."

An audience did not intimidate Betty. She had been addressing an audience of fifteen children for nearly ten months, now. Her hand went up. After two teachers presented some carefully-worded flattering questions to him, it was Betty's turn. Her compatriots watched her with intense interest; they were seeing a braver Betty than they were used to.

"Mr. McIntyre, I would like to address the issue of trying to teach three science, three geography and three language courses at once. I heard what I considered to be a very practical solution from an experienced teacher, who suggested we teach only one of each of these on a revolving basis, co-coordinating our efforts with the teachers who have preceded us and the ones who will follow. I was impressed with the practicality of the idea. Would you give us your opinion on this?" She sat down, delighted with her daringness, her display of intelligence.

"Miss Wheatley...I have been presented with this dangerous proposition before. And...I must tell you it pains me that this idea of circumventing the prescribed courses still surfaces. Let me reiterate, with deep sincerity, that there are no shortcuts to knowledge. No shortcuts. None. You must—and I emphasize the word—you must teach all that is listed." He surveyed the room. "I hope you have all heard me clearly."

Kate's face had a wry smile on it. Edwin's looked troubled. Mrs. Allan whispered in Betty's ear. "Don't take it to heart, dear. He's just another version of the old saying, 'Don't do as I do, do as I say'. You can bet your boots that when he taught rural, he didn't cover everything, either. However, when one breaks the written rules, it's best not to vocalize it. I shouldn't have told you my easy way out. It's all my fault."

Betty did not remember a single word that was spoken during the rest of the conference.

~ Ж ~

"Alec. Would you lend me your jack-knife over night? I promise to return it first thing in the morning." As soon as the bus left, Betty pulled out the odious strap and slashed it into pieces.

To heck with Inspector McIntyre! Teaching by fear is not teaching by courage. If he comes back, I'll say one of the boys cut the strap up, right after his visit. No one will replace the thing for years, anyhow, if ever. Just like the clock.

Although Inspector McIntyre did not reappear in her class, she felt unsettled for days. She was sure she had talked herself out of a decent evaluation.

~ Ж ~

The days marched by much faster now that May had arrived. Betty could actually see ahead to the finish line, the end of the school year. Because the curriculum had to be completed by the year-end, she began to plan the lessons backwards, moving from the end of June up to the present day. She made adjustments, such as hurrying up the progress of the fifth-graders' arithmetic. Slowing down that of the sixth-graders'. Preparations for the spring concert, which was only a week away, ate into her teaching time, as did the softball practices.

She had them practicing softball basics—catching ground balls, stealing bases, batting low and high balls, bunting. She selected Alec and Bruce to practice pitching and back catching. They made a great team and were clearly the best for these positions. She guarded her well-thumbed coaching book as if it were heaven sent.

As her rapport with them on the field grew, so did her rapport in the classroom. Ever since the bullets in the stove, ever since the local 'history and commerce' projects, ever since she had lost her fear of an another Inspector McIntyre visit, she had been discovering new things: the value of praise, of initiative, of a relaxed attitude, of participation, and of being on stage. There was an upward learning-spiral in the classroom. She and the class had become a team.

She waited for them every morning on the school steps to hear their bits of news. And frequently got more from them than she should have.

"Miss Sweetly, could Hell freeze over? My ma says that's when my pa will stop drinking so much."

"Miz Sweetly, Jake made my ma laugh so hard her teeth fell out, an' he took out his own teeth and made them be puppets! My ma and me sure like Jake."

"Mr. Sunders, the trapper, says his wife, Mrs. Sunders, has turned night into day. How does she do that?" asked Raymond.

"I know," replied Helena. "She sleep walks all over town. Even on the ferry. My dad says she's a streetwalker."

"Is Nina Trent going to jail, Miz Sweetly? My pa saw Constable Kayke pat her bottom and she smacked him in the kisser!"

"The high school teacher Mr. Chalmers is really weird, Miz Sweetly. He just sits and sits at his window at the boarding house, watching everyone who gets off the ferry. With binoculars!"

The line between teacher and pupil was blurring: Betty joined them in the playground more often, and when her Bulova said it was time, she waved her hand and, without the bell and line-up ceremony, her flock followed her into the classroom.

Now, comfortable with the mechanics of manipulating three grades, she threw orthodoxy out the window.

"Twelve. A special number. Can you guess why it's so special?"

"We sell eggs by the dozen?"

"Good."

"There's twelve inches to a foot."

"Yes. Anything else?"

"Twelve months in a year."

"Super! There are many ways to make twelve by adding, subtracting and multiplying. Grade fours. How about you getting together and figuring out how many ways you can make twelve, using the numbers from one to eleven? Grade fives, list all the numbers that are divisible by twelve but are less than 360. Use lots of crazy colours to do so. Grade sixes, would you write a story, a rhyme, a song—your choice—about Farmer Brown and how he uses the number twelve in his approach to farming? Go to it, everyone! Remember, we're going out this afternoon on the school bus to see the Whatshan Dam."

Every other week she arranged for a tour: the Arlada Cheese Factory, the Kokanee Box Factory—even Kurt Guttemann's tombstone factory. Kate's new beau Kurt won the award for philanthropy: he handed out round magnifying glasses so they could see the different minerals in granite, see the mica, quartz and felspar, showed them how marble bubbles when a drop of acid is placed upon it, how slate splits easily along flat cleavage planes, then gave each child a bag of samples and a chunk of peanut brittle to take home. Kurt—not at all what he had appeared to be, thought Betty. Don't judge a book by its covering; he's not a Gloomy Gus after all.

It was her own brand of progressive education. She kept half her brain on the curriculum and let the other half twist the details into challenges. Despite the freer approach, she was covering more ground. The children were more alert and receptive. She could feel the progress; she was pleased with her performance.

~ Ж ~

The night of the concert arrived. When Betty entered the community hall, she saw groups making proud-parent noises as they gazed at the photographs, write-ups and drawings on the posters her pupils had designed and prepared. The parents had got caught up in 'Initiate and conduct explorative projects regarding local geography, history and commerce'. And the end results far exceeded her pupils' abilities.

Margie was sharing the limelight with her grandmother, whose lively personality eclipsed the shy girl's. "...and I waited tables at the old Halcyon Springs Hotel, a real grand place. Old General Burnham, he fancied me. Told me I was 'a fine specimen of a gel'. And..." Margie's grandmother was the loudest, but not the only relative indulging in showmanship.

"Yep, me and my brother learned what we needed, not from no book, but from Charlie Flick, down at Edgewood. Real skookum fella. Best durn cattle breeder in this here valley. We lets a Highland bull have a go at our Shorthorn cows, and, sure as a dog will sniff another dog's arse, we got ourselves some dandies..." It was once-dour Mr. Detweiler! His eyes flickered when they spotted Betty, but he did not miss a beat in his proud dissertation. Alec's father, Mr. Detweiler, the unlikeliest of show barkers.

Later, he sidled up to her. "Got to thinkin' 'bout yer question 'bout how much land I got. So I bought mesself some more. Yuh haven't fussed my boy. 'preciate it." He left as he had come, leaving Betty no time for questions. She could only assume from the civility of his manner that in his critical eyes she was doing some things right.

Betty was learning from the displays, too. Mr. Detweiler's cows were not ordinary cattle but 'Snowlanders', a crossbreed developed here in the valley from 'Polled Shorthorn' and 'Highland' cattle. Wooden boxes, Eric's poster explained, were made from spruce because it held nails well, and the lids were made from cottonwood because it bent easily.

Teacher Edwin Chalmers approached her. "Damnably fine example of teaching excellence, Miss Wheatley. You have inspired your young plodders admirably! Ah, 'study is like the heaven's glorious sun', my dear. You deserve la Légion d' honneur."

"Not quite, Mr. Chalmers, but they have done well."

"Indeed they have, Miss Wheatley. My highest commendations. I admire your leadership."

Praise at last, she noted with gratitude. Gratitude that inspired her to a generosity she never had meant to give. "Why don't you pop down to my school for the odd game of chess?"

"What a magnanimous invitation! I shall bring my board next Friday, then, if I may?" His eyes shone.

"Yes. That would be fine." Oh well, she thought, there's only a few weeks left. It won't kill me to be kind.

Mr. Detweiler approves of me and Mr. Chalmers has praised my teaching. Hah! Inspector McIntyre. What the heck do you know?

~ ɔɪc ~

Piano duets, recitations, Mrs. Allan's winsome innocents—all surpassed by Betty's pupils. Their musical skit stole the show—at least until Betty and Jake's son-in-law Curley McCloskey came on stage to jitterbug. Betty in her twirly pink felt skirt with a black felt poodle appliquéd to it. Curley in zootsuit pants, pulled chest-high by red suspenders. Betty with black and white saddle shoes and an exaggerated ponytail. Curley with a red bow tie and grease-slicked hair.

They started dancing just as they had practised. He twisted her under his arms, over his arms, slid around her, had her slide under him, forced her into faster footwork than at any practice. And then, for a finale, creative Curley discarded their rehearsal routine. He tried the back flip. He swung Betty high, high in the air, over his back. There was just a fraction of a second more needed for the move to be spectacular.

But her heels hit the floor first, her feet skidded, and down on her backside she went, like a sack of potatoes dumped on the dock. The crowd gasped. Curley lunged forward and, with a final super effort, pulled her to her feet, held her by the arm and led her into a low bow. The tail of her spine stung; she wondered if she would be crippled for life. Suddenly, the audience exploded, cheered, whistled, thumped. That was all she needed. With a burst of show-biz adrenaline, she righted herself, beamed, waved and pranced off the stage.

Curley caught up to her. "God, we were good, eh? Next year, we'll do a French Apache dance. Lots of gymnastics. Okay?"

"Not in a million years!" Betty rubbed her tailbone. "I once had the idea of going to Hollywood, Curley, but tonight has changed my mind for good."

She left him for an unscheduled, quiet act at the back of the room. A real-life drama about real-life love. The starring role was that of the newly returned and pregnant Vivian, holding onto the arm of janitor Len, the husband she had discarded nearly six months ago. Vivian's eyes sparkling as she patted her large, rounded belly.

Playing the main supporting role, standing at Vivian's side, a happy, grinning Dot, with a matching tummy and her own proud husband. Betty moved into the welcoming circle they opened up for her. Her friends. Four of many, if the kind words of the community were any indication.

How come they like me, if I'm known as the town's she-devil?

Chapter 22

I call a fig a fig, a spade a spade.
- Menander

Screeches clawed the air as trapper Sammy Sunders loaded caged cats onto a pick-up truck. All the doors and windows of the hotel were wide open: Sammy's efforts to clear the stench from the zoo.

"Hello, Mr. Sunders," called out Betty as she approached the truck.

Sammy looked like a man choking on a chicken bone. "How do," he muttered, then plodded back to the hotel for another load of yowling cats.

Betty entered the store. "Mrs. Johnson, I saw Mr. Sunders packing up his truck. Where are they going?" Betty momentarily flushed as she realized how involved, how much like the locals she was becoming; it mattered what her neighbours were doing.

"Only Sammy's going. Not his wife. Just Sammy and the cats. Poor Mrs. Sunders has been dreading the move back to the bush, to the log cabin. She loves Narrows, God bless her. She's asked him to let her stay a few more days."

How strange, thought Betty. Mrs. Sunders thinks Narrows is a metropolis. "Her husband doesn't look too happy about moving all the cats."

"Sammy? Why, he loves them as much as she does. Why else would he put up with them?"

"Darned if I know, Mrs. Johnson."

"There's a message here for you to call home, Miss Sweetly." Mrs. Johnson snapped a super-white storekeeper grimace at Betty. "Ha, listen to me! I keep calling you Miss Sweetly, just like the children. Can't imagine why I should."

Has she just insulted me, wondered Betty. Is Mrs. Johnson making an oblique Georgika-Betty slur? I doubt it. I mustn't be so suspicious. I mustn't take offense so easily.

"It's a flattering name. I don't mind at all." Here it was late May and the children were still using the kind misnomer. Betty tensed. "I'm supposed to call home?" Long distance meant bad news. Something horrible happening.

She yelled into the mouthpiece. "Mother, I'm so sorry I was rude to you at Easter. Are you okay?"

"Betts, my dearest Betts. Oh, I just don't know how to tell you! You know how things are with your father and me—"

"It's Dad! Oh no, what's wrong with him?"

Betty's sympathy for Glen hardened Nora's voice. "There's nothing wrong with him. Nothing his floozies can't fix. I'm going, Betts, leaving him. For good."

Leaving? For good? Betty sifted through her parent's captious marriage, looking for some reason, any reason to save the union. She found none. Nevertheless, she decided, she must try. "Mother, perhaps—"

"Betts. I'm leaving him for someone else." Now Mother's voice was revving up. She's in a hurry, thought Betty, she wants to toss out her explanation and hit the road. "Fred Ross. I'm leaving with Fred Ross."

"What? Who? Fred Ross? Mother. No. Not Hop-along Freddie, Mother!"

"Please, Betts. Don't call him that odious name. I'm really surprised Betts, that you can't appreciate my situation. Fred is a man I've always admired. So different from your father. Kind. Gentle. Not a critical bone in his body. He positively radiates understanding and I absolutely adore him. And he's got money, Betts. We're moving to Spokane. He's buying a small aluminum casting business. Making cookware. You understand, don't you, Betts? You must. A whole new exciting life for me—I just adore Spokane..." A nervous, girlish giggle with undertones. Nora was waiting for an endorsement.

Betty, in befuddlement, could only repeat: "Not Hop-along Freddie, Mother?"

Go ahead, live your own life and I'll live mine, Nora had said at Easter. *It's my fault,* thought Betty, *and now my mother is leaving us. I'll never ever argue with her again. My unkind words must have been the final straw that forced her onto the road to perdition.*

~ Ж ~

The effect of Nora's unsettling announcement was greatly offset by the most welcome of gifts: Storekeeper Mrs. Johnson handed Betty a letter from Cameron. Betty hurried away, off to a nearby stump, clutching her letter to her breast. It's an apology. Yes. A logical explanation to end all my foolish fears about him. Betty read the letter. Read it again. Then read and reread sections of the letter until indignation and pain flowed from her like blood from a stab wound.

God, she wailed to the grey sky, he's as bad as my dad! Floozies!

> *...your letters have been sort of stuck in a rut Betts. You sure sound different than you did at Easter.*
>
> *Have we finally got things cleared up about the girl Kathy? I wish to God I'd never gone out with her at all. She is a nothing compared to you. Please, please Betts, don't bring her up as a subject again, the talk of her is getting annoying.*
>
> *As you can see by the address, I'm back in Trail again; I've got the same summer job in the leadwells. Damn depressing.*
>
> *I needed cheering up, and I ran into Leona, an old pal from Kamloops. Did I tell you before that she's teaching here this year? She invited me to a party with a bunch of teachers. I guess I should have known better than to go, because she kind of hung around me, got drunk, and I had to take her to her apartment. Don't worry, I was a perfect gentleman. Quite frankly, I can honestly say I've got her completely out of my system. Even her body isn't a patch on yours.*

That Cameron! Damn! He's never seemed like a Casanova. But first a Kathy and now a Leona? The...bastard! Are there others? Ones he hasn't told me about? If gullible me had got pregnant, would he marry me? Probably not — I'm used goods. He'd use his stand-by phrase: 'Betts, be reees-sonable!' Red-hot anger, fueled by a vivid imagination, raged inside her. She strode home and dashed off a heated reply.

> *May 16*
>
> *Cameron.*
>
> *I promise not to mention either your Kathy or your Leona again. I don't want to <u>annoy</u> you any further. I guess I have no claims on you, anyway. You can go to all the parties you want, with whomever you want, and get a bunch of floozies drunk and pregnant whenever you want. I don't care anymore!!!!*
>
> *Not yours,*
>
> *Betty.*
>
> *P.S. How do <u>you</u> know what Leona's body is like, or shouldn't I ask and risk <u>annoying</u> you???*

If Mother can drop Dad, then I should smarten up, too. Drop Cameron and get my own Hop-along Freddie!

~ ж ~

She took the letter to the store and handed it to Mrs. Johnson. There was an odd twist to Mrs. Johnson's face as she placed Betty's letter to Cameron with other outgoing mail.

In Betty's short absence from the store, some Jekyll and Hyde transformation had taken place in Mrs. Johnson's demeanour. Not one admirable tooth showed through her clamped lips, but her eyes bored into Betty's, as if she were attempting telepathy. She picked up a textured, ivory-yellow envelope and placed it upon her open bible. Right on top of Moses and the stone tablets, all the while keeping a mute, fierce hold on Betty with intense eyes.

There was no doubt about it this time: Mrs. Johnson was definitely making reference to she-devil notes! Betty turned hot, then shivered. Her eyes bugged out. Her mouth opened and closed, but she could not speak. Mrs. Johnson's visage relaxed. As though she had made her point. She retreated into her unlit storage room.

Betty opened the envelope. She fully expected to see an ivory-yellow hate-note inside it. But there wasn't one. The envelope was empty. She followed Mrs. Johnson into the dark back room, looked behind the large cartons piled there, but couldn't find her. It was as if she'd vanished. Just as well, thought Betty, her heart pounding, her breathing almost painful. What would I ask? Or say? Do I even want to hear her responses?

~ ж ~

The photo of Cameron was still thumb tacked to the wall beside Betty's pillow. She rushed to the bedroom, yanked the photo off and turned it around, dooming Cameron's bright eyes and charming smile to darkness; then choked when she read what he had written on the back of it: To dearest Betty, I love you with all my heart, Cam.

~ ж ~

Kate stood by the sink, beside freshly washed pots and pans, wearing a knowing, I've-got-you sneer. Swinging Betty's glasses in her hand. "Betty, you fake, you're as big a fraud as that windbag Edwin Chalmers and his pedantic speech!"

Betty wondered what had set her off this time.

"Ever since Easter you've hardly worn your glasses. So just now I tried them on—they're nothing but plain glass! What a phony, you sly little bitch, trying to look so bloody bright and bookish!"

Kate's words bit like bee stingers, snake's fangs, shark's teeth. Still aching and raging from Cameron's letter, and from Mrs. Johnson's mute acknowledgement of the hate note-writer, Betty pulled the pin from her recently cultivated self-discipline, pulled the pin from her lifetime of timidity, pulled the pin from her position of rent-controlled serfdom and hurled at Kate a hand-grenade of abuse.

"Me a bitch? Me a bitch? A fake? You. You...you're the biggest, darndest fake of all! And you're the bitch, yes! A one-hundred percent certified bitch, Kate, the snoopiest, rottenest, crabbiest bitch there ever was!" She emphasized her harangue like her father would; she banged her fist down on the sink ledge so hard that the pots jumped to the floor and hid under the stove, so hard that the pot lids gyrated and rolled into the bedroom.

"Crutches? Hah! Headaches, hard time sleeping? Hah! Appointments in Nakusp? HAH! I don't need the stupid glasses but you–you phony baloney don't, and probably never did, need the stupid crutches! Or... or the money you got from that poor kid who bumped into you, you vile wretch. I bet it was your fault anyway. You're a road menace, the worst driver on earth."

Now that she had started, she was like a boulder rolling downhill, gathering momentum; she could not stop. She charged toward Kate and pushed her index finger under Kate's nose. "It's your own fault no one up here likes you, your own fault they carried you off in a straitjacket last year!"

Kate's eyes bulged like a bullfrog's. She ran down the stairs and out the back door, slamming it. The whole house shuddered.

For a brief moment, astonishment lit up Betty's face; she had finally done it, called a spade a spade. Applause for her own performance resounded in her head as she beetled down the stairs to find Mrs. Allan. She just had to tell someone she had battled with a tyrant and won. What sweet victory!

But halfway down the stairs she stopped and sat. Victory? It seemed Pyrrhic at best, an escalation of a squabble like that of nine-year olds Helena and Ingrid fighting over who would clean the black boards.

Oh, Lord, I have probably sent Kate down to the lake to commit suicide! She rushed back upstairs to a window. Kate was outside, but she was not heading to the lake. She was leaning against Granny's fence, talking to her beau Kurt Guttemann in a voice that was not only steady, but downright coy.

Kate glanced up at the window from which Betty peered and saw Betty's pale, anxious face. From her pocket Kate pulled a white handkerchief, which she waved at Betty, waved as though it were a flag of truce, of unconditional surrender! And then Kate grinned. Grinned at Betty from ear to ear. With as much resilient audacity as those classroom plagues, Howard and Alec and Bruce, rolled into one. A flag of truce. The war was over. A wary Betty waved back and then smiled; began to laugh. *Will I always misjudge people? Will I never understand them?* Then she frowned as the ghost of Mrs. Johnson's tight lips floated by.

Chapter 23

The higher the monkey climbs, the more he shows his ass.
François Olivier

H ot days. Every afternoon, Betty abandoned the art, the music, the science and took the class outside for softball practice. She hoped that if Inspector McIntyre showed up again, he'd prove to be a sports lover.

Keith Evans: asthmatic, Margie Sloboda: butter-fingered, Donny Rodman: clueless—he usually wandered about the field, his back to the game—and Helena Stevens and Ingrid Johnson:–only interested in serving refreshments. That left her with just ten willing players. She knew they had no chance of winning.

They practised daily, no matter how warm it got. The gods smiled on the ill-assorted class and its undersized teacher, and allowed the month of May freedom from afternoon rain.

Betty demonstrated her interpretations of how to grip the bat, how to choke up if they swung late. How to cock the bat behind the shoulder, push off from the back foot, stride forward, whip the bat around level with the ball. She found the best location for each player; taught them all to shift positions to cover for errors. When Daisy abandoned second base for left-side grounders and Eric, shortstop, moved to cover for her, Betty decided maybe they did have a chance, and kissed the cover of her ragged coaching book. "Class. I think you should choose a name for our team. What will it be?"

Without hesitation Alec said, "Miz Sweetly, we're… The Narrows Skunks."

Skunks? So much for democracy, she thought.

~ ж ~

On the first Saturday of June, bus driver Len dropped off Betty's students at the high school, then drove to Kokanee to pick up teacher Leslie Bedford Jones' team.

Keith, Margie and Donny were the 'water boys', in charge of pails and dippers for each team, running back and forth to the pump for refills. Helena and Ingrid squeezed a dozen lemons into a galvanized tub, added a bag of sugar, poured in pump water, topped the mix with a block of lake-ice. Wide-mouth Mason jars would serve as drinking glasses.

Betty had hand stitched bright red armbands, morale boosters, to distinguish her class from Leslie's. "Come on, Narrows Skunks, let's have a warm-up before Kokanee arrives." They raced to the field, strutting their red-striped arms.

Betty patted her freshly curled hair as the bus returned from Kokanee, hoping she looked attractive enough to impress handsome teacher Leslie Bedford-Jones. But she forgot about her own appearance when 26 fourth, fifth and sixth graders piled out of the bus. Betty moaned. They all wore bright yellow ball caps emblazoned with machine-stitched words: Kokanee Colts. Her arm-banded class was stunned, already out-psyched.

Bus driver Len, as umpire, ambled toward home plate. Alec, as Skunk's captain, shook the hand of his yellow-capped counterpart—a fat boy who looked like a miniature Babe Ruth. Alec towered over him. Having a fourteen-year-old in grade six had its advantages.

"Where the heck did you get the caps, Leslie?" asked Betty.

"Arlada Cheese Factory. Our sponsors." Spider webbing seemed amateurish compared to Leslie's veil of modesty.

Betty stood by her silent group, feeling like a mother hen. An inadequate one. She wanted to tuck them under her protective feathers, out of sight.

"Okay, now. Play ball!" Called out Len.

Leslie Bedford-Jones' players were up to bat first, with an all-boy line up. Betty shook her ruffled feathers. "Just a minute, Mr. Bedford-Jones. We can't have an all-boy team playing against a mixed one."

Leslie reluctantly rearranged his batting order. The Kokanee Colts looked confused. Complained. "Mr. Bedford-Jones, we didn't practice this way. It ain't fair."

"Isn't," he corrected.

Betty's players took to the field: Alec was pitcher, Bruce, catcher, and Eric, shortstop. Grant, Daisy and Raymond covered the bases. Three outfielders. Jenny Carson was the only spare.

First inning. The Kokanee Colts scored four runs before the Skunks could put them out. When the Skunks came to bat, they struck out. A group of Kokanee girls cheered: "Our team is RRRED HOT! Our team is RRRED HOT!". Betty felt like strangling their saucy little necks.

Next inning. Morale began to lift for the Skunks when first Alec, then Bruce hit home runs. The Kokanee pitcher got flustered and Leslie pulled him out. He had let two players walk.

Third. Howard and Eric hit good ones near the end of the inning.

The Narrows water boys and hostesses united into a cheering squad: "Kokanee, Kokanee, yer never needed! You'll never win because yer too conceeded!"

Thunk! Raymond hit a grounder that brought Alec home from second and allowed him to round all the bases. The team rallied and for a glorious moment spunkily played their best.

But by the sixth inning, the Kokanee Colts were ahead by five runs.

Betty gathered her Skunks around her for a pep talk. "You're doing great."

"We're losing."

"Just a minute. Remember, this is a game: win or lose, the idea is to have fun. Go out there and imagine it's just a practice. Enjoy yourselves. Have fun! And win or lose, I've got a present for everyone."

Bruce gave Alec a conspiratorial wink. "Have fun? What do you say?"

"Hoo, boy! …let's!"

The Colt's captain, the waddling image of Babe Ruth, topped the line up again. He stood at the plate, loaded with confidence. Betty frowned. Darn kid will probably point with his bat to where he's going to hit his next home run.

"Hey, Alec. Throw the Spitteroo," called out Bruce.

"What's that?" asked the fat boy.

"Oh, he hawks a juicy one on the ball and when you hit it, it squirts on your face," said Bruce. Betty glanced at Leslie, saw his lips pucker with disgust.

Alec bulged out his cheeks, bent over the ball, made vulgar sounds. When he raised his head, drool hung from his lip; the fat boy was visibly unnerved. Betty stopped watching Leslie's face.

"Strike!" called Len as the ball splashed into Bruce's glove.

In no time, the fat boy was out. One down. Next up was a freckled-face boy with long arms. "Hey, measles. You hit like a girl."

"I do not." The freckled-face boy swung with all his might.

"See? I told you. You're a girl. Can't hit 'em." Soon number two was out. One to go.

Next up, a girl. Bruce cupped his hands. Pressed his thumbs together and blew. Pffffffp! "Whew. I smell something funny. Was that you? You fart?" Betty only dimly felt Leslie's outrage burning into her averted shoulder. Herr team had surpassed her coaching techniques by far; they were speaking their own baseballese, as if they had their own private, out-psyching, coaching manual. She hadn't a clue what teacherly reaction might be appropriate. Then she shrugged. What the heck. It's just a game. When in doubt do nothing, she rationalized.

The yellow-capped girl turned crimson. Even the Colts laughed.

"No, it couldn't be you. Must be the backhouse. Alec, throw quickly. I need some air."

Ping! She popped it. Bruce got under the ball and she was out. The Skunks hop, skipped, jumped off the field.

"Okay, team! Let's show 'em!" Betty could not contain herself. To hell with book rules; to hell with Leslie's yellow caps.

Alec stepped up to bat with a wide grin, thoroughly at ease. "Hey!" He called out. "See if you can throw it over the plate. You haven't yet."

Alec swung. Thwack!

"Run, Alec, run! You're good for two!"

Next up was Bruce. "Whattaya say. Throw a hard one. I always hit homers when they're hard."

A slow pitch - Bruce stepped forward, just like at practice. It connected. Pow!

"Go! Go! Bruce, go!"

Alec and Bruce pounced onto the wooden home plate, breaking it. Len put the pieces back together. "Batter up."

Grant Kieffer had caught the mood. He stepped up like a pro, chewing a wad of gum and spat on home plate. Betty pretended not to notice. The pitch went wild.

"Ball one."

"What's wrong? Can't pitch?" Grant called out.

"Ball two."

Two more balls. Grant sauntered to first. Next up was Daisy. The Colts looked relieved. Daisy cocked her bat, gripping it like Joe DiMaggio. The ball spun toward her and she whipped the bat in perfect timing.

Crack! The sound that every hitter wants to hear.

"Run, Daisy, run!"

The Colt's left fielder fumbled the ball.

"Go home. Go home. Atta girl! Way to go!"

Two more and the score was tied at eighteen all. None out.

Leslie Bedford-Jones looked sick. "What the heck is wrong with you, you ..." His body language conveyed his disgust with the disheartened Colts.

Before the Colts could put out the Skunks, two more runs came in and Betty's players were this year's champions: twenty runs to eighteen.

Leslie stomped across the field to reluctantly shake Betty's hand. "Of course they've won," he hissed in her ear. "In fact, you've absolutely no discipline over them at all, Betty!" Betty shrugged and smiled sweetly.

The deflated Colts sipped a few drops of lemonade; nibbled at the sugar cookies. Betty watched Leslie pace back and forth far from the party.

He can't even bear to look at his players; he's a poor loser. I would never have guessed. Look at him now: he's practically pushing them onto the bus.

As the bus left, she shook her head. The first time in ages I get to see Leslie, and I've upset him. You can't attract a man by beating him!

Betty's sweat-beaded, elated team belted down their Mason-jar drinks, demolished all the cookies.

As they boarded the bus, Betty patted them on the shoulder and gave each one a Babe Ruth chocolate bar. Like a general pinning medals on war heroes. When the bus rounded the corner, she dropped her teacherly smile, howled a cry of triumph and danced a jig on the dusty field.

~ Ж ~

When Betty emerged from the mail van, an exhausted looking Georgika, smoothing back freshly cropped hair, walked slowly over to greet her. Her drawn face was even paler than when they last met. She tried to lift Betty's suitcase.

"No, Georgika, leave it!"

"Old habits die hard, Betty. I keep thinking I'm as strong as an ox. I still haven't quite got myself back in shape since that surgery, but I'm working at it."

"What does the doctor say?"

"Not much. But I'm getting stronger every day, praise God. I just have to stop being so lazy—push myself a little harder to get my muscles back, that's all."

As they crossed Main Street, Betty eyes lingered on the town's civilized look. Its wide, well-flattened sandy road, its hitching posts, bits of wooden sidewalks. Kokanee has promise, she decided. It'll probably be a major city someday.

Georgika sighed. "I can't believe it's only three weeks until you leave, Betty."

"Neither can I."

"Your friendship has meant a great deal to me and I can't help saying that I wish with all my heart you'd be returning next fall." She sighed again as she opened the door to the restaurant. "Life is just one continuous round of hellos and good-byes. Friendships would be fine if only a person could stop themselves from giving part of their heart away every time." A tear slid down her cheek. She whipped it away. "Don't pay any attention to me, I just get soppy if I'm tired," she murmured. "Anyhow, I can visit you next year in Trail, when I'm better."

They passed a table of colourfully dressed Doukhobors. Georgika jerked her head toward them. "I have to stay here this afternoon and visit with my kinfolk. Leslie's come up with the idea of taking you up the mountainside for a picnic."

Kinfolk? How wonderful for me, thought Betty. A picnic with Leslie Bedford-Jones? Ahhh… He's forgiven me for the softball loss! Finally, to be alone with him in the wilds. The idea was irresistibly promising; she felt a slight animal twinge. Maybe there's still a chance for Leslie to be my Hop-along Freddie!

Georgika surveyed Betty's clothes. "You're not dressed suitably for mountain climbing." Betty wore a carefully selected skirt and blouse. And new shoes.

"These? These are old clothes. Really old."

~ Ж ~

Leslie stood in the doorway, his blue eyes seeking her out. He came to

232

the booth and sat opposite her. Georgika had gone to the kitchen.

Betty made her voice soft and feminine. "I hope you're not angry with me about the ball game, Leslie. I agree with you, my kids didn't exactly play like little gentlemen."

"Oh, the game." Leslie allowed himself only the briefest of frowns. "Of course I am not angry. Not at you, anyway. That bus driver, your janitor friend Len, in fact, was out of line. I am sure you noticed he favoured your team enormously. And those two older boys on your team ought to have been reprimanded. A couple of no-accounts—no manners, no futures. But I have put the whole business out of my mind. Did Georgika tell you of my invitation to go hiking?"

"Yes." The resentment in his voice made Betty feel terrible. Being the victor really had its downside.

But Leslie had made his point and now he was radiating camaraderie. "There is a beautiful spot on the mountain side that is my favourite place in the whole valley. Would you like to see it?"

See it? She would gladly climb a slagheap and stare at a smelter if Leslie asked her to. She said good-bye to Georgika and followed him. He looked wonderful: beige chino trousers, a T-shirt that showed off his muscular build.

Leslie walked to the side of the restaurant, where he retrieved a bundle wrapped in an Indian blanket and handed a picnic basket to Betty.

They passed through the town, then took a side street that led to the foot of the mountain and began to ascend a narrow, steep trail. Perspiration soon gathered around Betty's temples, her forehead. The basket began to feel heavy.

Leslie stopped periodically to wait for her.

"...stretches the muscles, this climbing. Keeps one fit. In training for the future. ... loaded with energy, and I am utterly comfortable in the role of principal, I seem to be a natural leader, but I can do more..." His voice kept swelling then disappearing as he climbed ahead, springing up the steep slopes with easy strides. "...and next move is principal of a bigger school," he shouted down to her. "Then inspector. After that well...who knows? Maybe I'll win a post in Victoria with the ministry—What did you say, Betty?"

"Nothing, Leslie. I'm fine," she puffed back. No use repeating her words. Too rude. 'Bloody show-off' would not exactly endear her to him. She shifted the picnic basket, grasped a small tree, and pulled herself up a difficult incline. She may have won the ball game last week, but today at this climbing game, he was winning with ease.

"Good for you, Betty. I knew you were a girl with grit."

"How nice." Gritty was more like it. Grit in her mouth, under her nails, on her clothes.

Fortunately, Leslie's favourite spot was not too far up, and after a half-hour hike, they reached a small plateau. Leslie gestured. "This is it. Ideal, isn't it?"

She glanced around. As she wiped her dripping face on her sleeve, she had to admit it was worth the climb. From behind a clump of mountain alder, a small stream splashed down over a rocky outcrop, formed a motionless pool, then, spilling over the rim, gathered momentum as it rushed down the mountainside. From here, the view of the town, the lake, and the adjacent mountains was postcard perfect. In a clearing among the tamarack, among rippling birch and aspen leaves, among scatterings of huckleberry bushes, nestled a vibrantly blue patch of cornflowers. She picked one and stuck it behind her ear. The plateau was rocky, but Leslie had previously cleared a space, and there he placed the supplies.

They rinsed their steaming faces in the mountain pool. Betty cupped her hands and drank from them. The cold water ran up her lifted arms and soaked her shirtsleeves. Leslie removed his shirt and splashed his torso.

"Go ahead, Betty, you'll feel cooler if you strip down a bit."

"I'm okay. Just fine, Leslie." Down to my bra? Here? Now?

"I've got my bathing suit on under my clothes. It's too bad you don't have one, too," he confided, then checked to see her reaction.

A bathing suit in the mountains! What next? Bare all? Does he think this is romantic? This was not the Leslie she had imagined.

Leslie spread out the Indian blanket. On it, he placed a small white tablecloth, set out a bottle of red wine. "I have managed to find us a claret, Betty. From Bordeaux. Wonderfully fruity. Ripe plums. Velvety. You'll see."

He unwrapped a roast chicken and homemade bread, placed them on china platters, flourished a huckleberry pie and set it inside an ornate silver pie dish. Then he unwrapped two of Georgika's wine goblets with the delicacy of a watchmaker. "Voila! We're in the French forests of Manet, now, n'est-ce pas?"

"Oui, monsieur." This picnic tableau she had to admit, was an exquisite creation. Well worth the climb, worth the feeling of being an inferior in the company of an Adonis. She sat on the blanket, kitty corner to him. "Your picnic is super. And this place? Well, it's the Garden of Eden. You do everything to perfection, Leslie." She held the glass of proffered wine high. "To

234

Mother Nature and her excellent helper."

"Thank you, Betty. I endeavour to improve; I live to excel." He looked at his handiwork with satisfaction. "You see, Betty, our lives are like mountains and valleys. Most people stay in the valleys, but I am one of those who climb. I..."

She had stopped listening to the actual words. She knew they would revolve around his favourite subject. She accepted another glass of wine, leaned back against a slanted rock and watched him as he cut bread and chicken and offered it to her, talking all the while. "As I said, being principal is just a stepping stone..."

He's so beautiful. And graceful. Until he speaks. Funny, I never noticed this blowhard side of him, before.

He held his wine goblet up to the sun. "What clarity and colour! Marvelously mellow. Not my choice of goblet, though. Overblown Victorian fussiness."

"Dot has six cross and olive wine glasses. And she has wonderful Fiesta Ware dishes—"

"Really. When I marry, we shall collect fine Swedish crystal. Very plain, you see. And Rosenthal or Limoges. Heavy Georgian silver. Can you picture it, Betty, contrasting with Swedish Modern? Marvelous! Perfect for cultivating the right sort."

"Sounds wonderful." Swedish Modern what? He was taking her down uncharted paths.

Leslie served her a piece of huckleberry pie on a cut glass plate. Another one of Georgika's treasures. "How generous of Georgika to lend you all her beautiful things, Leslie."

Leslie sidestepped Betty's remark. "Exactly so...I have such an affinity for beautiful things; I treasure her treasures more than she..."

At this moment, Betty stopped listening and started staring. While she rolled about mouthfuls of huckleberry pie, while her teeth and lips turned greyish-blue from the delectable berries, Leslie was undressing.

He's taking off his pants! Good God. What a form-fitting bathing suit! He's lying down. Right next to me.

Betty, fork in hand, no longer chewing, gawked at his nakedness, at the outline of his male parts. I'm the peahen staring at a peacock in full display. Such glorious skin. Such golden curly body hairs. Such perfect legs. Is this foreplay?

Be worldly. Relax. It is simply that we are in a Manet. Yes. Luncheon on the Grass à la Kokanee. Except we have a near-nude man on the blanket and a fully-clothed me.

I can't relax. It's my brain; it's a voyeur. Betty-the-student, studying Comparative Anatomy. Cramming for an A.

I blame the wine, the nearness, the thin material of Leslie's bathing suit. I blame the bump. The lump. Right...there. Leslie's...

Betty's capricious imagination darted off to Grampa Wheatley's Billiards Hall and Tobacco Shop. To the cigar smokers leaning over the billiard tables. To the stumpy remains of their cigars, discarded, upright, in the mounded, sand-filled ashtrays. The cigar stubs, their soggy tips just bent over ever so slightly ... Here, she thought, is a little cigar butt under cloth, pointing at me. And below it, also outlined by the thin cloth, are two billiard balls—bigger by a country mile than Cameron's.

"... and you would be right for me, Betty. You are so accommodating, so willing to assist..."

The cigar-butt temptation grew taller and thicker. Betty's hormones responded.

A shuffling noise. Betty looked up. Then, as she moved her hand, ever so slowly, toward Leslie, her fingers inadvertently brushed his bathing suit. The cigar sprung up to full size. "Leslie," she rasped.

"Yes, my darling," he whispered back, his voice thick as an eider down quilt.

"D-Don't move."

"No, I shall do as you wish, my sweet," he promised from his position of expectant bliss.

"Leslie. Play dead."

Play dead? Leslie, with an effort, brought his glazed eyes back into focus, turned his head and met a new set of eyes—fur-surrounded eyes and a black, wet snout. Leslie's newly arisen cigar shriveled, melted like puddling, acetylene-torched ice cream. His face turned to chalk.

But the rest of his athletic body had no trouble reacting. He leapt to his feet, jumped over a stone-still Betty, as his mouth screeched "Ursus Horribilis-sss!" As his perfect flanks flatulated loudly like a released balloon and his godly body spun erratically down the mountainside. He was gone in lickety-split with not even backward glance to see what fate might befall his beloved Betty.

Betty inched from the picnic blanket in controlled terror. Not making the mistake poor old Hop-along had. Not this time. Not like last fall's outhouse-black-bear-panic. Cautious step by cautious step, she descended backwards, her attention cemented to the grizzly's every gesture, every grunt, every growl.

However, the grizzly seemed neither interested in the huckleberry blue-mouthed Betty nor deterred by the stinky odor left behind by the aromatic and quick-footed Leslie. Each step Betty took coincided with a chilling sound issuing from the giant beast: a crunching, skin-popping, Hop-along's leg sound! The bear, with a discriminating pallet rivaling Leslie's, had chosen to be as civilized as the picnic before him demanded. A Canadian Manet. He now occupied centre stage on the tablecloth, in the warm picnic spot Leslie had so hurriedly vacated. It was his huge canines that were producing the heart-stopping sounds as he masticated the whole roast chicken. In his left clawed paw, he held the dainty pie aloft, ready to sample it next.

Now, in Leslie's footsteps, Betty plunged down the hillside; wondering if the bear would also enjoy Leslie's choice of wine: was he serving himself in Georgika's precious goblets? Giant jumps and strides, leaping off pointed rocks; she felt a new edge of exhilaration such as she had never experienced before, and she babbled shrill hysterics to the skies.

Me, Betty—eye to eye with a Goliath of a bear, brushing against Death! And winning!

Leslie cowered at the foot of the mountain, experiencing none of Betty's exhilaration. "My God, I am ruined," he moaned, as his hands cupped his shriveled privates. "I can't go through town like this! Betty, you must help me protect my reputation. Get up to the house and get me some clothes, quickly. And do not stop to talk to anyone! Please!"

Betty parted her tangled hair so she could see her bare feet. See the cuts and blisters on them. But she followed Leslie's command, she became his rescuer, she raced off.

~ ж ~

Tommy's mouth hung wide open as he listened to her story. His voice broke into loud guffaws before she could even finish. And by the time he had returned downstairs with an armful of Leslie's clothing, he was doubled over with laughter. "Holy cow, Betty, have I ever got one up on him, now! You stay here; Ma's coming any minute. I'll rescue the bathing beauty."

Betty had one frightening glimpse of herself in the long hall mirror before

Georgika opened the door. Dark purple huckleberry lips and teeth echoed a spectacular series of splotches on her blouse and skirt, where she had spilled most of her pie. Dust and blood from tree-branch scratches mingled on her cheeks and arms and legs.

She poured out the whole story again. Georgika did not chastise and she withheld a grin until she had heard enough to know that Leslie, too, was safe. Then her laughter spilled out.

Georgika fussed over her, insisted on pouring her a cool bath. "Look at you. Face and feet all torn up, and sunburned as hell. Huckleberry pie and bears. In June, no less. That boy. And he just left you there to fend for yourself? More nonsense in one day than in two whole years."

Betty's teeth chattered, although she was warm. "I think he might have sort of been proposing to me, but he never will now. Not that I care. I'd rather die an old maid than marry that namby-pamby."

Georgika looked at her as though she had sunstroke. "Marry? Leslie? He won't marry for years. Not even you, Betty. He's too ambitious. You need some food. A good dinner – and maybe some hair-of-the-dog that bit you—wine, I mean!" She left Betty to undress and bathe.

Through the floorboards, as she lay soaking the stinging slashes, Betty could hear a different Georgika. Yelling at Leslie. A torrent of angry words relating to missing heirlooms taken without permission and imperilling naïve little Betty. "... and I'll deal with you later!"

Georgika's voice mixed in confusing conflict with that of Tommy's: "... and when I got there, he had half the town around him, asking if he was practising for some kinda races...haw, haw, Les, you looked like you'd just ate shit and you smelled like it too."

She lay there in the soothing water, a smirk pulling up one side of her mouth. The Olympics, Leslie. That's all you had to say. Helsinki. Poor Leslie. No imagination.

Chapter 24

What would the world be like without men?
Free of crime and full of fat, happy women.
—Nicole Hollander

B etty log-rolled the HB pencil between her fingers. On Sunday afternoon she had made a considerable dint in her preparations—despite, or maybe because of, the end of Leslie-dreams--he of the skimpy bathing suit and even skimpier bravery. Today's problems, however, were another matter: grade six arithmetic problems, a chapter full of them.

She could not solve them without resorting to high school-level algebra. Who, she pondered, could she ask for help? Not Kate, she'd sneer. Edwin Chalmers? But she would not see him until Friday's chess game. She pushed the answer book aside and blew enough space clear of eraser crumblings for a fresh sheet of paper. She would try once more.

A rolling, squeaking wheel, whispers and footsteps, disturbed her concentration. She stepped outside to peals of laughter ringing from two bell-shaped girls: pregnant Dot and Vivian, each pushing a handle of a blanket-covered wheelbarrow.

"Surprise," shouted Dot. "If Mohammed won't come to the mountain, the 'mountains' are coming to her!" Vivian clamped a cautionary hand over unaccustomed spurts of laughter. Dot belly-laughed.

Betty broke into a smile that matched theirs. "What are you two up to? Coming to steal my outhouse or something?"

"We two super-dooper bakers have come to have tea with you, because you never come to have tea with us," said Dot.

"Tea?"

"Well, no romance—just a safe little tea-time picnic, really, and without any bears" said Vivian. She looked at Dot and both giggled. The story of Betty's mountainside tryst had, predictably, already made its way to Narrows.

Dot waggled a teacherly forefinger. "Betty, you are in need of an antidote! Shut your books and join us—Miz Sweetly." They turned the heavy wheelbarrow around, heading it to the shade of a large tree.

Betty fetched the grade-six math text. When she caught up to them, they were setting out a red blanket and a white tea cloth. She dismissed a fleeting flashback to the ursine picnic with Leslie.

"Where's baby Harry?"

"Nina's daughter is baby-sitting him. She's very good with him. It was Dot's idea." Vivian flashed Dot a grateful look.

Awkwardly, reaching over their large, firm stomachs, they set out side plates, cups and saucers, dainty napkins. They kept glancing at Betty, looking for her approval as they did so, like her pupils now did. She sat cross-legged at one end of the blanket and watched them. Vivian's big teapot was wrapped in two large towels. She placed it with both hands and a grunt in the centre of the tablecloth. Dot unwrapped an iced, coconut-covered cake and set it on a cutwork glass pedestal.

"Ta-Duhhh!" She sang, heralding this triumph of kitchen art. Vivian, not to be outdone, removed from the wheelbarrow a plate of sliced matrimonial bars and a small bouquet of flowers.

"My gosh, I'm thunder-struck dumb. This is incredible," said Betty. She glanced over her shoulder. No, no bears around. And no huckleberry baking to tempt them, either. She relaxed.

Dot beamed at Vivian. "Congratulations, Missus Wilson."

Vivian curtseyed. "Congratulations to you, Missus Fielding." They began to laugh again.

"Congratulations to you both," said Betty.

Dot and Vivian tried to sit cross-legged like Betty. "Being pregnant is like having thick tapioca pudding tied around your waist," said Dot.

"Or ... like having a balloon inside your stomach stuffed full of turkey dressing," Vivian volunteered. Betty grinned. Food seemed to be their prime interest. Vivian continued. "Will you pour the tea, Betty, it's too awkward for me. I don't know why I put the pot in the middle of the tea cloth."

Dot cut huge slices of cake. "Look at it. It's so light and airy," she said reverentially.

"It's your best yet, Dot. Delicious." Vivian took another big bite. "We should have brought forks." She licked her fingers. Eating was serious business for the two mothers-to-be; no talk until they had eaten large amounts. Betty basked in the warmth of their new friendship with each other, felt the healing powers of their efforts—this, their combined gift to her.

"Sorry, Betty—I have to ask— we heard you had quite a time in Kokanee this past weekend, Betty. Surely you're not interested in fancy-dancy Leslie Bedford-Jones?" asked Dot.

"No. Absolutely not. Well… not now. Leslie's only interest is…Leslie. He would have fed me to the bear to save his own skin…" Betty moaned dramatically. "In fact, I'm through with all men. Through! I'm going to teach at a nunnery next year."

Vivian's eyes widened. "Really, Betty?"

"Don't pay attention, Viv, she's just pulling our legs. She's got that special beau in Vancouver. At least she did have." She scrutinized Betty.

"I sent him a real nasty, good-bye forever letter after he told me he dated two different girls."

"Told you? Guys with something to hide don't tell you, you dodo," said Dot.

"I've wondered about that myself a few hundred times since I mailed the darn letter. But I did and he hasn't written me since. I've chased him into the waiting arms of a gorgeous, wealthy coed, I'm sure of it."

"Oh, dear, we better have some more cake. I don't think she'll want the matrimonial squares," said Vivian.

"Call them 'date' squares, then, and give us all one, Viv," said Dot. "Start looking around again, Betty. There's more than one Mister Right for every girl. I might even find one for you—one of my many cast-offs." More laughter.

"Well, my life is a shambles. I can't even do the grade six arithmetic problems. Would you listen to this one? 'A grocery store owner has five pounds of tea from Ceylon that sells for twenty-four cents a pound and ten pounds of tea from China that sells for eighteen cents a pound. If he blends the two teas together, how much can he charge for the blended tea?'"

"Call it 'The Queen's Own Blend' and charge a dollar a pound," replied Dot.

"Oh, Dot, be serious. She needs help. But don't ask me, Betty, I taught the early grades because I'm terrible at arithmetic," said Vivian.

Dot looked up. "Is that right? Me, too. You better ask Farmer Detweiler." Peals of laughter again.

Betty put down her math text. "Be serious. What am I going to do?"

"Fake it," said Dot. "Let the grade seven teacher worry about it!"

Betty decided she'd have to wait for Edwin, after all.

"Did Dot tell you we've joined the Trent's Landing Women's Institute? They put on fairs and card parties and have guest lecturers and lots of interesting women belong."

"Yeah. And they sure let their hair down once the men are out of sight. We decided shortly after Viv got back from her mother's. It'll help us get through the winter with our new babies."

"Are things okay for you, now, Vivian?" Betty asked.

"Uh ..." Vivian pondered over her answer, examined her fingernails, which were no longer chewed raw. "Yes." She nodded emphatically. Unequivocally. "Yes, they are. Dot visited me at my mother's in April. We talked a lot about marriage and other things. She helped me." Vivian glanced down at her enlarged middle. "I can't even believe I was praying for a miscarriage at Christmas. I couldn't stand the thought of returning here for another winter, cooped up with yet another child. I thought I'd go crazy."

"I was quite helpful, actually," Dot said without a trace of modesty. "It's funny. As I tried to convince her of the merits of married life, I kinda brainwashed myself." She moved the tea things to the centre of the tea cloth and lay down.

"I don't know about you, Viv, but my back is killing me. I think the answer to our problems is in the old proverb, 'Misery loves company.' We both were disillusioned with our lives and our husbands and our dreams. Now we can deal with them again. We're The Two Musketeers. Mumketeers, actually."

"I think a woman has to have more than a husband. She needs a female friend," said Vivian in her high, earnest voice.

"It's more than that. A woman needs a man, a husband; and then she needs a girlfriend to complain to about him. That makes for a perfect life." Dot lifted her head and grinned. Vivian looked doubtful. Dot grinned again. "It's true, Viv, you know that."

Betty put a doleful look on her face. "Well, all I can say to you is this: if being pregnant at the same time has brought you two together...you'd better synchronize your watches and get pregnant at the same time every year!"

"Sure, and you can join us, Betty, you don't have to get married, just get pregnant," said Dot.

"Well join us, but do try and get married, first," said Vivian.

"No babies for me. Maybe I'll run away and join the circus. A circus of single women. I'd have even more fun than you two."

"I think you're jealous."

Betty's bravado crumbled. "You're probably right, Dot, I think I am, too. It would have been nice to be married to Cameron."

~ ж ~

"Kurt is taking me to Nelson Saturday. Do you want to come along?"

"No thanks, Kate. It's only two weeks before the end of the term. I'll be finishing up my marking. Perhaps you could ask Mrs. Allan."

"I'm not that desperate for company, for Pete's sake. She's happiest with Granny, anyhow."

"That's true. She's sure settled into the community well," Betty replied. "She loves teaching the lower grades; she's got the energy to cope with them, and her evenings with Granny seem to be enough. They've almost become a couple—going to church together every week and dinner at Nina's every Sunday night. It's quite wonderful for them both. What a pity Inspector McIntyre isn't letting her come back for next year."

"She's too old," Kate snorted.

"Only in age, not in any other way. Anyway," Betty continued, "Saturday night is the last dance in the community I'll ever attend. I want to say good-bye to my friends."

"You've been the one to make all the friends up here, and you're going. I can't be bothered, and yet I'm the one that's staying."

Ever since the day Betty had blasted her, Kate had been treating Betty as an equal. Tonight, protected by the anonymity of the pitch-black bedroom, she had taken the chip off her shoulder.

"It is ironic, isn't it? You know, you could be going to the dances, Kate, now that your leg is better."

"I only liked going when I didn't have to dance. I would have preferred more of the musical evenings, like the one at Georgika's last fall."

"Me too. It's too bad Georgika stopped liking poor old shaky Elaina Maleyna. She was such fun. I never could understand that."

"You couldn't? Elaina's a pain-in-the-ass. I gather she raised a hornets' nest in Kokanee and won't be coming back next year—by popular demand."

That shows how well I can judge people, thought Betty. I'd have thought they'd worship her. "Poor soul. She must be like a traveling Gypsy schoolteacher, changing schools each year, making an instant community hit, then spiraling downward for the remainder of the year."

Kate lifted her head, stared at Betty in the night shadows. "You're an oddball. You really can make a big deal of people's affairs. Personally, I have no interest in what becomes of her. The only one up here I'm compatible with is Nina Trent. And Bill. Him I really like."

"Well, now you've got that undertaker fellow Kurt Guttemann, I guess."

"Yes. Talk about irony: I was crazy about Roscoe Taylor, and I couldn't have him; I don't give a tinker's damn about Kurt, but he'll stick like glue. Lucky, lucky me. I've got a great future."

She'll marry Kurt for nothing but the security of his businesses, thought Betty, so she doesn't have to teach anymore. How sad.

~ Ж ~

The evening was warm. Betty put on a light summer dress, a devil-may-care coral-coloured cotton one that laced up the front, and two-toned, high-heeled sandals. Off she went alone, down to the ferry to await a ride to the Trent's Landing dance.

The McCloskey's stood outside their truck. Curley, Betty's exuberant stage partner, held his child, who was fighting to free himself. The baby wanted to lurch about on his own feet, now, and his vocabulary had advanced beyond "berbert". Freda, from the looks of her, was expecting the new baby any day.

"How are you feeling, Freda?" asked Betty.

Freda groaned and rolled her eyes. "Not very good. I can hardly wait to dump out this bundle."

"I can imagine. Is the heat bothering you?"

"Yeah, you can say that again. I'm not going to have any more kids, you can bet your boots." She looked resentfully at Curley, who responded with a guilty flush.

"Have you heard from your sister Charlotte?"

"Yeah, she's doing good in the nursing school. She wrote that she's got some swell friends and she's enjoying the schoolwork. That could have been me, eh, Curley?"

Curley hardened against her second accusation. "She's different from you. She's smarter."

Freda zapped him with a look of pure hate. "The only difference was she had me to advise her. Any more pregnancies and I'm taking my own advice."

Kate was right last winter about Charlotte and abortion, decided Betty.

"Did you hear I've got a job? I'm writing the *Notes from Narrows* column for the Arrow Lakes News. They don't know it yet, but they'll get no nicey-nice pieces from me—I'm writing meatier stuff."

"Good for you, Freda, people will love it. Will you write about politics? World crises?" Betty looked at Freda with new respect. Freda the crusader! A tantalizing job, Betty thought, one I would like. What a dramatic position, what power a reporter for a newspaper would have!

"No." Freda's face was resolute. "I'll report on the real happenings around here. Not the usual who-visited-who stuff; I'm going to make people squirm. Tell it as it is." Betty wondered where this might lead Freda: to heady success, or ostracism and instant firing?

Another truck pulled up. In it was pregnant Dot and her husband Lou. "Hop in, Betty!" She did so, relieved to leave the hostility behind.

"Look what I made," said Dot. "Three-layers! I'm going to wow everybody." On the remaining edge of her lap, she clutched the rim of a plate that held a large cake. Curlicues of chocolate icing gleamed in the low rays of the evening sun.

"That's going to be one big baby in there," said Lou. He studied Dot's belly with as much pride as Dot was bestowing on her cake.

~ ж ~

Betty recognized every face. And it seemed that because she was leaving, every man in the hall wanted to dance with her. Even the handsome farmer from King City danced a short polka with her, heehawing with abandon all the while.

Later in the evening, Dot motioned to her. Beside Dot stood a new arrival, someone whose face looked familiar. "Betty, this is Sparks Thornton. You met him. Remember?" Dot spoke in a voice reserved for matchmakers.

Betty picked up on it and checked over Sparks like a judge at a dog show: Taller than me. Good. City clothes. Good. Water-slicked blond hair. Good. Shiny shoes. Good. And handsome. Good, good, good!

"No, I don't think so..."

Dot laughed. "He's the fresh guy that complimented you on your first day here." Betty still looked puzzled.

Sparks Thornton spoke for himself: "I'm the one who called you 'Red'. Do you want to dance?" The musicians were playing a waltz. "I can't dance any of those complicated square dance things," he said as he moved her to the dance floor. "So I'm grabbing you while there's a slow one." He guided her around the room with a practiced, polished step. He smelled nice.

"You used to have red hair, and I called you 'beautiful Red'. Remember?"

"Oh, yes, I sure do, now. You're the truck driver." The fellow, she thought, that Dot once said was the best catch in the valley. How very promising! My luck has changed.

"I've seen you around town many a time, as I've been driving by. But I never tried to speak to you again. I figured you were the stuck-up type. It was Dot who suggested I come here tonight and ask you to dance. I said I figured you had me down for a jerk."

Betty laughed. "What an awful impression I made! I was just trying to be a model schoolmarm."

They danced every one of the remaining slow dances. When she danced the folk dances and squares with others, he watched her. What joy! A room full of friends and an admirer.

"Can I drive you home?" he asked, after they had eaten pieces of Dot's magnificently rich cake. The musicians were assembling to continue; it was only twelve-thirty.

"Yes, you may." She knew, as they slipped out the door, she was forfeiting her last chance to say farewell to her friends, but she continued to follow him, drawn to him.

They stood outside his blue Chevy pickup, on the ferry, and the cool evening breezes wafted away the heat radiating from her body. She had "danced up a storm", as Gramma Beaton would have said. As she prattled nonstop in a way that matched her upbeat mood, he kept staring at her.

"I sure never figured you to be so friendly," he finally said. "We could have had a friendship going all this time—and now I'm leaving. Tomorrow. My job here is over. Got a new job starting Monday."

"Oh." She wondered about the wisdom of having left the dance so soon.

They returned to his truck when the ferry docked. "Do you want to stop for a beer? I've got some beer in the back of the truck. It might be warm, though."

"I don't mind."

"I'll drive up to the sand pit road. It's private there. No one will see you. Keep up your 'model schoolmarm' image."

They sat in his truck, drinking Revelstoke Lager and listening to the urgent love calls of croaking frogs. By the time she finished the second beer, Betty's head was mildly fuzzy. Sparks had been chain-smoking. Then, as though he had solved a riddle, he stubbed out his cigarette, locked eyes with her, touched her cheek. "What do you think of me, Miss Schoolmarm?"

"I think you're great. So different from the other fellows at the dances."

"So I'm not an unacceptable truck driver?"

She breathed in the nearness of him. His fingers on her face felt so satisfying, so hypnotizing.

"I'm not a trucker, anyway. I'm a first-class electrician," he whispered as he moved closer and began to kiss her.

She blotted out everything. Self-centered Leslie, far-away Cameron, the past, the future; blotted out all in favour of this perfect, delicious moment, this surge of excitement. She pressed her breasts against him; she arched her body toward him. Sparks loosened the laces on the bodice of her dress. Slowly. She began to breathe in shallow gasps. One warm hand caressed her left breast; one warm hand began moving elsewhere. She shut her eyes and savoured the deliciousness; did not open them even as he began stroking her inner thigh. Ecstasy. Anticipation.

But, in the seconds he took to one-handedly undo his zipper, the prudent area of her brain tore through the layers of bliss, and reminded her of the dangerous, baby-making game she was about to play. "Sparks," she panted, trying to push away his hands, " Sparks, you've got to—don't—don't touch—I can't; I—"

Thumpff! Thumpff! Sparks pulled away so quickly he tore loose a handful of Betty's laced bodice, uncovering her left breast. Someone was pounding on the hood of Sparks' truck, pounding on the windows, screaming: "FORNICATORS! WHORE OF BABYLON!" Sparks quickly stashed his wilting member back into his trousers as he flashed on the headlights, as Betty jolted to an upright position.

A black-haired, black-gowned hulking figure shielded his face from the blaze of light and barrelled in the opposite direction down the dirt trail of a road.

"Good God," Betty shouted, "It's the minister of the New Testament Tabernacle Church!" Like Estelle Patten, she would have taken an axe to him if she had one.

"Fucking peeping Tom!" Sparks roared, as he revved his engine, backed up his truck, ground through a heavy thicket and gave chase to the fleeing man. Sparks' truck, now without a muffler, roared like a mountain lion and shot out flames. They lost sight of the black gown, but met up with him again as they rounded the road to Narrows.

The hotel lights flashed on. Granny's lights flashed on. Bill and Nina gawked from their porch.

Sparks jumped from his raucous truck. Stood nose-to-nose with the captive goggle-eyed minister. "Bloody spying loony!"

"W–w–word of G–G–God! Y-young women exposing their fleshly t–temptations...s–save you from s–sin..." It was warm out, but the round-faced New Testament Tabernacle Minister was shivering.

Sparks grabbed the ecumenical collar and positioned his fist to smash it into the fearful face. The New Testament Tabernacle Minister braced himself. His eyes gleamed with fervour; he was eager to be martyred for his efforts to save souls from damnation. "Only the good shall—"

"STOP! Unhand the minister. This instant!" commanded a familiar voice. As one, the audience—now including Granny and Mrs. Allan—turned to the commanding voice, to the flea-bitten, mothball-odoured figure who stood as sternly as General Patton before his troops, singling out some private for particular punishment, turned to the transformed—but still flea-bitten—Mrs. Sunders. Sparks lowered his fist. Hastily zipped shut his trousers. Mrs. Sunders strode towards them and placed a hand on Reverend Hanginger's arm. "Come with me," she said in her new-found voice of strength. Come where? Betty, still in the truck, dimly wondered, before she looked down and saw her torn bodice, a chilling reminder of her barely cooled off moment of passion. Everything was happening so fast! She clutched the dress front with two hands, and crouched low in Sparks' truck cab.

The New Testament Tabernacle minister had ceased his high-pitched rant the moment Mrs. Sunders had taken charge. Now, as if she were a holy lifeline flung from a heaven-sent sternwheeler, as if she were the very Saviour Himself, he grasped her hand with two of his and followed her into the hotel. And one by one the stunned townsfolk slipped away.

Sparks slipped back into the truck cab and looked at Betty with despair. "God damn the preacher! Damn the timing! If I just only had a few more hours, a few more days..." He pounded the shuddering steering wheel so hard, Betty thought he would break it. "I've thought about you all winter, you know. I've dreamt of you. But I never, never imagined I had a snowball's chance in hell. Then look what happens on my last night here. Paradise! All screwed up by a crazy preacher."

Dreamt of me? Betty let go of her torn dress front, which parted to display her charms. Batted her eyes in the semi-dark.

Sparks did not notice. "Oh, Christ, I've got just enough time to get back and pack up and get going. I've got to get to Vancouver and be on the boat by tomorrow night. I'll write immediately, though, and—"

"Uhh...just where are you going?" Betty was pulling her dress front together again.

"To Kitimat. To the new development up there. I'll write you every day, Betty." His voice was filled with ardour. "It's one hell of a primitive set-up up there, now, but in just two years or so, it'll be decent enough for a nice girl like you to come and live there—"

"Kitimat? Way up north? Two years?" Betty's voice was nearly a squeak. Her father's words returned with a vengeance: to hell and gone. Kitimat. A smelter town-to-be. No road to anywhere. Accessible only by boat. Oh, no. Not again. Not for me.

"Yes. But if you can be patient with me, I ..." He talked on in a coaxing, wooing voice.

Shades of Cameron, Betty thought. And nearly the same words. Me, Betty, doomed to a life of waiting. Waiting for any man, all men. Men who could find countless other women in the meantime.

She interrupted his earnest plea. "I'm sorry, Sparks, you're really great, but...I'm leaving, soon, too." She took a deep breath. "For Hollywood. To be an actress. You see, my mother wants me to. She has great faith in my acting abilities." She was easing herself out of the truck as she spoke.

Once she was back her apartment, the bright lights rushed any ounce of arousal that might have survived the crazy night rushed from her body, as if routed by a pail of ice water.

My God, my God, I am sex-crazed! I nearly did it with a complete stranger!

Maybe the Reverend Hanginger had been an angel in disguise! The Peeping Tom saviour... Possible coitus interruptus decreed by the Windshield Thumping Hand of God!

She climbed into bed and spoke to the ceiling. "Two weekends in a row I've been indulging in dangerous lusts. Sliding into promiscuity. And punished for it! First by a ravenous bear and second by a lascivious peeping-Tom minister...Betty Casanova. Betty-the-Wanton. Never again. NEVER!" She sighed: "If Cameron had given me those Woolworth rings, I'd probably never have sunk to such dangerous lows. It's his fault." But trying to place the blame on Cameron's shoulders did not work. She tossed and turned all night long.

~ ж ~

Morning came and Betty continued castigating herself. No Kate around to lecture, thank God. She was still in Nakusp. Sensible Kate had the prudence to carry on her love affairs in the far-off Leland Hotel. Normally voluble Mrs. Allan, after a quick assessment of Betty's burning face, stumbled through breakfast-time small talk.

Later, downstairs, Betty had to pass Granny and Nina. "Boyz-oh-boyz, that was some sideshow last night, the likes of which we haven't seen before! And this morning, you could have knocked me down with a feather: Mrs. Sunders and her suitcase took off with the preacher. Arm-in-arm on the ferry. Going to God-knows-where."

Betty was barely listening. She waited for Nina's scorn.

Nina continued. "Mrs. Sunders looks like a new woman. Even had a bath, by God. Lordy, Betty, you took a real shine to that guy from the power plant, eh?" Nina's eyes danced as she spoke. "Is he gonna give your Vancouver boyfriend a run for his money?"

Betty felt tremendous relief at Nina's nonjudgmental casualness. Maybe the darkness had hid Spark's telltale gaping fly front. Maybe. She tried to respond in a light manner. "He's a very nice person, Nina, but he might as well be heading off to the moon on a spaceship. He's gone to Kitimat."

Nina's gaze telepathed empathy. "Well, if you're going to drop the old boyfriend, I'd rather you picked a guy who's going to stick around. It would be great if you stayed up here for good, Betty."

"Thanks, Nina, but I guess there's not much chance of that."

Betty darted a look at Granny. At the stiffness in her lips. Disapproval. I knew it, thought Betty. Granny's disgusted with me. And so she should be.

~ ж ~

After a full night of heavy rain, the roads and paths had become streams of mud. She waited alongside Kate for the bus to arrive. When it splashed to a stop near them, the windows were so steamed up they could not see inside, nor could the passengers see out.

They climbed aboard and sat in the front seat, the one reserved by mutual consent for Kate. The children, as usual, chatted animatedly.

Little Donny's high, piping voice carried all the way from the back of the bus. Betty gradually became aware that he was talking about her. She selectively filtered out the voices of the other children and froze. "I'm not kidding. I tell you, Howard, I heard my ma telling my pa. Old Lady Sweetly was out all night long after the dance with one of those guys from the power station! And the preacher caught her and gave her hell!"

A highschooler chimed in. "My old man says 'school teachers are easier to bang than falling off a floating log.' " Laughter broke out at the back. Giggles and shushes swept down the aisle.

Kate paid no attention, if, indeed, she had heard at all. She continued to stare down at her hand, at her spectacular diamond engagement ring.

In a place deep within her heart, Betty began chastising herself viciously. God, even the Trent's Landing people know. And Jake's sullen daughter Freda will no doubt write it up in her new column for the Arrow Lakes News, with a 72-point headline enshrining my transgression:

Board Demands Wheatley Resign
Bad Example to School Kids

By Freda Patten

Betty Wheatley, middle-grades teacher, disgraced the village of Narrows last night. Pastor Hanginger spotted the sinners on Sandpit Road ...

251

Chapter 25

Life is a terminal illness. We'll all go.
Joe Slovo

"Y ou don't look well, Georgika. You're pushing your luck; it's not that long since your surgery. Shouldn't you slow down?" Although Georgina did not look as drawn and pale as the last time Betty had seen her, she had lost a great deal of weight. The solidity of her had gone; the look of sturdiness had been replaced by flaccid muscles, which danced about as Georgika moved at her usual kitchen high-speed. Drips of perspiration ran down the sides of her face.

"Betty, I just can't." Georgika pulled out one gold-brown loaf of bread after another from her cavernous ovens and began reloading them with trays of cinnamon buns. "Now that my son Tommy's added on a bakery to the restaurant, we need more stuff than ever—the dough's rolling in, pardon the pun. I'll finally get a bit of cash to fix up this old place, praise God. When you come back up here for a visit, you'll—" Georgika tilted a stove lid. "Drat! I'm low on wood."

"Visit? Cripes, Georgika, I've worn out my welcome up here. I'm lucky not to have been tarred and feathered."

Georgika's whole body strained as she lifted the entire cast iron firebox cover and clunked it to one side. Fiery embers lit up the room. "Nonsense. You're a prude." Her chest heaved like pumping forge bellows. "And I'll come to Trail—"

Now Georgika hoisted an armful of unsplit logs. But she staggered, and the logs crashed to the floor.

"Stop, Georgika! I'll do that! Georgika! Stop! Now!" Betty heard her own voice—the authoritarian one. The teacher one. The one she used on Howard to stop his temper tantrums. When had she changed? Now she commanded adults as if they were children, in a take-charge voice; she liked the sound of it. She moved to the fallen logs.

Ever ready to respond, Georgika opened her mouth. But only an odd gurgle emerged. From her crouched position beside the woodpile, Betty glanced up. At Georgika's eyes that were no longer focusing.

At a fixed grimace. Georgika lurched slightly, righted herself and, with tremendous effort, attempted once more to speak. Then stiffened. And like an old tree with a rotted core, she snapped and fell slowly forward. Her outstretched arms smacked the fervid stove surface; her breasts straddled the hot firebox; her head plunged into the open blaze.

Like darting snake tongues, the forked flames licked her face, seared her hair, scorched and crackled her skin; her fluids began dripping into the firebox and acrid oily smoke rose from her burning flesh.

Betty grabbed the back of Georgika's plaid flannel shirt, and pulled. But the shirt came away without Georgika. Shreds of it.

She clenched her teeth and clamped her arm around Georgika's neck—the only part of Georgika not welded to the firebox—and with the same hidden strength she had summoned to drag Howard to the cloakroom so long ago, she wrenched Georgika's heavy body from the stove, fell with her to the floor. Georgika's deadweight forced the wind from her lungs; Betty struggled free. Layers of Georgika's skin sloughed off and clung to Betty's hands and arms as if Georgika did not want to let her young friend go.

Betty could not look away from her seared and smoldering friend, could not hear her own high-pitched wailing, as she jumped up and ran about, ran here, ran there, wetting tea towels and wetting table cloths, filling jugs of water which she threw onto Georgika, as she raced for heavy coats and wrapped them around Georgika's lower body. Her mind sped through Constable Kayke's first-aid lessons, through everything he had said about burns—first-degree? Second?

Third-degree. Nothing you can do. Take the patient to the hospital. That's what he had said.

The fetor of burning hair and charred flesh, blood vessels and bone, blended into an unholy alliance with the aroma of cinnamon buns.

~ Ж ~

Unseasonable rains fell all night, fell all day; the grey skies were grieving. A line of rain-coated, dark mourners gathered round the gravesite. Behind them, a contrast: Georgika's Russian relatives, five women, dressed in boldly brilliant colours. Behind them a deep green solidity of ascending mountain firs.

Kurt Guttemann, Kate's fiancé, directed the funeral proceedings. Here, in his business habitat, he exuded yet another side of himself: a suave sureness, a dependability. Betty wished Kate was here to see him.

Once the Fire Valley minister finished his delicate eulogy, skirting around Georgika's gruesome immolation, it was Tommy's turn. It was not easy for him; he spoke as one stumbling over unfamiliar, uneven terrain. "My ma...she'd be pleased to see so many friends here... Last Sunday she was telling me how she was counting her blessings..." His voice failed and he could say no more. Leslie moved beside him and found the words Tommy struggled for. Calm, soothing words, extolling Georgika's virtues.

Betty restrained a sob and wiped tears onto her bandaged arm. Carefully. Her face still felt sun burnt. It's too bad men mustn't cry, she thought. Tommy is only a boy. He should be able to let the tears flow when they want, without having to dam them until he is alone, out of sight of all who care for him. Her tears continued.

While the minister gave the final blessing, while the Russian women dirged polyphonously, the audacious, animal side of Betty came to life and refused to be contained. She caught herself staring through wet eyes at both Leslie and Tommy, drinking in their somber good looks, as they stood there in their white shirts and dark raincoats. White and black, black and white; browned, angular male flesh and two boyish, curly heads side by side, just as they had been when she had first met them. Such beautiful handsomeness.

Betty looked at the coffin. You were so very kind to me, Georgika, and I was so suspicious. Now here I am at your funeral, doing you another wrong: having libidinous thoughts. Forgive me.

It was as if Georgika still lingered; hovering, wanting to comfort them, dispel their gloom. A soft wind whispered by, carrying the scent of late lilacs. It brushed her face, pushed away the guilt, filled the air around her with grateful memories.

Such kindness, such generosity. Georgika shared her home with me and shouldered my loneliness—even my health concerned her, while her own was declining. She catered to me as no one else has ever done.

The distaste and doubts about Georgika's preferences were merely inconsequential conjecture in other minds, now, not in Betty's. Regardless of what anyone thought, Georgika was a true friend.

As the minister finished praying, the promising summer blue of the skies began to push away the last memory of burnt flesh, push aside the wisps of cloud that hung low on the mountains, push them up to join the hard, dark rain clouds, push them all out of sight. A breeze began to dry the sodden, grateful earth.

~ ж ~

The subdued crowd began to move, some to talk, some to leave. Betty stood still, immersed in reminiscence, absorbed in comforting, reassuring thoughts of Georgika.

Without warning, a force yanked at the neck of her raincoat, jerked her backward, and just as abruptly let go of her.

"Die!"

Thwack! Pain shot across her back. She staggered. Her foray into the past vanished; her brain focused only on the violent blow, unable to make any sense of it. Then another excruciating strike caught her across the shoulders.

"Die!"

Whack! She raised her arms to protect her head.

"Abomination!"

Cruel blows struck her bandaged arms. Betty wailed. Instinctively, she sought closeness to the ground. Like a soldier hearing an incoming round, she could think only of self-preservation.

Those at the gravesite stood frozen by the bizarre scene before them. Raincoat statues. Doukhobor statues. Stunned. Horrified.

Whack! Betty's buttocks stung as another blow found its mark.

"She-devil!"

Smack! As Betty pulled her body into an even tighter ball, her head twisted sideways.

"Go to the grave with her!"

Betty glimpsed her attacker: a swivel-headed fury with a strap in her hand, a leather classroom strap, a classroom instrument of torture, Inspector McIntyre's recommended source of discipline.

A fedora and a battered briefcase thumped onto the ground next to Betty, and the beating ceased as abruptly as it had begun. The corporal punishment ended.

Betty staggered to her feet to see a pair of plump arms gripping her attacker around the waist. See high school teacher Edwin Chalmers lift flailing, screaming Elaina Maleyna off the ground as easily as a hawk snatches up and carries off a mouse. Elaina's invectives deteriorated into babble as others crowded around Edwin, as others took a firm hold on Elaina's wild limbs and carried her off.

Edwin Chalmers reached Betty just as she reeled, fell into darkness...

~ ж ~

"It has indeed been a hobby of ineffable satisfaction, Miss Wheatley. A welcome relief from my dalliances with William Blake. And from my sentinel's post—my boarding house window—I have had the opportunity to play Sherlock Holmes with unparalleled pleasure."

Bill Trent was driving Betty, his wife Nina and the grandiloquent hero Edwin Chalmers back from the funeral. Betty, wrapped in a blanket in the backseat of Bill's car, listened with all her might, despite the pain radiating from her battered shoulders, arms and back. She did not want to miss a single word of Edwin's astounding story.

" ... and Mr. Trent and I had a most satisfying talk with the school board trustees..."

Betty kept nodding her head, as she began to get the gist of Edwin's explanation: It had not been an anonymous member of Fire Valley Gospel Church who had written the She-devil notes. Or the Reverend Hanginger. Or the storekeeper, Mrs. Johnson.... It had been Elaina! My absolutely delightful Elaina Maleyna, thought Betty, who, behind her sunshiny mask, has been nurtured a— a poisonous brew of hate and jealousy!

"Humhh… and I mostly thought it was Mrs. Johnson; she has cause to find me wanting. And she's been giving me cryptic messages through her bible," mumbled Betty.

"Mrs. Johnson? She thinks you're the cat's meow!" interjected Nina. "Just a few days ago she brought one of those damn nasty notes up to show Bill. Seems it was mailed to her, with a request to post it on the store's bulletin board. Mrs. Johnson was furious."

" ... and " continued Edwin, "By process of elimination, Elaina Maleyna was the only one who travelled to Nakusp on the right days to mail the unpalatable letters—the postmarks were her undoing, and when I confronted her with my evidence, she confessed." There was a long scratch on Edwin's face. Courtesy of Elaina. "Constable Kayke said she had not committed any crime: calling people unsavoury names through letters is not slander under the law. And Inspector McIntyre concluded it was best all round to let her complete the school term. I unfortunately agreed. I should have anticipated today's outburst. Such truly egregious behaviour. Outrageous."

Outrage. Betty was incapable of outrage; despite the violent attack, despite the venom of the letters, despite the turmoil they had added to her life, her early admiration of the woman still persisted, although now twinged with pity.

Elaina Maleyna. Leslie's 'Elaina Complaina', Betty recalled. Free and easy on the surface. Insanely complex inside. Denying her aging body, seeing herself as an enchantress capable of charming Leslie. Punishing both Georgika and me for stealing the affections of her Leslie; affection she wanted, needed desperately. Affection she felt she deserved. Oh, yes…she got her revenge; but she got it at a high price.

"Where is she now?"

"Kurt Guttemann has her well strapped into his hearse and is driving her up to visit Constable Kayke. Imagine. Off to jail in a hearse," said Nina. "You owe Edwin a vote of thanks, Betty, he saved your bacon with the school board. She'd sent notes to them, too. Good old Bill told the other trustees way back in February not to pay the notes any mind, but it was Ed, here, who saved the day, with his proof. Today was icing on the cake. The whole community saw her in action. And saw Edwin come to your rescue."

Betty, despite the pain in her bandaged arms, pumped Edwin's hand up and down as she poured out words of thanks.

"Think nothing of it, Miss Wheatley. Just a magnificent opportunity to play in the game of life. A whole community as pawns, several odd moves by one of the bishops and a malevolent queen. I suspect every chess player would welcome such an opportunity."

Nina chucked Betty on the chin. The compassionate touch was enough to undo Betty's stoicism. Back came the tears. Nina put an arm around her. Gently. Afraid to offend Betty's bruises and tender skin. "Got a silver spoon in your mouth, kiddo. You sure were up the creek without a paddle last winter."

Chapter 26

Dear, damn'd, distracting town, farewell!
–Alexander Pope

"**K**ate's moving Kurt like a house afire," said Betty. "He's got to buy Colonel Farnsworth's old mansion in King City, arrange a honeymoon in California, and marry in July!"

Mrs. Allan shook her head. "It's a terrible thing to say, Betsy, but I can't see their marriage lasting. Marriages are a little bit like minefields. You have to always tread cautiously through them."

"Quite so, Edna, I couldn't have put it better myself." Granny nodded emphatically. "When my husband Charles was alive, he didn't dare tread on me."

Betty suppressed a smile. She loved Granny's skewed logic. "You two are going to miss each other."

"Oh, we've made plans to visit regularly. I have some lovely friends I'm going to introduce Maudie to in Nelson. We old girls have to look after one another." Mrs. Allan looked fondly at Granny, and Granny radiated back a look akin to hero worship. Mrs. Allan turned to Betty. "And you, my dear, you must keep us informed. Write us, won't you?"

"And let us know when you get married," added Granny. There wasn't an iota of hypocrisy, a hint of condemnation on Granny's face—or Mrs. Allan's, for that matter. Not one single admonishment or snide comment had come Betty's way since her well-known trysts with Sparks Thornton and Leslie had taken place. But then, she remembered, there had been no village mention of Charlotte's behaviour. Or Kate's. Where was the fallen-woman scorn she had been brought up to expect? It must be there, buried beneath their outer civilities, she felt, and yet… and yet… . Not a trace.

Married, Granny had said. That treasured word. Betty shrugged. Even aging roués wanted virgin wives. "If I ever do."

"Good heavens, there's no doubt about that—you're the marrying kind, Betsy. Just be patient with that engineer of yours."

"Not much hope there. I burned my bridges with him. I've got to find someone else."

"Check him out when you get home, Betsy. You may have your facts wrong. Remember, a bird in the hand is worth two in the bush."

"My sentiments exactly," Granny added. She patted Betty's healing forearm most gently.

~ ж ~

"Omigosh, Kate, it's our achievement reports from Inspector McIntyre!" Betty unfolded the single-sheet report with trepidation. "Hoh! Wow, Kate, I can't believe it! Look at this. I got some 'excellents'. And not even one 'poor'. I thought he'd written me off as a big-mouth who couldn't discipline. And he knew about Elaina's she-devil notes!"

"It says here 'Edwin Chalmers, the principal of the school, commends Miss Wheatley for carrying out her duties most cheerfully'. Gee. Mr. Chalmers has been my principal all along. No wonder he played Sherlock Holmes for me. I just thought it was because of the chess games. Huh—he's been the principal of us all!"

"Yeah. Big deal. There's me, with an equal degree to his, I'm a better teacher, a better disciplinarian, I get lower pay, and I'm his subordinate. And now he's getting another plum job on Vancouver Island. It's the usual story: men looking out for men, no matter how inferior they are." Kate shoved her unread report into her slacks pocket. "Do you want my books?"

"What?"

"My books. My Book-of-the-Month Club books, remember? God, Betty, clean out your ears. You waited for your selections every month like some wide-eyed kid at Christmas. You can have all of mine, if you'd like."

"You mean it? Really? Those two boxes full?"

"Yes. Kurt's got a houseful of leather-bound books that have never been opened."

"Oh, my, thank you, Kate, I—"

"And if our paths cross, don't ever show them to me. The way you treat dust covers just sickens me." There she goes again, thought Betty, gives with one hand and slaps with the other.

Kate clapped Betty on the shoulder, then stood up. "Kurt's coming to get me any minute. See you around some day. By the way, happy birthday."

What a crazy world. I've just completed a fifth of a century, and the only one who remembered my birthday is Kate. There's a heart inside her after all. It's just that it's buried awfully deep. She needs all the good wishes she can get.

"Good luck, Kate. I hope you and Kurt have a really good life."

Kate turned back, as she reached the corner of Granny's house. "By the way—you should wash out your gossipy mouth with soap and water. I did not get carried off in a straitjacket last year. That was my roommate!" A wicked chuckle accompanied Kate as she vanished from sight.

Betty tore open the other letter she had received, one written with a shaky hand, much shakier than usual. From Gramma Beaton.

June 1952

My dear Betty.

Satan's work is afoot among us all. I am banished by your Mother just like the Israelites. Banished to Mount Pleasant Home. I should come first, I told her. A Mother comes first. It says so in the Bible

But she's gone off to the States, to the Land of Warmongering Capitalists. Hop Along Fred Ross thinks he's going to make aluminum pots and pans. The Yankees will make him produce war helmets.

The same villains have released germ warfare on the Koreans and now the Chinese Yellow Hordes will spill over their borders in countless millions and send forth their Atomic Fires of Hell that   will end the world any moment now. The Book of   Revelations was right. The

Final Plague has begun.

Betty, be one of the servants of God who are sealed and predestined to go with the angels to meet our Maker. Aim to be among the hundred and four-four thousand that will go to him. Examine your mind and your soul my girl. Quickly. Have you finally learned your lessons about Life?

So reflect, my girl, the Time is coming

Your Grandma

Just like Gramma Beaton to believe the world is ending as her own life crashes.

Billions of people on earth and only a hundred thousand or so to be saved. Fat chance I have of being saved. With all the sins I've committed.

And lessons? What lessons have I learned, Gramma Beaton? I always thought that people believe you are guilty until you're proven innocent, and maybe not even then. But up here, I've learned not to generalize.

And I've learned that if you work hard enough at anything, even if you thought you'd hate it, you'll learn to love it. Look at me: go to Hollywood, that was my dream. Teaching the basics to children was never my goal. Reading, arithmetic, spelling—mere stepping stones, with the little green school as a place to practice acting techniques until I could push ahead to stardom.

Now I think that stardom lies in the mind, it can be anywhere. And anyone can be a star. Edwin Chalmers is a star. Jake Patten's a star. Even Mrs. Sunders is a star. Sort of.

Am I a star? A classroom one?

Betty recalled her early inadequate performance, her inability to discipline, her failure to inspire her pupils. It was only in the last few months that she had shown any ability at all. She stuffed the question into a pigeonhole in her head.

I've also learned, Gramma Beaton, that no matter how immoral I've been, I'll wither away, if I don't get someone to love me.

Thanks to a gift from the Women's Institute (not from Inspector McIntyre), twelve wonderful books, the nucleus of a school library, had arrived. Brainy Helena and Ingrid couldn't leave them alone. Even Alec had taken one home to read.

Betty watched them each in turn, dipping their pens in their inkwells, trying to keep the stiff, rusty pen nibs from scratching through the surface of their lined paper. Helena and Ingrid are definitely university material, Betty concluded, capable of real degrees, not just 'MRS'es. Eric and Keith are UBC material, too.

"Hurry up, Donny, we could be having one last game of scrub softball before the bus arrives if you'd hurry."

"Just leave him here, Miz Sweetly, the rest of us can go play," called out Howard, who, as he turned to see if the class appreciated his leadership, knocked over his sister's ink bottle onto her exercise book, and grinned when the ink soaked into it. It was Jenny Carson whose eyes filled, who ran to get rags to clean up the sodden mess.

I wish she were mine, thought Betty, I wish I could adopt her. Give her confidence and shake out all that timidity.

"....and here are your report cards. I'm pleased to say you have all passed. Congratulations. Here's your report card, Alec. I'm proud of you, and your dad will be, too." She beamed at him; he was her biggest success story. From big-bugger troublemaker to motivated student.

"Daisy—well done." Blonde little Daisy. If she were a boy in the city, she'd be in the Little League, batting the hell out of life.

She handed out each report card as though she were conferring degrees. And with each card, she recalled incidents with each student, realizing with growing delight as she did so, the escalating changes she had wrought in the child's life. She prayed for each one, prayed he or she would continue to move ahead, fulfill their dreams, succeed. Become stars. She handed the report cards out with a sense of reluctance, with a feeling of finality. They were farewell cards.

She gathered them around her after the softball game and studied each and every face, trying to etch them into her memory.

The bus pulled up to the school. A lump formed in her throat. "Good-bye, class. Have a wonder-filled summer."

"G'bye, Miz Sweetly," shouted a chorus of voices that rang in her head with all the power and resonance, the significance, of the school bell.

~ ж ~

She looked around the empty room. The silent clock on the wall still read the same time that it had in September: nine-twenty. It's sort of like me, she thought. I've been suspended in time for the year, too. But then maybe not. Maybe this has been the most important year of my life.

"I'm leaving here sooner than you," she said loudly to the picture of the deceased King George. "No one gives a hoot about what happens to your picture now that you're a dead king." It was true. No one had told her what to do with the old photo, or bothered to send her a picture of the young queen.

The bottom drawer of the desk was slightly ajar; empty once more, except for telltale strap fragments. The welts on her back and arms cheered as she threw the pieces out.

She walked over to the Heintzman and ran her fingers over the forlorn keys. Next year, she promised herself, in a new school, I'll play God Save the Queen every morning. To a new audience.

Audience? A teacher always has an audience, is always on stage. And I'm a bona-fide teacher. That look of wonder and joy on their faces when they grasp what I'm getting at? It's silent applause.

She stretched her arms out to the empty seats, as if to embrace the spirits of all the students who had ever sat in them. And then she shouted at the top of her voice: "Miz Sweetly—Star of the Green School!"

~ ж ~

Mrs. Allan was on the ferry, gone off with her nephew from Nelson. Betty carried a paper sack of odds and ends round to the front of the house. All of her other possessions were waiting down on the dock, waiting for the Minto.

Bill Trent lingered just outside Granny's gate. "Come over here, Betty, and have a look-see." Betty moved next to him. He waved his arm in a broad sweep. "Isn't that view something?"

"It certainly is, Mr. Trent." She was distracted by smiling Nina, waving from the bustling café, which was open for the tourist season again. Strawberry pie scented the air. "It's probably one of the prettiest places in the whole world, and it's also got some of the nicest people," said Betty.

"I think so, too. Come on, Betty, why don't you stay one more year? You've had fun up here. How about it? It can be arranged, you know. One call to Inspector McIntyre..."

Betty blinked as rapidly as hummingbird wings. Despite everything, Bill wants me to come back! The screen door of the café opened and out stepped storekeeper Mrs. Johnson. She flashed a warm, shiny-toothed smile at Betty as she headed back to her store. Even Mrs. Johnson defended me, believed in me, thought Betty. Mrs. Johnson and Bill, the community arbiters. On my side. These are a forgiving people, these valley dwellers, tolerant of others far beyond expectation. Beyond reason, even.

She looked at the ice-blue waters below and at the crystalline sky above. At the pristine Selkirks, the Monashees. Familiar friends, now, these gentle giants. She inhaled the pungent freshness of the evergreens and listened to their psalms. Funny, she thought, I've never appreciated how beautiful it is, until now.

She looked over at amiable Nina. She thought of Granny and her kindness, of the vivacious Dot and the gentle Vivian. She thought of the earnest young faces, as they called out their last good-byes to 'Miz Sweetly'...

Then she remembered the near-breakdown she had had before Christmas, the tormenting letters, the painful strapping from Elaina, the confining winter snow falls, the ordeal of the outhouses, the longing for home, for a lover.

Another year up here? I'd be even more desperate for male attention. I'd probably fall for Tommy, and then I'd be stuck here forever, baking cinnamon buns. In Trail, there's my dad, my sister, my friends. A chance to win Cameron back. And if that fails, I'll visit my mother in Spokane and scout around for a rich American, warmonger or not.

She smiled placatingly at Bill Trent. "Part of me would like to stay, Mr. Trent, but a bigger part of me wants to go."

"Too bad, Betty." He turned toward his home. Belched.

"Mr. Trent?"

"Yes?"

"Try to get my pupils someone who isn't a beginner for a change, will you? It's not fair for them to be guinea pigs every year."

"That's a tall order, Betty. I'd hoped you'd be the experienced teacher. But I'll try."

As Bill left, Granny appeared. She had been waiting behind her living room curtains for him to leave. She bustled over to Betty. "I could tell he didn't succeed. He was trying to talk you into staying, wasn't he?"

"Yes."

"That Bill. I could have told him it was no use, he could have asked me." There was a hint of embarrassment in Granny's face. Betty watched her gathering up courage. Granny, she could tell, was going to express an emotion, and her English upbringing did not allow such excesses. "I shall miss you, Betty, you're a nice girl. A good girl."

On impulse, Betty hugged her and kissed her cheek. Granny fished up her sleeve for a handkerchief and dabbed at her eyes. "Oh, I hate to see you go. Please, please keep in touch," she said and rushed off.

It was the first time Betty could remember initiating a hug. No one in her family hugged one another, ever. It felt good, she realized. No wonder Georgika did it. It's 's so simple, so pure – a nice way to say something words cannot.

~ Ж ~

A sharp horn blast from up the lake. The stately Minto was bearing down on the town, boastfully, as usual. Betty licked at a dripping vanilla ice cream cone—a farewell gift from Nina and her café—as she walked down the steep hill for the last time, in step with the sounds from the paddlewheel. The ferry, too,   thrummed   and

266

hooted, converging on Narrows. And behind her, a car horn honked insistently. The tranquil place was as noisy as midnight on New Year's Eve! She looked over her shoulder as the honking car pulled up behind her and stopped. Tommy and Leslie emerged. Just as the Minto cut its engines. Just as the ferry docked.

"Did you hear of my good fortune, Betty? I'm to be a principal in New Westminster. I'm—" Another insistent blast interrupted Leslie. Another horn, from a car roaring off the ferry. Betty swept by the sky-blue eyes of Leslie as she turned to the annoying sound, so uncharacteristic of the peaceful town.

It was a Henry J.— Dad's car! Why, Betty wondered, had her father decided to make the mountain journey he swore he would never take again? The same nerve-testing trip along the same rough roads that had jolted and dented his ass-backward Henry J.? Because of Easter? When he had paid her the compliments of compliments: 'Did real good, just like I'd expect of a...a son.'?

The Henry J raced toward her, kicking up a cloud of dust, then braking face-to-face with Tommy's car. Confrontationally, defiantly. The car door opened.

Sudden, distracting electrical charges flew about inside her, erupted into static, just like Granny's radio. And Betty's brain waves began bumping into each other, wholly confused—a constellate of opposing emotions: anxiety and ardour, perplexity and passion, but Betty, as ice cream dripped down her arm, had no time to compose her thoughts as she watched the last person she could have expected step out of the Henry J.

Cameron! ... He strode toward her confidently, a commanding presence. Only his pupils narrowed as he took in the scene: Betty with two handsome men. She remembered the heated letter she had sent to him, her 'not yours, Betty' letter. Hadn't he received it? What was Cameron doing here?

The same anxiousness she had felt on the first morning of teaching gripped her; butterflies flapping amok in the pit of her stomach. She threw the messy ice cream cone into roadside bushes and willed the return of her composure. "Leslie, Tom, this is Cameron, my—my boyfriend?" She watched Cameron as she said the words. He did not flinch, did not deny them. His face hung between a smile and caution.

"Hullo." Tommy pumped Cameron's hand. Leslie offered a reluctant one, then took a step back, away from them.

"I'm driving Leslie to the coast," continued Tommy. "Gotta sell my restaurant. Gotta chance to buy the Arlada Cheese Factory." Tommy's bark of a country-boy laugh filled the air, and as unexpected as its arrival, it departed. Cameron looked amused and relieved and a wide grin took over; he no longer looked concerned. Betty began to breathe again.

"Buy the Arlada? I bet you'll be the most successful man in Kokanee, Tommy." Betty grabbed Tommy's hand with both her own and pumped it, just like Georgika would have done.

Then Betty turned toward Leslie. His beautiful eyes in his beautiful face were glacial as they looked at her. No handshake from Leslie, the craven coward. Just as well, thought Betty, Cameron might misinterpret it. "Good luck on your climb to the top, Leslie. It won't be a picnic, I'm sure."

"Haw Haw—picnic! Climb to the top! Do it with more clothes on this time, eh, Les?" Tommy laughed all the way to his car.

Leslie whirled round and followed him. They drove onto the waiting ferry.

"Those guys were my competition? And I worried like crazy since Christmas about that Leslie. Geez, Betts. You never told me Leslie was a fruit." Betty's eyes widened at his rough remark, but she did not say a word. Cameron took her in his arms there, in front of the whole community.

The sternwheeler crew had been watching the roadside drama. Now they unloaded Betty's luggage, pulled back the gangplank and shoved off. Betty did not hear the Minto's departing blast, did not hear the rhythm of thumping engines as it moved away without her.

~ ӝ ~

Cameron parked the Henry J behind the green school.

"... and you never wrote," she concluded.

Cameron reached for her, pulled her close to him. Wiped dried vanilla ice cream from the tip of her nose. "Too   busy   working overtime, Betts. I needed some extra cash. Here. A birthday present from your mother and Hop-along Freddie." Cameron brushed his lips against her hair and handed her a velvet jewel case. From it, Betty pulled out a tinkling charm bracelet. She lifted it up to the light. No cheap piece of costume jewelry like the ones I bought, she observed. This is real silver.

Tiny pots and pans jingled from it.

"And, last but not least..." Cameron reached behind the car seat and brought forth a brown paper Woolworth's bag, and held it out, grinning. "Happy birthday from me."

Betty glanced inside, then cocked her head as a soft smile lit up her face. "Cam! You did get me a Woolworth ring, you do care!" She swung her arm around Cameron's shoulder and managed to plant a kiss on his ear.

"Scratch the windshield with it, then see if you still want one from Woolworth's! It was my grandmother's. Reset. You don't mind? It's no dime store imitation, Betts, it's the real McCoy: 14-carat gold and a decent diamond."

The narrow band and its humble stone illuminated the Henry J with bedazzling light. "Oh, Cam, you still want to marry me! And I thought I'd wrecked things with you forever." But out of the warm and promising haze she was in, a warning bell began ringing. "Uhh ... Cam," she said, in a voice as off-hand as she could muster, "where are you going to work when you graduate?" Please God, not Kitimat.

Cameron looked as satisfied as if he had just tasted a piece of Nina's fresh pie. "I've got a scholarship from A.V. Roe. And they hinted to me that there'll be an offer, when I graduate, of a job in Toronto, working on the Arrow—the Avro Arrow—a super-sonic jet interceptor. They're saying it will be the best in the world! We still have to wait two years, Betts, but we've a good future ahead of us, and..."

Oh, no, not that two years mantra again! Betty blocked out the words. Oh, well. Better than no Cameron at all.... and leaned against Cameron's protective arm. Cameron's future war mongering arm— Cameron, a big success, just like Hop-along Freddie?

High-speed thoughts whizzed through her head. Optimistic ones. Attitude changing ones... . New visions coalesced of herself in an organza apron, dusting a nice little Toronto house—just like Vivian's, except it would be finished from day one—with her own angelic baby Harry and his countless siblings following behind her, and hovering over all of them would be this unbelievably trustable, handsome, adoring Cameron, master builder of fighter jets, making Canada safe from Communist attack!

And in the meantime, fortified by the shining ring, only two years more of Green School-type success: teaching in the beloved, urbane City of Trail.

~ Ж ~

The ferry cut its usual blunt path through the lake. On board, Betty, with Cameron at her side, stepped out of the Henry J for one last survey of the brilliant waters. The breezes lifted her red/brown hair and whispered on her cheeks. What a comparison! When she had come by boat, last fall, filled with foreboding, she had arrived in darkness, unenlightened and alone. Now, she was leaving with Cameron. And more. She was leaving with a sense of accomplishment and a rosy future. As well as shining upon the waves of the pure Arrow Lakes, the sun shone with equal brilliance upon on her.

She waved good-bye to Bill, in the pilothouse. She hoped he could see the flashing sparkles of her tiny diamond.

What a pity I couldn't show it to Granny, to Miss Allen, to sourpuss Kate. Show them my handsome fiancé. Show him off to everyone. "Meet my jet-building future husband..."

Then, it was if a shadow had passed before the sun. Two years... wait for two years for marital bliss. Cameron's casual words resurfaced in her head. Two long years alone... She forced the thought into the furthest recess of her brain next to her memories of wayward romances with Leslie and Sparks Thornton. I can wait, she said to their handsome images. And I can behave myself. I'm infinitely more mature. Good Lord, I'm twenty now! She relaxed.

Jake was directing vehicles off the ferry, more like a cowpuncher than a traffic cop. "Hey, Miz Wheatie," he called. "You forgot somethin'!"

"I did?"

"Yup. Yuh never packed yer schoolhouse in yer suitcase. YOUR schoolhouse and all them kids who miss yuh already. Just don't set yer next school on fire... or blow it up! Eee hee hee..."

Betty smiled at this kindly man who made her feel so welcome in what seemed at the time to be a forlorn outpost in the middle of nowhere...even though he never did get her name right. She'd faced childish temper tantrums, a nasty room-mate, a peeping-Tom minister, unreliable paramours, cruel rumours and hungry bears-- and yet, she'd survived.

I think.... maybe.... I am leaving as a champion after all.

Well, hmm.... she pursed her lips... .mostly survived.

Maybe a semi-champion?

About the Author:

Author **Denise McKay** wrote *Sweetly*, an insightful engaging novel, based on her own real-life experiences as a former teacher at a one-room schoolhouse in the rugged British Columbia interior.

McKay, who was born in Vancouver and now lives in Ancaster, Ontario, has studied creative writing at Ryerson University and Humber College.

She is a gifted writer and a highly creative artist in oil painting, acrylic, sculpture and pottery with many awards to her credit.

Postscript

I am a temporary enclosure for a temporary purpose;
 that served, my skull and teeth,
 my idiosyncrasy and desire, will disperse, I believe,
like the timbers of a booth after the fair.
—H. G. Wells

The *Minto*

Its end was inevitable. Many people from the smaller towns had gravitated to the bigger communities seeking better jobs, better services and better schools. And the government had built new roads to major centres such as Nakusp, Castlegar and Nelson. The slow-moving Minto, the transport link between RobsonWest and Nakusp, could not compete and ceased as a viable means of transport for people and goods.

On Friday, April 23, 1954, she set off on her last voyage, steaming south from Nakusp to Robson West and then back again. Nostalgic locals and sternwheeler buffs had booked staterooms months in advance; the *Minto*'s decks and saloons swarmed with passengers. At each stop along the way—Bird's Landing, Needles, Edgewood, Broadwater, Renata, Syringa Creek—the villagers gathered to say good-bye. Men took off their hats and surreptitiously wiped their eyes, as they waved and watched the *Minto* steam to her final destination.

Across from Edgewood at Fullmore Point, Jock Ford, in full regalia, piped a Scottish lament. At the Narrows, the passage that separates Upper from Lower Arrow Lake, a dredge crew solemnly placed a funeral wreath on board, and draped a wide ribbon reading "Farewell *Minto* - Well done, old girl." [1]

~ Ж ~

The towns

Their end was inevitable too. Post-war progress demanded more electricity. And the Columbia River watershed, which covers an area twice that of the British Isles —260,000 square miles, spanning Wyoming, Montana, Idaho, Oregon, Washington and British Columbia—provided a huge source of hydro power.

By 1950, much of the potential power of the Columbia and its tributaries had been harnessed by dams in the States. Further development, stated engineers on both sides of the US-Canada border, required a cooperative undertaking to turn B.C.'s Columbia River watershed into a headwater storage. More dams on the Columbia would create reservoirs capable of increasing the flow during periods of low-water levels, and decreasing the flow during high. The

273

result: maximum power generation, minimum downstream flooding. Progress.

The Columbia River treaty, signed by Prime Minister John Diefenbaker and President Dwight Eisenhower on January 17, 1961, sealed the fate of the Arrow Lakes' villagers. (2, 3, 4)

~ ж ~

The world of the valley people changed abruptly when the second largest engineering project in North America, second only to the St. Lawrence Seaway, got underway. A storage dam built just north of Castlegar, called the Keenleyside Dam, raised the water level 36 feet higher than the highest flood level ever suffered by the valley. The rising waters completely drowned the little communities such as Edgewood, Fauquier, Needles, that had hugged the shoreline. More than 2,000 people were uprooted, torn from their way of life, thrown into a world not of their making. No piper played a lament, no crew laid a wreath. But many cried. (4, 5)

~ ж ~

The *Henry J.*
This car, the first post-war attempt in North America at small car production, started off in 1951 with promise: a first year production of 82,000 cars! (The famed Henry J. Kaiser, whose team of ship builders at Richmond California, had, during the war, constructed 368 Liberty and Victory ships, now turned his engineering genius and administrative expertise to domestic car manufacture.) In three years—from auspicious start to dismal finish—manufacture and assembly of the *Henry J* ceased. In the last year of production, 1954, Kaiser Motors sold only 1,113 units. (Unknown Website)

~ ж ~

The *Avro Arrow*
When the newly completed delta-winged, twin-engine Avro CF-105 *Arrow* flew at twice the speed of sound, Avro employees cheered: their efforts had paid off; they had designed and built the world's largest and fastest jet interceptor. But on February 20, 1959, Prime Minister John Diefenbaker stunned the Avro engineers and fellow employees when he cancelled government support for building *Arrows*. He had decided—upon advice of his Chiefs-of-staff— that there was no future for fighter interceptors: the space age had arrived, Sputnik circled the globe. The threat to Canada's security would be Russian missiles, said Diefenbaker, not Russian bombers. A.V. Roe closed, the workers and engineers were dismissed *en masse*. (6) The talented engineers left the country; they were snapped up by the American, British and French aeronautical and space industries. Diefenbaker decreed that not one *Arrow* and its advanced technological secrets was to be left for posterity: the air reeked of acetylene fumes as the last of the six beautifully crafted jets was torched for scrap at General Smelting's plant in Hamilton, Ontario.

~ ~ ~

The grizzly bear

They still roam the forests of the mountains, from Alaska through central British Columbia and western Alberta, to the northern parts of Idaho and Montana, but the future of the grizzly, Ursus arctos horribilis, remains in doubt. Man and bear cannot coexist because man, out of fear, will kill Grizzlies.

Grizzly attacks capture headlines: an innocent hiker, trapper, camper is mauled, sometimes killed by these enormous beasts, weighing from 500 to greater than 1000 pounds.

The grizzly explodes upon any animal it thinks is competing with it for food or endangering its young. Once captured, it holds its adversary down with one massive paw and rips out flesh with the other, chomps on the head or arm or leg.The grizzly find it more and more difficult to survive as their habitat, the high country, is invaded (clear-cut logging, expanding farms, summer dwellings), and their traditional food sources, depleted (over-fishing, man-stripped berry bushes). The grizzly are forced to leave the high country and, in turn, invade man's territory: his garbage dumps, his farms, even his towns.

Pulled to the aroma of waste food, animal remains, and unpicked fruit. Once a bear enters man's world, the bear must be destroyed. But no conservation officer, no policeman kills a bear without regret: he knows that part of our wilderness dies when a bear dies.[7]

Will the grizzly disappear too? Is their end inevitable like that of the *Minto*, the *Henry J*, the *Avro Arrow*, the little communities? That page of history has yet to be written.

References

- *Sternwheelers and Steam Tugs*, Robert D. Turner, 1984, ISBN 0-919203-15-9
- *Chronicle of Canada*, Jacques Legrand, ISBN 0-920417-16-7, 1990
- *Whistle Stops Along the Columbia River Narrows*, Editor Pat Philcox, Burton New Horizons Book Committee, 1982, ISBN 0-88925-305-6.
- *People in the Way*, J.W. Wilson, Toronto: University of Toronto Press, 1973, pp. 197.
- *Storm Over High Arrow*, Jack McDonald, Self-published.
- *The Globe and Mail: Flights of fact and fantasy*, January 11, 1997.
- *Bear Attacks, Their Causes and Avoidance*, Stephen Herrero, 1985, ISBN 0-88830-279-7.

Manor House
www.manor-house-publishing.com

Manufactured by Amazon.ca
Bolton, ON

42422518R00153